To Peter & Jill

Hope you enjoyed the holiday

George Jackson

George Jackson was born and raised in Liverpool. In 1986 he was tragically widowed and left with two young children. At the relatively young age of 54, George retired from his insurance based career, as he had always dreamed of trekking famous mountains and above all writing a novel. Those dreams are now a reality.

To Maureen

George Jackson

JACK

AUSTIN MACAULEY
PUBLISHERS LTD.

A CIP catalogue record for this title is available from the British Library.

ISBN 9781786121493 (Paperback)
ISBN 9781786121509 (Hardback)
ISBN 9781786121516 (E-Book)

www.austinmacauley.com

First Published (2016)
Austin Macauley Publishers Ltd.
25 Canada Square
Canary Wharf
London
E14 5LQ

Acknowledgments

My wife Sheila for her unwavering support.
My late friend Shirley Smith.

Chapter 1

He looked across the smoke-filled New York night club at his prey, a busty blonde he had been checking out for the last half hour, waiting for the ideal moment when he could talk to her on her own, separated from her two giggling girlfriends. He really liked a woman to have a bit of meat on her bones; she fitted the bill nicely with her figure-hugging dress, accentuating the shape of her breasts and then going in at the waist before curving out again and completing her hourglass figure. It gave him a warm glow in his groin that he thought only a man could possibly describe to another man.

The opportunity arrived as her two friends, presumably, went to the ladies, leaving 'blondie' to look after the drinks. He strode across to her purposefully with an inner confidence borne from being six feet two, with thick, black hair, dark eyes and an athletic body. "Jack Williams," he said smiling, holding out his hand for her to shake.

Jack was not a man to try the clever one-liners; he believed women preferred the direct, honest approach, and he never did anything without thinking it through thoroughly.

This had not always been the case with Jack, however. He was born and lived as an only child. His father had run away before he was born, leaving his mother to struggle on her own with him, and struggle she did. Both her parents were dead and she had no brothers or sisters. She and Jack lived in a two bed roomed apartment in the Bronx. She worked hard stacking shelves, cleaning, waitressing, taking in laundry, anything to get by. Life was so tough she didn't have time to give him the parenting that he needed. Consequently, as he was growing up, he seemed always to be in some kind of trouble. A little scam here, another one there. He would seize opportunities as they arose with little or no thought of the consequences. His education suffered of course, as he didn't think it was important. His teachers eventually gave up. It was obvious to them that he had a really sharp mind but simply didn't try hard enough. If they had known what his private life was like, perhaps they would have understood.

His life, as a boy, consisted of grabbing whatever food from the refrigerator that his mother had left for him. He would often see different men come and go from her bed. She would, at times, be drunk and completely out of control, swearing and fighting with them. Consequently he grew up with little respect for women. On one of the rare days that she actually sat down and talked to him, she explained that his father had been a student and, when told of the pregnancy, had run away. His mother went on to say she had never seen or heard from him since. The men coming and going would sometimes leave their coats in the hall and he would take this opportunity to rifle their pockets. As usual he wouldn't have put any thought into it, and so he would be caught and punished severely.

At seventeen, long after finishing school, he left his mother and the dingy apartment, moving into an even dingier apartment with two of his pals. Unlike most of his friends and associates, he didn't feel even the slightest bit proud to be called a New Yorker, "What the fuck had the so called Big Apple ever done for Jack Williams?" was his take on the subject.

Having little respect for the law, he and his friends were in and out of young people's institutions on a regular basis. At the age of twenty, having just served four months in a particularly bad one, his life took a change for the better. An older guy that he met befriended him. Tony Martin was a tall, good looking man in his fifties with a good head of hair that presented a package that belied his years. He immediately took to Jack. He was a really successful crook who cleverly was rarely in trouble with the law and he found Jack very funny and would call him 'Jack the Lad'. Tony became a big influence on his life. He convinced Jack that if you don't plot a job properly, there would rarely be a decent pot at the end. He drummed it in to him, 'No plot, no pot.'

Gradually Jack's attitude changed. He began to weigh up all the possible pitfalls, in order to avoid them. Consequently, he became much more successful which, as a bonus, kept him at arm's length from the law. As he earned more and more money, it allowed him the luxury of leaving his two dopey friends and renting his own rundown apartment in the Bronx. It also enabled him to afford amongst other things, good quality clothing that he could wear when visiting his favourite nightclub.

His blonde prey smiled up at him and reciprocated, "Catherine Morgan, pleased to meet you, Jack."

Keeping hold of her hand for much longer than was really necessary, he replied smiling, "You're pleased to meet me? Catherine, I've been waiting for more than an hour to get you on your own. They then chatted on as though they had known each other for a long time.

Her two friends soon returned and, although she introduced everyone, she made it obvious that she wanted to be with Jack. Her friends eventually accepted the inevitable and drifted off. However, an hour later, Jack was bored to tears with her. He liked a woman to have a quick mind and a good sense of humour and, although Catherine was very attractive, in his opinion, she had neither. He asked her for her telephone number and promised he would contact her the next day, as he felt a bit shattered and needed an early night.

The following morning, Jack had to go to a funeral. He didn't really want to be bothered. However, it was for an old and dear friend of Tony Martin's who had passed away, whom he had met a couple of times. In any case, if it was a big deal to Tony, then that was enough. So there he was, standing in a line of mourners, some upset, others confused when an embryo of an idea began to hatch in his mind. It struck him that people going to funerals could be a soft touch, as they would be at a low ebb and, therefore, might easily be conned out of their money.

Over the next couple of weeks, he visited numerous funerals at different venues and began to put together a plot. He noted that when mourners were arriving, or when they were leaving, there was never a priest or vicar, or indeed any official to be seen. He began to put things down on paper, mapping out all the venues in and around New York and proceeded to draw up a separate plan for each one.

He noted that it would be very unusual for any of the people at any venue to return the next day, and so there was no reason why any scam couldn't be perpetrated again and again. He then heeded Tony Martin's words; one of the main reasons people ended up in prison was greed and with this in mind he decided on a maximum of three days at each venue. Having visited every one of the chosen churches, he decided on St. James Presbyterian as the first one. It was near the Bronx and he had discovered they needed volunteers to collect the funds that were required to pay for a huge repair job on the bell tower. Having found out the name of the chairman heading the fund raising committee, he approached him with an offer to join them in their quest to raise the $500,000, which they had deemed necessary.

The following night he sat round a table in one of the local schools with five women and two men listening to the chairman, whose name coincidently was Mr. James, as he read out the minutes of the last meeting.

On the table in front of Mr. James, was a large graph showing a line from zero to the target of $500,000. Jack had to refrain from smiling, as he noticed the dates on the graph alongside the amounts raised so far, meant that in two years this committee had managed to generate the grand sum of just $1,600. He worked out quickly in his head that, at the present rate, it would take at least 25 years in order to reach their goal and by that time, most of the present company would be approximately 100 years old!

Mr. James, still reading the minutes, was congratulating a Mrs. Watson on the $45 and 50 cents that she had raised by baking cakes and selling them from a table at the end of her garden path. As Jack looked at her, gushing with pride in her huge, pink, floral dress, he had a cruel mental picture of her eating most of the cakes. Scolding himself, he refocused his mind on Mr. James who, having reached the end of the minutes, closed the book.

"Now, ladies and gentlemen," the chairman went on, "I would like you to welcome Mr. Jack Williams here to our little group. He has offered to raise money with us by singing with his guitar in the city centre."

The whole group clapped as one, along with encouraging shouts of. "Go for it Jack," and "The Lord be with you." He felt like a heel for a brief moment, but only for a brief moment. At the end of the meeting, Mr. James gave Jack a form to take away for him to fill in, along with what Jack was really after, a genuine official St. James Presbyterian Church badge. He laughed as he thought to himself, "God is charitable after all." Jack's plans were falling into place nicely and so he commissioned a local artist to create a dignified and classy poster in black and gold. After pondering long and hard on the wording, he finally settled on a message simply saying:

'We would like to bring tranquillity and beauty to your loved ones final resting place, then maintain it. Would you please, please help with a small donation?'

Although delighted with the finished poster, he was concerned that the people might feel awkward, not knowing how much to contribute, so he paid the artist to do another one, adding the words:

'Even if it's only a couple of dollars.'

He didn't like the second one, but thought it was a good back up.

His calculating mind devised two plans regarding his own presentation, the first of which was to refrain from saying anything to the people; his thinking being that they would be less likely to remember anything about him. He did of course have a backup which he was prepared to use. Everything was now in place. He had covered every angle that he could think of and had even worked out what the possible pot could be. After having visited all the venues on his list, he knew that, on average, there would be approximately forty mourners at each funeral and if only thirty of them contributed $3, the pot could be as much as $90. As there was a funeral every hour, a total of eight funerals could net him $720 a day! Jack's wicked sense of humour interpreted the pot as: 'Death Duties.'

Day one of the St. James account saw Jack up, showered and decked out in his black suit and tie ready for action. He looked at himself in the mirror and smiled coldly, as he pinned his official St. James Badge onto his lapel.

"A license to print money," he thought. Then he was off to work, having picked up a fresh flower on his way from the local florist to complete his outfit. With his poster on its polished wood stand, he stood back and admired it.

The first funeral arrived. Jack didn't feel the least bit nervous or guilty as the people began to drop donations into the small, beautiful cask that he had strategically positioned to make them walk around it. He didn't have to say a word and was pleasantly staggered at how easy it was.

After they had filed through, he quickly walked to his car and counted his ill-gotten gains. However, his face sank as he counted out only $28 and a few cents. He cursed himself as, at the last moment, he had used poster B. He quickly returned to his spot and exchanged poster B for poster A, returning B to his car. He then returned in plenty of time for the next funeral and a short time later they arrived. Jack, although sorely tempted, did not look once, as the people filing through dropped their donations into the cask. It seemed like an age before the last one was out of sight and he was able to go quickly to his car with the second pot. A couple of minutes later a huge grin was on his face.

"Yes," he whispered with a clenched fist. He had counted $85 and a few odd coins.

With day one at an end, Jack sat in his apartment counting the pot; a total of $780 plus a few cents. This was more than he had hoped for and easier, too. He had a shower, letting the warm water run through his thick, black hair and then down onto his fit, muscular body. The water seemed to penetrate into his very soul making him feel really good. He took his time in the shower, as there was no hurry. The decision never to go out drinking when he had to go to work the next morning (which is exactly how he thought about it) was a good one and he would stick with it.

He stepped out of the shower, dried himself and had a shave. He then put on a drab housecoat, a maroon one, which he fleetingly thought would be replaced soon. Then, going into his tiny sitting room, he looked around at the damp walls with flaking paint, thin, drab curtains and a cracked window.

"These, also, will have to go," he thought. He poured himself a shot of whiskey and lit up his first cigarette of the day. He had decided never to smoke at work in case of offending anybody. Now, sitting in his favourite armchair with Louis Armstrong grunting out one of his favourite songs, he took a big draw on his cigarette and, as he exhaled, laughed out loud. Then, still chuckling to himself, raised his glass. "Here's to you, Tony Martin!"

He poured himself another shot of whisky and sat listening to the incessant noise from the neighbours above and the constant drone of the traffic outside. Having then drunk the last drops of his whiskey, he stretched out his arms yawning. No matter how tired he felt, he still had some preparations to complete before going to bed. Opening out the local newspaper, he turned to the obituary column. Taking a pen, he went through it and circled each entry applicable to St. James, before then scanning them to see if he knew any of the entries and, therefore, any of their friends or loved ones.

"Excellent," he thought, "I don't know any of the poor saps."

Having completed this task, he then checked his suit was hung correctly and his shirt laid out. Finally, he polished his shoes enabling him to go to bed. His last thought before dropping off into a deep sleep was of the girl in the florist with her nametag on her left breast, 'Phylamina'"

Jack woke up the next morning with the irritating alarm ringing; at least that is how he used to think of it, but not anymore. He pushed the button down and leapt out of bed and, after a few warm up exercises, did his usual thirty push-ups and sixty sit-ups. His body was in great shape. He was now 22 and felt at his peak. His stomach was as flat as a board, and he was proud of it.

After showering and shaving, he carefully dressed and had his usual breakfast of cereal and fruit with his beloved cup of coffee. He looked at his watch and, as he was early, made himself another coffee and lit up a cigarette. He thought perhaps his presentation could do with a fine tune. He tried to imagine himself as one of the people queuing up, and considered the feeling of being with close friends and family, who could see how much money was being put into the small cask. Furthermore, he thought, it might in a way encourage a bigger donation if he himself was actually watching the money going in. The down side to that, however, being it could make him more memorable.

With that in mind, he opened a small cupboard and took out a long, thin box. After sifting through it, he decided on a smallish moustache and a pair of thin, horn rimmed spectacles. He put them on, donned his hat and nodded his approval. Not too noticeable, but enough of a change that (a) any description would probably be concentrated on the moustache and spectacles and (b) a person knowing him maybe wouldn't notice. His mind made up, he put the box back in the cupboard. Over the last two years he had become adept at disguise, but on this occasion he wanted simplicity. He removed his disguise, as he was looking forward to his visit to the local florist for his fresh flower and, in particular, a beautiful young lady assistant named Phylamina.

Jack walked briskly along. He almost had a skip in his stride as he visualized her with her long, brown hair tumbling down over her shoulders and her beautiful, blue eyes that seemed to dance as she talked and moved. He had noted, of course, that there was no ring on her wedding finger. He knew that he was not unattractive to women and was well used to them falling for him. He reached the florists and was delighted to be the only customer. Phylamina was serving on her own, as she had been the day before. He looked straight into her eyes with what he thought was his most endearing smile then, offering his hand said, "Jack Williams."

Averting his intense gaze and ignoring his outstretched hand, she simply asked, "Can I help you, sir?"

Not to be put off, Jack ordered his fresh flower and, as he paid for it, he commented on all the beautifully arranged flowers around the shop. The remark seemed to bring a sparkle to her eyes. "Thank you very much, sir," she said smiling, as she walked around the counter and over to a shelf, where she began arranging flowers.

That was enough for him. Taking it as a positive signal, he walked over to her and putting his arm around her waist, ploughed straight in, "Why don't you and I do something on Friday night, Phyl'?"

Her mood noticeably changed. She glared at him and pushed his arm away, as she replied "I'm afraid that is out of the question, sir. I think you had better leave now." She then walked over to the door and held it open. This made him feel like an idiot. He gave a choked cheerio as he left. As he walked away from the shop, he noticed the sign swinging in the breeze 'Phylamina D. T. Riley. Florist for every occasion'. He realized he had acted like a fool, presuming she was just a salesgirl when, in fact, she was obviously the owner.

"A lesson learned by Jack Williams," he thought, as he shuffled off to work with the skip noticeably missing from a little earlier.

Jack's second day at 'work' went well, which lifted his spirits. On his way home he purchased a deep blue, cotton housecoat; his favourite colour. He then called into a small restaurant where, having had a nourishing meal, he finished with an essential cup of coffee and lit up his first cigarette of the day. It relaxed him completely. He was trying to think positively about the Phylamina situation and he mused to himself "What brings a woman's defences down?" and then, as the lines cleared from his forehead,

"Of course, you make her laugh; it never fails". He took a deep drag from his cigarette and, as he exhaled, his face lit up, as he realized how best this could be achieved.

Before going home to his apartment, Jack called in to see an old colleague. This guy, nicknamed Benny the stamp, could fake anything from a stamp, to a passport, to a coat of arms. Jack, having reached Benny's front door, rang the bell. As soon as he spoke into the intercom, the front door opened and he entered and closed it behind him before bounding up to the third floor, taking two steps at a time. There was a lift of course, but he had always been sceptical of them and, in any case, he felt the exercise helped him to keep in shape.

Benny Mendez, a short, broad shouldered man with a receding hairline opened the door. Peering up at Jack, he smiled, as he asked, "What are you up to now, you thieving little swine?" Jack just chuckled and patted Benny on the head as he went through the hall and into a wonderful lounge, which was decked out in beautiful furniture, wonderful sculptured objects and quality paintings.

As Jack was sitting waiting for Benny to come back from the kitchen with a cup of coffee, he smiled as he looked around. "The trouble with Benny," he thought, "is that you never really know whether any or all of this grandeur is genuine or not."

After they had settled down and discussed old times, Jack took out a small, black bag from his inside pocket. He placed the contents into Benny's hand. Benny looked at the official badge bearing the name "St. James Presbyterian Church" and then looked up with a puzzled look on his face.

"Benny," Jack said, "could you make me a replica of that badge, but bearing the name, St. Thomas Baptist Church?"

After studying it for a short time, Benny replied, "Sure, man, no problem." Naturally, he didn't ask what it was for, nor indeed did he want to know. Honor among thieves and all that. They shook hands on a fee and Jack set off home, suddenly feeling tired. It had been a long day, but he walked to his car confident in the knowledge that Benny would never discuss his business with anyone.

When finally he arrived home, it was dark. He quickly had a shower before pouring himself a well-earned drink and lighting up a cigarette. Relaxing for a couple of minutes, he then put on his favourite singer, Louis Armstrong, and proceeded to enter into his file the takings for the day; an unbelievable $950! He didn't bother with the coins, preferring to pocket them.

His new presentation had been a terrific success, even down to shaking hands with each person saying "God bless you," which he had correctly calculated, would give the other people in the line a little breathing space to, hopefully, have their money ready. Having laid out his suit and polished his shoes until they were shining, he had completed his chores for the night and so took out the Yellow Pages.

Drawing a circle around an advertisement for a 24 hour floral delivery service, he rang and asked them to deliver a dozen red roses to Phylamina D. T. Riley, with the message: 'Phylamina, I'm guessing you never receive flowers as a gift. I figure even a bunch of red roses will be of more use to you than my tongue-tied schoolboy advances yesterday. Regards, Jack Williams. xxxxx. P.S. I've chopped off both of my arms.' He then insisted to the girl on the phone that the flowers had to be delivered at precisely 8.30 the following morning. After agreeing to pay an extra $12 for that special service, he gave her the address and said goodnight. He was just about to go to bed when he realized that he had not yet checked the obituary column. This really irritated Jack. The thought of Phylamina had lowered his guard. He made a promise to himself that it would never happen again. Work first, women second. With the obituary task completed, he went to bed shattered and was asleep within minutes.

Jack's alarm went off at 7 a.m., as usual, and he was soon up doing his exercises with relish. He then stepped under the shower. The hot water cascading down onto his hair made him feel good. He smiled as the water, he noticed, was running to the end of his penis and then sort of spouting down onto the shower floor. He began to feel excited as he thought of Phylamina. He had been so busy preparing for the funeral scam, there had not been any time for women.

As he thought of her, he stroked his neck and chest with his soapy hands, before carrying on further down across his hard, flat stomach and through his thick, tight, curly pubic hair, finally resting on his erection. Leaning back against the hard tiles, he imagined this was Phylamina in the shower with him, running her fingers gently up and down his erect penis. He then imagined her fingers encircling his testicles with one hand, as the other stroked his shaft, slowly at first, building up the pace faster and faster, until blessed relief left him gasping as he leant against the wall.

Finishing his shower, he put on his new housecoat. Then looking in the mirror, he consequently thought it would be a good idea to upgrade the rest of his wardrobe. After breakfast, which finished with a cup of coffee and a cigarette as usual, he began to think about the St. James account, as most of his clear thinking seemed to take place at this time in the morning. He thought it was time for more fine-tuning, deciding in retrospect, to increase the maximum days at each venue from three to four. This meant that he could work Monday to Thursday at each of them, leaving Friday for banking his takings and doing any preparation that was necessary for the next venue.

"Yes," he thought, "this really does make sense." He popped his diary into his inside pocket and, as usual, stopped at the front door for a minute in order to make sure he had not forgotten anything. Satisfied, off he went. He had on his most expensive aftershave, in order to hopefully impress Phylamina. He hurried along, as he had to be outside Phylamina's shop before the delivery van. Having arrived, he had only waited a few minutes when the van pulled up bearing the name 'Flower Power.' A lady with a bunch of roses disembarked from the van and stood looking at the flower shop, puzzled. As he watched, grinning, she seemed to double-check her documentation before shrugging her shoulders. She then pushed open the door and entered. Jack was at the corner of the window and could see clearly Phylamina's, at first, surprised look, turning into a huge smile and, as far as he could tell, a laugh, as she read the card. He waited until the lady had left, took his jacket off and fastened it around him, with the sleeves swinging free. He then entered, with some trepidation, into the shop.

Phylamina looked at him, as he stood there with his shoulders hunched and his bottom lip drooped like a naughty little boy.

"I suppose you think you're hilarious don't you, Jack Williams?" she asked laughing.

He was feeling pleased as he introduced himself to her properly.

"So, tell me, Mr. Williams, what do you do when you're not harassing young women in shops?"

"Oh I'm really boring then, Phyl'; I'm sure you wouldn't like me."

"So, Mr. Williams, you've made your mind up already that I like you?"

"I can see I'm going to have trouble with you," he replied with a smile.

"Here's my card."

She looked at the card before reading it out: "Import and Export Consultant? Impressive, Mr. Williams."

"I can assure you, Phyl', the word boring would describe it much better than impressive, and please call me Jack. Seriously though, Phyl', please accept my apologies for my pathetic actions yesterday. I was out of line." He purchased his fresh flower and, having put it into his lapel, took the plunge. "I'd ask you out again, but I suppose there's a long line of dead gorgeous guys in front of me?"

"Well actually," she said smiling, "the line isn't that long. By the way, my name is Phylamina." She then gave him her business card.

Jack waved as he left the shop, closing the door behind him. Although he hurried to work with a definite skip in his stride, he arrived a little late, which annoyed him.

"At least," he thought, "I have Phylamina's number."

The takings were not going as well as the day before and he thought to himself "Tight Bastards; I hope they all go to hell." In between funerals, he took the opportunity to ring Phylamina and make a date for the coming Friday. They decided to meet and have a meal in an Italian bistro that, in conversation, they had discovered they both knew very well. It being near Phylamina's apartment and, coincidentally, quite close to Jack's friends, Tony and Cindy. He then rang Benny the stamp and arranged to pick up his package on Friday afternoon. On his next break he made his final phone call to 'The Davies Trading Company' and asked to speak to Mike Tomlinson. After a pause, a girl came back on and asked who was calling. After giving her his name, there was another slight pause before Mike's booming voice came through. "Hi Jack, I didn't expect to hear from you until Saturday."

"Yes, Mike, that was the arrangement, but I needed to raise a couple of points with you and also to ask if it would be possible to pick up my order on Friday?"

"Oh I see, fire away then, Jack."

"I would like you to confirm that my order has been made to fit a 3 inch diameter pole and also a 4 by 4 inch square post.

"Yes, that's all in order. Anything else?"

"Well, only to confirm that it is adjustable only with an Allen key."

"Let me see," Mike said, as he read down the order book, "Yes, that's all taken care of and yes again, you can pick it up on Friday. Right, see you then," he said before hanging up.

Mike had been extremely abrupt, as usual, but Jack thought, "What the hell, he's also very efficient."

Jack was pleased when the day finally finished and he was on his way. The takings had not been too bad in the end and he still had to pinch himself to make sure he was not dreaming. He had hit on something so profitable, and yet so easy. On his way home, he called into a department store and enjoyed himself selecting some new clothes, as he obviously could now afford to. He then went for a meal before going home. After finishing his chores, he unwound with a couple of drinks and Ella Fitzgerald.

The following morning being Thursday, now the last day of his working week, saw Jack walking briskly to Phylamina's shop on his way to work. She gave him a smile as she put his flower in his lapel.

"This one is on the house, big boy," she said affectionately.

He put his arm around her waist and kissed her on the cheek, which made him feel as though he was marking out his territory; going on to ask, "Can I call you Phyl'?"

"You must call me Phylamina," she answered with a playful, disapproving look.

Leaving, he said laughing," I'll call you later, Phyl'."

Having left the shop, he cursed as he noticed it was raining. He had previously taken rain into account of course. In the back of his car he had a long canvas bag, which contained a collapsible canopy. Having erected it in approximately fifteen minutes, it kept him and his treasured poster dry, as well as the mourners of course. Even so, the rain tended to hit his takings very badly. He mockingly called it: 'An act of God.'

On his way home, he called in to see his mother. He thought that she looked dreadful, but he was used to it. She was 45 but looked much older. He explained to his mother that he had been to see old Tom, who had the grocer shop at the corner of the street, and had left some money with him for any supplies that she would need. He went on to warn her that old Tom, under no circumstances, would supply her with alcohol or money. He stayed with her for what seemed like an eternity but, in fact, it was no more than a couple of hours. He could never think of anything to talk to her about. He had, in fact, been thinking about the next day and the things that he had to do before meeting the beautiful Phylamina.

Friday morning was drab and rainy, but not enough to dampen Jack's spirits, as he banked $2,500 and then went off to the Davies Trading Company, as arranged. Having collected his parcel, he put it into his car and, as it was only 1.15 pm, decided to call on Benny the stamp a little earlier than planned. Benny gave him the new badge and he was so impressed with it, he immediately placed an order for another six venues. Benny didn't blink an eye when Jack presented him with six new names, as the golden rule applied; the need to know basis. They then both went out to lunch and had an enjoyable chat about old times and old friends.

Jack arrived home at 4.30 p.m. and immediately unpacked his parcel from the Davies Trading Company. He set the mechanical date and loaded the blank tickets into the machine, according to the instructions, before successfully trying it out with a couple of $1 coins. Having checked that the attachment would fit a 4-inch by 4-inch post, he packed the whole thing away. He then lay down on the sofa and within seconds fell fast asleep. He woke with a start and looked at his watch. Having seen the time to be 6.30, this surprised him as he felt as though he had only been asleep for a couple of minutes.

After showering, he dressed in his new, smart gear. It was a warm night so he decided he wouldn't need a jacket. He put on his black shirt, which the sales girl had said enthusiastically, "That makes you look fantastic, sir." He smiled, as he thought he had always been a sucker for a pretty face. The phone rang as he was looking in the mirror. Phylamina's voice came on, explaining that, as she only lived five minutes' walk from the bistro, it made more sense for them to meet at her apartment. She went on to give her opinion that they were a bit old to be meeting on the kerb like a couple of teenagers.

"Speak for yourself, old lady," he said laughing.

He wrote her address down with a glint in his eye. He thought she was a beautiful woman and he fancied having this particular notch on his belt.

Before going to pick Phylamina up, Jack went first to the bistro for a quick drink. He had travelled by cab, as he didn't want her to see his old battered up car. There were two guys serving and one of them was actually Italian. He gave each of them a $20 tip and asked them to make a fuss of him later on, when he returned with his girlfriend. They agreed of course and, having made sure they both knew his name, Jack went off to pick up his date.

Arriving at her apartment block, he was impressed, as it was situated in such a pretty rural area and looked really up market. He was happy to see that she lived on the first floor, as he didn't want her to know that he was afraid of lifts. Having spoken to him on her intercom, Phylamina was waiting for him at her front door. He took that as a sign that she was really keen. She invited him in and he gave her a kiss on the cheek. He then told her that she looked fantastic. She stood before him in an old pair of Jeans and a tight, blue top, finished off with a simple pair of sneakers. He was not aware, as he looked at her long, shiny hair falling loosely round her shoulders, that she felt as though she was being examined, until she commented. "I'm sorry, Jack. I hope you don't mind, but I have to wear silly dresses and girly things every day at work. I feel more comfortable like this."

He smiled and looked her up and down, licking his lips as though in anticipation. They both laughed and enjoyed a glass of wine, while chatting and generally getting to know each other, before then walking to the bistro.

On the way, she explained that she came from Irish parents, who lived approximately six miles away, going on to explain that she loved them both dearly, and made sure to visit them at least once a week. He lied of course, telling her that his parents were both dead.

"I noticed on your shop sign that you have two middle names," he said as he took hold of her hand. "What does the D.T. stand for?"

"Phylamina Donna Theresa Riley," she said with shoulders snatched back and standing her full height. They chatted on like old friends until eventually reaching the bistro. He, of course, had told a pack of lies. They entered the bistro and, to Jack's complete surprise, as soon as the waiters looked up, they began to make a fuss of Phylamina, hugging her in turn. Jack put his finger to his lips, indicating the need to keep their mouths shut.

Feeling like an idiot, he was introduced to Antonio Berezi and Sam Potts, as they were ushered to their seats. Phylamina explained that Antonio and Sam were old friends of her brother. She further explained that they had been to many family gatherings, and that she loved them both dearly. "Antonio," she then said, "works occasionally in the bistro in order to help out his best friend, Sam, his main job is actually a security guard."

Jack couldn't help but feel as though Antonio and Sam were judging him the whole evening, especially Antonio. Even so, he really enjoyed himself, as he loved being with Phylamina. He thought they had the same sense of humour, and that she gave as good as she got with her sharp wit.

They eventually left the bistro and walked hand in hand back to her apartment. It was a beautiful, clear night and, as Jack looked up at the stars, he pondered, "I'd better not blow this by coming on too strong". Having reached her apartment, she made them both a cup of coffee and they chatted and joked for at least an hour. Finally, she picked up the cups and took them into the kitchen. As she was washing them, he gently turned her round to face him, and placing her wet hands behind his neck, kissed her. He was sure he could feel her body tremble against his hard muscles. He was tempted to make the next move, but he didn't want to ruin it so he bade her goodnight leaving behind, if only he knew, a frustrated woman.

Saturday morning, Jack had his breakfast and then rang Phylamina, who was working in her shop until noon. "Good morning, Irish," he said. She reprimanded him tongue in cheek for calling her 'Irish.' Totally ignoring her, he went on, "Have you any plans for this afternoon, this evening, and for the next thirty or forty years, old lady?"

"I suppose, old man, that has probably been your opening line to hundreds of conquests that you have had in the past. Actually, I'm calling on my parents to pick up their dog, Alfie. He's my dog really, and he's adorable, but I didn't think it was fair on him with me being in the shop all day, so he lives with them now. Anyway, they are going away for a couple of days, so I am going to look after him, which means, of course, I can't go out tonight, as it wouldn't be fair to leave him alone."

Jack's heart sank. He immediately thought this was the old, 'I'm washing my hair tonight' or, one that he has used himself, 'I have to go out of town for a business meeting.' Phylamina sensed the insecurity in him and smiled; it was the little minx in her. She then broke the silence and lifted him again. "I'll be back from my parent's house by about three, though. Why don't you come and join little Alfie and me then? If you like, I could make us a nice meal later on this evening. What do you think?" His spirits lifted transparently, even across the phone, which made her smile again wickedly.

Jack called into a little wine shop on his way to Phylamina's. Looking at two particular wines that seemed rather expensive, he asked the proprietor the reason why. The old guy, having explained, impressed Jack so much that he chose a red and a white. He took a cab again, arriving at three thirty. She opened the door to him wearing a very smart skirt and a figure-hugging top, which took his breath away. She picked up on his look.

"I'm sorry, Jack," she said, "I'm still wearing my working clothes. By the way, this is little Alfie. He's going to look after you while I change my clothes." Alfie, a little black Cocker Spaniel, was wagging his tail furiously and started excitedly jumping up at him as he made his way into the lounge. Phylamina disappeared into what Jack imagined to be her bedroom, leaving him with, what he thought, was the friendliest dog on earth.

"If a burglar broke in here, Alfie, I bet you'd lick him to death wouldn't you?" The little dog wagged his tail even faster and then went off across the lounge and returned with a toy bone. Phylamina appeared wearing a pair of shorts down to her knees and an old baggy T-Shirt.

"I hope you're not wearing that horny gear in order to get me into your bed, Madam?" Jack said looking her up and down.

"You can skit all you like, Jack Williams. I wear clothes to suit myself, not to impress or titillate men. Apart from when I am at work that is. Right, let's go; we're off to Central Park," she added, picking up a poop scoop in the hall and handing it to him. "That will be your responsibility. It's strictly a man's job, as is cleaning drains, fixing cars, taking out the rubbish and the like."

"Is that right, Madam, and what exactly is a typical woman's job then?"

"Oh, we have to make ourselves beautiful of course" she replied as she tickled his rib cage. "Come along now, stop dawdling." He loved her sense of humour and laughed as they went down the stairs.

They drove to the park in her van with the name of the shop in huge letters on both sides. He had never really shared anything like this before with a woman, but thoroughly enjoyed it. They played with little Alfie, throwing sticks for him to chase, and berating each other unmercifully in a good-humoured way. He didn't even mind the mud on his new pants, which he had purchased in order to impress her. She knew, of course, and found it humorous.

They returned to her apartment at 6.30 p.m. Alfie, having run so much, looked tired; they had a cup of coffee on the balcony as he snuggled into his dog bed in the corner. Jack explained that he had only ever had a dog once in his life, a scruffy little mongrel called Patch, when he was about eight years old. "Unfortunately," he went on, "the poor little dog was run over by a truck."

"Oh dear," a soft hearted Phylamina said. "That must have been awful for you. So you do like dogs then?"

"Oh yes, I love them, but like you, I feel it would be unfair to leave a pet on its own while I am at work." He was sure he was scoring points by the minute, which of course he was.

"Jack, will you stay out here and keep Alfie company while I shower and change please?"

"Of course," he replied, giving her a little kiss and a hug, which she responded to warmly. Phylamina reappeared some time later wearing a very simple, but beautiful linen dress. He was quick to notice that she wasn't wearing a bra. He thought she looked the most beautiful woman he had ever seen, and found her perfume almost intoxicating.

"You go and have a shower, Jack. I've put out some clothing in the bathroom that should fit you." After noting the downtrodden look on his face, the little minx added, "They belong to my father. He left them here after painting my apartment and he's about the same size as you."

"I see," he replied, "that's another job men are supposed to do then?"

"That's right, Jack, now you're getting the idea."

Having reached Phylamina's bathroom, he looked around at the beautiful sculptured tiles and expensive looking paintings, which he hoped she hadn't bought from Benny the stamp. He walked into the large shower cubicle smiling at that thought. Standing under a huge showerhead, he turned on the faucet. A massive amount of hot water came cascading down, saturating him in seconds. The sheer volume and power had taken him by surprise.

"That's it," he thought. "When choosing a new apartment, this kind of quality will be my benchmark." Stepping reluctantly out of the shower, he noticed she had left a plastic razor for him on the washbasin. He proceeded with great difficulty in trying to shave, as little plastic razors were not designed for bristles such as his. Meanwhile, Phylamina was in the kitchen, giggling to herself at how easy it had been to bring Jack's bottom lip down onto his chest, with a simple line about there being some men's clothing that should fit him in her bathroom.

"Men are such idiots," she thought, "and women are so superior". She was feeling pretty good about herself; she had met quite a few men of course, but never one whom she could really relate to. One who could possibly be her one and only soul mate. She then thought of Jack with his sexy, dark eyes and thick, black hair. How her knees had turned to jelly at the feel of his rock hard body when he had kissed her. She looked down at her erect nipples pushing against her thin dress thinking "Let's hope he picks up the right signals tonight, the big dope." She felt her face flush and smiled, before carrying on to create a wonderful Irish stew, with dumplings and a thin wholemeal crust on top, along with grilled mushrooms and honey glazed carrots.

"Nobody can make this dish quite like mum," she thought.

She bent down and stroked Alfie, who was wagging his tail furiously. He took another little tit bit from her hand, having sat there patiently staring at her not even daring to blink, in case he missed something.

Jack came into the kitchen wearing her father's jeans and T. shirt. "How do I look, Turkey?" He asked, smiling.

"You'll do, I suppose," she replied, as she reached up onto her toes and kissed him gently on the lips. "Dinner will be about another hour. "I do hope you're hungry," she added as she proceeded to pour out two glasses of wine.

"I'm starving," he confessed as he followed her out onto the balcony with Alfie scurrying between his legs. When they were settled and relaxed, he began to pontificate about the wine saying. "The interesting thing about this wine is that for hundreds of years, it's been grown by a private family in Northern Italy. Apparently, it's a very tiny grape that reacts in a strange way when going through the process of fermentation..."

Phylamina, who had been listening intently with a smile on her face, interrupted him at this point.

"Enough of all that nonsense, Jack." she said, handing him $40. "Antonio asked me to return this to you." They both burst out laughing.

The meal went really well; he ate like a horse and she liked that in a man. He raved about the Irish stew. She liked that as well. His table manners, she noticed, were appalling, as she watched him, amongst other things, wave a fork around his head with a piece of meat on it. She could soon sort that out, she thought.

They chatted away, totally absorbed in each other's company, covering many subjects, as they shared a couple of bottles of wine. Much later, with the meal over, they took the dishes out into the kitchen and shared the chore of cleaning them. Having put the clean dishes away, Jack put his arms around her tiny waist and gave her a long, endearing kiss, which as before, made her go weak at the knees. With their bodies locked together, she was feeling quite hot and excited, until she was brought down to earth with a bump, as he stupidly asked, "Can I see you tomorrow, Phyl'?" She looked up at him and shook her head. She could hardly believe that he had not picked up on the right signals.

Taking hold of his hand, she proceeded to pull him along after her, as she walked down the hall and into the bathroom.

He watched in amazement as, having shut the bathroom door behind them, Phylamina simply opened the door to the shower cubicle and walked in. She then spun around and turned on the powerful jet of water. Within seconds she was absolutely drenched to the skin. Her erect nipples pushed at her thin linen dress, and it was obvious to the, by now extremely excited Jack, she was not wearing anything on the lower part of her body under the clinging dress. Jack thought it was by far the horniest thing that he had ever seen.

Discarding his shoes and socks, he joined her under the torrent of water and, like her, was quickly soaked. He kissed her passionately as she dragged open the buttons of his shirt and jeans, as their tongues hungrily sought out each other's lust. Having practically ripped the shirt off his back, she pulled down his jeans and boxer shorts which ended up on the shower floor.

He pulled her thin dress up to her waist, and lifted her effortlessly up and onto his rampant erection. She gasped with pleasure as she clung on tightly with her hands behind his neck. These were moments of raw passion under the cascading water. Jack managed to keep control of himself long enough to carry her out and lay her onto the fluffy white bathroom rug, where they rode out their crazed hunger together.

He felt sure that they had climaxed at the same time, which, he thought, always gives a man a terrific feeling, at least men who know and appreciate good sex. They eventually ended up back in the shower laughing, as they tickled each other and then having stepped out, towelled each other dry.

Phylamina looked at him sheepishly with her big, blue eyes. "You wouldn't like to do me a favour would you, Jack?" She asked. "My hair takes ages to dry and little Alfie needs to go out for a walk before he beds down for the night." He could hardly refuse, so he dressed in his soiled clothing that he had worn in the park that day. As he was heading for the door with a very excited Alfie, he heard Phylamina shout. "Don't forget the poop scoop, Jack".

On their return, Phylamina gave Alfie a biscuit, as Jack complained about having to clean up the pavement after him. In reality though, he was getting to like this little chap with the floppy ears and never ending appetite.

Chapter 2

Sunday morning, Phylamina woke up with Jack's big hands roaming all over her body.

"Mmmmm, Mr. Williams, what are you like?" she murmured, turning round and cuddling into him. Later, they had breakfast on the balcony with Alfie, who sat patiently waiting for a morsel of food, after having had his morning walk with Jack. They chatted about Phylamina's education. She told him that she had studied Law in England, in an all-girls college. Aside from that, she added, she had always been interested in antiquities, which she thought would be her chosen career, until on her 20th birthday when her father had given her the Florist's shop.

They then went on to talk about music, the weather, Phylamina's parents, even politics. However, Phylamina thought that dragging any personal information from Jack was like trying to get blood from a stone.

Phylamina then explained that little Alfie had a problem, in that he occasionally dripped blood from his penis. She told him that the veterinary surgeon had advised a course of antibiotics, in case it was simply an infection. When that failed to work, he had then advised castration, as in his opinion, Alfie was producing too much testosterone, and it was inflaming his prostate gland. There was no guarantee that castration would work, he had said, but it was the usual order of treatment for this problem. Jack butted in at this point, offering his advice. "Just put him with a load of bitches, that'll sort him out."

Phylamina looked at him and shook her head "You men make me laugh, you seem to think that cures anything and everything. Anyway, before you rudely interrupted me, I was about to tell you something. He's booked in to have the operation, and my parents are a bit worried about looking after him. I've decided to take care of him myself, even if it means taking time off work. I was thinking, perhaps you could help me with him?"

"Only if you pay me in kind, by pandering to my every wish, Turkey." He replied, winking his eye.

Phylamina smiled. "It's impossible to have a conversation with you, Jack Williams; you've got a one tracked mind." She then looked at her watch. "Goodness me I've loads to do."

Before Jack departed, they arranged to meet later at 4 p.m. They were in agreement that they both needed an early night because of work the next day and, with that in mind, had booked a table at Sam's Bistro for 6.30 p.m. Consequently, that gave them time to take Alfie for a good walk in the park, feed him, and then him leave settled on the balcony while they went for an early meal.

They arrived at the bistro promptly at 6.30 p.m. Antonio and Sam made a fuss of Phylamina, as usual, they then sat down to enjoy a meal in relaxing surroundings, which was going well until Antonio remarked. "I'm sure I know you from somewhere, Jack, I never forget a face."

Jack simply shrugged his shoulders, as he replied, "I don't know, Antonio, perhaps you do."

Antonio wouldn't let it go and went on to ask him about his occupation, which irritated Jack. He did his best to hide his annoyance and gave him one of his phony business cards. Antonio then pushed on further, making

Jack even more uncomfortable. Looking at the card, Antonio asked. "Have you an office in town?"

"No, in my line of business I tend to use agents, as it keeps my overheads low. I imagine Sam and Phylamina would appreciate that every month, when they have to pay out their biggest outlay, their rent." Sam and Phylamina enthusiastically agreed, which took the pressure off.

Jack walked Phylamina home before grabbing a cab, arriving at his apartment at 9 p.m. He did the rest of his preparations for the following morning, having studied the obituary column previously. He then poured himself a whisky and sat down in his favourite chair. As he relaxed, he thought about the wonderful weekend that he had spent with Phylamina, making a mental note that Sam's Bistro was now out of bounds.

Monday morning, having turned off his alarm, Jack leapt out of bed. He was feeling a little nervous, as it was the first day of the St. Thomas account. He set off earlier than usual and, after picking up a flower and giving Phylamina a kiss, arrived at work early as planned. Taking the package that he had picked up from the Davies Trading Company out of the car, he quickly read the instructions again, before then placing the machine against the post. He then swore, as it didn't fit! He had made a mistake, the post turned out to be 4-inch by 6-inch. Checking his watch, he swore again, before taking the machine back to the car and ramming it into the boot. Having set his precious poster up onto its stand, he calmed down, and by the time the first mourners came through, had recovered his cool, professional manner completely.

The first collection went well and on his first break he rang up the Davies Trading Company, asking to speak to Mike Tomlinson, making sure to give his own name in order to save time. After a few moments Mike came on.

"Hi, Jack, do you have a problem?" he explained what the problem was and Mike suggested he drop the machine off and they would put it right by the following week. In his most charming manner, Jack then explained that he needed the machine for the following day and asked would it be possible for a workman to stay behind, in order that he could do the alterations that night. Mike said he would see what he could do, and in his usual abrupt manner, hung up. Jack left his cell phone in the car and went off to do his next collection.

Later that morning, he rang up Mike again, who said he had arranged for an engineer to stay behind, adding that Jack would have to pay for the overtime and parts. He readily agreed and, having set a time, was just about to tell Mike how grateful he was, when the phone went dead. The incomparable Mike Tomlinson had struck again. Jack just smiled.

The first day at St. Thomas' had gone okay, but no more than that. Jack turned up at the Davies Trading Company, as arranged, at 6.30. He was eager get the job done and by 7.30 was on the road, with the machine having been altered to his satisfaction. He was so satisfied, in fact, that he gave the engineer a healthy tip.

Having eventually reached his apartment, he made himself some supper, Spaghetti Bolognaise, and settled in for the night. He rang Phylamina, who asked him how his day had been. He hated her asking awkward questions about his job, as it brought home to him how difficult it would be to sustain this wonderful relationship. He told her that he had encountered some problems, but kept it extremely vague. "The less lies you tell," he thought, "The less you have to remember."

However, to Phylamina on the other end of the phone this just served to raise more questions in her head; where did he live? Has he any family? Where is his car? Why does he never talk about his job? They said goodnight and hung up. She was feeling sick inside. She had fallen for him in a way that she had never before experienced, and it made her feel terribly vulnerable and a bit weepy. She went off to bed and fell into a fitful sleep.

Tuesday morning saw Jack scurrying to work. He had decided not to bother with the fresh flower, as St Thomas's was quite a bit further away than St. James's and, in any case, he needed to be there early to get the machine into position. Arriving in plenty of time, he took it out of the boot and fitted it to the post. "Perfect," he said to himself, as he tightened the clamps with an Allen key. He had decided that ordinary nuts and bolts would be too handy for some little two-bit thief to steal the machine. The need for an Allen key, however, meant that it was much safer. Satisfied, he stepped back and read the words on the machine: "Pay and display. $1.80 cents. No change given. Will not accept notes. He looked around him at the interior car park, provided free of charge by St. Thomas' and uttered to himself, "Thank you very much." He further noted that the position of the machine, under an archway leading to the service, was perfect.

Checking his watch, Jack smiled as he considered the approximate total of $50 that he would net from an average of 28 to 30 cars, paying $2 per car. He had reasonably considered that people upset, attending a funeral, would not bother looking for loose change and would simply put in $2. In fact, in his opinion, $2 represented good value for money. But more importantly, his business would prosper by approximately another $4oo per day.

He walked over to his position by the poster where, as the people arrived, he witnessed them first reading the sign and then putting their money in, before returning to their cars with the sticker. It was all he could do not to laugh. Especially, as they then filed past him putting more of their money into his cask, as he shook hands with them saying, "God bless you."

The day went well and, after the final funeral, he removed the parking machine from the post and loaded it

41

into the boot of his car, along with the stand and poster. He drove straight to his apartment and, emptying the machine, counted out $390 and a few cents. "Not quite as much as it could have been," he thought. "But a very nice bonus thank you!" He then counted the money from the cask, which totalled almost$900, making a combined figure of $1280 for the day. He entered this amount into his ledger with relish. Having poured himself a whisky, he sat down and, remembering the parking machine, smiled as he thought, "Where did I get that one from?"

Eventually, he showered and changed and was on his way to Phylamina's, as arranged.

On his arrival, Phylamina greeted him with "the meal won't be ready for quite a while yet" in a cool manner.

He noticed that she was a bit frosty towards him and wondered what he had done wrong. During the evening, he tried to lighten the atmosphere with his own brand of humour, but to no avail.

"What did you do at work yesterday, Jack?" she surprisingly asked, putting him on the back foot. This direct question really threw him and he was stuck for an answer, so he decided to buy some time.

"Will you excuse me, Phyl'?" he asked. "I need to go to the John." Returning soon after he sat down. "Sorry about that, Turkey," he apologised, having recovered his poise. "Yesterday? Well, I had quite a good day really. I fixed up a deal with some guy in Peru, who wants to export his afghan clothing into the U.S." She just stared at him, her eyes cold. He could stand it no longer and so asked her directly what was wrong.

"Why do you never tell me anything about your life?" Before he could answer she carried on, which pleased him as it gave him a chance to think. "I don't know where you live, what car you drive, your friends, family, nothing."

He took hold of her hand and gently squeezed it." My darling, Phyl', it's simply that I'm not proud of it all. I live in a run-down apartment in the Bronx, which I will be leaving behind pretty soon. My mother is not dead; she's a raving alcoholic. I run an old, clapped-out, two door saloon, which also I will be changing soon, as my business is doing very well. I work hard and my job is really, really boring. I would much rather talk about your life, as I find it so much more interesting I suppose."

He could see that he had hit all the right notes, as her eyes cleared and her face softened. She put her arms around his neck, and kissed him. "Jack Williams, I don't care about those things, I'm not that shallow." She leaned forward and kissed him again only this time with much more passion. He slid his hand up the inside of her T-shirt and deftly unhooked her bra. He could feel her heat as he cupped her breast. Running his fingers over her swollen nipple, he whispered. "Thanks to you, sexy lady, I seem to have lost my appetite." Picking her up in his arms, he carried her into the bedroom. Later, as Phylamina lay contentedly cradled in Jack's arms, with her head dreamily snuggling onto his hairy chest, Jack whispered in her ear "I treasure every moment I spend with you, Irish. By the way, did you remember to turn down the heat on the meatloaf?"

"Oh my God, the meatloaf!" she screamed, scrambling out of bed. They both ran full pelt for the kitchen like a couple of streakers. On opening the oven door, the kitchen immediately became engulfed in plumes of choking smoke.

"Open the window, Jack, I'll try and save the meatloaf"

Having donned the oven gloves, she lifted the roasting dish out of the oven. Looking at the meatloaf with Jack peering over her shoulder, she uttered in a defeated tone "it looks like an incinerated prune!" The pair of them broke into a fit of laughter. When their infectious laughter had died down, Jack shrugged his shoulders "well, we can always use it as a doorstop, Turkey"

Thursday morning, Jack was up bright and early fixing the parking machine to the post. It was his last day at St. Thomas' and he made a mental note of his need to ring Benny the Stamp, in order to make arrangements to pick up his new badges. As he stood looking at the machine, he went sick inside as he heard a car drive into the car park behind him. He kept his cool and, thinking quickly, put his hand into his pocket and getting out two $1 coins, put them into the machine and ripped off the parking ticket. He then turned round praying that he wouldn't be looking at the cops, only to thankfully be looking at an elderly gentleman walking toward him.

"Good morning." Jack said as he walked past the old guy and put his ticket on the inside of his own windscreen. Then retracing his steps, he walked past the guy who was busy putting his own money into the machine. Carrying on under the arch, he then walked quickly past the church and out of the way. Luckily, he had not yet set up his poster and cask. Waiting for the funeral to end, he knew that he could get set up for the next one, but this episode had unnerved him and he just wanted away. He waited until the first funeral had been done and dusted so to speak, before removing his machine and putting it into the boot of his car.

Jack had taken it for granted that nobody would ever arrive before the hearse carrying the coffin but, shaking his head, he thought, "I reasoned without that disrespectful old bastard." He decided, as he drove out of St. Thomas' car park for the last time, that really there had been no cause for panic, but it was the last day and perhaps he needed a day off anyway. He decided to use the time to visit his mother. He stopped off at Old Tom's grocery store to see if he needed to leave more money. There were a few customers to be served before he could have a word with Tom, but he was in no hurry. He was feeling more relaxed about the incident in the car park. "No job runs smoothly all the time" he concluded.

"Sorry to keep you waiting, Jack," old Tom greeted him, smiling, "How are things?"

Jack had been looking at Tom serving the customers thinking how unfair it was. The poor guy had been as bald as a coot for about the last 25 years and, consequently, had been known as Old Tom since he was approximately 40 years old.

"Fine thanks, Tom," he replied, as at the same time he began counting some money.

"You can put that away, Jack. Your mother hardly eats a thing; in fact, I still have about a $100 left over from what you left last time." He shook Tom's hand and thanked him and at that moment he felt true regret for all the things he had rifled from Old Tom's store, as he had been growing up. Having sorted things out with Tom and left the store, he firstly made arrangements with Benny the Stamp, regarding the picking up of the new badges the following afternoon. He then went and spent an impossible couple of hours with his drunk of a mother. He explained again, in vein, that she could have food and other provisions from Old Tom's store any time she needed them.

There were two messages on Jack's answer phone, when he arrived home One was from Phylamina shouting. "Hello, my darling, I was just thinking of you and I wanted to hear your voice on the answering machine. I have taken pots of money today from the plebs. Yahooooooo, byeeeeeeeeee."

Jack laughed; he found her sense of humour very funny. The second message was from Tony Martin, which simply said. "Will you give me a bell?"

"I wonder what Tony wants," he thought, "I can't tell him what I'm up to at the moment, as he's very religious and certainly wouldn't like it." Having rang his number; Tony's voice came on the line. "Yeah?"

"Hi, Tony," Jack said. "What's goin' down, man?"

"Not you I hope, you womanizing little thief. Listen, I want you to do me a favour on Saturday night. Be at my place at 6.30 p.m. and bring with you an overnight bag with smart casuals and a dinner suit. On your way, call in to the Blue Lagoon club and ask for Guy Peters. He will be expecting you at about 5 p.m. You will know him when you see him, he's the cocktail waiter and he's served you and me before. Now, he's going to teach you how to make a special cocktail. I have all the ingredients that you will need in my kitchen, so you don't have to worry about them".

"Hang on," Jack broke in. "What the hell are you goin' on about? Why would I be worried about the ingredients for a cocktail?"

"Jack, all will be clear to you soon, now don't be late." The phone then went dead.

"Favour?" Jack thought, looking at the dead phone, "that's no favour, that's an order." His shoulders sagged. "What the hell, there's nothing I can do about it. Problem is, what do I tell Phylamina?" All of a sudden he felt shattered. He had been through a traumatic day and now this. God knows what Tony had in store for him. He had a shower and settled down for the night with a bottle of wine and a plate of pasta. He soon felt a little better and thought he should give Phylamina a bell. The problem being that, for the first time in his life, he found it extremely difficult to tell a lie.

As he was deep in thought the phone rang and it gave him a start. It was Phylamina's cheery voice. "Jack Williams, why have you not rung me?"

"I was just about to, Phyl'."

"Phylamina," she reprimanded, "my name is Phylamina."

"Listen, woman, that name, like everything else about you, is too good. You have everything going for you, beautiful face, sleek body, shining white teeth and a fantastic boyfriend. As a matter of fact, I think you should give all the rest of the women a chance, by maybe putting some spots on your face, or knocking out a couple of front teeth."

"When you've finished with all the crap, Jack Williams, perhaps you can tell me when we can see each other."

He smiled, as he loved the banter between them. With a lump in his throat, he lied. "Well actually, gorgeous, I know that we planned to spend the whole weekend together, but I have a major problem at work. I have to go to Boston on Saturday and I won't be back until Sunday afternoon. I'm really sorry, but I don't have a choice. Can I take you out for dinner tomorrow?"

"That will be fine, don't worry," she replied. He knew from the sound of her voice that she was disappointed and he felt a heel, but what could he do?

He owed Tony so much. He then shuddered at the thought of what this latest escapade could be.

Friday morning, Jack was at the bank depositing his takings, which were building up very nicely. He was nearly at the target that he had set himself before taking a chance and renting an improved apartment, so off he went to a Real Estate Agent to check some out. After checking out a couple of disappointing apartments in the price range that he had set himself, he decided a rethink was in order.

Having picked up the new badges off Benny, they went for lunch and a couple of drinks. He loved Benny's company, as they usually ended up having a laugh about old times. When eventually he reached home, he thought about Phylamina and how he had needed to lie to her.

"At times like this" he thought, "my lifestyle makes me feel old, really old." Ringing the bell on Phylamina's intercom later, he was pleasantly surprised to hear her sounding chirpy. The buzzer sounded and unlocked the door. He bounded up the stairs, as usual, three at a time, to find that she had already opened her front door for him.

"I'm in the kitchen." He heard her shout. He crouched down onto his hands and knees and crawled into the kitchen panting for her with his tongue out. She laughed out loud and jumped onto his back. He crawled as fast as he could across the lounge carpet with her still on his back laughing, before collapsing. They finished up rolling over and over like a couple of teenagers.

"You're a nutter, Jack Williams," she laughed.

He looked her up and down and said in a cheery voice. "I thought you'd be ready to go, woman."

"Oh, I thought as we were going to Sam's bistro, I would be fine like this." she said looking down at her usual T-shirt and jeans. He had already thought of an excuse not to go to Sam's bistro.

"Well, I wanted to make up for ruining our weekend, so I've booked a table in the Old Hall Hotel restaurant in town to make a fuss of you."

"You are a big softy aren't you?" She kissed him on the cheek, stood up then pronounced, "I'll have to change then, won't I?" Running to her bedroom, she shouted back, "Pour yourself a glass of wine." Coming back a few minutes later, she posed in front of him "Well, do I scrub up okay?" He looked at her with hungry eyes as she twirled around and around like a young girl going to the High School prom. She had on a figure-hugging dress that made the most of her stunning charms. He licked his lips and then whistled at her.

"Don't do that, Jack Williams, I'm a woman not a dog."

He just laughed and took hold of her hand. "C'mon," he said, "I'm starving."

They grabbed a cab and went off to the restaurant. Phylamina was really impressed with the Old Hall but gradually, as the night wore on; she became quieter and quieter, which puzzled him. Eventually, he asked her if there was anything wrong. She whispered in his ear. "It's a bit embarrassing, but I seem to have my period earlier than expected. I've tried to sort myself out in the John but really, I feel uncomfortable. I'm sorry, but could we go home please?"

Having paid the bill, they grabbed a cab and went to her apartment. He made them both a cup of coffee and a few minutes later, she came back from her bedroom looking much more relaxed, wearing her jeans and T- shirt.

"I'm so sorry for ruining the evening," she apologized, "I can't understand it, as I am usually spot on time with my periods. It must be all the wonderful sex I've been having."

"Oh yes?" he said laughing. "Who have you been having wonderful sex with then?"

She punched him in the arm and scowled at him, as it hurt her more than it did him. Sometime later, he explained that he would have to go, as he had preparations to make for his trip the following morning. She acted hurt but really she was relieved, as she had terrible period pains and simply wanted to go to bed with a couple of painkillers. As she was seeing him out he grinned, "I'll give you a bell on Sunday afternoon and, perhaps if your period has finished, we might do something together."

Scowling at him again, she replied while pushing him out of the door, "Get out of here, you, monster!"

Chapter 3

The following afternoon, Jack packed his overnight bag and put a suit and shirt on a hanger. At 4.30 he went down to his car and hung his clothes carefully on the back seat. Having made sure he had everything he needed, he tried to start his car. The motor seemed to be turning over but for whatever reason, it just would not start.

"Fuck," he swore to himself as he pulled the lever to unlock the hood. After checking the spark plugs, Jack tried again but to no avail. He banged the hood down, took his bag out of the car and with his clothes over his shoulder, scurried down the street in the direction of the Blue Lagoon, praying he could catch a cab. Luckily, he was not long in getting one and climbed in sighing with relief. He thought about Tony's reaction if he turned up late and shuddered, as Tony hated tardiness. He had often heard him say, "If you're late for something, it's because you don't care enough about it, end of."

As the cab pulled up outside the Blue Lagoon, Jack looked at his watch. It was 5 o'clock and he was running a bit late. He paid for the cab and went into the club. Looking around he thought that he recognized the guy serving behind the bar, so he approached him, "Guy Peters?"

"As I live and breathe, man," the bartender replied staring at the clothes draped over Jack's shoulder.

Jack removed them saying. "Don't ask, Guy, and by the way, I'm Jack Williams."

As they shook hands Guy said, "Put your gear over there in one of the cubicles and come behind the bar. I'm gonna teach you how to make a terrific cocktail."

Having rejoined Guy, Jack asked him why it was so important that he should learn how to make this particular cocktail. Guy just shrugged his shoulders.

"That, my friend, is between you and Mr. Martin; I just do as I'm told. Now, we don't have much time so, if I were you, I'd pay full attention." At 5.45 Jack was fully versed and now wondered what all the fuss was about. Although he had never seen this cocktail before, it was pretty straightforward and simple to make. He jumped into a cab and finally rang Tony's doorbell ten minutes late. Before the door opened, he knew that his host would be annoyed. Sure enough, as Tony opened the door, he made a point of looking at his watch. Jack didn't bother making excuses, as it would rile him even more.

As he entered the lounge, Tony's girlfriend came out of the kitchen smiling, "It's wonderful to see you, Jack" she said, as she hugged him fondly.

"It's nice to see you, too, Cindy. That's a better welcome than I received from Tony."

"Oh, don't worry about him, he's a right grump. Come on, I'll show you to your room."

Having hung up his clothes, Jack went back into the lounge where Tony, having brightened considerably, put his huge arm around Jack's shoulders and gave him a hug saying, "Thanks for this, it really does mean a lot to me." Then noticing the puzzled look on Jack's face, he went on.

"Patience, patience, my young friend, come out onto the patio and I will explain all."

Jack sat down facing Tony across a small table on the patio, which was bedecked in fresh flowers. Tony didn't seem in any great hurry as he picked up a box of Havana cigars and, as usual, refrained from offering one to his guest, which Jack always found to be very strange. Tony was taking his time cutting off the end of the cigar, as Jack looked out across the huge lawns. The gardener was tending to the flowerbeds in front of the impressive lawned tennis courts, which were about 100 yards away. He had never seen anyone play on them and, although he would never say so, he had always thought they were simply a status symbol.

Cindy appeared with a pot of coffee and some biscuits.

"Here you are, boys, I'll just leave you to it."

Having put them down on the small oak table, she went back inside. Jack surveyed Tony, wondering if he should pour out the coffees. Tony had his eyes closed puffing away on his cigar. The front of his shirt was wide open as usual, showing the thick but greying hair on his barrel chest. He sat there seemingly oblivious to Jack, who went ahead and poured the coffee.

Eventually, Tony put down his cigar and, after having sipped his coffee, leaned back, "Right, Jack the lad."

Jack went sick inside as Tony always used this address when he had a particularly difficult task for him. "I have a very important job for you. One of Cindy's friends is staying the night as her husband is away on business. Now, this is where you come in. She is having dinner with us in town tonight and this is the bottom line. I want something on this bitch. It's very important to me that I gain some power over her and I know that I can rely on you not to let me down."

This immediately put pressure on Jack and Tony was well aware of it.

"This is the story" Tony went on. "Her name is Tracy Fielding. You may have heard of her, as she is a high court judge. When she arrives tonight, I want you to play the role of Greg, my nephew. Now you know Greg very well so, if the conversation gets difficult, it should be easy for you, as you know his job, his family and where he lives. Now, we are going to tell her that you are staying with us for a few days."

Jack broke in, "Hang on, Tony, I can't stay here that long."

"No, no, you're missing the point, I don't expect you to, that's only for her benefit." Jack relaxed back in his seat, dreading what was coming next.

"When she arrives, I want you in your casual clothes but I want you showered, shaved and smelling real nice. Now, before going out for dinner, we will be having a drink with you out here on the patio. I've never seen a woman who can resist you, so I want you to flirt with her big style okay?"

Jack rolled his eyes, "Just carry on please, Tony."

"Right, after a while, Cindy will suggest that you make us one of your special cocktails. Now we already know that Tracy loves cocktails, so she will be delighted. You will make it very cleverly in front of us, but before you pour the cocktail, I want you to insist that we each of us must drink a small, glass of water. You will explain to us that this guarantees our taste buds being clear and receptive to your masterpiece. Right, Cindy will give each of us a glass of water, then you will serve the cocktails. Now, with that out of the way and before we leave, Cindy will ask you what your plans are for the evening, to which you will reply, 'I'm having a night in watching television. At this point, I'm pretty sure Tracy will suggest that perhaps you would like to join us for dinner. If she doesn't, then Cindy will suggest it anyway. You, of course, will politely say that you don't wish to impose and we will then politely say that of course you must join us. You will then get changed and off we'll go."

Cindy appeared and enquired if they wanted any more coffee, to which Tony declined without even consulting

Jack. He then went on, "Now, is that all clear, or is there anything that you don't understand?"

"Well yes, Tony, it's very clear, what I don't get is the outcome."

"Yes, yes, please don't be impatient, all will be revealed. On the way to, and in the restaurant, I want you to flirt unmercifully with her. Cindy assures me that she will love it. During the evening, I will complain about cramps in my stomach, something I suffer with anyway, as you know. Cindy will suggest that we return home, where it would be more comfortable for me. I will object a few times before eventually bowing to her insistence.

Now, on returning home, I'll go straight to bed leaving Cindy to have a couple of drinks with you both. She will use the opportunity to explain that a couple of sleeping tablets and a good night's rest usually does the trick when I suffer with stomach cramps. She will then bid you both goodnight. Before going up to bed, she will say to you 'Greg, you know where everything is so please make yourselves at home.' Now look, I want you to woo the pants off her. I want you to take her to your room and give her a good fucking."

"Hold on, Tony, this is too much, you're not really expecting me to shag this tart?"

"Jack, I wouldn't ask you to do this for me if there were any other way. I'm desperate to gain some power over her, and you are my only chance, I'm sorry but that's it. Now, do you have any questions regarding the plan?"

Jack excused himself and went to the bathroom. His head was spinning and he needed time on his own. He felt nothing but revulsion for what he was being asked to do, but he also knew that he owed him big time, and Tony Martin knew it. Particularly, for one incident that happened in the early days of their friendship, which was now running through his mind as he rinsed his face with cold water. He had been working for one of the big hoods in town named Clint Hastings, with another two-bit thief like himself.

After one particular job, the pair of them felt aggrieved. They hadn't been paid anywhere near what had been promised and so decided on a course of action. This was to break into one of the warehouses owned by Hastings, in order to steal whatever they could for recompense. Unfortunately, they were caught in the act by one of Hastings's henchmen, who consequently shone his flashlight into Jack's face and, of course, recognized him before being knocked out by Jack's young accomplice from behind with a piece of wood. They then ran away leaving the guy in a heap on the floor. Luckily he recovered but, of course, reported this to Hastings, who immediately put out a contract on Jack.

Over the next week, Jack went into hiding in fear for his life. The news eventually reached Tony Martin, who contacted Hastings on his behalf and somehow sorted out a deal. This lifted the contract off Jack's head. Ever since, Jack felt he owed him his life, which he more than likely did.

Jack dried his face and hands and, with his head now much clearer, returned and rejoined Tony on the patio. Cindy immediately stood up and walked into the house as Jack approached.

"Okay, Tony, I'll give it my best shot, but what if this Tracy woman doesn't go for it?"

"She will no problem. Cindy has told me that she likes a bit of hanky panky on the side and I don't blame her, as she's married to that boring bastard Grant Fielding. In any case, after having drunk the small glass of water, before sampling your special cocktail, she will be as horny as fuck for a good few hours, as it does have a special ingredient, which, by the way, is tasteless when mixed with water.

"Ah, I see, I was just going to ask you what all that was about. I suppose it goes without saying that you already have my room bugged?"

"You bet your sweet life I have. There are three cameras in your room strategically positioned for maximum exposure. I want the bitch's face on view, so be careful not to hide it. I want really strong stuff. I want to clearly see you fuck her without a condom. This part is important. I would like the whole scene dirty, the dirtier the better."

Jack cringed, "Tony," he pleaded, "I have a beautiful girlfriend and, for her sake, I simply must use a condom."

"No chance, it must be bare shagging, it wouldn't have the same impact otherwise."

Jack knew from past experience that it was a waste of time arguing with him when he was in this mood, so he reluctantly agreed.

"Okay, Tony, you win. How will I activate the cameras?"

"As soon as you turn on the light in your room, the cameras will be activated automatically. If Tracy wants the lights off, the cameras will still roll. Naturally, I'd prefer to have them on, but the cameras are fitted with infrared, so it won't matter."

"What if she insists on going to her room?"

"No problem, her room is fitted out as well but that will be most unlikely, as your room is downstairs, and therefore more discreet."

"Well, Tony, you seem to have thought of everything as usual. Hang on though, what if it's the wrong time of the month for her?"

Tony laughed out loud at this. "There's not much chance of that, Jack. The lady is sixty four years old."

"Oh, no," Jack screamed, "Please, my girlfriend is twenty one years old and you are asking me to shag a pensioner?"

"First of all, she's a very attractive woman, and in any case, this is a job, and you are a pro. That's all that matters and, by the way, you'll walk away tomorrow morning with $3000 in your pocket."

Jack nodded his head "Okay, I just want you to promise me one thing."

"If I can, I will. What is it?"

"I want you're assurance that Cindy will never see or hear the video, as I imagine there is sound as well?"

"There sure is, it'll pick up the slightest noise and yes, you have my word."

Having laboriously gone over every detail again, Jack showered, shaved and dressed in his smart casual gear. Later on, standing on the patio, Tony drenched him in expensive aftershave saying." Great stuff, champ, she won't be able to resist you."

"No, no, no," Cindy said laughing, "You have far too much aftershave on. You men really don't have a clue do you? For goodness sake, Jack, go and wash some of that off." He took her advice and on his return, she kissed him on the cheek. "That's better," she said, "Much better."

When Tony and Cindy were dressed and ready to go out, they sat with Jack and went over it all again, but for Cindy's sake, left out the bedroom scene.

The doorbell rang. Jack, now sitting on the patio on his own, could hear them greeting Tracy and exchanging pleasantries. He then heard Tony say. "Come out onto the patio, Tracy, my nephew Greg is out there and we are going to have a drink with him before we leave." Jack stood up as the group approached him. As Cindy introduced him to Tracy, he gave her a warm smile and said that he was pleased to meet her. As he was looking at her he couldn't believe that she was sixty-four years old as she had a terrific figure and, probably because of face-lifts, looked no more than forty five to fifty. He also thought she had lovely eyes and a pleasing personality. She wore little make up and sported a very nice tan.

"Flirting with this chick will be no problem," Jack thought to himself.

For the next half hour or so, Tony and Cindy took every opportunity to leave Jack and Tracy alone by attending to drinks and the like. Jack tried one of his outrageously sexist and chauvinistic lines, which some women found really funny. Luckily, she found it hilarious and he was on his way, up and running.

With all four of them together again, Cindy suggested they all try one of Greg's special cocktails and Tracy seemed really keen.

"I see you're a man of many talents, Greg." She said giving him a smile. Jack proceeded to mix the cocktail in front of them with some style, juggling a couple of lemons with one hand and also showing them a trick that Guy had shown him in the Blue Lagoon Club. They all clapped him for his efforts as he finished making the cocktail.

"Right, my friends, before I allow you to sample this masterpiece, I must insist that you all drink a small glass of water as it needs to be tasted by a clean, fresh palate." He had acted out the whole scene with panache, and Tony noticed that Tracy was lapping it all up. For the first time since she had arrived, he began to relax. Cindy served the water, which they drank. Then, after a toast from Jack holding up his glass of, "fun, fun and more fun." They each drank their cocktail in one go, before congratulating Jack on his hidden talent.

"So far so good," thought Tony looking at his watch. "I think we had better be hitting the road, folks."

As they were preparing to leave, Tracy came in right on cue. "Have you any plans for tonight, Greg?"

"No not really, Tracy, apart from a couple of beers and television."

Tracy then went on, turning to Tony and Cindy. "Maybe Greg could join us for dinner?"

"No no, please," Jack intervened, shaking his head, "I wouldn't like to impose." Of course they all insisted and so off he went to change.

Jack, standing in his bedroom, looked at himself in the mirror, thinking that he looked quite dapper. There was a tap on the door. Tony walked in and said. "I don't want you to have too much to drink tonight "I'm not having brewer's droop ruining everything."

Jack looked at him in amazement. "You cheeky bastard" he replied before turning on his heel and walking out of the bedroom laughing.

The cab arrived and whisked them off to the restaurant with Jack in the back, between the two ladies. This gave him the chance to make his physical presence felt; allowing his strong, muscular thigh to lean firmly against Tracy's, which she didn't flinch from. As the evening progressed, he carried on flirting with her, but tried not to be too obvious. Tony periodically complained of stomach cramps, and Tracy was suitably sympathetic. Cindy suggested a couple of times that they return home, where Tony would be more comfortable.

Eventually Tony agreed and off they went in a cab. As soon as they arrived home, Tony went straight to bed as planned, leaving the other three in the lounge having some drinks. Cindy explained that this was a recurring problem with Tony's stomach and it was nothing to worry about. He would take a couple of sleeping pills, and after good night's sleep, would be fine. After a suitable period, Cindy said that she should go to bed, as she was shattered and still a little worried about Tony. After taking a couple of sleeping pills herself in front of them, she kissed them both goodnight. As she was leaving, she shouted to Jack. "You know where everything is, Greg, please make yourselves at home."

Jack made him and Tracy another drink and said that, although he was very fond of Tony and Cindy, the night was young. He then proceeded to pull a coin from behind Tracy's ear. "An old trick" he thought, "but it never fails." She lapped it up. He then put on some background music.

"Could I have this dance, my lady?"

"Of course, kind sir," she replied and joined him in the middle of the lounge. They had a few dances over the next hour, slow ones of course. He gently teased her and plied her with more drinks, until he sensed that the time was right. As they danced with their bodies locked together in the middle of the lounge, he stopped and kissed her gently on the lips. He didn't want to blow everything and he knew that this was the moment of crossing the line. He needn't have worried as she responded, pushing her tongue hungrily into his mouth. His plan now was to hopefully allow her to make all the moves, and it couldn't have gone better.

She whispered in his ear. "Where's your room, Greg?"

He took her hand and led her along the hall and into his room, where he immediately turned on the light, which of course started the cameras rolling. He leaned her against the door and kissed her with passion, as he was extremely aroused himself. He then unzipped her dress and slipped off the shoulder straps. Without any sign of protest from Tracy, it fell to the floor. He was pleased to see, in the bright light, that she was wearing only her bra and pants. He skilfully removed her bra. Then, kissing her nipples with her breathing heavily, he slid her panties down. She entwined her fingers in his thick, black hair as her breathing became more pronounced. He then stopped and exchanged places with her, so that his back was to the door. He then put her fingers onto the buttons of his shirt.

Tracy undid them and slipped the shirt from his muscular body, before kissing his chest, as he had done before with her. She then undid the buttons of his pants and they dropped to the floor. His manhood was pushing his boxer shorts out so much; she had to pull the elasticated waistband out and over. With her breathing heavily he kissed her and deftly manoeuvred her over to the bed

He positioned her just on the edge, as he wanted the cameras to be able to see the full penetration. Then lifting her legs up and apart, he pushed into a very willing partner.

Turning her over onto her hands and knees, he did the same doggy fashion. Jack felt for sure that the audio recorder would easily pick up the noises she was making. He then turned her onto her back again as he wanted the cameras to be able to see her face, when and if she came. He helped this become more probable by gently rubbing her with his fingers. Then taking hold of her hand, he encouraged her to take over; as he thought that she obviously would know how to bring herself off, which she did with plenty of moans as the pleasure waves engulfed her. Jack was not far behind; he had been holding himself and couldn't have lasted much longer. He came with terrific passion as she dug her fingers into his skin, and raked them down his back.

They lay in bed for a while teasing each other and having a laugh until, to his surprise, he became aroused again and wanted more. She was definitely ready as well, so the cameras got a bonus session. Eventually, she dressed and kissed him before going up to her room. He fell into a deep sleep.

Jack's slumber was broken the next morning by Tony shaking his arm at 7 a.m. with a glass of water and two painkilling tablets in his hand, "Here, take these, they'll cure your headache."

Suddenly, Jack felt the pounding in his head and the pain behind his eyes. He swallowed the tablets and lay back with his eyes closed.

"I'm sorry, champ," Tony went on, "You had the same ingredient in your water as Tracy. I couldn't take the chance of anything going wrong. Don't worry, though, I take them myself. At my age you sometimes need a bit of help. The down side is the horrendous headache that you are suffering with now. Enough of that, though, what I want to know is, how did it go last night?" Jack scowled at him but told him what had happened. Tony was delighted and gave him an envelope containing his $3000.

"Now look, Jack, I know how rough you are feeling, but I don't want you here when Tracy comes down, so with that in mind, I've ordered you a cab. It will be here in 15 minutes. Don't worry about paying the driver, as that's been taken care of."

Jack smiled sardonically "You're all fucking heart, Tony, do me a favour and take me off the payroll in future."

As the cab sped along Jack thought about the night before. He now realized why he had become aroused so soon after climaxing and, with a mental picture in his mind, murmured, "Bastard."

The telephone ringing seemed to Jack as though it was miles away and woke him up. He opened his bleary eyes and checked his watch; he had been asleep for five hours. The answering machine clicked in with a message from Phylamina.

"Hi, Jack, I don't know what time you will be home, but I'm going to my parent's house for Sunday roast at 2.30, and they asked me to bring you along. God knows why they would want to meet a rough boy from the Bronx, but there you are.

Hope you managed to sort out the problem in Boston. Give me a call on your return, byeeee." The machine then went dead. He lay there for a while thinking how nice it would be to go with her to meet her parents, as he loved being with her. In fact, he thought that he loved her. Jack had never felt this way about a woman before and it made him feel good. The problem being, there would be searching questions from her parents and, not wanting to risk that, he decided that it would be wiser to ring her on her cell phone at about 3.30, and arrange to meet later.

"My life's a mess," he thought, as he lit a cigarette to go with his cup of coffee. He thought of Phyl' as being wonderful, fantastic, beautiful and sexy. She was, in fact, everything that he had ever wanted in a woman. She turned him on, made him laugh and had a very strong character. In fact her strong character made her very hard to handle sometimes but that's what she was made of and he loved her, end of. Even so, he faced up to the harsh truth. Because of his lifestyle, he couldn't see a future for them. He couldn't see a light at the end of the tunnel. Even if he tried living within the law, what would he do? What could he do? If he could figure out the answers to those things he still would have the problem of explaining to her the loss of his Import and Export business. He could come clean and tell her the truth, but with her background, being educated in England in one of the top boarding schools and, in general, having lived a life that he could only have dreamed of, he felt sure it would spell the end for them, as she was as honest as the day was long. In any case, what could he do? No training, very little education, not even a history of another job, never mind a résumé. The whole thing seemed impossible. All this negativity made him feel depressed and lonely. Then a thought lifted his spirits considerably. The possibility of building up a sizeable lump sum from the proceeds of the funeral scam filtered through his mind. Why couldn't the lump sum be used to finance a legitimate business? No reason why not! Of course, for the scam to last long enough, meticulous planning for each and every venue was crucial. All this was going through his mind when he was startled by the phone ringing. He didn't answer it in case it was Phylamina. The answering machine clicked in and he picked it up as soon as he heard Tony's voice, which was really upbeat.

"Terrific job, champ, the bitch will have a copy within the week and then I'll have her by the fucking tits. Oh by the way, Cindy was very impressed with your performance on the video. No, I'm only kidding," he then added and laughed, "But seriously, I won't forget what you've done for me. Speak to you soon." The phone then went dead.

At 4 p.m. Jack rang and, after a brief chat with the usual greetings, he asked her what time she would be returning home. She replied that she would be home by five o'clock and that she would have little Alfie with her, as he had been castrated in order to cure his problem.

"Are you coming over?" She went on.

"Of course I am. I can't wait to see you," he said truthfully. At 5.30 he was bounding up the stairs to her apartment three at a time as usual. He had done all his preparations for the following morning. There was no interior car park at this new venue and he didn't want to disrupt the daily amount that he was raking in. With this in mind he had decided to take the parking machine and mount it at St. Thomas' on the way. He considered his plan to be risk free, and he could pick the machine up on his way home that night.

Phylamina was waiting at the top of the stairs for him. She put her arms around his neck. "I've missed you, Jack Williams."

He kissed her tenderly then looked down to see what was banging into his leg. It was little Alfie with a lampshade around his neck. "He needs that in order to stop him licking or biting his fresh wound." Phylamina said stooping down and stroking him. "The trouble is, he hates it and he doesn't understand, I feel so sorry for him."

Jack bent down and stroked him, "C'mon, little fella, it won't be for too long."

"The trouble is, Jack, the vet wasn't very clear on how we are supposed to deal with the situation. Do you think it would be wise to remove the shade?"

"I really don't know, Phyl, but probably, if he were mine, I would be afraid of him disturbing his wound."

"You're right, but we'll have to give him lots of love and attention." They walked into the apartment with Alfie banging into the frame of the door and the wall. He then tried to run between Jack's legs and in the act of trying to avoid stepping on him, Jack went sprawling headlong in the hallway.

"For goodness sake," Phylamina said laughing, "you're worse than a two year old." She helped him up as Jack complained of having hurt his groin, suggesting that it might need a massage.

"There's obviously nothing wrong with you, Jack. Come along, Alfie, I'll give you a little biscuit." They then spent the evening together. Alfie settled down well and fell asleep. At 10.30 p.m. Jack said that he would have to go, as he had to be up for work early the following morning. She crunched her face up to show her disappointment and asked him to stay the night.

Jack found it almost impossible to refuse her anything but said, "Phyl', I have to be up at 7 a.m. tomorrow morning.

"Oh come on, Jack, I have to be up early, too. I'll set the alarm for 6.30 a.m. You will be home before 7.15. Come on, please, please, pretty please?" He of course gave in and they took little Alfie for a short walk. She insisted on taking the lift, as she didn't want Alfie overdoing things. He of course hated that but said nothing.

Phylamina sorted Alfie's bed out on the lounge floor and, with him settled down for the night, they went off to bed. Jack made each of them a cup of warm milk and placed one on each of the bedside tables. As he then proceeded to undress, his world collapsed as Phylamina leapt from the bed screaming like a banshee. With her eyes wild and tearful, she began to pummel his hard muscular body with her tiny fists in a frenzied attack. Jack had a startled look on his face as he tried in vain to calm her. "What's wrong, Phyl'? He asked while holding her wrists as gently as he could"

She shouted hysterically. "What the hell are those scratches on your back?"

He usually reacted to things quickly, but on this occasion was completely stumped. He had totally forgotten Tracy Fielding digging her nails into him, "Phyl', it's not what you think." he said in panic.

"What do you mean, it's not what I think?" She asked hysterically. "Now I know what your problem was in bloody Boston. I told you when we met that I deal in truth." Then, with tears rolling down her cheeks, she went on. "Now put your clothes on and clear out of my life." He tried to soothe her, but she became hysterical. "Take your hands off me," she screamed. "If we don't have trust, we don't have anything."

"But, Phyl', it really is not what it looks like," he shouted. She became even more hysterical and, picking up his clothes, marched out in a rage with him in pursuit still pleading with her. As they went through the lounge, Alfie was barking and running into the furniture with his lampshade. She opened the door and threw his clothes out onto the exterior landing. He tried to take hold of her but she screamed at him and pushed him out of the doorway. She then slammed the door shut and ran sobbing to her bedroom. Jack felt sick inside as he dressed. His glimmer of hope, as the door reopened, was soon brought down to earth when she threw his shoes at him and slammed the door again violently. He could hear her crying and tried again to reason, but it only made her worse. He gave up and reluctantly went home.

Jack lay awake on his bed the whole night. "What have I done?" he thought. "This is really not my fault. Why does my life always get fucked up?" His mind was in turmoil. "What if I tell her a watered down truth? Or even the whole truth?" His alarm went off and he hadn't slept a wink. He picked it up and threw it at the wall with all the force he could muster but, of course, it didn't make him feel any better. He lay back on his bed with tears rolling down his cheeks. He decided he couldn't go to work, instead he made his mind up to go and see her and beg her forgiveness. "Perhaps," he thought, "She may have calmed down". He wondered whether or not he should come out and tell her the whole truth and beg her forgiveness? He thought of the wonderful times that they had enjoyed together. At the park with Alfie, watching television, their first lovemaking session in the shower, times that they had sat on the patio with a bottle of wine chatting; wonderful, simple moments that he had never dreamed possible, until he had met Phylamina.

He fell into a fitful, restless sleep, and eventually woke up feeling shattered. He checked his watch, 9.45 a.m. He had a banging headache, and felt a hundred years old as he dressed. He sat picking at his toast and tried again to figure out what he was going to say to Phylamina. Eventually he gave up, threw his toast into the trashcan and decided it was time to face up to her.

Arriving at Phylamina's shop, he looked in the window. There were two women in the shop so he waited, standing in the pouring rain, until they picked up their flowers and left.

Phylamina looked at Jack with cold eyes as he entered. The rage had gone, only to be replaced with something worse, total indifference. He began to utter some words of regret, but she stopped him in his tracks.

"Look, I told you when we met, that I deal in honesty and truth. I don't think that you know the meaning of the words."

"Okay, Phyl', I'll tell you the whole truth but not here, can we meet for a coffee or a drink somewhere?"

She slowly shook her head, "There really would be no point. You have removed something from our relationship as though with a scalpel and it can never be replaced. I would very much like you to leave now please." He looked into her cold eyes as a customer entered the shop and knew that there was no point staying. Having concluded she obviously needed more time, he turned round and walked out of the shop feeling depressed. He then went for a long walk, before ending up in his local bar, eventually becoming totally smashed.

As the week went on, Jack tried twice to talk to the still extremely cold Phylamina. The second time, she threatened to send for the police, so he wrote her a letter, which she returned in shreds.

In his despair, Jack drank more and more. He had lost his drive completely. Although he still went to work in order to earn enough for his boozing, he didn't care about anything and was beginning to take chances. He no longer checked the obituary column, and often didn't bother with the moustache and spectacles. Then, he made one mistake too many. He forgot to change the official badge from the venue the week before. Consequently, as he was standing watching the people file through, putting their hard earned money into his cask, he noticed that one of the mourners seemed to be taking an unhealthy interest in him. As the rest of the people passed, this guy stayed back and enquired. "Excuse me, sir, but what is an official of the Church of the Good Shepherd, doing collecting in the grounds of St. Marks?"

Jack, without even looking at his badge replied, "Our two churches are working in conjunction, sir. We have been for about a month now." The man looked at Jack and then his watch before walking on to the funeral service. As soon as the guy was out of sight, Jack quickly removed his poster, stand and cask, then threw them into the boot of his car and was away before the funeral was over. Cursing himself for a stupid mistake, he then went to his local bar as usual to drown his sorrows.

The following day, Jack went back to St. Marks bedecked in his disguise. He joined a group of mourners going in to a funeral, suitably dressed in his black suit. As he had expected, the game was up. There were three men dotted about who very much looked as though they could be police officers, even though they were in plain clothes. The following week, Jack visited another church that was on his hit list, only to find church wardens in attendance. The word had obviously hit the church grapevine, rendering this fantastic scam inoperable.

As the weeks and months went by, Jack continued to drink his way through the money he had saved. A new apartment was now out of the question, but didn't seem that important anymore. His twenty-third birthday came and went, but that didn't seem important either. He never answered his telephone; even messages from Tony were ignored.

A large envelope arrived, containing newspaper clippings of a trial in the high court, presided over by Judge Tracy Fielding. There was a picture of the accused, a Mr. J. Draper. He was a close friend of Tony Martin's. Jack had met the man a couple of times and remembered him well. He was extremely influential in all the rackets and the police had done him for tax evasion. According to a reporter in one of the clips, the expected punishment had been a custodial sentence of between six and ten years in the state pen. However, he had inexplicably escaped with a massive fine and three years community service. It all became crystal clear to Jack. Tony had ruined his life for the sake of keeping this murdering bastard out of prison. He crunched the clippings up in his hands and threw them violently against the wall, before sitting down with his head in his hands.

A few miles away, outside of town in her apartment, Phylamina was sitting with a magazine on her knee. She had just finished reading it and was now looking through the kitchen doorway at her boyfriend, Antonio Berezi. He was singing one of his many Italian songs, as he toiled away completely in a world of his own, cooking one of his special Pasta meals. She smiled as she looked at him with his receding hairline and trim figure, sporting a Paddington Bear apron. She found it amazing that such a kind, gentle, romantic guy, trained three times a week for kickboxing. It seemed to her so out of character. At that moment he turned and winked at her with a huge smile on his face, then carried on singing at the top of his voice, looking very happy, as was the future Phylamina Berezi.

Gradually, Jack's attitude changed from total despair, to total indifference. He had not seen his mother for months now, when yet another bombshell hit him. A message from old Tom on his answering machine said, "I'm very sorry to have to tell you like this, but your mother passed away on Friday night. The funeral, which has been arranged by the local church charity group, is on this coming Wednesday. I have the keys to your mother's apartment, so will you give me a ring?"

Jack dashed over to see old Tom. He apologized for not having been in touch, but said he had been through a rough time. Tom gave him the keys and he went up to the apartment.

Jack unlocked the door and entered. His memories of growing up in this so-called home were not good ones. Although the apartment was a bit of a ramshackle, desperately in need of some maintenance, he was always taken aback by the quality of the furniture and fittings, which to him looked like they could be antique, as could the collection of figurines and the velvet lined box of strange spoons. He didn't have a clue himself, but wondered whether Phylamina would help him.

Wednesday arrived; the funeral was a small affair with just a few people. No family of course, apart from Jack. Old Tom had told him that the keys to the apartment had to be handed in by the following Monday, which didn't leave much time. Jack rang up a dealer and made an appointment for the following evening at 8.45, before then going on to his local bar, to hopefully find the answer to his problems, at the bottom of a glass yet again. The following day, he went over to the apartment to pick up any paperwork he thought he should keep. After sifting through it all, he didn't have a clue what was essential and what could be thrown away, so he left it all there and returned home.

At 6.30 p.m., he sat by the phone trying to muster the courage to ring Phylamina and ask for her help with the paperwork, furniture, and possible antiquities. With her knowledge of antiques and law, he thought that she would know exactly what to do and he didn't have the remotest idea of anyone else he could turn to. He poured himself another shot of whisky. He had already drunk about five shots but, "what the fuck" he thought as he downed it in one and picked up the phone. Phylamina's voice came on, "Hello?"

"Phylamina, its Jack. Please don't hang up. I need your advice on something very important."

There was a pause before she answered. "I don't think so, this is…" she started to say until Jack broke in.

"Please, Phyl'. My mother has died and I don't know anyone else who could help me."

After another pause she came back on, "I'm very sorry to hear about your mother and I'm not promising anything, but how on earth can I be of help to you?"

He felt a little easier. It was the first time that they had really spoken since that fateful night, which now seemed like another lifetime away. He told her what the problems were and went on to say, "Please believe me, Phyl', if there was anybody else I could ask, I would. It's taken me all day to pluck up the courage to ring."

After another long pause, she came back on and agreed to help.

"What would you like me to do?"

He told her about the appointment with the dealer, the spoons, the furniture and the paperwork.

"I can't drive tonight," she said, "I've had a couple of glasses of wine."

"Can I pick you up outside your building then, Phyl'?" he asked. Another long pause ensued before she reluctantly agreed but warned him not to get the wrong idea. She told him he was not to come up to her apartment under any circumstances, but instead to call her from his cell phone on arrival. He put down the phone and poured out another double whisky, which he downed in one and then cleaned his teeth. Grabbing his keys, he then went down to his car. Before starting the motor, he reached into the glove compartment and took out a small canister of Gold Spot. He sprayed his mouth a couple of times so that she wouldn't be able to smell the alcohol. As he neared the district where she lived, he noted again how pleasant it was compared to his own, with trees, flowers, and even fields.

Arriving at her apartment block, he gave her a call and sat back and waited. It was now 7.35 p.m. and he hoped she wouldn't be long as it would take at least 35 minutes to reach his mother's apartment, it being just on the New Jersey side of the George Washington Bridge. He watched her approach the car five minutes later and smiled as he noticed what she was wearing. She had on jeans, plain brown shoes, a t-shirt and a throw around her shoulders. To him she looked fantastic. Getting into the car she said shyly, "Hello, Jack."

They then went through the usual pleasantries that people do when they haven't seen each other for a long time. It seemed odd to both of them as they had been so close. It was a cool, gloomy night with drizzle beginning to fall and probably because of the atmosphere, forgot to turn on his lights. The amount of whisky that he had downed no doubt played a part in that oversight.

The strange atmosphere was broken as Jack started the motor and drove down the avenue. They went over a small crossroad before turning right. They then travelled approximately one hundred yards with Phylamina trying in vain to fasten her seat belt. She was not to know of course, but it had been jammed for two years. Suddenly, and as if from nowhere, a police officer appeared out of the gloom waving his flashlight from side to side. Jack panicked. He put his foot down and accelerated past the startled officer with Phylamina screaming for him to stop. They had only gone a short distance, when another two police officer's appeared waving flashlights. More screams from Phylamina went over his head, as he tried to veer past them. The car didn't react on the greasy road and they went into a skid, hitting one of the Police officers as they careered on past and rammed very hard into, and then onto, a high kerb. The motor consequently stalled.

Jack, now crazed, restarted the motor and ramming it into gear, accelerated down the lane and away. His mind was a blur as he drove crazily in sheer panic. There was no sound from Phylamina. He thought she must have passed out. The car was lurching from side to side on every bend, until he took one too fast and it went completely out of control. It skidded straight through the bend on the greasy surface, smashing a fence down in its path, before taking flight through the air and belly flopping into a river. He was doing his best to hold Phylamina back as she was not wearing a seat belt. Panic changed to absolute terror as the car sank and the water began to rise inside. He tried to open his door, but it was jammed. Unbuckling his seat belt, he tried to bring Phylamina round, but to no avail. After feeling for a pulse in her neck and wrist without success, he tried crudely to administer mouth-to-mouth resuscitation. Having failed, and with the water getting ever higher, he screamed, "Oh my God, what have I done?"

Then, self-preservation took over. Scrambling into the back seat of the car, he lifted the tiny frame of Phylamina up and over to the left, placing her into the driver's seat. He then put the seat belt on her. The water was now half way up the window as he took deep breaths and exhaled slowly, trying to keep calm while he waited for the water to clear the top of the glass. With his head in a pocket of air between the top of the door and the roof, he took a deep breath before winding the window down as fast as humanly possible. He then extricated himself through the small space and out into the cold, dark, murky water. He swam frantically to the surface where, gasping for breath, he seemed to be covered from all angles by flashlights. As he was dragged out of the river by the police, they were shouting, "Is there anyone else in the car?"

"Yes," he cried in anguish, "but she's dead." He was taken straight to hospital for an examination and also a blood test, which was requested by the police.

When the medics had finished with him, the police asked him to make a statement, which he did. His statement read.

"At 6.45 p.m. this evening, I drove over to Miss Phylamina D.T. Riley's apartment to pick her up. She is actually my ex-girlfriend and had kindly offered to go with me to meet a dealer at my mother's apartment, where she

was going to advise me on all my mother's belongings, in order that I would receive a fair price. Stepping into the car, she said she could smell alcohol on my breath and so refused to go with me unless she was allowed to drive. I assured her that I had only had a couple of beers, but she would have none of it and insisted again.

I agreed, of course, and so we swapped places. She drove down her avenue, across a small crossroad and, after a short distance, turned right. We had not gone far when a cop appeared out of the gloom waving a flashlight from side to side. Inexplicably, Phylamina roared past the terrified cop with me shouting for her to stop. After another short distance, another two cops appeared also waving flashlights. Ignoring my screams for her to stop, she tried to go around them at great speed. At that point we must have gone into a skid as we hit one of the cops as we careered on past, before slamming into, and then onto, what seemed like a high kerb. Consequently, the motor stalled. Her head now completely gone, she restarted the motor and ramming the car into gear, accelerated away.

My pleas to her were going over her head, as she lurched through bend after bend like a mad woman, until eventually, we took one too fast, probably in the wrong gear anyway, and went into a skid. We screeched straight through the bend, burst through a fence and then we seemed to be flying, until we belly flopped into a river. Panic in me now turned to absolute terror, as the car sank and the water began rising. I tried to open the door but it was jammed. Having unbuckled my seat belt, I then tried to bring the slumped figure of Phylamina around but to no avail. It was pitch black down there as I checked for a pulse in her neck and wrist without success. I then tried to give her mouth-to-mouth resuscitation. Unfortunately, I've never been trained in that kind of thing. The water was rising fast. I think I screamed out.

"Oh my God," and I suppose then, self-preservation took over. "The water by now was almost up to the top of the window. I was able to breathe from the pocket of air between the top of the door and the roof, while trying to remain calm. As soon as the water reached above the window, I took another deep breath and wound the window down as fast as I could. I then managed to squeeze through the small gap out and into the murky water, then swam as fast as I could up to the surface, where, gasping for breath, I seemed to be covered by several flashlights. You then dragged me out of the water."

The statement was dated, signed by Jack, and witnessed. He was then allowed to go home but warned not to leave town, and to report to his local police department every day at 10 a.m. The days that followed saw him hating himself, thinking he should come clean and admit everything, take his punishment and start his miserable life over again. Then he would think, "What would be the point? Nothing would bring poor Phylamina back from this tragic accident." She was never out of his thoughts. He could neither eat nor sleep. He had strange feelings of wanting to commit suicide, and then he would berate himself for not having the courage to do so.

The phone constantly ringing was a nightmare, as the accident for whatever reason, had captured the imagination of the media, big time. It was always some reporter wanting an interview. Every day reporting to his local police department the greedy unfeeling press harassed him. He was by now drinking even more heavily than before, still looking for an answer. Waking up from drunken stupors left him depressed and even more suicidal. Eventually desperate, he rang Tony Martin for help. Cindy answered the call and told him that Tony was at work. She then asked, "Are you okay? Jack?"

"No, Cindy, I desperately need somewhere to stay for a while."

"I'll contact Tony and get back to you. He has tried to reach you on a number of occasions but your phone has been constantly engaged."

"Yes, I know, Cindy, this is all a nightmare." She promised that they would contact him real soon and hung up. An hour later, a knock came on Jack's door. He shouted through the door, "Who is it?

"It's Danny," a voice replied. "Tony told me to pick you up."

Jack opened the door and was packed and ready to go within a few minutes. He asked Danny if it would be okay if they stopped at old Tom's store on the way.

"Sure, man, no problem. By the way, Tony said you're not to tell anyone where you're going."

Jack looked in the mirror at himself as he put on his jacket. He was shocked to see a white, hollow face, with sunken eyes staring back at him.

Having reached Old Tom's store, his friend pointed out how terrible he looked.

"Yeah," Jack replied, "tell me about it. I'm sorry I've not been in touch, Tom, but you probably know why anyway."

"Yes, Jack, I did hear the news on the grapevine. I have left all the stuff from your mother's apartment in the back of my brother's garage and I have handed the keys back."

"Thanks, Tom, here's a hundred bucks for your trouble. Would it be okay if I leave my stuff there for a while? Naturally I'll pay your brother for the inconvenience." Old Tom thanked him for the money, adding that he could leave it there for as long as he wished. They shook hands warmly, and then Jack left.

On arrival at Tony's house, he was ushered onto the patio by Cindy, who then made him a sandwich and a coffee. He had just finished eating the sandwich when Tony arrived home and slapped him on the back saying, "You can relax now, champ."

The three of them sat down on the patio as Jack went through the same pack of lies that he had put in his statement. He found the truth hard enough himself, never mind Tony and Cindy. Having listened intently, Tony put his arm around his shoulders saying. "Try not to worry; you did your best for this dame. You have to get on with your life now. Cindy glared at Tony in disgust as she stood up and walked into the house.

Jack, for his part, was also extremely unhappy with his friend's attitude but he had nowhere else to go, so he bit his lip and stayed. He continued to report to the police every morning, which from Tony's house meant a forty odd mile round trip. He purchased a copy of the *New York Herald* in order to find out the funeral arrangements for Phylamina in the obituary column. There was a picture of Antonio Berezi with a cover story of his and Phylamina's wedding plans for the future, which of course were now dashed. Jack immediately felt a surge of jealousy, which he knew was ridiculous and then conversely felt genuinely sorry for Antonio, as he looked at a face that had aged considerably. The story ended with the funeral arrangements for the following Friday. He decided to go and pay his last respects to Phylamina, even though he knew that he shouldn't. Friday saw him dressed in his black suit and tie. Tony and Cindy were against it, but he wouldn't listen to their protests. Donning his disguise, he joined the people who numbered more than he had ever seen at a funeral. Sam was consoling Antonio, who was really distressed. Next to them were Phylamina's parents, who Jack recognized from photographs. He looked at the tears rolling down their cheeks, and suddenly felt like an intruder, so he made a discreet exit. He went to Central Park, still in his disguise, and sat for hours where he, Phylamina and Alfie, had spent such happy moments together.

Saturday morning, the day after the funeral, Jack went to the police department to report in as usual. On this occasion, though, two plain clothed police officers, having identified themselves, arrested him, before then charging him with the manslaughter of Miss Phylamina. D.T. Riley. They then read out his rights and allowed him to make one phone call before putting him in a cell. Tony Martin made a point never to have any dealings with the police, so he sent Cindy. Her visit was quite short. She told him that Tony was in the act of getting him the best attorney that money could buy, and that he was not to worry. She then went on to say that Tony would foot the bill for all the legal fees, no matter how much. Sure enough, a couple of hours later, Jack was introduced to a Mr. Wilson Smyth, who very quickly had him released on bail.

They then went on to Tony's house where Wilson Smyth went through the whole sorry tale of that fateful day with his new client. Then particularly through Jack's statement piece by piece, slowly and methodically. Wilson Smyth then looked at his client square in the eyes, "If all this is true, then I think we have a really good chance. Now, is there anything you have missed out? As I don't want any surprises in court."

Jack shook his head. "No, Wilson, that's it. You have it all." Wilson then left.

"He's the best attorney in the state of New York," Tony said "and he's costing me a packet, but you're worth every penny of it, champ."

These were harrowing days for Jack, as his Attorney was putting together a case for his defence and, presumably, the District Attorney was doing likewise for the prosecution. For his part, he just reported daily to the police department, before then spending his time waiting in Tony's house, away from the public eye. His first day in court lasted no more than an hour. After pleading "not guilty," his case was sent to the Supreme Court. On his way out, as he was trying to avoid the press, an irate Antonio Berezi confronted him. Looking at him through hate-filled eyes, Antonio said in a quiet, steady voice, "I'll make you pay for this, you murdering, cowardly bastard. Somehow, somewhere, I'll put a bullet through you."

Jack was then pushed into Tony's car as the press ran alongside trying to take yet another picture of him.

The media coverage, for some reason not understood by Jack, had not abated since the day of the tragedy, but now as the weeks went by leading up to the trial, gradually the press found other sensationalistic stories to write about. Jack was glad of the respite. Sitting having a coffee with Tony, he raised the possibility of a "guilty" verdict and hence, the possible prison term that he would have to serve.

Tony offered the view. "From what Wilson Smyth has told me, a guilty verdict is unlikely. However, I have always advised you that it doesn't do any harm to be prepared for the worst. Perhaps one of the main things you would need to do if you were to end up in the state pen would be to get on the right side of the 'Top Dog'. That would make your life inside much easier. How you could achieve that, of course, is the million dollar question."

Chapter 4

The advice given by Tony had at least given Jack something to occupy his mind. He began jotting down notes in his pad as he tried to picture everyday life in the state pen. The daily routine of life behind bars. It became apparent to him that the best way to befriend the 'Top Dog' would be to be able to give him information on what could possibly be going on behind his back. He thought this could be achieved, in the early weeks of a prison term, by keeping one's eyes and ears open to idle gossip. Having decided on the carrot, namely Information, he then tuned his mind to methods of contacting the donkey, so to speak. He began to make notes of possibilities. Sitting by the 'Top Dog' at mealtime? Could prove difficult. Recreational periods? His henchmen would more than likely be present. Watching television? Not good enough. Toilets? Showers? Work time? No, no, no.

The only place that would be suitable, he jotted down, would be a place where he had the 'Top Dog's' undivided attention. With that in mind, he began to jot down everywhere that he could think of in the whole prison. Cell, dining hall, library, kitchen, gym, exercise yard and so on. Eventually, an idea began to take shape. He didn't have the answer yet, but for the first time in months, he was using his imagination. Once he had decided on the best place to isolate his quarry, he then went on to try and figure out how best this could be achieved. He used his tried and tested method of jotting down situations and possibilities, before sifting through them bit by bit. After a few days he began to see daylight. Benny the stamp, who knew practically every contact in New York, provided him with a name and address. Troy Devlin, a chemist in Manhattan. Jack went to see this chemist twice. On the second occasion, he came away with a small parcel and put it in a safe place. As was his way, he then began plotting plan b and c; hoping, of course, that neither of them would be necessary. He began working out in Tony's gym for two hours every day. He wanted to be in perfect physical shape so that he would look good in court to any woman on the jury and also capable of looking after himself physically in the event of probable fights in prison. He had stopped drinking and was eating healthily for the same reasons. Furthermore, looking in the mirror, he decided that his shoulder length hair would have to be cut short, thinking he would get more respect in court from any follicley-challenged, jealous, baldy bastard on the jury. He also considered that men or women over forty would be more likely to see him as the boy next door; 'butter wouldn't melt in your mouth' type.

He was getting fitter and stronger by the day. He still had the inconvenience of being restricted to Tony's house and gardens, but Cindy was great company. With Tony, as usual, out of the house a great deal on business, she seemed really happy to have someone to keep her company. Tony's indoor gym and pool were a real blessing. Jack got into a routine of daily two hour workouts in the gym on the running and rowing machines, before finishing off on the weights, and finally a swim. Cindy was inspired so much by Jack's efforts; she decided to join him in the gym each day for an hour's workout. Sure enough, the following day, as Jack was going onto the running machine, after having already done a workout on the other apparatus, she walked in with a pitcher of iced water. He was amazed at the amount of energy that she had as he watched her first on the rowing machine, then on the skiing simulator. His two-hours complete and with sweat pouring from every pore in his body, he drank a glass of water before then walking out and into the large outbuilding, which housed showers, changing facilities, and a swimming pool. He stood under the cool cascading water and washed the sweat from his body, and as he then walked out of the shower into the changing area, Cindy surprised him as she waltzed in as cool as you like and proceeded to strip off her sweaty track suit in front of him. She casually chatted about the gym, the pool, and her friends. He quickly wrapped the towel around his waist feeling extremely uncomfortable. Cindy picked up on his embarrassment as she stood before him in all her glory, and laughed. "Jack, please don't feel uncomfortable, Tony and I are naturists. We have been for years." She then carried on with her chitchat as she walked over and stepped into the shower. He was stunned as he put on his swimming trunks.

"I'm going into the pool, Cindy," he shouted as he left.

Powering through the water doing the crawl, he tried to get his head round what he had just felt as he had looked at Cindy, totally naked, standing in front of him. He had always thought of her like you would an older sister, but the feeling that he had just experienced bore no resemblance to that. "But she is," he thought guiltily, "an extremely beautiful woman." Cindy dived into the pool naked and began swimming up and down with grace and power, seemingly oblivious to him. As the days went by with this routine, he began to feel a little easier. Sometimes she would wear a bikini and sometimes nothing. Like him, she was a strong swimmer. They got into the habit of doing several lengths of the pool, before then going on to a diving competition or a race. Her diving technique left a lot to be desired, a sort of belly flop was all that she could manage. She still, however, demanded a mark of nine or ten from Jack, before giving him three or four.

Each time they would have a race over a couple of lengths, he would begin with the words, "Ready? Steady?"

She would always dive in before the word go, and would finish every race laughing and splashing him as he finished second. They had great fun together and it took his mind off the forthcoming trial. He was not aware of it, but she was teasing him ruthlessly. She knew exactly how stripping off in front of him made him feel awkward, like a little boy lost, not knowing what to do. She was well aware of his plan each day of staying back in the gym, giving her time to shower and get into the pool, but she liked the tease. She hadn't had so much fun for years and would look forward to it every day.

On another typical day, Jack, after having reported in to the police department, had his workout on the running machine and had just started on the weights, when Cindy entered. She immediately hit the running machine, which she normally spent most of her time on in the gym. After an hour she said, "Come on, champ, let's go and have a swim." They had a glass of water and Cindy as usual went to have a shower first, but on this occasion felt like teasing him again. She sat in the changing room and rang a friend on her cell phone while waiting for Jack. He was surprised, on entering the changing area, to find her still sitting there with a towel round her waist talking on her cell phone, as he thought she would have been swimming by now.

She really enjoyed his little boy lost look as he quickly stripped off his gear, before practically running into the shower. Cindy immediately said, "Bye for now, Sue, speak to you tomorrow." She then dragged the towel from her waist and joined a totally bemused Jack under the shower, making sure that she touched his naked body as she pushed past him. She then carried on chatting about everyday things pretending not to notice his rising erection, as she ran her hands through her long blonde hair. Having turned off her shower, she smacked him hard with the palm of her hand across his butt saying, "You naughty boy, Jack Williams," and ran out laughing on her way to the pool, where she jumped in naked. He joined her and they had another frolic like a couple of teenagers. At the end of the session, he stood on the side offering his hands to help her out of the pool, which she accepted reaching up. He pulled her out and as she said. "Thank you, sir." He promptly turned her round and smacked her rear end as he pushed her back in.

"That'll teach you, turkey," he said as he ran to the showers.

Cindy didn't bother with her bikini anymore and carried on teasing Jack as, apart from her having a good laugh, it was turning her on. Tony was getting the benefit of this every night, but of course didn't know the reason why. Jack for his part was getting regular erections thinking about what could happen between him and Cindy. He was nervous, as he knew this was wrong; he was living in Tony's house and his legal expenses were being taken care of. These thoughts were building up his resolve not to take advantage of Tony's hospitality and trust. He made a decision to break him and Cindy's daily routine, in order to remove temptation. The following day was a perfect opportunity to begin backing off, as Tony had arranged a meeting that morning, so that Jack and Wilson Smyth could go through the court proceedings. He returned having reported to the police at 10.30 a.m. There was no sign of Cindy. He thought she probably would be in the swimming pool but decided not to check. Wilson Smyth arrived late at 11.45 full of apologies and they settled down in the lounge. They then went through every court procedure laboriously, with Wilson insisting on Jack making notes. They were then just about to cover his testimony when Cindy arrived home. She pointed out to them that it was 1.15 and she would make them some sandwiches and coffee. With her busy in the kitchen, Jack pointed out to Wilson that his head was spinning and he needed a break. They decided to resume the meeting at 2.30. Cindy served lunch. The three of them gelled really well. Cindy was an interesting, charismatic lady and surprisingly to Jack, Wilson turned out to be quite a character himself, with a good sense of humour. He told them of mistakes that were often made by his colleagues and also by himself. "We're only human you know," he said laughing.

"Oh well, if you make a few errors and I end up in the slammer for about fifteen years, we'll just put it down to a bad day at the office then," Jack said, now laughing himself.

The atmosphere was light and enjoyable. Eventually Cindy stood up and cleared away the dishes leaving Wilson and Jack to carry on with their meeting. She then went for a swim glancing at Jack on her way past.

The meeting resumed and quickly took on a more serious note, as Wilson went through his statement, practically word by word. Jack had a copy and knew the statement off by heart, but it made him uncomfortable and he was relieved when they eventually put that part to rest. Wilson then went on to say they had found out, after hiring a private detective, that Phylamina had gone to a wine bar with a girlfriend straight after work on that fateful day. "Furthermore," he went on, "we have a witness, the guy who served her, who is willing to testify that she drank four glasses of wine in the space of approximately thirty minutes." The attorney was in full flow now, as he went on. "They had also found out that at the age of 16, she was charged with driving a car under age and fined $600.

Wilson I'm not comfortable with you ruining her character." Jack said, "She was a wonderful girl and it's simply not right."

The attorney took off his reading glasses and put them down on the coffee table with the paperwork. He then paused for a moment looking into Jack's eyes.

"Let's get something straight. If you get found guilty of your charges, you're looking at anything up to thirty years in the slammer. I'm only putting evidence in court that's true, so if you try to tie my hands, then maybe it would be better if you hired yourself another attorney."

Jack put his hands up, "Wilson, I've got the message; we play it your way."

The attorney then picked up the paperwork, put on his reading glasses and carried on, "The guy who served her will also testify that Phylamina had her ignition keys on top of her pink handbag. We are going to get her friend, in the event of her refusing to give evidence, subpoenaed in order to back this up. We can also prove that on the afternoon in question, she closed her shop early in order to go to the wine bar. This will show her to be irresponsible. Right, Jack," he said standing, as he put his paperwork away.

"We have agreed an approximate date with the prosecution for the trial, which will be in about two weeks. I'll be in touch as soon as the exact date is known."

They shook hands and Jack went to the door to see him off.

He then went to his room and lay down on the bed suddenly feeling shattered. He couldn't understand how everything that had been so wonderful between him and Phylamina had turned out so bad. "I'm not an evil person," he thought, "Yet this lovely girl is no more." The reality of the trial was almost upon him and his mind was racing. "What did the prosecution have? The truth had gone down with Phylamina into those murky waters, yet they must have enough evidence else they wouldn't have charged me surely?" He fell asleep and was woken up by Cindy shouting his name, as she knocked on his bedroom door.

"Yes, I'm coming out now," he shouted. He went out and into the lounge just as Tony arrived home. Cindy made them both a cup of coffee and as they sat down, Tony noticed the terrified look on Jack's face.

"Try not to worry, champ, everybody goes through bad times at some point in their life. You'll come through this, I promise."

The following morning, Jack reported to the police and then went shopping for two presents, a box of Tony's favourite cigars, and a huge bunch of flowers for Cindy. He knew a word with Cindy was necessary in order to clear the air, as he wanted their friendship to be as strong as ever. He returned with the presents to find her in the kitchen busy making some lunch for them. Her hair was damp so he knew she had been for a swim. He gave her the flowers and kissed her on the cheek. She smiled as she began putting them into a glass jug. He then somehow knew that there would not be a need to bring up the delicate subject of the swimming pool and showers. It made him feel much easier as he settled down for lunch, in the knowledge that temptation was now a thing of the past.

All concerned agreed the date for the trial. It would begin on the eighth of November. That left just nine days, and Jack was dreading it. He had practically given up cigarettes, but with the stress he now felt, was smoking as much as ever. The press were now building up pressure, after having left the case alone for a while, and he was finding it all extremely difficult. He decided to tie up some loose ends before the trial, in case he was found guilty. He went to see Old Tom and gave him some money for the inconvenience of keeping the stuff from his mother's apartment in his brother's garage. Having it there was a load off his mind. He went on to tell Old Tom that he had made arrangements with a friend to periodically keep up the payments, in the event of the worst happening. He shook Tom's hand warmly and then left in order to go and pay another month's rent on his apartment. He then went home to pick up items that he felt necessary to leave in Tony's house, such as paperwork and other personal things. As he packed them into a bag, he looked around at the apartment, which he thought looked so drab and lonely, before then turning off the electric and gas. He managed to catch a cab and arrived at Tony's house late afternoon.

Whilst sorting out the bags with Jack, Cindy commented, "Jack, you don't look well, come and sit down and I'll make you a stiff drink," she then disappeared into the kitchen.

While waiting for her to return, he looked around him at Tony and Cindy's beautiful, house, with fresh flowers as usual, giving off a wonderful aroma. It struck him that the difference between this place and his apartment couldn't be greater.

"Here you are, Jack," she said, giving him the drink. "That should make you feel a little better."

The phone rang and Cindy excused herself before picking it up, "Hello?" she answered.

After a few moments she went on, "Oh I see, no don't worry, Tony, yes he's fine. I'll see you tomorrow, darling, love you," she put down the phone and picking up her drink, crossed the lounge and sat next to Jack on the big, white settee.

Clinking her glass against his she toasted, "Here's to you, kid" and then laughed as she noticed that his was empty.

"Tony is flying to Boston tonight on business, Jack, he sends his apologies and said to tell you that he will be back tomorrow night. He has booked a table for the three of us at a top restaurant," she then picked up Jack's glass and disappeared into the kitchen. On return she told him a funny story about one of her friends, who was fleecing her new boyfriend. Her friend described him as a five foot two little runt, who thought he was God's gift to women. Jack was beginning to feel better. He told her in confidence about his funeral scam, and she thought it was hilarious.

"Tony would do his nut if he knew about that one, Jack, right; I'll have dinner ready in just over an hour, so you go and get yourself showered, shaved and changed. That'll make a new man of you."

He took her advice and, yes, he did feel much better. She was stirring some meat and vegetables in a sauce as he entered the kitchen. He tried to have a taste but all he got was a rap on the hand with a wooden spatula.

"Open a bottle of wine you, naughty boy," she said laughing.

By the time he had opened the bottle, she had the food on the table. They enjoyed the meal, the wine, and the conversation. The trial was not mentioned, as they stuck to much lighter conversation. Jack's days on the funeral scam had Cindy in hysterics. She laughed so much it made her sides hurt. They finished off the meal with coffee, which she served with chocolate covered, mint biscuits. He then wanted to finish with a cigarette but she would have none of that.

"No, no, no. You must have one of Tony's Havana cigars."

Having fetched one, she popped it into Jack's mouth and lit it for him (after having chopped off the end.) She then gave him a glass of Tony's best Bourbon to go with the cigar.

He took a long draw on the cigar and, looking up at the ceiling said, "You can take me now God."

They both laughed. A few more drinks and several funny stories made for a perfect night. Cindy then said with a much more serious face, "It was very nice of you to buy me the flowers, but there really was no need. I'm not daft you know. You felt uncomfortable because of Tony and I understand that. I also know that the flowers were given as a way of showing your respect for me. You backed off for all the right reasons, but you don't know the half of it. I met Tony when I was just eighteen years old. The fact that he was forty and much older didn't seem to register with me, as I was infatuated with him.

"You wouldn't have known me then, Jack, I was quite a shy girl and, in fact, I was still a virgin. You can lift your jaw off the floor now, you cheeky bastard," she said, as he exaggerated shock and disbelief.

"Anyway, I fell in love with him and in fact, I'm still very much in love with him. The last few years though, and I'm telling you this in the strictest confidence, he doesn't want to make love to me as much as he used to. No, that's not strictly true, the fact is, he has never had a high drive in that way. Don't get me wrong, I'm not complaining; Tony Martin hasn't a selfish bone in his body. He satisfies me in whichever way is necessary, his touch, his kisses, whatever. I don't think I have to spell it out for you. Now you're not going to like this, but I've seen the video of you and Tracy Fielding. Jack's jaw dropped open as she went on, "I know, Tony made a promise to you, and he has kept his word.

"I made a point of finding it when he was at work. In fact, I have seen it about eight times now. The reason that the video got to me is quite simple, I have never made love to anybody else but Tony and it has become a bit of a fascination for me. My friend Sue thinks I'm mad, she's been trying to get me to have an affair for ages now, but I couldn't do that to Tony. Then you moved in and we started to have a laugh together, as we always do. I began to tease you unmercifully. I would really look forward to you seeing me naked. I knew that you were getting excited of course, and that made the game even more enjoyable. At the same time that I had been teasing you, I'd been watching your video, which was turning me on. I began to imagine myself being there instead of Tracy. In fact, I probably became jealous of her. How crazy is that?

"I even began to crave for an exact rerun of that night, with me there instead of that bitch, cameras and all."

Jack was amazed by these revelations as Cindy rose and replenished their drinks. She put them onto the coffee table and said she would be back in a few moments, before then walking out of the lounge. He took a gulp of his drink and went to the kitchen for another refill. He had just sat down when she returned and did a twirl in front of him. She had on a dress that was an exact replica of the one Tracy Fielding had worn that night.

"Do you recognize this dress?" she asked, twirling again. He looked at her and thought that she looked fabulous.

"Wow," he said, "it looks so much nicer on you."

She knelt down between his legs and kissed him warmly on the lips, as she gently pushed her tongue into his welcoming mouth. She could feel her hardening nipples pushing against the thin dress. She took hold of his hands and placed them onto her breasts as she pushed her tongue deeper. He firmly squeezed her nipples, which made her gasp. She then stood up in front of him and pushing the straps of the dress down and off her shoulders, slowly pulled the zip down the back, allowing it to drop to the floor. She was now standing there in just her leopard skin bra and panties; which also were exact replicas of the ones worn by Tracy Fielding. Jack ran his fingers up the inside of her thighs. She opened her legs a little as she stood in front of him and then moaned with pleasure as she felt his strong fingers move the delicate panties to one side. He then stopped, picked her up in his arms and carried her to his bedroom. With Cindy standing with her back to the door, he flicked on the light switch as he had done with Tracy. He kissed her hungrily, while bringing moans of pleasure from her with his hands.

He then undid her bra and slipped it off, kissing her rock hard nipples. He then ran his tongue down and across her flat stomach, then further down, as he slipped off her panties. She opened her legs almost begging for penetration. He didn't disappoint. Just as he had done with Tracy, he then stood up and turned them around so that his back was to the door. She quickly understood and began to undress him. She did this slowly and deliberately, while kissing his body, then ran her tongue down and took him by complete surprise. He was anticipating the feel of her warm lips, but instead, she took both of his testicles into her mouth, consequently bringing him to fever pitch.

He didn't want that so he pulled her up and carried her over to the bed. As with Tracy, he positioned her on the edge. Whispering in her ear he said, "I want the cameras to get a good view as you are finally fucked by somebody else, bitch."

He then went ahead, trying to remake the scene that he had acted out with Tracy. First, turning her over and taking her doggy fashion, before then roughly turning her back to the missionary position, where she experienced an orgasmic shudder coursing through her body. He couldn't control himself any longer and succumbed with final frenzied thrusts. They then collapsed in each other's arms, breathless and laughing. They eventually enjoyed a full night of passion, which Cindy had never experienced before. Finally, they both dropped off into a deep sleep.

Cindy woke up the next morning in bed on her own. There was no sign of Jack. She put on her bra and panties, which were the only articles of clothing she had, and then picked up her dress as she went through the lounge and up to her bedroom. As she stood under the refreshing, warm, water in the shower, she thought of the night before, which had more than fulfilled her expectations. Having stepped out of the shower, she dressed and went down the stairs hoping he wouldn't be embarrassed about what had happened between them. Having checked the lounge and kitchen, she looked in the gym, before going out to the pool, where she found him sitting on the diving board.

"Hi. Jack," she shouted.

"Good afternoon, lazy bones; are you coming in for a swim?"

"No, I'm afraid I can't, I have a luncheon date with my friend Sue. I'll be back at about 3 p.m. would you like me to leave you some lunch before I go?"

"No thanks, Cindy, you go and have lunch with Sue, I'll sort myself out," with that he stood up and dived into the pool with what he hoped was one of his best dives, showing off like a teenager. Cindy felt relieved as she waved to him on her way out. It seemed to her that things were going to be fine between them.

Jack pulled himself out of the pool and went for a shower. He looked around at the changing room and showers as he towelled himself dry. The expensive looking Italian tiles that oozed class from floor to ceiling, and the delicate balance of practicality and beauty. There had obviously been no expense spared by Tony, who was now a wealthy man. He owned four casinos and two nightclubs outright. The days outside the law were now passed for Tony Martin, though he and his colleagues still sailed close to the wind. Jack dressed and went into the house, where he made himself a coffee and lit a cigarette.

The trial was never far from Jack's thoughts now. Just a few days away before the legal battle, which would decide his fate; freedom or the state pen? His mind drifted back to when he was last in a young person's correction institute. The drab walls, with peeling paint and the awful smell of bleach everywhere. Bent screws, who seemed to enjoy dishing out mental and physical pain, to what they obviously viewed as low life and who cowardly, picked on week-minded inmates. Horrendous feelings of being trapped, as a day seemed like a week, and a month, a year. So called 'food' that you had to eat in order to survive, after having listened to the screws hint that they had spat in it or worse. Low self-esteem becoming even lower, as you were made to clean out yet another rat infested John. Endless fights between inmates, as they wrestled to be 'Top Dogs.' The sight of wimps sobbing, as they were bullied unmercifully. Yet all of these things, he thought, were probably nothing to what lay ahead in the state pen if he were to be found guilty. The thought of the probable fights made him wary. Preparation, as always, could be the key to survival in a place such as that. He decided to have a word with Tony on his return home. A couple of hours later Cindy arrived babbling on about Sue, the lunch, the crowded restaurant, the waiters, in fact anything but an embarrassing silence.

He stopped her, "It's okay, Cindy," he said, "Everything is fine. I hope we are going to be great friends, as always."

She smiled back and relaxed, "You're right, Jack," she said as she walked into the kitchen, "It was just sex after all."

A couple of seconds later she popped her head round the door, "Mind you, it was bloody good sex!" she shouted and laughed.

Jack heard a car outside and looked out of the window. Tony was getting out of his dark, blue Buick. As he entered and walked through the hall, he was whistling to himself obviously in a good mood, as he put his arm around Jack's shoulders." Are you okay, champ?"

Jack forced a smile, "Yeah, did you have a good trip?"

"I certainly did, my friend," he replied, as Cindy handed him a whisky and soda. Tony gave her a hug. It was obvious to Jack that Tony loved her very much, and her shining eyes made it plain to see that she felt exactly the same. Jack didn't feel the least bit uncomfortable, as he strangely felt as though he and Cindy had acted out a film or a play.

During supper, Jack asked Tony if he could bring in a karate teacher a few times this coming week. He said he felt the need on two counts. One, the threat from Alberto Berezi, being a kick boxer, and two, if the worst were to happen in the trial and he ended up in the state pen, he would really need to be able to protect himself.

"No problem," Tony replied, "in fact, leave it to me and I'll sort it out."

The following morning, having been to the police department, Jack went again to see Old Tom. The shop was really busy so he had to wait. Looking around at the drab shop, with the peeling walls and wonderful smells that seemed never to have changed since he had been a young boy, he noted that the place, as always, was immaculately clean. Old Tom had always been a stickler for that. He would clean his scales and counter several times a day with great pride. Looking at Old Tom chatting to the customers as he served them, he thought to himself that it must be satisfying to be so content in your job and also in your life. He decided at that moment, guilty or not guilty, he was, in future, going to lead a normal life, inside the law. His days of being Jack the lad were over.

The last customer left and Tom apologized for keeping him waiting. Jack smiled, "Don't be daft, Tom. I don't like to bother you anymore, but I have one more loose end before the trial, which I'm hoping you can help me with. I was wondering if I could leave some more stuff in your brother's garage? I'll pay him for the extra inconvenience of course."

Tom picked up the phone and rang his brother. After a few seconds he was exchanging pleasantries before saying, "Marco, Jack is really stuck and he needs to put some more stuff in your garage. Is there any chance?" After chatting a bit more with Marco, Tom put the phone down. "Yes, no problem; now you know where Marco lives, just ring him when you want to drop the stuff off." With that, he wrote down Marco's number on a piece of paper and gave it to Jack. "Now I have something to tell you, I've been subpoenaed by the prosecution to give evidence at your trial. I don't want to, but I don't have a choice. I haven't a clue what they want from me, but I have to tell you now, no matter what, I will tell the truth, do you understand?"

"Yes, Tom, of course I understand, I wouldn't want you to do anything else." Jack then hugged him and thanked him for everything. They shook hands and Jack left Tom with tear filled eyes, and his fingers crossed.

After ringing Marco, he went to his apartment in a cab and picked up the parking machine and poster. Having dropped them off, he arrived at Tony's at noon, to find a guy waiting to teach him karate. The guy introduced himself as Gus. Cindy made them both a coffee, as Gus firstly wanted to chat to Jack about what to do and what not to do, when fighting. The first thing Gus told him was that most people make the mistake of going for the head and regret it. "The head," he went on, "is a difficult target, and even if you succeed, ninety nine times out of a hundred, your opponent will be able to come back at you." An hour later, having finished advising Jack, Gus added, "We only have five days, which is not nearly enough, but I will do my level best to teach you as much as possible."

They worked really hard every morning in the gym, until the last session was finished the day before the trial. Jack thanked Gus for all his help, but not all of his bruises. Gus smiled as he was leaving and wished him good luck.

That night, after going to bed, Jack lay there reflecting on everything that had happened to put him in this mess. Was it all down to bad luck, bad judgment or just plain stupidity? The death of Phylamina had fallen into all of those categories. Here he was being tried for manslaughter and he couldn't make up his own mind of his guilt or innocence. It was clear to him that if he had been able to find a pulse, he would not have left that car without her. He would have rescued her or died trying, as he really had loved her and, indeed, still did. He then fell into a fitful sleep.

Chapter 5

The eighth of November, nineteen ninety-seven, the first day of the trial, saw Jack Williams in the shower at 7.30 a.m. He had in fact been awake since five, going over and over his life, now he just felt numb. Later on at breakfast, all the kind reassuring words from Tony and Cindy went straight over his head. It was now time to leave. Tony, as usual, would not be going to the court with them; he just walked out to the car to see them off. More optimistic words from him were wasted on Jack as the car pulled away.

As Tony's driver pulled up outside the Supreme Court, Jack felt sick inside. He looked around as he stepped from the car. Pond Park, which is situated right in front of the criminal court, was packed with fascinated onlookers. He and Cindy pushed their way through the hungry press, whose cameras were flashing furiously. Every couple of yards, the police would push back yet another reporter, as he or she tried to thrust a microphone into Jack's face.

They entered through the massive, wooden doors into the now faded marble halls of the New York Supreme Court, leaving the mayhem behind them. Then, after ascending in what Jack thought surprisingly as a grubby and basic elevator, they stepped out among groups of people stood huddled together, whispering and staring: Witnesses, police, lawyers, court officials and of course the general public, both friends and enemies. With Cindy tightly clutching Jack's arm, they approached Wilson Smyth, who ironically was talking to Nicky Forrester, the Deputy District Attorney, who was obviously going to do her level best to put Jack away for a long time. A stunning looking woman immaculately turned out in a smart, navy blue suit, with blonde hair and sparkling, blue eyes, being just five feet four with a model's figure, she was looking up at a completely captivated Wilson Smyth. Having reached to within ten feet of them, Jack and Cindy waited until Wilson realized they were there. Wilson shook hands with Nicky and, as she walked away, he joined Jack and Cindy.

"We'll be going in soon," he said, shaking Jack's hand and warning him yet again not to look flippant or serious in court, but to try and show a healthy interest at all times. He commended Jack on his appearance. Cindy had chosen well: a smart, single-breasted blue suit with a darker, blue, tie and a white shirt. He looked extremely handsome with his freshly cut hair being, in his opinion, just long enough to avoid looking like a thug. Wilson informed them about Nicky Forrester; who she was and her exact role. Jack immediately hoped that there would be more women on the jury than men, otherwise he thought he had no chance, as Nicky would have the poor saps eating out of her hand in no time. Ten minutes later, Wilson led Jack to their seats in court behind a huge wooden desk, covered with lots of paperwork, jugs of water, glass tumblers, and various other items.

On their right, facing the bench, sat Nicky Forrester and two of her aids. Further right on the front row sat three sketch artists and behind them a dozen reporters. The public gallery was filling up fast. The atmosphere in the courtroom was now electric as Jack looked into the public gallery at Cindy, who was smiling at him holding two fingers up in a victory salute. The whole situation now seemed unreal and he wanted to run a mile. Suddenly he felt faint and asked Wilson for a glass of water. As he gulped the water down, his hand was shaking. Once again,

Wilson warned him not to drink too much water, as judges become extremely irritated if recesses have to be called because of the defendant needing the toilet. The murmuring in the courtroom died down and an air of expectancy hung over the whole scene. Judge Stuart H. Hyde entered and sat down. Above his head and slightly to the right of the United States flag, were the words: "In God We Trust." The room came to its feet.

The judge's docket clerk, a weedy little man with not a hair on his head and bifocals ridiculously perched on his pudgy little nose, made his announcement.

"Oh yea, Oh yea. The people versus John E. Williams. The Superior Court for New York is now in session. The honourable Stuart H. Hyde presiding. Draw near and give your attention and you shall be heard. God save the United States of America and this honourable court."

The judge then banged his gavel and announced, "When everyone is seated, the trial will begin."

Wilson had explained to Jack that the first day would be taken up choosing a jury of twelve people, from what is called a venire. This being a group of people called for jury duty, who would be questioned by the judge and lawyers, in order to determine whether or not they should serve in the case at hand. When everyone was seated, the docket clerk called Jack's case to trial.

"Are we ready to call for the venire?" the judge asked.

The docket clerk promptly phoned the clerk's reception room and asked for the venire. He then whispered to the judge that they were in the corridor. On the judge's say so, the venire entered; Forty-five people, of whom only twelve would decide Jack's fate. The docket clerk then called for the first sixteen to sit in the jury box, ordering the remainder to sit in the first row of the public gallery, which had been set aside for them. The judge began by telling the venire about the case, as he had on numerous occasions before. He was extremely canny when questioning prospective jurors, always seeming to know exactly what questions to ask in order to root out unsuitable people. Indicating to a middle-aged woman in the front row, he asked her if she had read about the case in the papers.

She replied, "No, sir."

Judge Hyde simply said, "You may step down now, Madam. You won't be needed on this jury."

He then pointed to a young, black man and asked, "Do you think the defendant is guilty?"

"I don't know, sir. Maybe yes, maybe no," he replied. The judge then told him to step down also.

He then went on at length explaining to the whole court that the defendant was totally innocent, until proven guilty beyond a reasonable doubt.

"There is no room whatsoever for pre-empting your judgment, before you have heard even a scrap of evidence. That is the law and you must keep that in mind ladies and gentlemen, throughout this trial."

He then picked out a young woman, "Do you think the defendant is good looking, young lady?"

She hesitated for a moment, looking at Jack, then turned to face the judge and replied, "Yes, sir, I do."

He then moved on one seat to a middle-aged man who was sitting next to her, "Do you know what is meant by circumstantial evidence?"

The man licked his lips, as he thought about the question, and then replied, "Yes, I think so, if you had a lot of circumstances pointing to guilt, then the defendant, probably, could be guilty."

"You may step down now, sir. We won't be needing your help," Judge Hyde said smiling, as the sniggers went around the court.

This went on and on until after lunch, until eventually, questions about the potential jurors' backgrounds began.

This is called 'Voir Dire', or truth telling; questions from the judge and the legal representatives, pertaining to their private life. "What papers do you read?" "Do you have any children? If so, how old are they?" "What is your occupation?" "Are you a member of a union?" "Private body?" "Were you born in this country?" "What are your feelings toward the police?" "What is your stand on capital, corporal punishment?" Finally Judge Hyde called a recess and said the trial would resume at 10 a.m. the following morning.

During supper that night, Jack and Cindy filled Tony in about the proceedings that had taken place in court, as they enjoyed a meal and shared a bottle of wine, before going to bed early.

Day two, and with everyone ready, the questioning of the prospective jurors continued. Just before lunch on the second day, the jury was chosen, seven women and five men. Wilson Smyth whispered to Jack that he was reasonably happy with the choice of the final twelve, which included a couple of housewives, a quantity surveyor, an environmental consultant, a creative manager, a lady who owned a gift shop, a retired financial consultant, an industrial chemist, a clothes shop owner and two casual labourers, who changed jobs frequently. Judge Hyde also seated four alternates, who would hear all the evidence in case one of the chosen twelve fell ill or were excused.

At two in the afternoon, standing in the hallway, waiting to go into court for the trial to get under way properly, Cindy tried her best to lift Jack's spirits. Wilson Smyth told him not to worry, but instead to stay alert and listen intently to the evidence given by the prosecution witnesses, in case they said something that was questionable. Finally, they were called into court and the trial began. Everyone was waiting for the opening statements, first from Nicky Forrester for the prosecution, and then secondly from Wilson Smyth. There was tension in the air; it was as though two gladiators were going to do battle. Nicky stood up and strode purposefully forward. She stood in front of the jury with her hand resting on the wooden plinth in front of them. She had changed her suit. She now wore a cream one with the skirt slightly shorter. Her choice had been motivated by what she considered to be a comparatively youngish jury. As with every opening, she made sure to make good eye contact with every male juror. She used her sexuality unashamedly for all that it was worth. Then looking slowly at each and every juror, she created an intentional silence to facilitate maximum impact. You could hear a pin drop in the courthouse as she began, "A young woman has lost her life. This, ladies and gentlemen of the jury, is a reality that you must remember during all the legal wrangling and all your deliberations. We, the prosecution, will show that the defendant before you," indicating Jack as she pointed directly at him with her finger, "John E. Williams, ended Phylamina D.T. Riley's life through criminal neglect and is therefore guilty of manslaughter. It will not be for you to have to think of any possible punishment, no. You must simply decide on guilt or innocence. Just a few months ago this lovely girl was happily running her florist business, until she met the defendant standing before you, who entered her life only to snuff it out like a candle."

She then went on about points of law for the jury's benefit for a long time. Wilson Smyth sat there impassive; delighted that she was taking so long. He was hoping that there would not be enough time for him to make his opening address. His thinking being that the jury would be tiring and, in any case, a new day would lessen the impact of Nicky Forrester's offering. With this in mind he began jotting down some points of law of his own that he could take up with the judge and the prosecution, in order to clog up the proceedings.

Nicky eventually finished her address and with her usual poise, walked back to her seat. Judge Hyde then invited Wilson to conduct the opening for the defence. He stood up and instead, asked if he and the prosecution could approach the bench. An hour and a half later, they were still there wrangling over unimportant points, until the judge called an end to the day, leaving Nicky Forrester looking extremely irritated, as she knew full well what Wilson had manipulated.

"First round to us," Wilson thought.

Day three, the whole court waited with bated breath. Wilson stood up, tidied the paperwork that was in front of him, then strode forward. Although not particularly tall, he was nevertheless an impressive looking man. His dark hair, immaculately groomed, was beginning to grey at the temples. He approached the jury and, standing with one hand in his trouser pocket, gave a big smile. "You probably noticed the omission from the prosecution's address regarding 'reasonable doubt.' Well, of course, they know full well that they have to prove beyond reasonable doubt, that this young man standing before you is guilty. The law is quite clear. If you have any doubt, the law requires you to set him free by bringing in a verdict of 'not guilty.' For my part, I truly believe the defendant is innocent."

Wilson, at that point, took his hand out of his pocket and strolled over to the bench, this done with perfect timing in order to allow the jury to digest what he had just pointed out. Judge Hyde was smiling, as he had seen Wilson in action many times before. The attorney then strolled back, and smiling at the jury again with meaningful intent, pointed out the omission of the words, circumstantial evidence from the prosecution's address. "You will find, ladies and gentlemen, that as the trial unfolds, their whole case is built up on the said 'circumstantial evidence.' Well, in a case such as this one, that is all they have. How could they have anything else? This tragedy occurred on a riverbed. There was only the defendant and the deceased. This young man did everything he possibly could in terrifying circumstances. After attempting mouth to mouth resuscitation, he went on to look for a pulse. All this in pitch darkness with the water rising fast. Panic then gripped him and, not being God, he did what seems to have been made out to be a cowardly act. He saved himself." Then, lowering his voice a little, he repeated, "Yes, he saved himself. Circumstantial evidence as we all know can be important, but it's not absolutely reliable."

Wilson walked away again allowing the jury to – hopefully – begin to feel sorry for Jack. Approaching them again, he went on, "Because of what happened, the witnesses in this case will only be able to talk about circumstances. That is, of course, apart from one person; the defendant, Mr. John E. Williams. The only person under oath who can possibly know what happened on that fateful night."

The whole courtroom was riveted; Wilson had them all in the palm of his hand. He then strolled confidently to his seat and sat down, having noticed Nicky looking a bit flushed on his way past. Murmurings all around the courtroom were brought to an abrupt end, with Judge Hyde banging his Gavel down hard and calling for a recess until after lunch.

At 2.15 p.m., the court rose as Judge Hyde entered the courtroom from his chambers and sat down. The docket clerk announced, "The court is now in session. Please be seated."

The first hour was taken up by the opposing lawyers arguing about points of law, which everyone found incredibly tedious until at last, the prosecution opened its case, by calling Thomas Granger to the stand. He entered, looking a bit shaken as he took his place. Standing in the box, he was sworn in with his hand on the bible. Judge Hyde warned him, "You are now under oath Mr. Granger."

Old Tom, feeling a bit upset, looked across at Jack with tears in his eyes. Nicky Forrester walked over, stood in front of Tom and asked, "How long have you known the defendant, Mr. Granger?"

"Well, all of his life really, he is a good man and…"

"Just answer the questions please", Nicky butted in. "Did you know his mother, Mrs. Stella Williams?"

"Yes, I did."

"Was your relationship with her a sexual one?"

Wilson Smyth objected. "That question has nothing whatsoever to do with this case, Your Honor."

"Sustained. Please keep your questions relevant to the case, Ms. Forrester."

Nicky, unperturbed, went on, "Have you ever known the defendant to be gainfully employed?"

"Objection", said Wilson standing up.

Judge Hyde overruled. "The witness will answer the question."

Nicky went on. "Now, I'll ask you again. Have you ever known the defendant to be gainfully employed?"

Old Tom looked sheepishly at Jack, as he quietly replied, "No."

"Will you speak up?" Nicky said forcefully.

"No," Tom replied, a bit louder this time.

"Did you see the defendant on that fateful day, the fourteenth of April, nineteen ninety seven?"

"Yes, he had been up to his deceased mother's apartment, and came to see me. He told me he intended selling most of the contents of the apartment to a dealer. He then left."

"Could you smell alcohol on the defendant's breath, Mr. Granger?"

Old Tom asked for a drink of water before going on. "Yes," he said finally.

"I see," and what time of the day was this?"

"I think it was about 11 a.m.,"

"And was the defendant driving that morning?"

"I don't know, Madam,"

Nicky glared at Old Tom, "Did you get the impression that he was driving then?"

Wilson was immediately on his feet again, "Objection," he said with feeling.

"Sustained," said the judge, who was beginning to warm to the proceedings.

"You know very well, Ms. Forrester, that the witness' impressions are irrelevant."

Jack wrote something on his notepad and handed it to Wilson, who having read it, smiled. Nicky then walked back to her seat. "I have no more questions for this witness."

Wilson Smyth stood up and walked over to Tom, without being invited to do so by the judge. Then, smiling at the witness, to make him feel more relaxed, asked, "How far away from the defendant were you, when you thought you could smell alcohol on his breath?"

Old Tom thought for a moment before answering, "About three feet?"

Wilson then put his own face 18 inches from Tom's and asked, "Did you at any point, have your face this close?"

"No, sir, I didn't."

Wilson backed off and removed his spectacles. He wanted a moment of silence, in order to make the whole court hungry for his next question, so he took a handkerchief from his jacket pocket and cleaned the lenses of his spectacles, before putting them back on.

"Tell me, Mr. Craven, am I wearing aftershave?"

"Objection," said Nicky, now on her feet.

Before the judge could rule, Wilson got in first, "Your, Honor, the prosecution knew full well that the defendant admitted in his statement to the police, that he had alcohol in his blood on that fateful night. They have put Mr. Craven on the stand, wasting the court's time, for no other reason than to discredit the defendant. If you will bear with me, you will soon see where my question is leading."

"Objection overruled. The witness will answer the question."

"Thank you, Your Honor. I will ask the question again. Am I wearing aftershave, Mr. Craven?"

"I really don't know," said poor old Tom, looking baffled.

Wilson then asked, "Am I correct in saying that you yourself are certainly wearing aftershave?"

"Yes I am. I always do."

He actually reeked of it.

There were a few sniggers going around the court before Wilson then went on, "Is it possible, Mr. Craven, that you couldn't smell mine because of your senses being full of your own aftershave?"

"Yes, I suppose so."

Wilson went on, "Have you found this morning leading up to your testimony stressful?"

"Yes, sir, I have."

"Am I correct in saying that you yourself have had some alcohol before coming to court?"

"Yes," Tom replied sheepishly, "I've had two shots of Bourbon."

More sniggers from around the court.

"Mr. Craven, on the day you attended the funeral of Stella Williams, were you stressed and in need of alcohol?"

"Yes, sir, that definitely would be true."

"And the morning after, when you thought you could smell alcohol on the defendant?"

"Yes, sir, I had had two or three shots of Bourbon."

"I put it to you, Mr. Craven, that as you didn't get any closer than three feet from the defendant, it's possible that you didn't smell alcohol on him at all, your senses being full of your own aftershave and Bourbon; just as you couldn't smell my aftershave a few moments ago, not from three feet, but from eighteen inches."

After a brief moment Wilson then said, "Mr. Craven, you testified earlier to the prosecution, that you could smell alcohol on the defendant's breath on that fateful morning. Do you now wish to withdraw that testimony?"

"Yes, sir," Tom replied. Then looking up at the judge, he repeated it, "Yes, I do."

Wilson walked over to his seat feeling like he had just hit a home run on his opponent's patch, "No more questions, Your Honor."

The Judge looked across at Nicky, but she didn't move, so he told the witness he could stand down. Old Tom walked toward the exit feeling much better. Wilson Smyth had made him out to look like a doddering old drunk, but he didn't care about that. Wilson had negated his testimony against Jack's character, and that was all that mattered to him as he glanced across at Jack on his way out.

"The people call Dr. Niles J. Sawyer," cried the Judge's docket clerk.

The doctor, who was a tall lean man with a pencil moustache, walked confidently across the court to the stand. He was tanned and well dressed with a thick head of silvery gray hair. Wilson took an immediate dislike to the witness who had a constant smirk on his face, which smacked of arrogance. Having been sworn in, the witness was then irritatingly warned by the Judge "You are now under oath, Dr. Sawyer."

Nicky Forrester walked over to him, "Doctor, are you the Pathologist that performed the autopsy on the deceased, Phylamina D. T. Riley?"

"Yes, I am."

"Will you tell the court what you determined to be the cause of death?"

"The deceased died from drowning," he replied with a casual air. At this disclosure, lots of murmuring went around the court, but on this occasion Judge Hyde allowed it time to evaporate. Jack, for his part, felt sick inside and his eyes filled up.

Nicky went on, "Did you find any fresh wounds on the body?"

"Yes, on the right hand side of the deceased's forehead."

"In your opinion, Doctor, if the deceased had been wearing a seat belt, would it be true to say, she probably would not have received the said wound?"

"Objection!" cried Wilson, "The prosecution is leading the witness."

"Sustained," said the Judge, beginning to enjoy the battle.

"I withdraw the question," Nicky said gloating inside, as she knew she had achieved her goal, "In your opinion, Doctor, could this wound have caused unconsciousness?"

"Yes, in my opinion, it could have."

"Finally, Doctor, is it absolutely definite that the deceased would have been alive prior to being engulfed by water?"

"Objection," cried Wilson.

"I withdraw the question," Nicky said before the Judge had time to rule, again happy to have made her point. Wilson was fuming inside, but he knew that by and large, he usually gave more than he took in these exchanges.

Nicky walked over to her seat, "No more questions," she said as she sat down.

Judge Hyde ended the day at this point and ordered a resumption at 10 a.m. the following morning. Wilson and Jack did a debriefing session in a small office that had been allocated. Cindy then took Jack home.

Day four, the jury entered from the room that they would eventually use for their deliberations, and sat down in their usual places.

Judge Hyde reminded Dr. Niles J. Sawyer that he was still under oath, before then inviting Wilson Smyth to cross-examine. The doctor had on a completely new outfit, but in Wilson's mind as he approached him, wore the same pathetic smug, arrogant smile on his face.

"Have you studied the deceased's medical records, Doctor?" Wilson opened.

"Yes, of course I have."

"Well then, did you not think it relevant so far in your testimony to mention the fact that the deceased, periodically in her life, suffered with epileptic fits?"

"No, actually I didn't. I thought it was your job to ask the questions and mine to answer them."

At that point Wilson could quite easily have put his fist right through the doctor's smirking face. Instead he made the comment, "Well, I must admit, you should know, Doctor, as this is the fifteenth time this year that you have given evidence at $2000 a time."

Nicky was on her feet in a flash shouting, "Objection, Your Honor."

"Sustained, Mr. Smyth, please keep your schoolboy remarks to yourself," said the Judge as the sniggering all around the court died down.

Wilson had really enjoyed embarrassing the arrogant doctor. He then carried on with the questioning.

"Is it possible that the wound on the deceased's forehead could have been caused by banging it against the steering wheel?"

"Objection," said Nicky, "That is leading the witness."

"Sustained," said the broody looking judge, which surprised Wilson.

He returned to his seat, "No more questions."

The judge called for a ten-minute recess and disappeared into his chambers. On his return, the trial continued with the docket clerk announcing, "The people call Alberto F. Berezi."

Jack looked into Alberto's hate-filled eyes and it sent a shiver down his spine. He thought that he looked gaunt and even thinner than he had remembered him. His normal tanned face now took on a sallow look. After he had been sworn in, Ms Forrester asked him, "Is your name Antonio F.Berezi?"

"Yes, it is."

"In what capacity did you know the deceased, Phylamina D. T. Riley?"

"We were to be married. She was my fiancée."

While pointing her finger at Jack, Nicky asked, "Have you ever met the defendant, John E. Williams before today?"

"Yes, I have, on four occasions. The first time I met him, I was serving in my friend's bistro. He came in and bribed my friend and myself into making a fuss of him on his return with his new girlfriend. He returned later to the bistro, and to our complete surprise, was with a very good friend of ours, namely Phylamina, the deceased. I didn't trust him from that moment and I told Phylamina so, as I gave her his dirty money."

At this point Wilson considered objecting but decided not to; as he considered that the amount of hate and jealousy shown by Antonio left an opportunity to discredit him as a witness.

"You say you have previously met him four times?"

"Yes, the third time, he came in again with Phylamina. We were a bit slack on that occasion and it gave me a chance to ask him some questions. I asked him had we met before, as I had a strong feeling that we had. He just shrugged his shoulders. I then asked him what he did for a living, to which he replied, "I'm a consultant in the Import and Export field."

I then asked him where his office was. He said he didn't have an office and then gave what sounded like a good reason why. He then gave me his card."

At this point Nicky drew the court's attention to exhibit one, which she removed from the evidence cart. Showing the card first to the Judge and Jury, she then finally passed the card, which was in a plastic sleeve, to Alberto.

"Is this the card that he gave you, Mr. Berezi?"

"Yes, ma'am, that's the card," she then put the card back into the evidence cart. Wilson Smyth sat uneasily in his seat. He had been dreading this witness, as the whole testimony showed Jack up to be a calculating liar.

Ms. Forrester carried on with the questioning, "Did the deceased ever wear spectacles?"

"Yes, she did, but only when she was driving," Nicky drew the attention of the court to exhibit 4, a pair of spectacles, which she took out of the cart and again passed round to the Judge and Jury, finally showing them to Alberto.

"Do you recognize these spectacles?"

"Yes, I do, ma'am. They belonged to Phylamina."

"Now, I want you to be sure on my next question, Mr. Berezi, as it is an extremely important one. Did you ever witness the deceased drive her car while not wearing these spectacles?"

"No, never, I'm quite clear on that."

Nicky, holding up the spectacles for all the court to see then went on "As the police report states, these were found by the police in the deceased's apartment, where she had left them, as she was obviously not intending to drive that night." Nicky then placed them back into the cart and went on. "Was it common knowledge, among the deceased's close friends, that she had an idiosyncrasy whenever she travelled in a car?"

Alberto smiled, "Yes. She would always take off her shoes and place them under her seat."

At this point Nicky brought Exhibit 2, the said shoes, to the attention of the court, following the same procedure as before. She then highlighted the police report, which stated that they were found under the passenger seat, on recovery of the vehicle from the river. Murmurings around the court were brought to an abrupt end by Judge Hyde's gavel. Jack was as white as a sheet, as Nicky then asked, "You said that you had met the defendant on another occasion?"

"Yes, Ma'am. It took me a while, but finally I remembered where I had seen him before. In my full time job I work as a Security Guard and four years ago I gave evidence in a young offender's court regarding an attempted break in at the office block that I was guarding at the time. The defendant was one of the youths found guilty."

"Objection, Your Honor," cried Wilson.

"Sustained," the Judge said glaring at Nicky Forrester. "The last statement will be stricken from the records and you, the Jury, will completely ignore it on your deliberations."

Nicky, feeling she had shown Jack up as a compulsive liar, sat down and said, "No more questions."

After being invited to cross-examine, Wilson walked over and said to Alberto, "Mr. Berezi, do you admit that you would very much like to see the defendant behind bars."

"Yes I would, but I wouldn't lie in order to put him there," Alberto replied in a cool, unruffled voice.

Wilson decided that it was pointless having this witness sit there any longer, as he was doing so much damage to Jack, so he sat down and said, "No more questions."

The rest of the day was spent discussing points of law that the Judge wanted the Jury to consider. Finally, Jack sat opposite Wilson in the tiny debriefing office.

"Look, Jack," Wilson said, "today went badly for us, but that's how it goes in trials such as these. If there are good days and bad days, its common sense to believe that there is reasonable doubt. Now, that's all we need. Don't let it get you down. Go home and have a relaxing weekend; I want you back here on Monday morning looking fresh and sharp.

Jack had a restless weekend; he was nervous, twitchy and unresponsive. Tony and Cindy understood and just gave him some space to sort his head out. On day five of the trial it was pouring with rain as Jack and Cindy were driven to the court, which did little for his morale. Cindy reminded him that Wilson Smyth was recognized as one of the best in the business, but her words were falling on deaf ears

The trial restarted with the Docket Clerk calling for the first witness of the day, a Mr. Daniel G. Golding, who was the mechanic who had inspected the car when it was dragged from the river. Having been sworn in, he was irritatingly reminded by the judge, that he was now under oath.

Nicky Forrester strolled across to him wearing a beautifully tailored, peach coloured suit. "Mr. Golding, will you tell the court in what capacity you are giving evidence in this trial, please?"

Mr. Golding, a short, stocky red-faced man with long, straggly hair and a rugged complexion, was looking straight at Nicky's ample breasts as he answered, "Sure, I was responsible for the inspection of the defendant's car when it was fished out of the river. My report is actually on that cart over there."

"Now, Mr. Golding, will you tell the court the position of the driver's seat on your inspection? By that I mean, was it forward or back? Also, the condition of the seat belts in the car?"

Nicky turned round and looked at the Jury while waiting for the answer. Mr. Golding was too busy admiring her figure, so the answer didn't come. She turned back to him with a quizzical look as the sniggering in the court abated.

"The position of the driver's seat?" he finally asked and went on, "It was as far back as it could possibly go. As regards the seat belts, the condition of the belt on the driver's side was in good working order. However, on the passenger side, the belt was extremely tight, practically seized up."

"What was the condition of the tyres, Mr. Golding?"

"The two rear tyres were fine, but the two front ones were badly worn."

"In your professional opinion, would the car have retained control on that bend, if the front tyres had been in good condition?"

Wilson was on his feet in a flash. "Objection, Your Honor, the prosecution knows full well that an opinion such as that would be pure speculation."

Nicky didn't wait for a ruling from the judge. Instead she quickly went on. "Let me put it another way. A set of tyres with a good tread would have had a much better chance of holding the road. Is that not true?"

"Yes, of course it's true," he replied.

"Now, was the passenger door in good working order? That is to say, could it open and close without difficulty?"

"Yes, Miss. It was fine."

Nicky glared at him for having the nerve to call her 'Miss,' before going on, "And the driver's door?"

He thought for a while before answering, "I would describe that as very stiff."

"Finally, Mr. Golding, was the interior light switch in the on or off position?"

"It was in the on position."

Nicky walked back to her seat. "No more questions."

Judge Hyde looked across at Wilson Smyth. "Cross-examine, Mr. Smyth?"

Wilson stood up and sorted some paperwork out on his desk before cross-examining the witness, as he wanted him to be as nervous as possible. Looking at the Jury instead of the witness, Wilson asked him. "Were you present when the body of the deceased was removed from the vehicle?"

Having to look at the back of Wilson's head, the witness replied, "No, I believe I arrived about 30 minutes later."

Still looking at the jury, Wilson smiled and went on, "Then we are asking the wrong person regarding the position of the driver's seat, are we not?"

"Er, I don't know. It's not for me to say."

"You are quite correct there, Mr. Golding," Wilson said sarcastically, noticing a few of the jurors smiling. "It most certainly is not for you to say. Now tell me, as you were on dry land when you inspected the doors, is it possible that the action of opening and closing them would be different to when the vehicle was on the river bed?"

"Er, maybe, but if…"

"Please just answer "yes" or "no," Mr. Golding," Wilson said interrupting him.

"Yes," he said grudgingly. "I suppose so."

Wilson was really enjoying this cross-examination. "How many years' experience have you had as a mechanic?"

"I've had thirty years."

"Right then, perhaps you can clear something up for me with all your experience. If a pair of shoes were under the driver's seat and the car had a heavy collision with a high kerb, then driven in a wild state through different bends, crashing through a fence and belly flopping into a river, is it not possible for the shoes to have shifted position?"

"Well, possibly I suppose."

"Yes, Mr. Golding, 'possibly' is the right word. Now then," Wilson went on, while looking at the Jury, "if a car goes into water, which side of the car ships water faster, driver's side or passenger side?"

"It would be the driver's side," he said to the back of Wilson's head, "because of the way the chassis is formed."

"You're extremely knowledgeable, Mr. Golding, I'm impressed. So therefore, if the water gets into the car faster on the driver's side, it surely would be possible for the water to float a pair of shoes toward the passenger side, would it not?"

"Well really, I don't know," Golding answered with a shrug of his shoulders.

"No, Mr. Golding you don't. And neither does anybody else." Wilson felt that he was scoring heavily. "I didn't ask you if you knew. I asked you if it were possible."

Golding was fed up to the back teeth with Wilson's line of questions and now just wanted to get out. "Yes," he answered, "I suppose so."

Wilson carried on. "I'm not going to ask you about the position of the seats when the body was removed, as you have already told us that you were not there, but tell me, Is it true that the holding mechanism of car seats has changed in the last few years?"

"Yes, the mechanism used to be called slide and hold, and now it is called slide and lock."

"Well I'm just a mere Attorney, so correct me if I am wrong. I take it that the slide and hold version was obviously more prone to the seats sliding into a new position?"

"Yes, that's correct."

Wilson, turning back again to look at the Jury, then asked, "Did the defendant's car have the old unreliable slide and hold version?"

"Yes it did."

"So a heavy collision could have moved the seat?"

"Yes, it could."

"Thank you for clearing that up for us. Now finally, the seat belt on the passenger side of the car. I know that you testified earlier that..." Wilson paused, as he got out a document and read, "the belt on the passenger side was, to quote you, 'tight, almost seized up'?"

"Yes, that's what I said."

"Would it have been at all possible, for a strong man to have been able to pull that seat belt out?"

"I suppose so, Mr. Smyth, just possible."

Wilson then picked up exhibit 5 out of the cart and having gone through due procedure, read out a passage from Mr. Golding's inspection report. "'The retraction mechanism of the safety belt on the passenger side of the car is not impaired.' That is what you put in your report?"

"Yes. That is correct."

"Well then, in that case, the retraction mechanism being in good working order, could in fact have retracted?"

"Yes, I suppose so."

Wilson walked over to his seat. "No more questions, Your Honor."

Nicky Forrester was fuming. She hated surprises in court. She had no idea that Golding had not reached the scene until 30 minutes after the car had been fished out of the river. She had also not been informed of the change of mechanism in car seat movement. "Heads will definitely roll," she thought to herself.

Judge Hyde then called a recess for lunch. The colour had returned to Jack's face and he was upbeat over lunch with Wilson Smyth.

"Now look, Jack," Wilson cautioned, "we have had a good morning in court. The prosecution made mistakes and we were able to exploit them. But remember what I said about good and bad days. It's important that you stay alert in case a witness makes a mistake. The slightest error could be of help to us. Having said all that, I am happy with Judge Hyde. He is an intelligent and reasonable man and, most of all, Nicky Forrester's tits or ass don't faze him. I haven't decided yet whether or not to put you on the stand. We have to weigh up the down side, that being; Nicky Forrester might rip you apart. On the other hand, if we don't put you on the stand to tell your side of the story, people may take that as a sign of guilt. It's a difficult one, but the law is clear on this. Although the jury would obviously think that, as an innocent man, you would want to put your side of the story forward, the constitution of the United States of America clearly states that you don't have to. The fact is the State has to prove your guilt; you don't have to prove your innocence. You don't have to say a thing if you don't want to. In the event of you not taking the stand, the Judge will remind the Jury of the constitution.

However, we don't have to decide yet. Let's just leave it for a while and see how things go."

After lunch the prosecution called Detective Inspector Wayne Thomas Bridge to the stand. A not too happy Nicky Forrester approached him. "Will you tell the court your responsibility regarding this case, Detective Inspector?"

"Certainly, I have been in charge of the police procedure and subsequent arrest of the defendant."

"Thank you, Detective Inspector. Now, in the period between the defendant's car being dragged from the river, and the arrival of Mr. Golding, the inspecting mechanic, were you present the whole time?"

"Yes, I was, the whole time."

"So Inspector, if anybody were to have moved the driver's seat, you would have known about it?"

"Yes, I would."

After a pause Nicky asked, "Did you see anybody move the driver's seat?"

"No, I didn't."

"When the body was removed from the driver's seat, were there any gloves on the deceased's hands, Inspector?"

"No definitely not."

"You will see where I'm leading to now, Inspector. Did you find any of the deceased's fingerprints on the steering wheel?"

"No, we did not."

Jack, who had been listening intently, wrote a message on a note pad and passed it to Wilson. It simply said, "I wore driving gloves every single time that I drove that car." Wilson made a note of it in his memo pad.

Nicky went on, "Were there any of the deceased's fingerprints on the ignition key?"

"No, Madam, none."

"Now tell me, Inspector, regarding the seat being back as far as it would go. Could the deceased's feet have reached the pedals?"

"No, not if she were sitting correctly on the seat."

At this point Nicky went to the evidence cart and retrieved exhibit 4, the deceased's spectacles. "Can you tell the court where you found exhibit 4 please?"

"From the deceased's apartment."

"Were there any spectacles found in the vehicle?"

"No, Madam."

Nicky walked back to her seat saying, "No more questions, Your Honor."

Wilson was on his feet and on his way over to Detective Inspector Bridge before being invited to cross-examine. Judge Hyde, not being pedantic, let it go.

"Detective Bridge, you have just testified that the deceased's fingerprints were not on the steering wheel or the ignition key. Is that correct?"

"Yes, it is."

"I put it to you, Inspector Bridge; you have led the jury and this court into believing that, although the deceased's fingerprints were not on the said items, the defendant's were, and you have done this quite deliberately."

"No, Mr. Smyth, I have not done that."

"Really?" Wilson said sarcastically

"Then tell me, Mr. Bridge," deliberately leaving out his Inspector status. "Did you find any of the defendant's fingerprints on the said steering wheel or ignition key?"

"No."

"Then I put it to you that there was no point, apart from deception, and there is no room for that in American justice."

Although this seemed a bit over the top, Wilson liked to fly the American nationalistic flag for all it was worth. In this case he hoped the Jury would take an immediate dislike to Inspector Bridge. Wilson then asked if he and Nicky could approach the bench. In a huddle between the three of them, the Judge then ordered a recess and an audience in his chambers.

Judge Hyde sat down behind his big leather covered desk in his chambers.

"Please sit down," he said to the two Attorneys, before taking a big draw on his cigar. After exhaling, he spoke through foul-smelling cigar smoke. "What have you to say, Ms. Forrester? And please don't come out with any crap in my chambers."

Peering through the smoke, she replied, "When I asked those questions, I had no idea the defendant's prints were not on the said items. My aim was simply to show that the deceased's were not, but I can see how it could have looked like deception."

"Mmm, the Judge muttered, as he leaned back, blowing little rings of smoke toward the oak panelled ceiling. He then leaned forward and, after blowing out another cloud of smoke, asked, "What have you to say, Mr. Smyth?"

"Well, your Honor, I'm not going to accuse Ms. Forrester of lying, but at the same time, I believe that this part of Inspector Bridge's testimony should be stricken from the records and the jury told why."

More little rings of smoke emanated from the Judge's mouth as he leaned back in his seat, considering both sides. He then leaned forward. "I tend to agree with Mr. Smyth and therefore, I'm going to agree to his request. Furthermore, Ms. Forrester, I want you to re-cross-examine the Inspector in order to tie up any loose ends."

As Judge Hyde entered from his chambers, the court rose to its feet. The trial restarted with Judge Hyde advising the jury of the reasons for scrapping part of Inspector Bridge's testimony, and hence, the re-cross-examination. Nicky embarrassingly cross-examined and put the problem to bed, before then sitting down and allowing Wilson to carry on where he had left off.

Wilson looked at Inspector Bridge, now feeling that the Jury suspected collusion between the Police Inspector and the assistant District Attorney. He then asked him, "In the police report, it said that the deceased's purse was found on the rear seat of the car. Is that correct?"

"Yes, that is correct."

"Would you agree with me, Inspector, that it would be extremely unusual for a passenger in the front seat of a car, to leave their purse on the rear seat?"

"Yes, I suppose so, but who knows?"

"Precisely Inspector, who indeed? But that's the problem with circumstantial evidence, wouldn't you agree?"

"Objection," Nicky said standing up. "That is leading the witness."

"Sustained," said Judge Hyde, as Wilson walked back to his seat saying, "No more questions."

Nicky Forrester then stood up. After a few moments of silence, she said, "That concludes the case for the prosecution, Your Honor."

Wilson and Jack's debriefing session took much longer than usual. The question of whether or not he should take the stand was now at hand, and was vital, as it could swing the case either way.

"Having gone through the trial so far," Wilson said, "This is how I see it. I believe that the prosecution has failed to prove guilt. If I were in Nicky Forrester's shoes, I would be champing at the bit to cross examine you, hoping to blow you out of the water so to speak. At the moment, I see us with possibly a 70% to 30% advantage. If you don't take the stand, some of the jurors may waver a bit, therefore reducing our advantage to possibly 60% - 40%, which is obviously more than reasonable doubt. The judge in his closing direction to the jury will point this out. The reasonable doubt I mean, not the rest," he added laughing. "So, you can decide, or you can leave the decision to me."

Jack sat there thinking. "What shall I do? I've kept these lies inside for so long now, who knows, under interrogation I may break up? Then, on the other hand, as Wilson said, not testifying may swing them against me." He made up his mind; "I think I would like you to decide, Wilson."

"Right, Jack that settles it. I will sleep on it tonight and make my decision in the morning." Jack then went home for yet another restless night.

Day six, Wilson took Jack into the debriefing office to tell him of his decision. "I have decided not to put you on the stand, is that okay with you?"

"Yes, of course, Wilson," he replied, relieved. "I'm totally in your hands." They then went into court, which again was packed. The sketch artists quickly began doing drawings of Jack, as they obviously thought the time was fast arriving when he would take the stand. The court rose to its feet as the Judge entered and finally, with everyone seated, the trial restarted with the defence calling for Mr. Clive Wheldrake. Having taken the oath, he stood there in his brightly coloured clothes. His hair was shoulder length and tied back into a ponytail. He actually looked as though he was enjoying his moment of stardom.

Wilson began. "Will you tell the court where you are employed please, Mr. Wheldrake."

"Sure, Man," he replied. I'm a bartender in Kidd's wine bar."

"Thank you, Mr. Wheldrake. Now, did the deceased in this case, namely Phylamina D. T. Riley, enter your wine bar on the fourteenth of April nineteen ninety seven?"

"Yessur, she did."

"Do you remember for how long she stayed, and also what she drank?"

"Yeh, she wus there for about a half hour and drank four glasses of white wine."

"Did you actually see her drink the four glasses of wine?"

"Sure, Man, she wus sittin' with a girlfriend on a bar stool right in front a me."

"Was she a regular customer, Mr. Wheldrake?"

"She would frequent the bar once or twice a week."

"At what time did she enter the bar on the said date?"

"It would have been about a quarter before five in the afternoon."

"Did she place anything on the bar?"

"Yeah, she put her bag on the bar with a set a car keys on top."

"Why did this catch your attention, Mr. Wheldrake?"

"Well, the keys were attached to a huge Mickey Mouse figure that was almost as big as the keys 'emselves. I actually made a remark about 'em, sayin' 'there ain't much chance-a you losin' them, babe'."

"Thank you, Mr. Wheldrake, no further questions." Wilson then walked back to his seat.

Nicky Forrester stood up and surprisingly announced "The Prosecution has no questions for this witness, Your Honor."

Mr. Wheldrake looked disappointed, when asked to stand down by the judge. The defence then called for Phylamina's friend, Joanna C. Cole, who took the oath and stood there glaring at Jack, as she waited for the questions to begin. Wilson knew she would be hostile to him, as he had been forced to subpoena her. He began by asking her name.

"Joanna Cole" she replied curtly."

"What was your relationship to the deceased in this trial, Ms. Cole?"

"We were very good friends," she said as tears began to well up in her eyes.

Wilson genuinely felt sorry for her and said. "Now, I know this must be extremely difficult for you, but remember, you have taken the oath." He then carried on. "Did you go into Kidd's wine bar at approximately 4.45 p.m., on the fourteenth of April nineteen ninety seven, with the deceased?"

"Yes, I did."

"Ms. Cole, can you remember what you both had to drink on that occasion?"

"As far as I can remember, we had three or four glasses of wine."

"Is that three or four glasses of wine each?"

"Yes."

"Had you driven to the wine bar, Ms. Cole?"

"No. Phylamina picked me up and then dropped me off on her way home."

"Now, this is important, was Phylamina wearing spectacles when she drove that night?"

After a delay thinking about the question, the witness finally answered. "I'm not sure, I can't remember."

"Did you ever witness her driving without wearing her spectacles?"

"Yes, not very often, but a few times."

"Would she frequently drive her car having had that much to drink?"

"No, I wouldn't say frequently."

"At what time did you both leave the wine bar?"

"It would have been about 5.15."

Wilson walked back to his seat saying. "No more questions, Your Honor."

Judge Hyde then invited Nicky Forrester to cross-examine, who only asked one question. "Ms. Cole, on the occasions that you witnessed the deceased driving, having had two or three glasses of wine, was she a careful driver in your opinion?"

"Yes, she was an extremely careful driver."

Nicky Forrester then walked back to her seat and sat down.

The next witness for the defence was called, a Ms. Martha C. Henderson, who was in charge of the trainee nurses in New York General. Having taken the oath and informed the court of her name and status, Wilson asked her, "Ms. Henderson, would it surprise you if someone, who had never had any medical training whatsoever, had trouble finding another person's pulse?"

"No, it certainly wouldn't surprise me, in fact that would be the case the majority of the time."

"If this action took place in total darkness and in a stressful situation, would I be correct in thinking that it would make it even more difficult?"

"Yes, sir, absolutely."

With no more questions from either the defence or the prosecution, Ms. Henderson stood down. The whole court was now tense. The atmosphere was electric as the expected call for Jack to go on the stand drew near. Wilson stood up. You could have heard a pin drop in the courthouse as he said unexpectedly. "That completes the case for the defence, Your Honor." There were gasps around the court. Nicky Forrester was disappointed. She had felt sure that she would have been able to cross-examine Jack. She knew in her heart that they had failed to prove guilt and now, Wilson had taken her last chance away.

The judge brought the court to order with his gavel, and called a recess until after lunch, when the closing statements would take place. Nicky Forrester rose and left the courtroom fuming. The strategies she had worked out to trash Jack's character were now no more. She had been caught unawares. Expecting the case for the defence to last at least until then end of the day, she consequently had only a couple of hours to finalize her closing statement with two aids.

Wilson Smyth contentedly puffed on his cigarette. He had finalized his closing statement the night before and knew it off by heart, unlike Nicky Forrester, who he knew at that very moment, would be working feverishly putting hers together.

Consequently the need to keep looking at notes during her statement, would lessen the impact. He laughed at the very thought of it all.

At 2.15, the court waited with anticipation, along with an impatient judge, as Nicky fiddled with pieces of paper on her desk. She then walked over to the jury, having recovered her poise over lunch.

"Ladies and gentlemen of the jury, we have heard testimonies showing the defendant as a liar, a cheat, and an imposter who has never legally worked. The law states quite clearly that he did not have to take the stand, but people will have to work out for themselves his reasons for not doing so. An innocent man, in my opinion, would have wanted to take the stand in order to clear his name. But no, he decided to say nothing. Circumstantial evidence, as a single entity, of course is not proof, but a series of it can prove conclusive. The defence, when faced with all this evidence, would have us believe in flying shoes, moving seats and a seat belt with a mind of its own. We know from evidence that the deceased died from drowning, as the defendant single-mindedly thought only of himself. But of course, that's exactly what he has done for the whole of his life. We, the prosecution, have shown that the defendant, not the deceased, was driving that car and, consequently, was responsible for her death through criminal negligence." Periodically looking at her notes, Nicky then covered again the most damaging evidence, and ended finally. "Our job is finished now, but yours is not. He won't get away with this crime if you good people do your duty and bring in a guilty verdict of manslaughter." Nicky then walked back to her seat with seemingly the whole court whispering.

Judge Hyde simply waited for the whispering to die down before then inviting Wilson Smyth to complete the case for the defence with his closing statement. Wilson took his time. Unlike Nicky, he had no notes to read from. He put his hands on the plinth in front of the jury, took a deep breath and, as he exhaled, began. "Ladies and gentlemen, let me first tell you why the defendant decided not to go onto the witness stand. Simple really, I advised him against it. The reason being, in my opinion; the prosecution has failed to give one scrap of factual evidence to, now wait for it, prove the defendant's guilt beyond reasonable doubt. Yes, they would have done a character assassination on my client, of that there is no doubt. They have proved he was not employee of the year and that he told a lie in order to impress a beautiful lady. He even gave a false identity card to further impress her. However, I say to them; hello? He is not on trial for those things and, if he were, we could have half the population of America in court standing trial!"

At that point, Wilson walked back to his desk in order to give the court time to laugh at the prosecution's expense. He then returned and carried on. "He is a young twenty three year old man, who has been through a horrendous experience. We have heard the opinion of a qualified medic of high esteem, explaining to us how it can be difficult for a trainee nurse to find a pulse, even in a brightly lit hospital. This young man, however, was in a car at the bottom of a riverbed with water rising quickly. He was in complete darkness and in fear of his life. Is it any wonder that he failed to find a pulse, in what must have been a stressful, panic stricken experience? He then did, what has been interpreted by the prosecution as a cowardly act, he saved himself. Is that a crime? Perhaps we should try him for that next! Let's now look at this so-called 'damning evidence' that is supposed to prove his guilt beyond reasonable doubt; I'll repeat that, beyond reasonable doubt.

"Firstly, the position of the driver's seat, which they claim was too far back for the deceased to have been able to drive the vehicle. After a heavy collision with a high kerb, the car was driven wildly through bend after bend before crashing through a fence and belly flopping heavily into the river. This, by the way, with the old slide and hold system, which, as you now know, has been updated to a much safer system; namely, the slide and lock. The change having taken place, as the previously mentioned one was prone to seat movement. Beyond reasonable doubt? I think not. Furthermore, even in the unlikely event of the seat not having moved under all that duress, when it was fished out of the river, there was a period of approximately thirty minutes before the mechanic arrived to inspect it. He, Mr. Golding, then gave evidence here in court of the seats position on his arrival. Well, of course, by that time the deceased had been removed from the vehicle. It could have been moved to allow for the removal of the body, who knows? Beyond reasonable doubt? I think not, Ladies and gentlemen.

"Secondly, the 'immovable shoes', which we are led to believe, could not have changed position, having gone through all the action previously mentioned: Their steadfastness was further threatened by water entering the car on the driver's side before then moving toward the passenger side, much as a tide would." Wilson then threw his hands in the air as though in exasperation, as he said with a distinctly louder voice. "I don't know, for goodness sake, were they nailed down or made of solid lead?" He then walked over to his desk and had a drink of water, again allowing the jury and the rest of the court time to laugh at the prosecutions expense. He was really enjoying himself now.

"Beyond reasonable doubt?" He went on, "I think not." Let us now look at another so-called piece of damning evidence; the seat belt on the passenger side being tight. The prosecution would have us believe, by guesswork, that whoever was in that seat could not have been wearing a seat belt. Therefore, according to them, that person must have been the deceased, as she had suffered an injury to the head. I must point out to you the evidence given by Mr. Golding, the mechanic with thirty years of experience. He admitted under oath that, in his opinion, the belt could have been pulled out by a strong man and indeed, because of the retraction mechanism being completely independent, a retraction could have taken place even though the belt was tight! Beyond reasonable doubt? They must be joking! I would now like to point out something very important that the prosecution must have overlooked, as they were building this case. I refer to the deceased's purse, which was found on the rear seat of the car, in which they insist she was the passenger. Yes, on the rear seat of the car. Now, if the deceased was, as they claim, in the passenger seat, why on earth would she have put her purse on to the back seat? No, it doesn't make sense does it?" Then, with a clenched fist for maximum effect, he continued, "In fact, but for this oversight, I believe the prosecution would not have even brought this case to trial. I'm sure it would have looked obvious even to them, that the only reason for the purse to be on the rear seat of the car was because the deceased had put it there so that she could drive." Then he lowered his voice.

"Finally, we come to the last piece of —so-called damning evidence, the deceased's spectacles that were found in her apartment by the police. Well, ladies and gentlemen of the jury; it was obviously not unusual for the deceased to drive without her spectacles. Her friend, namely Ms. J. C. Cole, testified in this court that she had herself been present on previous occasions, when the deceased had driven whilst not wearing spectacles." Wilson then changed pace and spoke in a slow, even tone. "Yes, as I said when I first started, not a shred of factual evidence to prove guilt beyond reasonable doubt. I thank you for your attention and trust you will bring back a verdict of 'not guilty'." He then turned on his heel and returned to his seat with the artists still sketching him.

Although there were plenty of people whispering around the court, Judge Hyde allowed some respite before bringing the court to order and ending the day. He would prepare his closing address to the jury that evening.

On day seven of the trial at 9.45 a.m., with Wilson briefing Jack on the procedure that was to follow, a knock came at the door. Wilson opened it to find one of the bailiffs looking a bit perturbed.

"I'm sorry to disturb you, sir," he said, "One of the jurors has taken ill and has, in fact, been taken to hospital with possible appendicitis. Judge Stuart Hyde is swearing one of the alternate jurors in at this very moment, and the trial is expected to resume at 11 a.m."

"Thank you very much," Wilson said. "Can you tell me which of the alternates has been chosen?"

"Yes, sir, Mrs. Paula C. Marcantonio." The bailiff then left and Wilson sent for two cups of coffee. Jack, of course, feeling nervous took this news as a bad sign.

"Relax," Wilson said. "These things happen, it can't be helped."

Finally, at 10.50 a.m., Wilson and Jack were in their designated places. The court was packed out as usual. It rose to its feet yet again as Judge Hyde entered from his chambers. With everyone seated, the jury entered from the deliberation room and took their places. The new juror was a beautiful 32 year old wife and mother, with a promising career as a copywriter in the advertising industry. Her shoulder length brown hair, framed her pretty face perfectly. She looked extremely nervous, which of course was understandable, as she had been thrown in at the deep end.

Judge Hyde brought all the murmurings to order with three sharp taps of his gavel. Wilson was feeling optimistic, as the day before had gone so well and Judge Hyde, he felt sure, would direct the jury to Jack's advantage.

After a short pause the Judge began his direction. "Ladies and gentlemen of the jury, you have sat patiently listening throughout this trial, as the testimonies have been put to you and this court. Now of, course, it is your responsibility, if possible, to reach a verdict. As the prosecution pointed out in their opening statement, a young woman has indeed lost her life at the tender age of 22. You have to decide whether or not the prosecution, with the evidence that they have put before you, have proven guilt beyond reasonable doubt.

There are key points that you have to deliberate on; firstly, the position of the deceased's shoes, being under the passenger seat on recovery of the vehicle. You must bear in mind that we have heard testimony under oath that the deceased, due to an idiosyncrasy, always placed her shoes under her seat. Secondly, you must take into account the position of the driver's seat. If, having deliberated, you feel that the seat had been deliberately positioned to the extreme rear of its forward, backward motion then the driver, of course, would have had to have been a lot taller than the deceased. Finally, regarding the seat belt on the passenger side of the car. We have heard from a witness under oath that it was, in his opinion, extremely tight, almost seized up. Yet, in his statement to the police, the defendant claimed he was the passenger, and he was wearing his seat belt."

Wilson Smyth sat there with a disbelieving look on his face; he had never before heard such a blatant direction from a Judge. A direction, arguably, encouraging a guilty verdict. Right through the trial, in Wilson's mind, Judge Hyde had been fair and just in all of his rulings and, up until this morning, had his total respect. He simply could not understand why the judge seemed to have done a somersault overnight and neither could Jack, whose heart was now sunk into his boots. The colour having drained from his face, he felt sick as he scanned the public gallery looking for Cindy. Instead, he froze as the hate-filled eyes of Tracy Fielding bore right through him. Jack was full of anger and frustration. He now realized what had happened to the judge overnight. Tracy, a fellow Judge, had got to him. "I've got no chance now," he thought, "as I can't even tell my own attorney what has happened. These bastard Judges, solicitors and attorneys are all in the same boat, and will always stick together." The unwanted sexual encounter with Tracy Fielding, having lost him his beautiful Phylamina, could now be about to lose him his freedom.

"The fact that the defendant refused to take the stand in order to defend himself," the judge continued, "cannot enter into your deliberations, as the constitution of the United States of America states that he doesn't have to. I would like you to go now and, if possible, reach a verdict. God bless the United States of America and this court."

Sitting in the small debriefing office later on, Wilson said. "Look, Jack, I have to be straight with you. The judge's direction to the jury inexplicably went very bad for you. When we came in this morning I believed you had a 60% to 40% chance, but now I think it has gone completely the other way."

After countless cups of coffee and cigarettes, the message came through from the bailiffs at 3.30 p.m. that the jury were about to return. Wilson shook Jack's hand warmly and wished him luck. They then went back into court to hear his fate.

Murmurings all around the Supreme Court were brought to an abrupt end, as Judge Hyde banged his gavel down hard. Wilson could not understand it. The Judge's demeanour had, in his opinion, completely changed overnight.

"Have the jury reached a verdict?" the Judge barked out.

Stephen Jackson, the foreman of the jury, stood up. A stocky, handsome thirty year old Environmental Consultant, with bright blue eyes and a strong jaw replied

"Yes we have, Your Honor."

Chapter 6

"How say you to the charge of Manslaughter?" The judge asked with a look of real intensity.

As Jack waited for the answer, he felt sick. Stephen Jackson, the foreman, replied "We find the defendant "not guilty," Your Honor."

Glaring at the foreman through narrowed eyes the judge asked. "Is that the verdict of you all?"

"Yes, Your Honor, it is."

Judge Hyde banged his gavel down even harder than previously. "Case dismissed, the defendant is free to go." He then disappeared into his chambers leaving behind a totally bemused and numb Jack Williams. He was being hugged by Cindy, his face wet with tears. He was not sure if they were Cindy's or his own. Everything was a blur to him as well-wishers were pumping his hand; some he knew, some he didn't. He was still shaking as they were being ushered out of the court by the impatient bailiffs. Wilson wisely took Jack to the debriefing room in order to get him to relax. Jack did this with a cup of coffee and the most enjoyable cigarette that he had had since the whole sorry mess had begun.

"Jack, we have a small gathering with refreshments arranged at my office, is that okay with you?" Jack would much rather have gone quietly back to Tony's house but he agreed, as he felt that he owed Wilson Smyth big time. This gathering was obviously for his benefit, in order that he could preen himself in front of the press. At the gathering, Jack picked at a cheese and pickle sandwich, had his picture taken shaking Wilson's hand and gave a short statement to the press. Finally, he was in the car with Cindy, being driven home to peace and quiet.

Tony Martin welcomed Jack home with a big bear hug. "Thank you for Wilson Smyth, big fella," Jack said hugging him back.

"It was the least I could do, if it hadn't been for me, you would never have been in that predicament in the first place. For which I am truly sorry. To make up for it, I'm going to cook a special roast for you tonight."

"I don't know about that, Tony." Jack said laughing. "I've just had one narrow escape and don't forget, I've tasted your cooking before and, unlike a cat, I only have one life."

"Well, there's gratitude for you. I should have let you go to slammer"

Cindy interrupted the boyish banter. "I'll cook the roast, but not until we open that bottle of Champagne and have a toast."

Tony poured them each a glass of Champagne and, holding his glass up, toasted. "A new beginning." They then all chirped in together, clinking their glasses. "A new beginning."

"That nightmare is over at last," a relieved Jack thought, as he stepped into the shower. He closed his eyes as the warm water cascaded down onto his extremely tired mind and body. The never ending thoughts, as usual, were of Phylamina and the terrible trail of events that had taken her young life. He knew that it was his fault but he would never have intentionally hurt her in any way, as he had loved her dearly. The tears flowed freely down his face mingling with the warm water. It felt good to let it all out, convulsing involuntarily with sharp intakes of breath, until finally, the tears subsided. Having finished showering, he dried himself on a huge, fluffy, white towel with Donald Duck smiling at him from both sides. Then, having put on his beloved jeans and t-shirt went out and joined Tony and Cindy in the lounge.

For the first time ever, Tony offered Jack one of his Cuban cigars, as they chatted about the events that had taken place in court that final day. When told of the Judge's final direction to the jury, and the fact that Tracy Fielding was in the public gallery, Tony was amazed. "Man, somebody up there is sure looking after you. That took some balls for the jury to defy the old bastard and go with their true feelings. Good for them."

Cindy left them both chatting and went into the kitchen to see to dinner. Tony smiled, looking at her as she left "She's quite a lady ain't she, Jack?"

"She sure is, Tony. You're a lucky man."

Sitting down later that evening for dinner, which was wonderfully cooked by Cindy, the atmosphere couldn't have been better, as the meal was washed down with copious amounts of good quality wine.

"You must be mightily relieved at not having to go to the state pen."

Jack burst out laughing as he replied, "I don't know who the 'top dog' is in there, but I tell you what, he's a fuckin' lucky dog. Do you remember, Tony? A few weeks ago you made a suggestion to me regarding the 'top dog'?"

"Yes, I remember vaguely. Why?"

"I acted on your suggestion. I went to see a bent chemist in Manhattan named Troy Devlin. Do you know him?"

Tony thought about it. "Troy Devlin? No, I don't think so."

"I want to show you both something," Jack walked briskly to his bedroom and, returning after a couple of minutes, sat down and handed Tony a package.

"Open that." Tony opened the package with a quizzical look on his face and took out a packet of cigarettes.

"Open the packet, Tony." Jack urged.

Having opened the package, Tony removed four small vials. Two red ones and two green, and looked even more quizzical than before. "What the hell are these for?"

"Well, through a process of deduction, I decided that the only place in the pen I could get a private audience with the 'top dog' was in the prison hospital.

Tony and Cindy were now totally captivated, as he went on. "I intended to pay someone to create a diversion, in order that I would have time to drop the contents of one of the red vials into whatever drink the 'top dog' was having. The chemist assured me the contents of each vial were completely tasteless. So far, so good. Now, at the same time, I intended to consume the contents of the remaining red vial. After approximately 30 minutes, we would both be rushed to the prison hospital with suspected severe food poisoning, where we would definitely need to have our stomachs pumped. Right, the two green vials contain the antidote needed so, having taken one myself, I would then have dropped the other one into the 'top dog's' water. If the plan worked out, I would have him all to myself. I hoped to befriend him by giving him information that I had gleaned during my first weeks in the pen, keeping my eyes and ears open. My thinking being, I could possibly offer to become a plant for him during my stay in the pen."

Tony burst out laughing. "What are you like, Jack? You were going to poison the fuckin' 'top dog'?" Tony's laughter became infectious and they all laughed so much that their sides were hurting and they each had tears in their eyes. "Oh dear," Tony went on, trying to quell his laughter, "knowing you, there would probably be a plan 'b' in case the poison plan failed to work."

"Well, yes of course, in that event I intended, with the help of a diversion, to nip the top off a gas lighter and throw the fuel over him, therefore setting fire to his clothes. Making sure there was water nearby in order that I could arrive like the cavalry and put the fire out, becoming a hero and possibly a close friend."

Tony, now laughing out loud, struggled to get the words out, "so, if the poor bastard hadn't been poisoned to death, he wouldn't so much have been a 'top dog', as a fucking 'hot dog'?" All three of them broke out into pleats of laughter.

"You're incredible, Jack." Tony remarked, regaining his composure and wiping his eyes. They finished off with some coffee before relaxing in the lounge, where Tony and Jack each enjoyed a brandy with another Cuban cigar. Tony settled back in his seat, blowing out tiny rings of smoke. "Would you like to come and work for me on a permanent basis?"

Jack took a sip of brandy before replying, "I appreciate your offer, I really do. However, I promised myself before the trial had even begun, that I would start a new life with a normal job and go straight. Crime does pay, we all know that, but it makes you grow old very quickly. I've had enough, I really have."

"Well, as you seem to have made your mind up, Jack, I may be able to help you on that score. A guy I know named Quinton Spencer owes me a favour and, as it happens, he owns a factory that makes security doors or something. He's actually a real English Lord. Leave it with me and I'll try to sort something out. Okay?"

Jack's eyes opened wide and he smiled. "Yes, that sounds great, Tony. That might put me on the first step of the ladder. By the way, I'm starting my new life tomorrow morning, when I return to my apartment."

Cindy, who had been listening to the conversation, suddenly became more interested. "Jack, there really is no need for you to go so quickly. As far as we are concerned, you can stay here for as long as you like."

"You have both been very good to me, Cind', but it's time that I sorted myself out."

"It's your call, you do what you think is best, but as Cindy said, you are always welcome here with us. Now let's do some serious drinking."

Jack woke up the next morning and checked his watch. Noting that it was 9.15, he quickly showered and dressed before going into the kitchen. There was no sign of Tony or Cindy as he settled down to some breakfast. Sometime later, as he was relaxing in the lounge, Cindy, who had been for a swim, walked in wrapped in a white towel. She was carrying another smaller one in her hands, which she was using to dry her hair.

"Will you dry my back please, Jack?" she asked, handing him the smaller towel. Turning her back to him, she then unwrapped the towel from around her naked body and allowed it to drop to the floor.

As he was drying her back, she turned to face him and looked into his eyes. "Tony has gone to work and he won't be home until six tonight." Then looking down at the bulge in his pants, she smiled and began unbuckling his belt as he stood there motionless. She then pulled the belt from its loops and proceeded to unzip his fly.

Jack stopped her. "No, no, we can't do this. You know, as well as I do, it's not right. As much as I find you attractive, you and Tony are my best friends and I'd very much like to keep it that way." He then took her into his arms and hugged her tightly before letting her go and rearranging his clothing. "I'll call for a cab now, Cindy"

"No, Jack, that won't be necessary. I will drive you home. Just give me a few minutes to dress."

Having loaded his boxes into the car, they drove over to his apartment like two strangers making small talk. Entering into the apartment, he thought it looked even dirtier than he had remembered. "I'm going to clean every inch of this dump, Cind'. Then, I'll redecorate completely; curtains, carpet, furniture, the whole works."

"You seem very positive, Jack,"

"Yes I am. This is the first day of my new life. I'm sorry about what happened between us this morning but from now on I'm going to be straight down the line with people, especially when those people are my dearest friends."

She kissed him on the cheek. "Come on, let's go and pick up the rest of your stuff from Marco's garage and then stop at the supermarket." Having driven over to Marco's house, they loaded Jack's stuff into the car. He shook hands with Marco and thanked him before then paying him handsomely. The shopping completed, they were back at Jack's apartment by 4 p.m.

"I don't like leaving you here on your own, Jack, why don't you stay with us at least until you have this place looking like a home?"

"I'll be fine. You go now, and thanks again for everything. I'll give you a ring later, as I'm hoping Tony will have some news regarding that job he was talking about."

He closed the door behind Cindy, sat down and lit up a cigarette that he intended would be his last. With the cigarette package crumpled up and thrown into the trashcan, still containing several cigarettes, he stubbed out the final one into the ashtray and shrugged his shoulders. He then began the long, laborious task of cleaning his apartment from top to bottom. Starting in his small kitchen area, he began with the oven and hob, cleaning them with real gusto before moving on to the sink unit, which he left shining. There was a half-bottle of Bourbon on the kitchen shelf. Picking it up and unscrewing the top, he poured the contents down the plughole.

"From now on," he muttered to himself, "beer will do for me." At 7 p.m., he stopped cleaning for the night and settled down with a healthy chicken salad.

As the days went by, Jack carried on with his task of cleaning his apartment thoroughly. Ceilings, floors, bedroom, bathroom, all were eventually left in pristine condition. Tony rang and gave him the name and address of the company, along with the telephone number of the personnel manager; Mr. Drew Rickets. Jack was delighted as he thanked Tony and promised he would ring Mr. Rickets the next day, which he did. His interview was arranged for the following morning in reception at 10 a.m. Having received directions regarding the nearest subway or bus to the factory, he thanked Mr. Rickets and put down the phone, punching the air with delight. Drew Rickets had sounded friendly on the phone and that made Jack feel optimistic. Having grown up in the Bronx, Jack was aware that West.111 St. was situated in a reasonably pleasant part of Harlem, not too far from his apartment and, as a bonus, right on the edge of Central Park. His best travel arrangements were simply a direct run on the subway to 110 St East, followed by a walk of just a few blocks. If everything worked out, he thought, he might consider leaving his apartment, his beloved Bronx and, in fact, his old life behind.

The next morning, Tuesday the twenty third of November, Jack arrived for the first interview that he had ever had and, of course, was far too early. The factory was a lot bigger than he had expected. As he watched the delivery vans leaving the huge yard, he made a note of where reception was and, looking at his watch, smiled. It was only 9 a.m. He went and found a diner that was scruffy but suited his needs in order to kill time. Having picked up a newspaper on the corner, he settled down in the diner with a mug of coffee in order to kill 45 minutes and settle his nerves. He had a deep feeling Inside that a turning point in his life was about to take place, and he was determined to give it his best shot. How would his fellow workers react to him? Should he keep a low profile as he had lived the life of a hermit for months now? How did the general public view his trial? He really had no idea what the public at large thought. He only knew what the destructive press had printed in order to sell newspapers, with little care for truth. Jack was shaken out of his thoughts by a voice a million miles away, asking him if he wanted another cup of coffee.

He looked up at a huge black woman with a cigarette hanging out of her mouth. Firstly looking at his watch, he then smiled up at her, as he replied. "No thanks, I have to go." Arriving at reception, still a bit early, Jack entered what he thought to be a very smart lounge with soft, pastel coloured walls, ruined by 'in your face' advertisements for security doors. On the far side from the entrance was a reception area with a stunning blonde busily typing. As he approached across a thick, plum coloured carpet, she stopped typing and stood up.

"Can I help you, sir?"

"Yes, my name is Jack Williams and I have an appointment with Mr. Rickets." The stunning blonde, with a nametag on her ample left breast, bearing the name 'Della' smiled and asked him to take a seat.

"Is there a John I could use, Miss?"

"Yes, Mr. Williams," she replied, flashing her blue eyes. "It's down the passage, on the right."

Having relieved himself of the contents of the huge mug of coffee, Jack checked himself out in the mirror. He was wearing the same clothes that he had worn for the first day of his trial. From his inside pocket he took out a toothbrush and cleaned his teeth for the umpteenth time. "Right," he thought, "here we go."

On his return to reception the beautiful Della said, "Mr. Rickets is ready for you now. His office is just past the restroom on the left. His name is on the door."

He walked down the passage and lightly tapped on the door. A cheery voice shouted, "Come in, Jack." As he entered, he was taken aback by the interior. Everything in the small office was blue, including the walls, ceiling, doors, even the desk, that Drew Rickets sat behind with a piece of paper in his hand, was blue. Drew stood up and offered Jack his hand and, as they shook, he laughed, "How do you like my décor?"

"Well, it's certainly unusual, Mr. Rickets, but interesting as well."

Drew sat down and gestured for him to do the same. "Don't look so nervous, Jack, I'm not going to bite you. If you don't like the décor just say its crap, end of. We don't stand on ceremony here and, by the way, call me Drew. I can't stand this Mr. Rickets rubbish. Now, I'll order us a couple of coffees before we start." Jack was feeling much easier as he watched Drew pick up the telephone. Drew, a skinny little man with hollow cheeks and thinning hair that looked too long, spoke down the phone. "Della, could you fix us up with two cups of coffee when you've finished doing your nails please?"

Jack was feeling more relaxed by the minute. This skinny little guy, with greasy hair that looked like it needed a good wash, had an infectious smile and personality.

"Here, have a look at this," Drew said, passing him the piece of paper that he had been reading. Jack took the document off him as Drew picked up a plastic file from his desk and walked over to the filing cabinet. Having put the file in the bottom compartment, he returned and sat down. Jack was laughing as he was reading the document with the heading, 'Rules for Men.'

1.   It's okay for a man to cry under the following circumstances: (a) the moment Angelina Jolie begins

unbuttoning her blouse or (b) when a woman is using her teeth on his pecker.

2. If you've known a bloke for twenty-four hours or more, his sister is off limits forever, unless you actually marry her.

3. No man shall ever be required to buy a birthday present for another man. In fact, even knowing your mates birthday comes across as a bit dodgy.

4. Friends don't allow their best mate to wear Speedos, ever, issue closed.

5. The girl who replies to the question. "What do you want for Christmas?" with, "If you loved me, you would know what to get me." gets a Play Station 2, end of story. And so on and so on. The two men were laughing as Drew, leaning over Jack's shoulder, pointed out the ones that he found to be the funniest. Their laughter was interrupted by a knock on the door. Drew immediately went and sat behind his desk.

"Come in, Della," he shouted. In she came with a small tray. Bending forward slightly in her tight, short skirt, she placed it on Drew's desk in front of Jack's admiring gaze.

"Will there be anything else, Mr. Rickets?"

"Yes, will you pass me Jack's file please? It's in the bottom draw of the filing cabinet over there." The same file of course, that he had placed back in there only five minutes previously.

"Yes," she replied with a smile, as she proceeded to walk over to retrieve the file. She stooped as 'lady like' as she possibly could with Jack and Drew watching her every move. After Della had gone, Drew wiped the tears from his eyes, chuckling to himself. Jack for his part, enjoyed this guy's company so much, he had almost forgotten that he was here for a serious interview. Passing him his coffee, Drew picked up Jack's file. "Well, I've read your file, such as it is. There ain't much in it of course, but I'll still get

Della to file it back down there later. Just describe yourself to me in your own words, Jack."

Having gone right through his upbringing, Jack told the truth about his lack of work experience. He then went on adding that he was a quick and willing learner and that, if given the chance, he would give of his very best. Drew leaned back in his seat, jotting down notes onto a pad that was cradled on his lap.

"You've not mentioned the trial once, Jack, but of course, you don't have to."

"Well, Drew, what can I say? I lost the woman I loved in a tragic accident and now I'm trying to put it all behind me and start again."

"Fair enough, you obviously know the right people to have even got this interview and, having met you, I like your attitude. So, yes, providing you pass the medical, we are going to give you a chance. Obviously, if you start work before Christmas, you won't get paid for the holidays. Do you accept that?"

"Yes, of course I accept that."

"Well you won't have to, as I was only jerking you off. Of course you'll get paid for the holidays." Drew picked up the phone and, looking in his note pad, rang the doctor's surgery that was responsible for the company medicals. After asking for the possibility of a medical within the next couple of hours, he jotted down the time of 12.45. p.m. Giving a card to Jack bearing the name of the doctor's surgery and the time of the medical, he went on to explain that, if he went out of the main gate and turned left, the surgery was only two blocks down on the left. Drew then shook Jack's hand. "You have some time to kill, so if you just want to sit in reception and watch Della for an hour and a half, you're quite welcome."

Jack laughed. "Well, as tempting as that offer sounds, Drew, I think I'll pass on it this time." Then more seriously he went on, "I want you to know that this job means a great deal to me and I promise you, I won't let you down."

He left leaving Drew to finish off the 'rules of men'. Passing reception, he thanked Della, whose eyes never left him as he walked to the door and returned back to the diner to kill some time. Having read his newspaper, he then went through his life comparing how he felt now about starting this new job, against times in the past when he would be starting a new scam or robbery. Where he had felt tense before, he now felt optimistic; pessimism was now replaced by excitement, uneasiness by pride. If only, he thought, he had been working in a normal job when he had met Phylamina, everything could have worked out so differently. He pictured her face with that cheeky smile that he remembered so well, her eyebrows crunched when she would be reprimanding him, her flashing eyes when feeling horny, the warmth that he had felt simply sitting watching television holding her hand. The tears welled up in his eyes.

"Yiss orright, boy?" A voice boomed out to him. Jack looked up at the huge black woman who was looking concerned.

"Yeah, sure, I'm fine."

Not to be put off, she tried again.

"Wud y'all like anodder coffee, boy?"

Jack checked his watch. "No, I'll have to go now, but thanks for your concern anyway." Picking up a new paper tissue, he went off for his medical wiping his eyes, as he walked along. Having arrived at the surgery five minutes early, he approached a tiny receptionist. She was wearing a huge pair of spectacles that appeared to Jack to be hiding a very pretty face. "I have an appointment to see a doctor," he said, as he looked round the waiting room.

"Watcher name, boy?" The bossy little receptionist asked loudly.

"Jack Williams. I've come from Spencer Security Doors."

Looking in the appointment book, the bossy little midget said, "You gonna 'ave ta wait a spell, boy. Doctor Cashmen is a might busy, set yesself down."

He sat down feeling extremely intimidated by the curious stares from four women and one man, all of them black. One of the women had with her a small child of about five, who strangely, was carrying a white baby doll. The little girl walked over, stood in front of him and looked at him with her big eyes open wide. She just stood there unmoving, as he nervously fidgeted on his seat for what seemed to him like an eternity. Then moving even closer, she plonked the baby doll onto his lap and tried to climb up his legs, consequently smearing the contents of her nose, which was all over her hands, onto his navy blue pants. He tried his best to smile down at her, but with his mouth seemingly set in cement, it was more like a grimace.

As he tried to gently keep her off with his hands, the little monster became more and more aggressive. She trampled all over his shiny shoes, while her mother carried on talking to anyone who would listen about her cold, headache and sore throat She was oblivious to the war being waged on Jack by her little treasure. Eventually, after what seemed to him like world war two, the little monster allowed her snotty hand to touch the leg of the man sitting on Jack's left.

The man, while pointing his finger at the enemy, turned and said sharply to the oblivious mother, "Lisa."

Without stopping to take breath, the mother carried on moaning about her backache, as she leaned over and gave her offspring an almighty smack on the back of her legs. She then dragged her screaming little girl off a grateful Jack, who was then left holding the little, white, baby doll.

Not knowing what to do with the doll, he was mightily relieved when the midget unexpectedly shouted to him, "You kin go in now, boy."

He was puzzled as to why he was going in before all the others but cared little. He quickly placed the baby doll onto his now vacant seat and walked briskly down the passageway, before the midget had a chance to change her mind. Stopping at the door bearing the name 'Dr. Cashman', he tapped gently on the door and entered when invited to do so by a female voice. Dr. Cashman was a black woman in a white, knee length smock which couldn't hide her curvaceous figure.

"Please sit down, Mr. Williams," she said. Having gone through his medical history, she then indicated to Jack the screen in the corner and asked him to undress down to his underclothes. He did as he was told and returned in just his boxer shorts. She checked his height, weight and blood pressure, before then asking him to sit down, where she proceeded to examine his throat. She pushed what seemed to Jack like an enormous wooden spatula as far down his throat as possible, making him balk.

"Say ah," she said. He did as he was told.

"And again please."

"Ah," he said, choking.

"Right, Mr. Williams, that's fine. You can stand up now." She then put on a pair of thin, surgical white gloves. "I would like you to stand with your feet apart please, Mr. Williams."

He did as he was asked and she laughed. "No, not that far apart, about 18 inches is all." Having followed her instructions, she then told him to drop his shorts. He did as she asked, and as they lay on the floor around his ankles, she cradled his testicles in her hand, and instructed him to cough, which he did. "And again please?" He coughed

152

again. "Now, will you bend over with your legs apart and try to relax, Mr. Williams?"

He then got the shock of his life as he felt her finger go up his back passage like a submarine and proceed to feel around inside. After what seemed to him like a period of five or six years, she removed her finger.

"You can get dressed now. We are all finished," she said, peeling off the surgical gloves and discarding them into a flip up trashcan.

Having dressed, he sat down at her desk, as she continued writing out the report.

She looked up. "You may go now."

"Will I live, Doctor?"

She looked up again and smiled at him, "Oh, I think we may get a couple of months out of you, Mr. Williams."

He thanked her and left. As he was walking past the waiting room, moaning Lisa was now going on about her ankles being swollen, while her one man war machine of a child, was pulling a glass vase containing flowers off the midget's desk. Jack chuckled to himself as he walked out.

A couple of days later, Drew rang Jack and told him that he had the job, before then going on, "You are to report to reception on Monday morning at 8 a.m.

Mr. Dalton the foreman will meet you there. You should wear respectable working clothes. The company will, of course, provide boots, gloves and a boiler suit. Good luck, Jack."

He thanked Drew and then immediately rang Cindy to tell her the good news.

"Tony's at work, as usual. I'll tell him as soon as he comes home. He will be delighted for you. By the way, are you still coming for the weekend?"

"Yes, Cindy, I'm really looking forward to it."

"We have been invited to a party on Saturday night by one of Tony's friends. I hope you will be up for it, Jack."

"Err. I don't know about that, Cind'."

"You listen to me, Jack Williams, you must start mixing with people again, especially as you have to go to work in a factory on Monday. In any case, there could well be lots of nice women there for you to meet."

"Oh, I'm not interested in that, Cind'."

"Yes, and my name's St. Theresa, and Tony's never going to have a bet again. I've decided; you're coming with us and that is the end of it. Now, I'll pick you up on Saturday morning at 9.30 a.m., so pack some nice clothes, okay?"

"Yes, Miss Bossy Boots. Have you ever thought about taking up politics?"

Cindy just laughed as she hung up.

Chapter 7

When Cindy walked into Jack's apartment, she was amazed. "Glory be," she remarked. "You have been a busy boy." Jack stood there as proud as punch as this was a new feeling for him and he liked it. They then left and, after completing their shopping chore, reached Cindy's house at 11.45 a.m.

Tony welcomed Jack as usual with a hug. "Come in, champ, it's good to see you." They went into the lounge and Tony immediately fetched his Cuban cigars and a bottle of Bourbon. He put them down onto the table and opening first the cigars, offered one to Jack.

"No thanks, Tony, I don't smoke anymore and, in fact, I only drink beer these days. We've just picked up a couple of six packs in the mart so I'll have one of them if you don't mind."

Tony looked at him, shocked. "I just don't get it. How did you manage to pack in smoking so easily? It makes me feel so pathetic."

Cindy interrupted. "You are pathetic, Tony," she said sarcastically. "The only thing you ever managed to pack in, was giving up packing things in."

"Right," Tony said rubbing his hands together. "We're off to Fifth Avenue. I'm going to buy my beautiful wife a new dress and, as for you, Jack, I'm going to treat you to some new clothes so, at the very least, you will look smart as you begin a new chapter in your life." Putting his hands up, he then went on, "Please don't put up any arguments, as I have just gone deaf. Phone for a cab please, Cindy. I don't want you driving, as we are going to have lunch with a bottle or two of wine." Then, looking at Jack, he added, "Oh yes, and some beers, too"

The cab whisked them away at 12.30 and, after a couple of hours shopping, they had lunch in the ritziest building in New York, the impressive Trump Tower. Jack offered the view that Tony must have spent a fortune, but lifting his glass, Tony shrugged his shoulders saying, "What the hell. If I can't make a fuss of the two most important people in my life, then what's it all about?"

They arrived back at the house at 4.30 in the afternoon where Tony and Cindy, feeling tired after the wine, went for a nap. Jack tried to relax but he was so hyped up he couldn't sit still so he called for another cab and, after leaving them a note, went off to see Old Tom. As Jack arrived, Tom was locking up his shop. He shook Jack's hand enthusiastically, obviously delighted to see him. Jack noticed a tear in his eye but didn't mention it. It's good to see you, Tom. Fancy a beer in your local bar?"

"I thought you'd never ask, youngen', let's go."

Over a couple of beers they talked and talked. Jack told Tom about his new job, his aspirations for the future, the fact that he had packed up smoking and his visit to the doctor's surgery. The visit made Tom laugh so much it brought tears to his eyes again. He then moved onto his interview with Drew, which Tom found even more hilarious. When finally it was time to go, Tom made him promise to keep in touch if and when he moved to Harlem. Jack finally left and arrived at Tony's at 7 a.m. Cindy scolded him jokingly and ordered him to hurry up and shower, as they would be leaving for the party soon, which was a mile away in a village hall.

Jack was absolutely delighted when they arrived to find that a jazz band, a really good one, had been booked. He was introduced to an attractive girl named Tina, who was the stepdaughter of the host and he thought that he detected a glint in her eye. However, he wasn't interested in getting involved with Tina or indeed any woman at that time, as he didn't want complications in his life. He did enjoy her company immensely as they danced and chatted together, but that was all. He had not noticed Cindy watching his every move and was oblivious, when she just happened to be passing by as he was talking to Tina. Oblivious again, when he went outside with Tina, in order that she could have a cigarette. Sure enough, Cindy appeared complaining that it was too stuffy inside. He still didn't put two and two together when she interrupted a conversation that he was having with her best friend, who happened to be Tina's stepmother, an extremely attractive woman. This happened again and again. Jack, in fact, didn't have a clue and, therefore, really enjoyed the party. Not one person had mentioned the trial, the jazz band were fabulous and he had felt totally comfortable in a social setting with lots of people.

Just after midnight, people began to drift off in cabs or in their own cars and, finally, Cindy broke into a conversation that he was having with Tina yet again, informing him that their cab was waiting. She then had the audacity to stand there waiting for him. This infuriated Tina, who by this time was sick of the sight of Cindy. She then became even more irritated when Cindy whisked Jack away before she had a chance to exchange telephone numbers with him. She cursed to herself as he could only shout goodnight from the cab.

The following day Jack spent a pleasant time with Tony and Cindy until late Sunday afternoon. When he was ready to go home, she refused to allow him to call for a cab. Instead, she insisted on giving him a lift. When they pulled up outside Jack's apartment, she said she would go up with him, as she needed to go to the toilet.

Having entered his apartment, she called to him, "Put the kettle on, Jack," as she herself went off to the bathroom.

They had a coffee together, chatting about inconsequential things. Eventually, Cindy put on her jacket and as she was leaving, he was just about to kiss her on the cheek when she pulled her body right up close to him and kissed him on the lips. He felt her body tremble against his own but pretended not to notice.

"Thanks for everything, Cind', I'll give you and Tony a ring and let you both know how I get on in my new job." He heaved a sigh of relief when eventually she left.

Monday morning and Jack arrived at the factory far too early for his first ever job, as he was determined to make a good impression. Looking at his watch, he decided to go to the diner again in order to kill some time. Eventually, returning to the factory, he looked up at the name on the main gate, which read, 'Spencer's Quality Security Doors.' He then walked into the reception, where the beautiful Della, flashing her big, blue eyes asked him to take a seat. He sat there waiting, actually doing what Drew had suggested, observing her as she went about her duties.

Eventually, a guy entered and spoke to her. Della called Jack over and introduced him to Leroy Dalton, the foreman of the machine shop. Leroy, a short thickset man, didn't utter a word. Jack for his part was just about to offer his hand when Leroy turned on his heel and gruffly ordered him to follow, as he walked toward the exit. Jack followed him, having taken an immediate dislike to this stocky little man, with his thickset jaw and bulging neck muscles. He had to remind himself of his intention to take everything in his stride, no matter how provoking. He was to find out that he was not alone in his dislike for Leroy. Every person who worked for him hated this lying, cheating, bull of a man.

Leroy saw Jack as nothing else but a threat. In Leroy's eyes, he was younger, better looking and probably more intelligent. Leroy would admit to himself that he had never been the sharpest tool in the box, but most importantly, he saw Jack as white. No black man or woman had ever been promoted to a staff position in Spencer's Security Doors. This, in a place where 75% of the workforce were black.

Lord Quinton Spencer and his son, Nigel, would always prefer a stupid, white person in a position of responsibility, before an intelligent black man or woman. This being the main reason for the company struggling under bad management, as Jack was soon to find out.

Leroy, with Jack in tow, walked out of reception and into a huge garage. They then turned right and went through another door before entering the machine shop. On the right, as they entered, was a desk strewn with lots of pieces of paper, dirty cups, pens, pencils, a stapler and many other things scattered around untidily.

Lying on the floor was a leather covered book with the words 'machine parts' written on the front, barely discernible under what looked like old coffee stains. Jack was unable to stop himself laughing as Leroy picked up the book, placed it on the untidy desk, and proclaimed it as his office.

"What's so funny?" Leroy asked, glaring at him.

"Oh nothing," Jack replied, trying his best to control himself.

Leroy's eyes narrowed. "Look here, pretty boy, let's get something straight before we go any further. I don't want any smart arse attitude from you, or you'll find yourself with a fuckin' busted nose. You won't look so pretty with a flat nose like all these lazy black bastards around here. Do I make myself clear?"

"Perfectly," replied Jack.

"Good. Now that we understand each other, this is your punch card which you place into the clock with your name facing you every morning when you start work and, of course, every night. Is that clear, Nancy boy?"

"Perfectly, Leroy."

"Mr. fucking Dalton to you. Now, go and put your card in the designated slot with your name on it.

Having sorted the card out, Jack returned to the laughable office. Leroy, with his bulging eyes now back in their sockets, gave him a piece of paper. "Go to the stores on the other side of the machine shop and give the big black bastard behind the counter these orders. He'll give you everything that you'll need and then come back here, but make it quick.

As Jack walked around the perimeter of the huge machine shop, he could feel several pairs of eyes following his every step. Finally, he reached the stores, which were diagonally opposite Leroy's desk. He entered and gave the order form to the black guy behind the counter, as instructed. The guy read the order and then looking up, asked, with a surprised look, "You a startin' work here, boy?"

"Yes, I am. Why? Is that a problem?"

"No problem to me, ma man," the black guy said, as he looked Jack up and down. Taking some overalls off the shelf, the store man then put them onto the counter in front of him. "They should fit you mighty fine, bring 'em here every Monday and swap 'em for a nice clean pair. Now what size boots yer take?"

"I usually take size eleven."

The store man then put a pair of boots on the counter, along with a pair of goggles and some gloves. "The broads a gunna be real pleased to 'ave you aworkin' here, boy," he said, as he offered his hand to Jack. "Duane Carter at yer service."

Jack put his hand into Duane's huge fist, which made his own look like a little boy's, as he replied, "Jack Williams, likewise."

160

Duane smiled, showing a shining set of white teeth. "Try 'em boots on, boy, then go pick yerself a locker on your way back to Leroy's office block." They both laughed before Duane went on "The locker room's through the canteen on the right corner of the machine shop. By the way, white boy, I wuddna' take too long about it, as Leroy won't be a fan a yourn, and he can be plenty mean." Jack tried on the boots, which fitted him fine. He then thanked Duane, a man he felt immediately at ease with, before making his way to the locker room, where he picked out an empty one.

Having donned his overalls and boots, he walked quickly back to see Leroy carrying with him his goggles and gloves. Leroy glared at him with hate-filled eyes. "Oh, so you've come back at last have you, Nancy boy? I thought maybe the big black bastard in the stores had taken a fancy to you."

Jack said nothing. He was determined not to rise to the bait, as he had decided that this thickheaded badmouthing bull of a man would keep for another day.

Leroy carried on enjoying himself at Jack's expense. "Well, seeing as you seemed to like it so much in the locker room, you can go and clean it up along with the stinking toilets and washroom. You'll find all that you need in the cupboard on the right hand side of the washroom, now get on with it."

As Jack walked to the locker room, his mind went back to the excited feeling that he had experienced that very morning on his way to work. His good intentions of working hard, while keeping a friendly attitude, now seemed like a joke. Here he was on his way to clean the john, sent there by an ignorant little prick whose face he would dearly like to restructure with a hammer. Feeling pretty low, he took a bucket and a mop out of the cupboard along with a cloth, rubber gloves, detergents, a sponge, a brush and a shovel. He was just about to begin cleaning the first toilet, when he heard a hooter sound. It became quickly apparent to him what the hooter was for, as within seconds, the washroom was full of people quickly cleaning their hands before going back into the small canteen. Realizing it was a pre-determined coffee break, he washed his hands and ventured into the canteen himself, which became silent as he entered. He froze, not knowing what to do, as he looked at rows of black faces examining him. Feeling ill at ease, he suddenly felt a warm glow as Duane's booming voice broke the silence. "Hey, Jack, park yer butt down 'ere a spell, boy."

He looked gratefully over at a corner table where Duane was sitting with a pretty black girl gesturing for him to join them. As he walked over and sat down, the people restarted their conversations, which was music to his ears. Duane introduced him to his companion named Bernie, whose big brown eyes lit up as they shook hands.

"Have you not brung any coffee, boy?" Duane boomed.

Jack shook his head. "No, I didn't think."

Duane was up in a flash and on his way to the locker room. He returned seconds later with a cup for Jack. Pouring some coffee into the cup, Duane laughed as he said. "As afraid I only takes ma coffee black man, if you'll excuse the pun." Jack was delighted with this gesture. Though small, it meant a great deal to him. Unfortunately, the hooter sounded before he had the chance to get to know Duane and Bernie properly. Even so, he went back to his chores in the toilets, now feeling a little better.

The next couple of hours cleaning the toilets until they shone gave him the chance to refocus his mind. He went over yet again what had happened to Phylamina, the months leading up to the trial, the twenty-five years that it seemed to last, the relief that he had felt as he walked free from the court. He began to realize that he had been a bit naive in thinking that his hopes and aspirations (which had since been dashed by an ignorant little runt) would fall easily into place for him. Now refocused, he thought to himself. "If it's going to be a long haul, then I'm ready for it." He thought of his first obstacle, Leroy Dalton. Jack thought the best way to handle Leroy would be to take everything he could throw at him, bite his lip, be respectful and finally win him over and of course deal with the little prick at a later date. Strangely, Leroy inadvertently had helped him to settle in by giving him the most menial task possible, as the mainly black workforce seemed to find him somehow more acceptable.

As Jack was cleaning the toilets, mirrors and washbasins in the surprisingly unisex washroom, people coming and going were complimenting him with friendly comments such as. "Great job, man. That looks pretty good for a honkey."

Just before lunch Bernie was washing her hands as Jack, was cleaning nearby. She enquired," What are you doing for lunch, Jack?"

"I dunno, Bernie, go to a local diner I suppose."

"Well, there's a burger van every lunch time at the main gate. If you want to, you're welcome to join Duane and me in the canteen."

"Yes, thanks, I'd like that. Would you like me to get you or Duane a burger?"

"No thanks, I'm a veggie, see you later." After she had left, he thought about her. She wasn't quite black, certainly not African, and didn't speak in their dialect. "Maybe Jewish or Arabic" he thought. But definitely not like the majority of her workmates. He put her age at early twenties but, whatever she was, he found her to be really friendly and he was grateful for that, as he was with her probable boyfriend, Duane.

The hooter sounded at five minutes to one for lunch, which was supposed to give everyone five minutes to wash his or her hands. Jack went to the main gate and, after a short wait in a queue for a burger, was back in the canteen by five past one. Duane and Bernie were sitting at the same table in the corner. As Jack sat down, Duane poured him a cup of coffee. They enjoyed a relaxed lunch break as all three of them seemed to gel. Duane told Jack that the whole workforce was amazed at the company employing him, as they were struggling and, in fact, redundancy was a real fear.

After lunch, as Jack was cleaning the locker room, his mind went over the reason why the company had employed him. He shuddered at the thought of the favour that Quinton Spencer owed Tony.

Having finished the locker room, leaving it in pristine condition, he put all the stuff back into the cupboard, checked that everything was in order and made his way to Leroy's so-called office. There was no sign of him so he just stood by the desk observing his fellow workers as they carried out their various tasks.

"What the fuck d'you think you're doin'?" Leroy barked from behind him.

"I've finished cleaning the John and the locker room, Mr. Dalton." Jack said in a respectful manner.

"Well it's taken you long enough. Let's go and see if you've even opened the fuckin' cupboard." With that Leroy walked briskly to the locker room with Jack in tow. Having inspected his work, Leroy looked at his watch then at Jack. "You can finish the day cleaning my office." He then turned on his heel and walked out. Jack took the brush and shovel out of the cupboard and went back to Leroy's desk. He was just about to start brushing up when the hooter sounded, signifying the end of his first working day.

On his way home Jack purchased a large flask and on reaching his apartment, collapsed into his favorite chair, mentally and physically drained. His first day at work had taken so much out of him that, by the time he had had something to eat and watched a bit of television, he couldn't keep his eyes open and so went to bed and was asleep by nine o'clock.

The following morning he arrived at work early with his flask, sandwiches and a mug. At eight o'clock prompt he was at Leroy's desk with a brush and shovel. Leroy was shouting and bawling at people in the machine shop. "Man management," Jack thought, "is definitely not one of his strong points."

Leroy sat down at his now much tidier desk (thanks to Jack's efforts) and, looking at him through a drunken haze, snapped. "When you've finished here, report to Benjamin Vignal on press number one. He'll show you the ropes."

Having finished cleaning, Jack went to the locker room and put the utensils back into the cupboard, before then taking his goggles out of his locker.

On his way back he passed Bernie, who was working in the file and trim area, along with a number of other girls. She called out to him.

"Hi, Bernie," he said as he walked over, aware of all the eyes examining him. "I'm supposed to report to a guy named Benjamin Vignal on press number one. Can you point him out to me, please?"

"Sure, Benjie's that guy with the yellow hat on the press nearest to Leroy's desk. I'll see you at coffee break, Jack?"

"Yes, sure," he said, walking away to a chorus of wolf whistles. Smiling gratefully, he waved back to them.

Benjamin Vignal was looking at some drawings and adjusting things on the press as Jack approached him. He waited for an opportune moment before making his presence known. "Hi, my name's Jack Williams. Mr. Dalton told me to report to you."

"Mr. Dalton?" Benjie said laughing. "I've heard that low life called many things, boy, but never Mr. Dalton, no sir." Benjie then wiped his hands on his overalls before

holding his palm up to Jack. "Lay some skin on me boy."
Jack held his hand up and they crashed their two palms
together before Benjie then went on. "Benjie is ma name,
but most people call me the donkey, especially yon women
folk over there.

"I'm a just settin' up this press for a set of doors, if you
makes your way to the sheet metal storeroom, you kin help
old Sheldon carry the sheets through when I'm ready for
'em."

Off Jack went to the sheet metal storeroom and
introduced himself to Sheldon.

"Sit yerself down a spell," Sheldon offered. "The
donkey'll give a holler when he's ready for the first sheet."
Sheldon was a skinny little guy, who looked like he would
struggle to lift a pot of coffee, never mind a sheet of
pressed steel. He explained to Jack that he was only one
year from retiring and, in the event of redundancies, felt
sure he would be the first out. He went on to say that the
workforce as a whole had become more optimistic about
keeping their jobs since they had found out about Jack
being taken on, reasoning that the company must have
taken new orders for doors. Jack of course couldn't tell him
the real reason.

Sitting there wasting time talking to Sheldon seemed
really odd. "Surely," Jack thought, "there's got to be a more
productive system than this."

After half an hour they heard the donkey yell for the
first sheet. Sheldon asked Jack to grip hold of one side of
the sheet, as he himself gripped the other. The heavy sheet
was really difficult to manhandle, as it naturally had a
wobble and, though Sheldon made it look easy, Jack
thought that this again was a total waste of manpower.
They struggled along going past press two and three. As
they got to press number one, the Donkey jumped down
and helped them load the sheet onto the press, then told

them they could go back to the sheet metal storeroom, until such time as another one was needed.

"Do you mind if I stay and watch?" Jack asked the Donkey.

"Sure thing, man, welcome aboard," replied the smiling Donkey as he activated the press, which consequently turned the metal sheet into a door, as though it were tissue paper.

"Wow, that was amazing," said Jack, startled. "What happens now, Benjie?"

The Donkey pointed at his watch. "I dunno about you, white boy, but the rest of us is goin' in for a coffee break real soon." He had hardly finished speaking when the hooter sounded and everyone rushed to the canteen with Jack following on thinking it was a bit odd. Here he was going for a coffee break and he hadn't really done any work yet. Taking his flask out of his locker, he joined Bernie and Duane at their usual table.

"How's it goin', pretty boy?" Duane asked Jack, smiling.

"Well, it's all a bit strange, Duane. I'll be happier when I know what I'm doing."

Bernie then chipped in, "Well, don't worry, the management sure don't know what their doin', so you're in good company. But never mind that, Jack, a group of us are goin' bowling on Friday night. Why don't you come along?"

"Yes I'd love to, Bernie. I must tell you though, I won't be very good at it as my social life usually involves going to the opera, visiting art galleries, lectures on Philosophy, that sort of thing."

"Sure you do, and ma names fuckin' Charlie Chaplin," Duane said, laughing. The hooter sounded and they all went back to work, moaning.

Jack looked closely at Leroy standing by his desk bawling and shouting at various people, his earlier suspicions now confirmed; Leroy was drunk, big time. "No wonder this place is a shambles," he thought, as he made his way to press number one. Four guys were extricating the newly pressed door as he approached, in order to move it on to the hole-punching machine. Donkey and Sheldon were standing watching.

"This is hopeless," Jack, thought, "it's a wonder this place is still in business." As the day came to a close, after several avoidable stoppages, Jack's astute mind began to click into gear. He decided that he would make a note of all the avoidable problems as soon as he arrived home, which he did. Reading his notes on the way to work the next day (having had only two day's experience) he realized with a surge of excitement, the potential for improvement .

On his third day, practically the whole workforce was made idle for the second time that morning, by the hole punching machine breaking down. Once again, it took the maintenance guy approximately an hour to put things right. This, of course, went into his notebook. He decided to find out who was in charge of the machine in order to have a word with him or her. This recurring problem, Bernie had explained, usually happened once or twice a day.

By the time Friday arrived, Jack felt as though he had worked at Spencer's for a month. By now he had helped out on most of the different areas of the machine shop and his note pad, which was only small, was nearly full. He decided to buy a bigger book on his way home that would be ideal for a calculated business study: His plan being to carry on making notes in a small book, before then transferring them into the main one at night.

At lunchtime, with his flask and sandwiches, Jack joined Bernie in the canteen where, unusually, she was sitting on her own. "Where's Duane, Bernie?"

"He's going to have a late lunch, as apparently a delivery has arrived unexpectedly."

"So, when we go back to work, the stores will be closed as Duane will be having his lunch break?" Jack asked looking puzzled.

"Yes, that's what usually happens in cases like this. Why, Jack?"

"Well, what happens if we need something from the stores like springs, bolts, files, etc.?"

"Well, obviously, we have to wait until Duane opens the stores," she replied shaking her head.

"Yet more information for my note pad," Jack thought, as he studied Bernie delicately eating her sandwich. She had dark hair and eyes, a slim petite body and a wonderful uncomplicated smile. He looked puzzled, as he asked, "Where do you come from, Bernie?"

She put down her sandwich. "I was born in New Jersey, where I grew up, but I now live locally. I have an apartment about a mile from here."

Jack pressed on. "Have you any family?"

"Yes, my amazing mother. She was born and raised in Iraq. When she was just fifteen years old, her father informed her that she was to be married three days later to a man she had never met. She was shown a photograph of him but it was not until just before the actual ceremony, that she was introduced to him. During the following three years, he treated her very badly. Finally, she had had enough and escaped, after borrowing money from her parents. She paid this to an underground organization who smuggled her out of Iraq. She arrived in America frightened and lonely but, eventually, she met my dad, who was Russian, and fell in love. He was kind and very sweet. Pretty soon, she became pregnant with me and they got married. So you see, I'm half Russian and half Iraqi. Some mix hey?"

"Fascinating, where's your mother now?"

"She's still in New Jersey and now remarried. Unfortunately, I don't get on with my stepfather. In fact I don't want anything to do with him. She has, of course, never been back to Iraq. Now it's your turn, Jack. What skeletons do you have in your closet?" Just as he was about to answer the hooter sounded, very much to his relief.

Bernie stood up. "Are you still up for the bowls tonight? Cause if you are, I'm in my car today and I still have one place left and can offer you a lift."

"Well thanks, Bernie, that would be fantastic. Mind you, I'd better check if my life insurance is up to date and covers being driven by a woman driver."

She slapped his arm playfully.

Jack later found out that the name of the guy in charge of the hole-punching machine was Glen Roach and, as a bonus, Glen, who was a white guy in his early fifties, was one of the group going bowling that night. He was also told that Glen was nicknamed the 'quiet man' as he very rarely spoke. If nothing else, he figured, the bowls night would give him a chance to get to know Glen.

They all met at the main gate after work, eight of them in all. There were two cars; Jack was to go with Bernie, Benjie the donkey and Duane. He was quite surprised when Benjie climbed into the front seat alongside Bernie, as he had taken it for granted that she and Duane were an item. So, all loaded up, off they went to Queens for a night of Pizza and bowls.

Eventually, they pulled up outside a small Italian pizza restaurant. As they were going in, Bernie asked Jack quietly if he could try and organize it discreetly, for him and Duane to flank her at the table. She added that Benjie had always had a thing for her and she wasn't comfortable with his attentions. He agreed, of course, and they entered the restaurant. The long table was ready, as they walked in and so they all began choosing their places. Bernie sat down immediately and Duane, who knew the script, sat next to her. Benjie the donkey moved deftly over and pulled out the seat on the other side. However, before he could maneuver his big frame around the seat, Jack swiftly sat in it and at the same time pulled out the next seat along, inviting Benjie to sit next to him with a smile. The donkey didn't look too happy but, nevertheless, sat down without making a scene. Jack whispered a sexist joke in Benjie's ear, hoping to appease him. The donkey laughed out loud and slapped him hard on the shoulder. He was a huge man and Jack really felt it, but said nothing.

On the other side of the table facing them was Glen Roach, the only other white person in the company. Alongside him were three girls who worked with Bernie named Tasha, Lila and Toni.

Jack enjoyed the meal, which was spent with lighthearted banter, all of it in good taste. Two hours and five bottles of wine later, each member of the group paid their share of the bill after Jack had worked it out in a flash. They were then off to the bowling alley.

Throughout the meal, Glen Roach had not spoken a word to anyone. Jack thought his nickname, the 'quiet man', fitted him perfectly. As the group were heading for their respective cars, Jack made a beeline for the front seat of the car next to Bernie, in order to keep the donkey away from her. Benjie opened the front passenger door, obviously not happy with Jack saying with a scowl on his face. "I think it would be better if I sat in the front. My legs are longer than yours."

"Oh we're only goin' just down the road, Benjie," said Bernie, now fearing trouble. The donkey grumbled as he made a meal out of the situation by pretending to struggle getting his legs into the rear of the car. Jack was a bit concerned. He had handled bigger and tougher guys than Benjie before, but he desperately wanted to avoid any trouble, which of course would ruin this fabulous feeling of going out for a bite to eat and a few drinks with his workmates.

A few minutes later they were in the bowling alley. Jack said he was going to the cloakroom to hand in his jacket and was immediately followed by Lila and Tasha. Lila promptly put her arm through Jack's saying. "Where do you live, honey?"

"In the Bronx," he replied smiling down at her.

Lila took this as a come on and offered, "Well listen, honey, why don' I drop you off on ma way home?"

"That would be great, Lila, as long as you're not goin' out of your way."

"No no, Jack, I'm a drivin' through there anyways. We'll sort it all out later."

By the time they rejoined their friends, Bernie and Duane were carrying two huge jugs of beer to the small tables next to the lanes they had been allocated. Glen Roach followed behind with a tray of glasses. Meanwhile, Benjie the Donkey had drawn pieces of paper out of an ashtray choosing the two teams, which by chance happened to team him up with Bernie, Tasha and Toni. Duane, having filled the glasses with beer, picked his up and made a toast. "To close friends, and that now includes you, Jack."

"Here, here," they all chorused together and drank to it. It made him feel warm inside.

"Right," said Benjie. "It's me an' Bernie against Jack an' Lila on lane seven, an' Tasha and Toni against Glen an' Duane on lane six. Let the best team win." With that, he put his huge arms around Bernie's trim little figure, practically squeezing the life out of her. Jack noticed her discomfort but felt he could do nothing. Despite the donkey being a bit pushy with Bernie, he was enjoying himself.

Jack and Lila easily won the first game with Lila posting five strikes, making Bernie feel uncomfortable in the process, by throwing her arms around Jack after every single one. They then changed over lanes with Jack and Lila now playing against Tasha and Toni, who had won their match against Glen and Duane, therefore reaching the final, so to speak.

On Jack's first bowl, he posted a strike. Lila threw herself onto him wrapping her arms around his neck and her legs around his waist, an action not gone unnoticed by the jealous Bernie, who was watching from the next lane.

Eventually, after approximately two hours, Jack and Lila won their match and so they all retired to the bar for some drinks. He had really enjoyed it; the banter, the beer, the competitiveness, in fact all the normal things most young people would take for granted. He was enjoying normality for the first time in his life and loving it.

Lila was sticking to Jack like a limpet, which he didn't mind, as she was a beautiful girl and he, being a typical man, obviously enjoyed his ego being massaged occasionally. This of course left Benjie the donkey all over Bernie like a rash as usual.

Glen was standing alone by the bar sipping his beer quietly, while the other three were trying their luck on the one armed bandit, too busy to notice Bernie's discomfort.

"I'm going to have a word with Glen," Jack said to a disappointed Lila, as she reluctantly let go of his arm before then going to join the other three on the Bandit. As Jack approached him, Glen didn't even bother to acknowledge his presence. He pressed on. "That was a great game of bowls, Glen."

"Yeah," was all that came back.

Not to be beaten, he tried again. "I believe you watch the Yankees a lot?"

"Yeah," was all that came back yet again, as Glen picked up his glass and downed his beer before belching.

Jack was finding this harder work than he had anticipated. He tried a few more pleasantries with the same negative responses and, just as he was giving up with a parting shot, "We'll have a chat on Monday, Glen, perhaps when the hole punching Machine breaks down?"

Glen perked up. "You're right there, man, that fuckin' machine a mine gets more breaks than the accident and emergency ward."

Jack was stunned. He had found something that Glen wanted to talk about and it happened to be the very subject he eventually wanted to get round to! Not to miss a chance, he pushed on. "What exactly is the problem with the machine, Glen?"

"It's the heads man, Glen said enthusiastically. "They're too soft an' they can't stand up to the hard steel in the doors."

"I see," replied Jack, feeling like he has just scored a home run. "Perhaps you could show me what you mean on Monday?"

"Sure I will, man, no other fucker's interested. I usually has ma' coffee break by the machine, so if you wants to join me, I'll show you then"

"I'll take you up on that, Glen, coffee time on Monday," Jack slapped him on the shoulder, as though they were now big buddies and walked over to Bernie and Benjie, feeling like a heel. He had been so wrapped up in Lila and Glen, he had completely forgotten about Bernie being at the mercy of the donkey.

"Hi, you two." He said. Bernie's face lit up, but Benjie just glowered at him.

Trying his best to defuse the situation, he congratulated Benjie on his amazing strength and power on the bowling alley. "You made it look like you were picking up little plastic balloons, Benjie. You must work out a lot."

Benjie was not bright enough to see what Jack was about and, as his head doubled in size, he replied, "Well, I do pump some iron back home."

Whoops of joy came from the bandit as the gang hit the jackpot. They rejoined their friends carrying a hatful of silver dollars and plonked them on to the bar. "This'll pay for the rest of the beers," Duane said with a huge smile on his face.

The group all enjoyed themselves for the rest of the evening. Jack didn't leave Bernie to the attentions of the donkey any more, even though he had Lila hanging on to his arm.

The bowling alley bar was closing and people were beginning to drift off, as Jack went to the men's room followed by Benjie. Back at the bar, Lila asked her passengers if they wouldn't mind taking a cab home, as she had promised Jack a lift to the Bronx and he had accepted. Bernie's heart sank. She could vaguely hear Toni say, "But you don't live anywhere's near the Bronx, girl."

Lila replied. "Yes, but I'm a sleepin' at my parents' house tonight, in fact I'm a stayin' there for the whole weekend."

Tasha then chirped in, "But your folk's live in New Jersey, girl. That's nowhere near the Bronx."

Lila, now getting fed up with her interfering friends, replied curtly, "Oh, it ain't that far out of my way. In any case, it's all done now." With that Lila went to the ladies room leaving her friends shaking their heads.

Meanwhile, Jack, who was standing at the urinal next to Benjie, got the shock of his life as Benjie turned to him with his trouser pockets sticking out, and his penis hanging down between his legs simulating an elephant's trunk. Benjie proceeded to put his hands on his hips and began swinging it around like a propeller. "Now you knows why I'm a called the donkey," he boasted, laughing out loud.

Jack was amazed at the sheer size of it. He turned away and, as he zipped up his own fly said, "I hope you don't have a soft inch in the middle, Benjie."

On leaving the men's room, Jack was on his way back to the bar when Lila, who had his jacket in her hands, intercepted him. "C'mon, she said, it's time we were a goin'."

"But what about you're other passengers, Lila?"

"They is all goin' to a club as usual. Don' fret none about them, Jack."

"I'll still have to say goodnight to them before we go," he said, pulling himself free from her clinging grip. He walked over to the bar and kissed each girl on the cheek before then shaking the hand of each of the men. He thanked them for inviting him and went on to say he looked forward to the next time.

"Are you ready to go then, Jack?" Lila asked, grabbing hold of his arm.

"Are you sure it's not out of your way, Lila?"

"Hell no, a couple a miles is all."

The rest of the group stood and watched them leave, knowing full well what she was about. As they were getting into Lila's car, Jack couldn't help thinking that the atmosphere hadn't been quite right with the gang. "Was there something wrong back there, Lila? I mean, was everybody okay?"

"Oh sure. They all said that they enjoyed 'emselves. A can see you is a born worrier."

As they pulled up outside of his apartment block, Lila put the handbrake on.

"Jack, I sure would appreciate a strong cup a coffee to clear my head."

Jack reluctantly agreed "Yes, okay, but you'll have to take my apartment as you find it." On entering his spotlessly clean apartment, Jack indicated to Lila where the bathroom was.

"Two sugars," she shouted, as she disappeared down the hall. As soon as she was in the bathroom with the door locked, she removed her top and took off her bra. Then, standing with her back to the door, proceeded to rub and caress her nipples until they stood out. After putting her top back on, she reapplied lipstick before rejoining Jack, who was in the kitchen area.

Leaning back with her hands on the kitchen work top and her breasts jutting out in front of her, she leaned her head as far back as it would go with her eyes closed and her long black curly hair tumbling down almost to the worktop. She said with a sigh. "Oh, I sure loves Fridays Jack don' you? No work in the mornin', we can sleep in as late as we wants ta." Lila knew how to use her sexuality and could feel his hungry eyes on her body. She was right of course. Jack was a virile young man and she was a beautiful young woman with an athletic, curvy figure. He was taking in the view, and of course, enjoying it to the full.

Not wanting to get involved, though, he steeled himself and, picking up the tray of coffees, walked into the lounge with Lila following behind. As she sat down, he immediately went and sat opposite, much to her annoyance.

"Have you lived here for quite a spell, Jack?"

"Two and a half years now. It's in need of some repair and it definitely needs new curtains and carpets."

"I could sure advise you on those things. I think you'd like ma woman's touch," she said with flashing eyes. "Have you got a girl friend?"

This question took him by surprise, unusually making him tongue-tied.

"Oh I'm sorry, Jack. A can't help my big mouth. You've endured enough questionin' in your trial."

177

Jack was now irritated by her, "Lila, I don't want to talk about that. I'm just trying to get on with my life."

"Sure you are, man. I could help you with that. Are you doin' anythin' this weekend?" He had now run out of patience with this pushy little madam and desperately wanted her gone so that he could go to bed.

"Yes," he replied, yawning. "I'm going to some friends for the whole weekend. In fact, I'm being picked up really early tomorrow and I feel a bit shattered."

She got the message at last. "Oh I see, Jack, of course you are. I better be on my way," she reluctantly said, standing up and putting on her jacket.

At the door Lila tried to kiss him on the lips but he wouldn't have any of that. He simply kissed her on the cheek. "Goodnight, Lila, I'll see you on Monday. Thanks for the ride home." As he closed the door behind her, he leaned against it, with a sigh of relief, before going to bed.

The following morning, with breakfast out of the way, Jack sat with his beloved cup of coffee waiting for Cindy to pick him up. She arrived bang on time at 9 a.m. and hugged him so physically, with her head buried into his chest, that it seemed to him to be way over the top. He briefly thought, "Women are like buses. None when you want one and two or three when you don't." She pulled her head back off his chest and began sniffing the air. "Is that perfume that I can smell?"

"Yes, I went bowling last night with some friends from work and one of them was kind enough to drop me off."

"Oh yes, I'll just bet she was."

"No, no, Cind'. You've got it all wrong. There was nothing in it."

He could tell that she didn't believe him but he refrained from trying to convince her, as he wanted her to think he was seeing other women anyway. On arrival at

Cindy's house, Tony came out excitedly hugging Jack. "It's great to see you, champ. How's the new job going?"

"It's really good, Tony. I like it very much, even though I had a few problems at first due to my own naivety."

"Well, you can tell us about it all later." Tony then took hold of Jack's bag and ushered him into the house. "Get yourself sorted in your room then come and join Cindy and me for a drink."

Having dropped his bag off, Jack rejoined his friends in the lounge. Cindy immediately went into the kitchen for the drinks.

"Just a beer for me please, Cind'," Jack called through to her.

"Oh, so you're still a saint then?" Tony said laughing, as Cindy rejoined them.

She glared at Tony. "It's a pity you don't take a leaf out of his book. Would you like me to bring you a bucket of Bourbon?"

Jack felt uncomfortable at this way over the top remark. He sat in the uneasy silence, as Tony had obviously only been joking. Having received his beer, he went on to tell them all about his new job, his night out with his workmates, the shabby way the factory was being managed, and his reasoning on why. He carried on. "Do you know Lord Spencer well, Tony?"

"Yes, he's a strange character, a bit difficult to read really. His son, Nigel is a smack head on cocaine and his daughter's a fucking nympho." Jack made a mental note about this bit of info on Spencer junior, another probable reason for the factory's mismanagement.

Tony then stood up. "I'm sorry, Jack. I'd love to stay and chat but, unfortunately, I have some pressing business to attend to. Cindy will look after you, won't you, darling?"

"Yes, of course, Darling," she replied, again sarcastically.

Tony ignored it and went on, "I've booked a table at Dino's for eight, I should be back by six, have fun, you two. Cindy, if you have any problems, contact me," he called out as he was walking through the doorway.

"Okay, Tony darling, you're great at solving problems, aren't you? It was really nice of you to spend an hour with us." With that she practically slammed the door behind him.

Jack looked at her pale drawn face. Her fists were clenched now and her eyes filling up. He put his arm around her shoulders and asked. "What's wrong? I felt like I was in the middle of a battlefield earlier."

"Oh, there's nothing you can do," she snapped.

He had never seen her like this before; he took hold of her trembling hands, "What's wrong, Cind'? Come on, tell me please?"

She broke down and went into hysterics. "It's all such a mess," she blurted out. Tony just says 'It's your hormones darling'; that's his answer to everything! Well it's not my hormones, darling. I'm pregnant, and you're not the father. I shagged Jack Williams when surprise, surprise, you were at work yet again, darling." She then buried her head into his chest and sobbed and sobbed.

He held her tightly with his own head now in a spin until her tears subsided. Sitting her down, he wiped her eyes with a handkerchief then took hold of her two hands firmly. "Right, Cind', we have to talk this through. Would you like to go and freshen up while I make us a pot of coffee?"

She walked out of the room without speaking. By the time he had made the coffee and set it down in the conservatory, Cindy had washed her face and regained control. She sat down facing him. He poured out the coffee and offered her a chocolate digestive biscuit. "Here you are; there's nothing that a chocolate digestive won't cure." She glared at him, her eyes filling up again.

"Cindy, I'm so sorry, that was my stupid way of trying to make you more relaxed. Can we begin again?" She didn't reply.

He waited for a while before asking, "Is it not possible that the baby is, in fact, Tony's?"

"No, Jack, it's not. We've been married for twenty years and never once have we taken precautions. We gave up on children years ago."

"Right, Cind', let's try and examine our options as calmly as possible. I hate to ask you this but have you considered a termination?"

"I was wondering how long it would take you to come up with that cop out. No, the answer is no. I could never ever kill an innocent child."

"I wasn't suggesting it, Cind', honestly. I was just trying in some way to simplify things. Okay, the way I see it that leaves us with only two options. One, we can tell Tony the truth..."

She jumped up out of her seat. "Jack, are you mad? You know very well, the cops would find you at the bottom of a river bed."

"Yes, I think you're right there. Well, that leaves only one option left. Do you think it would be at all possible for us to let Tony think he's the father?"

"He might ask for a paternity test, Jack, and in any case, I don't know whether I could carry off the lies."

"Cindy, Tony thinks of me like you would a son. He trusts me utterly and completely. The very trust that he also feels for you so, no, I don't think a paternity test would enter his head. Think about this, although Tony is quite a bit older than me, we are the same size and we have the same colour eyes and hair. You said yourself that you never

ever took precautions, so you both must have wanted children. This could turn out to be a blessing in disguise. Now, I don't want to be too personal, but did you and he have a normal sexual relationship at the time that you would have conceived?"

Cindy considered the question. "Well, more than normal because, at the time, I was secretly looking at the tape of you and Tracy Fielding. I was actually like a bitch on heat. Tony even joked about it at the time."

"Well there you are then, Cind', I could be sort of like the baby's uncle. I think this could work. Nobody would ever know. It would be our secret forever."

She looked at him with her eyes beginning to fill up again. "Jack, I can't think straight at the moment. I've had very little sleep since the pregnancy was confirmed and I'm exhausted. Do you really, really think this could work?"

"Yes I do, Cind', but you do look extremely tired. We will talk about this later after you have rested." He picked her up and carried her to the bedroom. Lying her down on the bed he whispered in her ear, "Everything will be OK, I promise."

She then fell into a much needed sleep.

Chapter 8

Cindy woke up alone on the bed and Jack was nowhere to be seen. After looking in the lounge, kitchen and conservatory to no avail, she went upstairs, showered and dressed. By the time she returned, he was in the kitchen making some coffee. "Are you okay, sleepy head?"

"Yes, Jack, I feel much better thank you. I've made a decision; I've decided to break the news tonight in the restaurant. Don't get me wrong, I'm absolutely terrified but I'll feel much stronger with you being present. Where have you been by the way? Not hiding from me I hope."

"No, of course not. I've been for a swim and a workout. I think you've made the right decision by the way; Tony would definitely be less likely to question the parentage with me there slapping him on the back and congratulating him. Now listen, Cind', from this moment forward and indeed forever, our conversation this morning, along with everything else that has happened, never took place. We must never even discuss it. Do you agree?"

"Yes, I do agree, Jack. Come on, we need some shopping from the mart."

Tony, Cindy and Jack arrived at Dino's in a cab fifteen minutes early and had a drink at the bar. Cindy felt relieved. The saying, 'a problem shared, is a problem halved,' now made total sense to her. She looked at Tony, who was smiling and chatting to Jack. She thought he looked really handsome with his thick, dark hair, which was now beginning to grey slightly at the sides. Although he was twenty-two years older than she, in her opinion, he certainly didn't look it. She then looked at Jack, the horniest looking man that she had ever known. She wondered if he was as nervous as she was. The prospect of dropping the bombshell on Tony in approximately two hours' time was scary.

Dino, the owner of the restaurant approached them "Your table is now ready, folks."

Cindy looked up at the smiling Dino, who gave her a private knowing wink.

"Come on, gang, I'm starving," Tony said, standing up and smoothing out his suit.

As the evening wore on and the last course had been eaten, Cindy became more and more nervous at the prospect of Dino (as previously arranged) bringing in a bottle of the very best Champagne, instead of the expected coffee and chocolates.

Tony broke her thoughts. "Are you okay, my darling?"

"Yes thank you, Tony, I was miles away. Inexplicably, I was bored listening to you two little boys prattling on about baseball."

"What a dame eh, Jack? Stunning looks, a heart of gold, and the patience of a saint to have put up with me for the last twenty years. You'll be a lucky man if you go on to find a gem like my Cindy."

She excused herself and went to the toilet, her insides ripped to shreds.

Having recovered, she returned and gave Tony a kiss on the cheek before sitting down. The table had been cleared of the dishes and Tony was just about to ask the waiter what had happened to their coffees when the lights were turned down low. The background music fell silent. Dino entered from the kitchen, pushing a trolley laden with a bottle of Champagne, brightly lit up by candles and stopped at their table. Tony sat there looking flabbergasted as their champagne glasses were filled. Looking straight at Tony, Dino said, "This, my friend, is on the house." He finished off by filling a glass for himself.

Cindy stood up on trembling legs, lifted her glass, and with tears now running freely down her cheeks, turned to Tony. "Congratulations, my darling, you are going to be a dad."

There followed an extremely stressful few seconds for Cindy and Jack, as Tony sat there transfixed. Eventually, he stood up. "Are you sure, Cindy?" he asked, not being able to take it in.

"Yes, darling, I'm sure," she answered, with her legs trembling.

Dino lifted his glass and made a toast to them both. The entire restaurant clapped as the group emptied their glasses.

Jack shook Tony's hand and gave him a hug. "Well done, big fella," he said, before then going on to kiss Cindy on the cheek.

Tony put his arm around Cindy, who was by now sobbing. He wasn't to know of course, that they were tears of relief more than joy. "Dino," he shouted, "champagne all round for everyone in the restaurant."

With the cheers of all the grateful people in the restaurant ringing in his ears, Tony gave Cindy a loving kiss on her forehead, before putting his arm around her protectively. Cindy for her part felt mightily relieved. It had gone better than she had dared hope.

Turning to Jack, Tony then said. "It looks like I'm gonna be needed at home, champ. Why don't you come and work for me? I'll groom you so that eventually you can take my place."

Jack slowly shook his head. "As much as I appreciate the offer, and please believe me, I do. I'm going to have to say no. I've found normality for the first time in my life thanks to you. Working in the factory and meeting new friends has been a revelation. If I had been living this life when I met Phylamina, there is no doubt in my mind that I would now be settled down with her for the rest of my life.

"Apart from that and, given half a chance, I intend to make Lord Spencer's ailing factory, a roaring success."

Tony clinked Jack's glass with his own. "If there's one thing about you, champ, your cup of life is always half full, never half empty."

The cab dropped them off at home and Cindy began to worry again. She knew that as soon as they were alone, Tony would want to talk about this incredible news. They had a nightcap before retiring and sure enough, as soon as they climbed into bed, he did. "This is amazing, Cindy. After all these years, I can hardly believe it."

She was ready with her answer. "Can you imagine how I felt? I couldn't believe it either. The doctor's view was that although uncommon, these things periodically do happen. But you are delighted about it aren't you, Tony? Please say you are."

"Yes, yes of course I am, my darling, I just wish that I were twenty years younger."

"So do we all, Tony, so do we all," she replied as they both laughed and snuggled together.

The following morning Jack was up at 7 a.m., working out in the gym before then going for a swim. By 8.30, he had the kettle boiling. He had just sat down with his coffee when Tony walked into the kitchen.

"Jack," Tony shouted, "how could you have done this to me?"

Jack froze, his stomach churning. His mouth dried up and he could hardly speak. "Tony I, erm…" was all that he could manage.

It was just as well, as Tony then went on. "That bloody video of you and that slag Tracy Fielding had me so

186

worked up, I've gone and put Cindy in the club." He then burst out laughing before he noticed Jack's ashen face. "Are you all right, champ? You look ill."

Jack was now getting himself together. "No, not so good really, too much to drink last night I expect."

Tony made a fuss of him, fetching him a glass of water and some painkillers. "Here you are. These should help," he said as Cindy walked in, smiling.

"I'm going to make you boys the best roast you have ever eaten this afternoon." Tony put his arm around her waist and gave her a hug.

Jack looked at her. She was glowing and looked happier than he had ever seen her before.

They spent a wonderful day together, until Cindy took Jack home at 7 p.m. As he was getting out of the car, she said, "Tony and I would like you to come and spend Christmas with us."

"Why, that would be great, Cind'. I did have other plans, but I'm sure Ronald Macdonald will manage quite well without me."

As Cindy drove off, laughing, she shouted "You're nuts, Jack Williams!" Monday morning saw Jack off to work with a spring in his step. A clear picture had already formed in his mind of changes that were necessary, in order to improve output and, therefore, greater profit for the company. The first and most important part of his overall plan was for him to come up with something that would really impress his employers. That, he hoped, he might find today, when he had a chance to examine Glen's hole-punching machine with the ongoing problems.

As usual, Leroy told Jack to brush round his so-called office and tidy his desk. He didn't actually mind this, as it gave him the chance to get an insight into Leroy's job. As each day passed, the job became clearer in his mind. Meanwhile, in the file and trim area, Tasha asked Lila whether she and Jack had hit it off on Friday after they had left the bowling alley. With Bernie's ears pricked she replied, "Mind-blowin', Tash'. He lives in a dump of an area, but his place is sure finger lickin' clean. Like most men, he needs a woman's touch a course. As a matter a fact, girl, he's asked me to help him with choosing curtains and the like."

Tasha's eyes opened wide. "You sure sound like you're well in there, Lila. You ain't bin a naughty girl have you?"

Lila just winked as she replied, "You know's me, Tash. I can't resist a horny man."

Bernie's heart sank into her boots as the two of them laughed, oblivious to her feelings.

At the morning coffee break, Jack joined Bernie and Duane. He had been looking forward to seeing Bernie, but no matter what he said, he felt as though she didn't want to know him.

It was obviously nothing to do with Duane, with whom she chatted to freely. "What the hell have I done wrong?" he thought. Maybe it was her way of telling him to back off. He decided that was what he would do.

After the coffee break, they had only been working for approximately thirty minutes, when Glen's machine broke down yet again. The security door's stoppage at Glen's machine meant that productivity on the file and trim, sanding area, and the locks, springs and fitting block, all came to a halt.

Jack, who was brushing around press 1, 2 and 3, was soon able to get to Glen's side. The maintenance guy arrived ten minutes later, which had given Jack enough time to go through the whole problem with an enthusiastic Glen. He was shown the punches, how they were attached and the problems facing the maintenance man, in order to remove them and fit new ones. He was even given an old set of punches by Glen, which he put into a small, plastic bag, along with a slither of metal that had come from one of the doors in the file and trim area.

At lunchtime, he didn't join Bernie and Duane; instead, he sat with Glen and picked his brains as much as possible. He made a detailed drawing of the arm mechanism that held the punches, noting down exact sizes of bolts and springs. By the end of the week, he knew Glen's machine inside out.

Sitting down with Bernie and Duane on Friday lunchtime, the atmosphere seemed a little tense, as he had spent every lunch break that week with Glen. Not being able to tell them why, he asked them instead would they like to go for a drink after work.

"Sorry, man," Duane replied, "we have agreed to meet the gang for a pizza, before goin' on to a club."

"Oh I see," Jack said, now with his chin on the floor. Maybe another time?"

The atmosphere went further downhill, as Lila joined them at the table." Are you comin' with us tonight, Jack?" she asked, with pouting lips and flashing eyes."

"I wouldn't like to impose, Lila." Jack said, his stomach now churning inside.

"Oh, don't be silly, Jack," she persisted, "you wouldn't be imposin'. We'd all love to have you with us, wouldn't we guys?"

Duane and Bernie were then in a difficult position and simply went along with Lila, who was now beaming.

"Right, that there settles it then, Jack," she went on. "You can come in my car with me and Tasha, okay?"

"Yes, okay." He replied embarrassed. "I'd love to."

Lila proceeded to flirt with Jack openly, which made Bernie almost puke. It was now obvious to her that he and Lila were an item, and that, she decided, was that.

They all met after work, Jack getting into Lila's car along with Tasha and Glen. Lila insisted that Jack was to sit up front with her.

At the pizza place, Bernie ended up with Benjie sitting next to her, as Jack sat on the other side of the table with Lila. He hated the thought of beautiful Bernie ending up with Benjie the donkey, but resigned himself to the fact that it was really none of his business, and he would have to accept the situation. They then went on to the club dropping Glen off at his home on the way.

The night continued as expected, but Jack hated every moment of it, so he decided to try and have a quiet word with Bernie in order to clear the air. If nothing else, he missed the camaraderie between them. At last his chance came as Benjie went off to the toilet, leaving Bernie alone. Jack extricated himself from Lila the limpet, explaining to her that he wanted a quiet word with Bernie. Which, of course, annoyed her.

He approached Bernie, suddenly feeling nervous. "Hi, Bernie, are you okay?"

"Yes thanks," she said in a quiet, muted voice.

He persisted. "How's your mum?"

Bernie, feeling really upset inside, answered curtly, "She's fine, thank you."

Jack had had enough of this atmosphere. "Listen," he asked, "have I done something to upset you? Because if I have, I'm really sorry."

She couldn't tell him that really, she was seething with jealousy. "No, Jack, nothing. I just have things on my mind at the moment."

"Well, if I've done nothing wrong, can we at least be friends again? I've really missed your company."

She looked up at his handsome, troubled face. 'It's not his fault if he doesn't feel the same way as I do,' she thought. 'I'm being a soppy cow; I'll have to pull myself together.'

"Yes, of course we can, Jack, I'd like that. Now, as we are friends, I'd like to give you some advice. I know it's none of my business, but if I were you, I would be very wary of Lila; she's a right little tart."

"Oh," he replied, with a puzzled look on his face. He was going to carry on with the conversation, but the dynamic duo of Duane and Benjie returned, so he went back to join Lila, at least feeling as though he knew where he stood with Bernie.

Lila grabbed Jack by the hand. "Let's have a dance."

"Sure, why not, Lila, but I warn you, I've never met a dame yet who could keep up with me on the dance floor."

The rest of the night went okay and, of course, when Lila offered Jack a lift home, he saw no reason not to. "Are you sure it's not out of your way, Lila?"

"No, of course not. I have to drive past your place anyways," she lied, now with a satisfied look on her face.

Toni, who had been listening, looked enviously across.

On the way to Jack's, they dropped Tasha off at her apartment block. Getting out of the car, Tasha leaned into the window. "Would you all like to come on up for a nightcap? I hate going into my apartment alone and I'm sure Jack would like to see it. Is that right, Jack?"

"Well yes, Tash, as long as Lila doesn't mind," he answered, very much hoping that she would.

Having turned off the motor however, Lila agreed but insisted it would have to be a quickie. With that, both girls went into a pleat of laughing.

Tasha lived on the third floor, and so pressed the button for the lift.

"I hope you don't mind, girls but I hate lifts, they make me feel claustrophobic, so I'll walk up."

"No," they both said, as they decided to join him.

Jack ushered them both in front saying, "Ladies first."

Lila giggled. "We haven't invited any ladies have we, Tash?"

Both girls laughed as they began to climb the stairs. Jack, for his part, was enjoying the view in front of him. They both had fantastic figures and, as they were wearing miniskirts (despite the freezing cold night) there was very little left to the imagination.

Having arrived at Tasha's front door, Jack stopped them. "By the way, girls, I don't have a thing about lifts; what I do have is a thing about miniskirts going up a flight of stairs in front of me."

Both girls pushed him through the now opened doorway. "You dirty little perv', Jack Williams." Tasha reprimanded. "I've a mind to tan your hide."

He was really impressed with Tasha's apartment. He thought the colors chosen matched up perfectly the walls, curtains, and carpets. Cushions were dotted about the furniture and an array of flowers made the room smell clean and fresh. The whole finish smacked of good taste and convinced him of the need to tap into it when he began redecorating his own apartment.

Tasha took his jacket. "What's your poison, Jack?"

"A beer would be nice, if you have one."

"Sure I do, would you like casked or bottled beer?"

"I don't mind, Tash. Either will do."

"Oh good," she said handing him a glass of wine, as both girls broke into another fit of giggling.

Lila put on some music and took off her tiny jacket, which showed again to Jack her revealing top. She took the wine glass out of his hand and pulled him into the middle of the lounge and proceeded to dance provocatively, pushing herself into him with little or no thought for Tash, who had disappeared into the kitchen. She then took hold of his buttocks with both hands and began to grind her body seductively against him in time to the music. He, for his part, didn't particularly like her as a person but "Hey," he thought, "what the hell, I'm a single man." Just then, there came the sound of drawers slamming in the kitchen.

Lila called out, "Tasha, what's all the noise for?"

"Oh, don' worry non', Lila, am' a just lookin' for a deck a cards. I thought we might 'ave a game of strip poker."

"Good idea," Lila replied as she sat down next to Jack on the sofa. Moving then onto his knee, she began to kiss him passionately.

"I've found 'em," Tasha said, walking into the lounge. She placed the cards onto a small coffee table next to the sofa. "C'mon you two, I'll bring us some more wine from the kitchen an then we'll start rockin'."

She returned soon after and all three of them sat cross-legged around the coffee table. Tasha, who had on a fitted mini skirt, had to hitch it right up so that she could cross her legs.

"Right," ordered Lila, "every time one of us loses an article of clothin', he or she as to drink a glass of wine straight off."

"Well, in that case," Tasha suggested standing up, "we'll need another bottle of wine." With her skirt high up on her thighs, she then ran into the kitchen and returned not with one bottle, but two.

Lila dealt the first hand. Jack smiled to himself as he noted that the number of articles of clothing being worn by the two girls was almost certainly four, while he himself had on five. He opened his cards to find himself holding a pair of kings. Tasha, who was on Lila's left, passed.

"I open, ladies" he said, putting three cards face down on the table. "I'll take three cards." Each of them took three cards and he looked at his hand to find himself still only holding a pair of kings.

"C'mon, Jack," Lila said smiling. "You opened; let's see what you have"

He put down his pair of kings. Tasha put down a pair of aces with a little excited squeal. Lila then put down a pair of Jack's and a pair of five's with an even more excitable squeal. He took off one of his socks to boos from both girls.

Tasha filled up his glass with wine and insisted, "Down in one, honkey."

As he stood up and put the glass to his lips, Lila stopped him. "Oh no, you'll have to drink it standin' on one leg."

He had already drank a few beers before leaving the club and together with the two glasses of wine that he had drunk since, he found himself tottering on one leg to cheers from the girls as he downed the glass of wine in one.

Lila pulled off his other sock saying, "You is a wimp."

Tasha dealt the next hand. Jack, after having drawn three cards again, finished up with just ace high. Tasha, who had opened, lay down three fours with a huge smile on her face. He was mentally getting ready to remove his shirt when Lila, with a groan, admitted she just had king high.

"Yes," Jack shouted laying down his ace high.

"Off, off, off," Tasha began chanting with Jack then joining in. Lila stood up and seductively removed her top while swaying to the music, revealing a tiny, black see through bra. Her nipples were jutting out like bullets. She then took the filled wine glass off Tasha and tottering on one leg, downed it in one, nearly falling over in the process. They were all laughing and having a wonderful time, as Lila sat down ready for the game to recommence.

Jack was next to lose and so stood up and removed his black tee shirt with hoots and squeals from the satisfied girls. Again on one leg, he downed a glass of wine.

Although really feeling the effects of all the booze, he was having the time of his life.

At this point, Lila excused herself and went to the bathroom. Tash crawled over to Jack and putting her arms around his neck pushed her breasts into his now bare chest. While kissing him, she ran her fingers down his chest and further on down past his belt, until her hand came to rest. Pulling her lips from his, she then whispered into his ear, "I had it wrong earlier, when I called you a 'little' perv."

Lila returned, "C'mon girl, get off him, we don't want him gettin' the wrong idea."

The two girls were laughing, as Tash crawled back to her place.

Tash was next to lose. She stood up and turned her back on them and with Jack expecting her to remove her top; unexpectedly unzipped her skirt, flipped the button open and allowed it to slip down to the floor. She then opened her legs wide in her tiny red panties and bent forward until she could see Jack between her legs. She winked at him smiling. Standing up, she then gulped down her glass of wine in one, standing on one leg as steady as a rock.

Lila lost next and stood up in her skirt and bra.

"Hold on a spell, I'm just goin to the kitchen. Returning with two cubes of ice, she put them inside her bra next to her nipples and swayed to the music for a few seconds, before then removing it. This had almost become a competition between the two girls and he was getting the full benefit.

He was next to lose, and not to be called a wimp again, unbuckled his belt, undid the buttons on his jeans and lay down with his legs high in the air. With his hands on his back for support, he invited the girls to pull off his jeans, one leg each. They did so with gusto, leaving him now with just a pair of jockeys. Another glass of wine on one leg left his head spinning.

Tash then lost twice, losing first her top, and then her bra. She was not so steady with the second of those glasses of wine. Lila then lost her skirt, leaving each of them with just the one item of clothing.

They all laughed as Tasha was about to deal, she stopped and suggested, "Why don't we all cut cards? Lowest loses their knickers. They all put up their hands in a mock vote of approval. Jack cut an eight of clubs. Lila cut second, a nine of diamonds. Finally, Tasha cut very slowly, a three of spades, "No, no, that ain't fair," she complained. "Let's have two out of three."

"I know," Jack offered, "let's all of us put on a blind fold and on the call of ready, steady, go, rip off our knickers at the same time, followed by our blindfolds.

"I agree," shouted a now relieved Tasha, as she ran into the kitchen shouting back, "I'll get three towels."

She returned with them and Jack proceeded to tie one around Lila's eyes. He then moved on to do the same to Tasha. With a wicked smile on his face, he then quickly and quietly put on his jeans, jacket, and shoes and dropped a fifty-dollar bill onto the coffee table to cover the wine.

"Is you ready yet, Jack?" said an impatient Lila.

"Yes, yes, I had a bit of trouble with my knot." Grabbing finally his tee shirt and socks he called out, "ready, steady, go, knickers above your head."

The two girls, with howls of laughter, whipped off their knickers and holding them high above their heads, pulled off their blindfolds. The girls' faces were a picture of shock, disappointment and anger, all rolled into one. They glared at Jack waving goodbye to them as he opened the door and bolted out and into the hall. Clutching his tee shirt and socks he ran down the stairs laughing. On reaching the bottom of the stairs, he stopped to put on his socks and tee shirt, knowing full well they were unable to follow him, being as naked as the day they were born. He was still giggling to himself thirty minutes later, when he finally managed to stop a cab.

Jack spent the whole weekend updating his business portfolio, with the main emphasis being the hole-punching machine. Having studied it in depth, he had ideas on how the re-occurring breakdowns could be prevented. He decided he was now in a position to take the problem to an engineering company. His plan was to thrash out a deal whereby they would produce a prototype for a small fee, which he was prepared to pay for, out of his own pocket. The small fee, along with a promise of ongoing orders for the finished equipment he hoped, would be enough enticement for them. If not, he would consult another, and then another, and so on, until success was achieved. He then made a list out of the yellow pages of possible companies; that he intended contacting the following week.

Monday morning saw Jack cleaning and tidying Leroy's so called office. Leroy, as usual, was shouting at people in such a way as to lower their morale. Jack could smell the booze off him from five feet away, and it turned his stomach.

Leroy walked over to the sanding area, swearing at one of the girls. Jack looked at him feeling only disgust and then carried on tidying the paperwork. As he opened one of the bottom drawers to look for some space, something snapped him to attention. It was an invoice for the supply and fitting of two security doors, which had been sent from a Manhattan address. Attached to it was a check made payable to L. Dalton for $2970. He quickly copied down the details of the check, the company, the invoice number and the pattern numbers of the doors. Looking further down, he found several more invoices, which further investigation he felt sure, would reveal fraud by Leroy

Dalton. Stuffing two of them into his pocket, he closed the drawer. As he then carried on brushing around the desk, he heard Leroy shout at him from behind. "When you've finished your fuckin' women's chores, Williams, go and help in the sandin' area."

Jack's mind was racing right up to the coffee break, by which time the strip poker saga had hit the grapevine, especially the part about him being phallically challenged and his inability to get it up when faced with two horny women. Lila and Tasha had wreaked their revenge cruelly and the best part for them was the fact that he knew nothing about it and so couldn't defend himself. Everyone was having a good laugh at his expense except Bernie who, on hearing the story, sadly shook her head. At the coffee break, she asked. "What do you think of Tasha's apartment, Jack?"

"Very nice," he answered sheepishly, now realizing it was common knowledge that he had at least been there. "Particularly the area, It must be nice living by Central Park."

"Well actually, Jack, I live in the same area as Tasha and an apartment has just recently become available in my block. If you're interested, I'll enquire about it."

He perked up. "Yeah, sure, Bernie, I definitely would like to see it."

"Right then, if you want to, you can walk home with me after work and I'll introduce you to the lady who has the key."

"Thanks, Bernie, that would be great."

They all went back to work with Jack oblivious of the cracks going round the shop floor. He wasn't aware of the names being made up like Jack Froze and Jack and the weenie stork. One of the girls even wrote a short verse. "Jack," said Jill "I'm on the pill and waiting for the come on."

"Jill," said Jack, "I'm only small and cannot get a hard on."

All the girls thought the verse was hilarious. The men, though, being fond of him, were delighted, as secretly they were all a bit fed up of listening to the girls describing him as the handsome honkey, before then giving an involuntary shudder.

Having met at the main gate, as arranged, Jack and Bernie trudged along in the pouring rain under her tiny umbrella.

"How long does it take to walk to your place?"

"About twenty minutes usually, but at the rate you're pulling me along, possibly five."

"I'm sorry, Bernie, I didn't notice, I get carried away when I'm walking. I used to be called the sergeant major back in the Bronx."

"Yes, sergeant, I can well believe that, but I thought you might have realized it by now as I have actually been running alongside you." They both laughed but, in Bernie's case, it was in spite of gasping for breath.

A sudden gust of wind blew the umbrella inside out and ripped it to pieces. Bernie threw it into a trashcan and they walked on with the rain falling down in torrents, soaking them both thoroughly in seconds. Bernie stopped, gasping for breath, as they both laughed at the situation. Being totally wet through, Jack suggested they ignore the rain and simply stroll to her place.

When finally they reached the apartment, Jack could feel the rain running down his legs and into his already soaking wet shoes. As they entered through Bernie's front door into a beautifully decorated hall, they both kicked off their wet shoes and socks. The apartment was nice and warm as Bernie ushered Jack into the lounge. "Right, Jack, I'm going to have a hot shower and change. It shouldn't take me long and then you can do the same." As she walked toward the bathroom she shouted. "Put the kettle on, I'll make us a hot toddy when I return."

He put the kettle on and then stood and took in the wonderful décor of the apartment. "Tasha's was really nice," he thought, "but this place was nothing less than sensational." The curtains, furniture and carpets were all brought to life by very clever lighting. It added up to a warm, homely, very smart place to live. Bernie appeared wearing a pair of jeans and a sloppy tee shirt with a towel wrapped round her head. He thought she looked beautiful and he fancied her like mad, but he had long since given up on that.

"Here you are, Jack, you can use this white bathrobe. Get yourself out of those wet clothes and into the hot shower." He did as he was told and, after stripping off his wet gear, was just about to step into the shower, when Bernie tapped on the door asking for his clothes. He passed her the clothes through the slightly opened bathroom door, then stood under the warm cascading water and closed his eyes, allowing the warmth to wash over him. Fifteen minutes later he walked into the lounge laughing at the size of the bathrobe, being way above his knees and the sleeves half way up his forearms.

Bernie went into a fit of giggling at the sight of him. "Stop moaning, think yourself lucky I didn't leave one of my little pink numbers out for you." She then sat him down in front of the gas fire with the imitation flames and gave him a hot toddy.

"Wow," he said, as he took a sip. "I thought when you made a hot toddy, you actually put some water in with the bourbon."

They sat sipping their drinks and chatting on about the vacant apartment, which she explained was identical to hers but needed a lot of work doing. "Nothing major of course, just cleaning and painting and the like. If you did decide to move in, I would be more than willing to help you with it."

"That's very good of you to offer, Bernie. By the way, I think the way you have decorated your apartment is absolutely fabulous. The cleaning and painting I could do myself, but your advice on everything else would be really great. I would follow it to the letter."

"Thank you, Jack. Actually, I was hoping you'd say that as, given free reign, I'd have the time of my life."

They chatted on and on about many things until he looked at his watch. With a sharp intake of breath, he exclaimed, "its 8.15, I had no idea it was that late."

"No, Jack, the time has flown by. I'll go and fetch your clothes, they should be dry by now" She returned after a couple of minutes and handed him his clothes. "Here you are, I think they're dry enough for a honkey." He went to the bathroom to change and, on his return; found Bernie on the phone arranging to meet a Mrs. Bateman, who had the keys to the vacant apartment. "Well, that's sorted, Jack; we're picking up the keys in ten minutes."

Mrs. Bateman, a huge woman in her fifties, with long blond hair that Jack thought looked ridiculous on a woman of her age, opened her door. After a few pleasantries, Jack was introduced to Mrs. Bateman, who handed the keys to Bernie.

"Thanks, Flo', I'll return them in about twenty minutes."

Having unlocked the door, they entered into a dilapidated apartment which smelled of dampness. Jack had the feeling that this was right for him however, even though the place was filthy and drab. As they went through the apartment, Bernie excitedly offered ideas on this and that until, eventually, she turned to him. "Well? What do you think?"

He smiled and spread his arms out. "I love it. What do I have to do now?"

"C'mon," she said, walking toward the door. He followed her out and along the passageway until they reached Mrs. Bateman's apartment, whereupon Bernie rang the bell. "He wants it, Flo," Bernie said, handing Mrs. Bateman the keys. Having written down the phone number of the owner, they went back to Bernie's apartment and rang him up. Within fifteen minutes Jack had his moving in date, which was to be after Christmas, but with permission to clean and decorate the apartment before then. Jack and Bernie hugged each other excitedly.

"I don't know about you, Bernie but I'm starving. Can I take you out for a meal, as a way of thanking you?"

"No, Jack, I don't want you to do that! Take your jacket off and I'll knock something up in no time at all right here."

"But you've done so much already, I can't allow you to make me a meal as well."

"Don't be silly, I love cooking. I tell you what, leave your jacket on and run down to the mart and bring back a couple of bottles of dry white wine and be quick about it."

"Yes, Madam," he said laughing, as he walked toward the door. Having returned, he put one of the bottles into the refrigerator and poured out two glasses of wine from the remaining one. He then sat on the breakfast bar and watched as Bernie, now oblivious to him, went about creating something with wonderful aromas from ingredients that she was taking out of different cupboards. She was completely engrossed, tasting, then shaking her head, before adding something else and checking the rice every few seconds.

This went on for some time. She did recognize his presence once though, as she chided him, "Come on, Jack, my wine glass is empty. For goodness sake lift your game."

Eventually, the meal was ready and Bernie said smiling. "Let's put this show on the road." Jack retrieved the other bottle of wine from the refrigerator and, having opened it, set it on the table. "I hope you like vegetable risotto," she said, putting the serving dish in the middle of the table. She served him first and he waited patiently until she had put her own meal out.

Having tasted the food, he looked up at her. "This tastes fantastic, Bernie." Her face lit up in the candlelight and, as he looked at her, he felt his usual frustration.

"Thank you, Jack. It's just something I threw together, a simple meal really."

"It might be simple to you, but this is the first vegetarian meal that I have ever enjoyed, apart from a Pizza that is."

"I can see there's a lot I have to teach you, Jack Williams."

After the meal was finished and, with both of them having had seconds, they carried on talking and talking, drinking the wine, and talking some more. She told him that she was twenty-two and that she had been treated badly by men in the past, which had left her with a deep mistrust of them. He for his part, told her in depth his version of what had happened to Phylamina. He had told it so many times, it was now almost the truth in his mind. He covered the tragedy, the trial, Cindy and Tony, even mentioning Old Tom. She was a good listener and the time flew. They were both shocked when they realized it was past 1 a.m.

"I'd better be off home and let you get some sleep, Bernie. Thanks for a fabulous meal, and a patient ear."

"Hey, what are neighbors for?"

He kissed her on the cheek and said goodnight, leaving her a bit bewildered.

When Jack had left, she looked at herself in the full-length mirror in her bedroom and mused. "I'm not bad looking, some might say bloody attractive, so why does he not fancy me? I give up. Maybe I should go out with Benjie or Duane."

The following morning, Bernie was working in the sanding area along with a number of other girls as Jack walked past on his way to the stores. As usual, all eyes followed him. Lila came out with one of her pathetic hints that she and Jack were very close. "That reminds me, I must call round to Jack's and measure up for his new curtains."

Bernie, almost gushing inside looked at her friend "It's strange he hasn't told you, Lila. Jack is moving into an apartment by me. In fact, he has asked me to design the décor in his apartment, as he liked mine so much."

"Is that right, Bernie, and when did this happen?"

"Last night actually, Lila, I made him a meal and we had a good laugh." Lila cringed as she carried on with sanding down one of the security doors

At coffee break, Jack noticed that Bernie didn't mention the night before. He figured she didn't want Duane to get the wrong idea and so he refrained from mentioning it himself.

"Well," said Duane, "just four more days and it'll be Christmas Eve, I wonder if Spencer'll close the factory for a half day again and let us go out for a few beers."

Jack looked surprised. "Is that what happens usually?"

"Yeah, man, unless of course, we're burstin' at the seams with orders, which ain't the case at the moment, I'm thinkin'."

"What are you doing on Christmas day, Jack?" said an unusually quiet Bernie.

"I've been invited to Tony and Cindy's for the day. As you know, I'm very close to them, and you?"

"It's New Jersey for me and a lovely Christmas lunch cooked by my mom. Unlike me, she's a wonderful cook."

She then gave a knowing look and smile at Jack, hoping that he would mention something about the previous evening but he didn't. Instead, he fidgeted a bit and asked Duane what were his plans.

"Well it's a toss-up between Nicole Kidman's and my brothers. It'll probably be my brothers, as Nicole's a lousy cook as well." Duane had lifted the tension with this reply which he himself wasn't even aware of.

Jack changed the subject. "I was thinking of giving Mr. Dobson a ring at lunchtime, Bernie. I thought I'd ask him if it would be okay if I kept the keys that he has left with Flo, so that I can come and go. What do you think?"

"It might be better if Flo were to give him a ring first. I'll ask her to give you a glowing reference. You know, like reliable, truthful, honest, the kind of thing men seem to be incapable of."

"You little madam, men are far more reliable and truthful than women. Have you ever heard a man tell a lie, Duane?"

"Never, man, never," Duane replied right on cue.

Jack smiled "There you are, Bernie. Proof positive."

The coffee break ended on that amusing note and they all went back to work.

At lunchtime, Jack rang two engineering companies, one of which worked late on a Wednesday. He made an appointment with a Mr. Windlass for 6 p.m. the following night.

First thing the following morning, Bernie handed Jack the keys to his new apartment. "Here you are; it's all been sorted. Don't forget to let me know when you begin cleaning, as I'd like to help you."

"Bernie, you're a gem, what would I do without you? I won't have you cleaning though. That's my job. Your job is all about creation."

Not to be put off, she insisted, "Jack Williams, you know as well as I that, when it comes to cleaning a kitchen, men don't have a clue, so I'm going to help you, whether you like it or not and don't bother to argue with me, my mind is made up."

"What can I say, Bernie? Thank you."

That night, straight from work, Jack went excitedly to see Mr. Windlass, carrying with him his sketches, samples of the broken punches and a slither of the door metal. Having gone through the whole story with Ted Windlass and discussed what was required and how much he was prepared to pay, Jack sat back. "What d'you think, Mr. Windlass?"

Ted Windlass, apart from being the owner of the company, was also an engineer. He sat there and thought for a moment before answering. "First of all, I'd like you to call me Ted. Now, what you have shown me is interesting. You have obviously put a great deal of thought and effort into this. The thing is, you are asking us to do official drawings so that you can patent the prototype, which you also want us to make for a paltry $300, plus possible ongoing orders. We are extremely busy at the moment, but even if this were a slack period, I would have to insist on dialogue with the owner of the factory that you work in, and probably a pre contract agreement. You, on the other hand, won't even tell me the name of the company." Ted then took off his spectacles and leaned back in his seat smiling. "I tell you what, though, Jack; I do admire your cheek and enterprise. If ever you want a job, come and see me." The two men shook hands and Jack thanked Ted for his time before leaving.

On his way home, he stopped at his local bar for a beer and a bite to eat. He couldn't face the rest of the evening alone in his apartment, on this, his twenty-fourth birthday. He had just finished eating and was contemplating whether or not he should have another beer, when a voice that he had not heard for a long time interrupted his line of thought. "Jack Williams, well you're sure a sight for sore eyes." Jack looked up at the smiling face of Tiggy Taylor, whom he had last seen four years previously in a young person's correction institute. Can I get you a beer, Jack?"

"You sure can, Tigg'. I think you owe me one for all the trouble you used to get me into." As Tiggy walked over to the bar laughing, Jack looked at him with his mop of ginger hair and the memories came flooding back. He remembered how he and Tiggy, apart from the color of their hair, were very much alike in looks and size. In fact, when they were both wearing baseball caps, they were like identical twins, and as such, often used to bamboozle the screws, who couldn't tell them apart

Tiggy sat down and pushed a beer over. "You know, Jack, this is an amazing coincidence meeting you like this. The reason I am here in the Bronx is quite simple, money, and lots of it."

"I'm sorry, Tigg', but before you go any further, I don't do the rackets any more, I have a normal job in a factory and I love it."

Tiggy looked at him wide eyed. "I don't believe I'm hearing this, Jack Williams. No, you're pulling my leg."

"It's true. During my trial, which you must have read about, I swore to myself that, given the chance, I would lead a normal life and I'm sticking to it."

"Oh yeah, Jack, your trial. You sure escaped from that one."

"What do you mean, Tigg'? Escaped from that one, I was innocent, you moron."

"Okay, okay, Jack, cool it man, and just let me explain how easy you could make about $5000. We have had a guy on the inside of our target for the last six months, in charge of security. He has been in involved in the act of transporting the takings to the main office, where they are put into three safes. He then sets the time locks. Right, on the night in question, he will set the time locks for the safes to open at 1.30 a.m., when the entire crowd will have well disappeared. He will then detail his security guards to other areas away from the main office giving us, and by the way you don't need to know who 'us' is, twenty minutes to empty the contents of the three safes into leather bags. Now, here is where you come in. You will pull up at the designated spot at precisely 1.50 a.m. We will walk out and put the bags into the back of your van. You will then simply drive off on your own and drop the bags off at your place before parking the van at a suitable distance. You will keep the bags for two weeks to allow the temperature to drop and then I will come and pick them up, and of course pay you your stake."

Jack, in spite of himself, couldn't help being intrigued by Tiggy's proposition. "What happens to your guy on the inside, Tigg'? Surely, he will be rumbled?"

"That's really not your concern, Jack, but he will be out of the country before the office opens at 9 a.m. He's here on a phony passport anyway."

"I don't get this, Tigg'. Are you sure you didn't know that I would be here tonight?"

"No, of course not, meeting you here is a pure coincidence; I'm meeting the guy who we had detailed for the pickup job that I have just described. The trouble is, we don't trust him completely and, as fate would have it, I walk in and find you sitting here, who I can vouch for one hundred percent."

Jack sat back in his seat, rubbing his chin. "I don't know, Tigg'. I won't lie to you; $5000 might enable me to possibly complete a project that I have been working on."

"There you are then. Do it! Your part in all this would be a piece of cake. You will, however, have to make up your mind now before the other guy comes in."

"Just out of interest, Tigg', what would you tell him?"

"Oh, that's no problem. I'd just tell him the job's been put on hold, as he doesn't know the details yet anyway."

Jack shifted about in his seat uneasily. He didn't like being pressurized into making a quick decision. "Look, Tigg', I know you said you're meeting the guy any moment, but I need a bit more time to consider everything and also for you to answer some more questions. Is it possible for you to put him off for twenty four hours and come up to my apartment for a drink?"

"Okay, I'll try. Where's your apartment?"

Jack wrote out the details of his address and cell phone number and gave them to him.

As Jack entered through his front door into the hall, he picked up his mail, hoping for a birthday card, but to no avail. An hour later Tiggy arrived, sat down and asked for a shot of whisky.

"Sorry, Tigg', I usually only drink beer these days."

"A beer it is then, Jack, and by the way, it's good to have you on board."

Jack returned with a couple of beers and settled down. "I haven't said I am on board yet, Tigg'. Now, first and foremost, how much dough would I be carrying in the van?"

"Jack, I think it's better to keep this on a need to know basis."

"Never mind the crap, Tigg', how much?"

"Okay, we estimate between $500,000 and $750,000."

Jack looked astounded. "Three quarters of a million bucks, and you want to palm me off with a measly $5000?"

"Jack, don't forget, when you've finished doing your sums, we have put six months' hard work into this heist. However, your cut is negotiable."

Jack had a sip of beer as he thought over all that had been said, before asking his next question. "I need to know what you and your playmates will be doing during the two weeks that I would be sitting on the dough and also, would they know my identity?"

"Why would you need to know that?"

"So, Tigg' my friend, I can weigh up the chances of you lot leading the cops to me in the event of anything going wrong."

"You have nothing to worry about on that score. We all live in Boston, where we will be before the office opens at 9 a.m. Not one of the others have ever been in trouble with the cops, they're all clean. Regarding your identity, they will have to know that in case of anything happening to me."

"Fair enough, Tigg', I can accept that. Now, regarding the van, I take it you are planning to steal one and, in that case, there surely would be a chance of the cops stopping me."

"No, we won't be stealing it. One of the boys bought the van six months ago and in any case, it will have phony plates."

"Well, Tigg', I'd like to sleep on it but I can tell you now, my cut would have to be $15,000, take it or leave it."

"Jack, I said it was negotiable, but I'd forgotten what a greedy bastard you are. Right, I'll be off now, I'll give you a call tomorrow morning." After Tiggy had left, Jack poured himself another beer and sat down with his mind in turmoil. He weighed up everything. There was no doubt in his mind that just a few months ago, he would have jumped at this opportunity but, after all that had happened to him, he knew that this decision could make or break him. He went to bed and fell into a troubled sleep.

The next morning, a little older and, hopefully, a little wiser, Jack was up early, showered and ready for work, having had his beloved cup of coffee. His mind was now much clearer having slept on his problem. He was breaking this decision down into simple options in his usual robotic thought pattern. Option one, he thought, take the chance with the obvious danger of imprisonment. Option two, stick to his life plan with the danger of going on and on for years, trying in vain to bring his plans for this factory to fruition. He turned off his cell phone and left for work, deciding he needed the whole day to make up his mind before speaking to Tiggy.

During the morning break, Bernie snapped Jack to attention. "Jack Williams, are you with us today?"

"Oh yes, sorry, Bernie, what were you saying?"

"I was just asking you if you were planning to start operation clean up in your apartment tonight. You, however, seem to be on another planet, I don't think you have heard a word that I've said."

"Yes you're right, Bernie, I have things on my mind. No, I can't tonight I'm afraid. I'm busy."

"Oh, what the hell, I'm wasting my breath here." With that she stood up and went over to talk to some of her friends on another table, leaving Jack alone.

By lunchtime, he had all but made up his mind, but thought a phone call to Mr. Windlass was necessary in order to clear up any loose ends. He took out his cell phone and called him. After a few rings, Ted Windlass answered. "Hi, Mr. Windlass, Jack Williams. I spoke to you last night about a proposition."

"Yes, Jack, what would you like us to do this morning? Build a couple of ships? Move Brooklyn Bridge? Or would you be happy with a simple reconstruction job, which you could pay us for in about ten years?"

"I suppose I deserve that, Mr. Windlass."

Ted Windlass laughed. "Please, call me Ted, and forgive my sledgehammer sense of humor. Now what can I do for you?"

"Well, Ted, I'd like you to be dead straight with me. How much would it cost me, cash in hand, for you to take up my challenge regarding the prototype that we discussed?"

"Well, obviously, this is only a –ball-park figure, Jack, but you would be looking in the region of between five and seven thousand dollars."

"Thanks Ted. I'll be in touch with you soon. By the way, if I were to get my company to pay you at a later date, would you refund my money in full?"

"Yes, I see no problem with that."

Having spoken with Ted Windlass, he put his cell phone into his pocket, his mind now made up, only for it to give off two beeps signifying a text message. He took out his cell phone again and was staggered as he read the message from Tiggy. "Sorry J but u ave been blown out of the job, I don't know why. C yer, Tigg'." Jack, puzzled, read the message again and again. He rang Tiggy only to get what he had expected, voice mail. He looked at his watch. He didn't feel the least bit hungry and needed to sort his head out so he decided to go for a walk. As he was walking past the loading bay, something strange took his eye. Ducking behind a stack of pallets, he smiled as he witnessed Leroy loading security doors into an unmarked van, accompanied by two huge black guys, whom he had never seen before. Jotting down the make and registration number of the van, he quietly slipped away.

Stepping outside into the bitterly cold and wet December weather, Jack tried again to contact Tiggy on his cell phone but to no avail "Prick," he mumbled to himself, as he suddenly felt a desperate need for a cigarette.

On his return to the canteen, Jack was told by Duane of the company's decision to close the factory half day on Christmas Eve in order to take all the staff to the Yankee Bar for the afternoon. It was the best news that he had heard that day.

Having finished, Jack left the main gate only to be taken by surprise again. Tony Martin was parked across the street waiting for him. In a split second, he had worked out what had gone wrong with Tiggy. Walking over he climbed into the front seat with Tony. "This is a nice surprise, how is the beautiful Cindy?"

"Never mind the bull shit, Jack. How come when I asked you to work for me you replied, "Crime does pay, but it makes you old very quickly." Then the first time some two bit hood hits on you for a piece of action, you can't wait to get your greedy little snout into the crap?"

"I know, I know, Tony. You're right and thank you yet again. My head is all over the place. I do know, however, that my problems at the moment are miniscule, compared to what I have been through. Thanks to you, though, I feel better already."

"C'mon idiot, I'll take you home. By the way, I hope you have a Christmas present for Cindy. If you're panicking about what to buy her, look no further than baby stuff, she never talks about anything else these days."

Jack entered his apartment feeling as though a huge weight had been lifted from his shoulders. He took out his cell phone and sent a text to Tiggy, which read, "Don't worry. No hard feelings. Will keep in touch." He then rang Bernie and apologized for his demeanor that day, blaming it on a throbbing headache.

"I'll forgive you this time, honkey," she replied, "but I'll expect you to buy me a cocktail in the bar tomorrow afternoon."

Having agreed and chattered on further, Jack hung up and took out his file on Leroy Dalton. He added to the file the time, date, and details of what he had witnessed in the loading bay; details such as registration, make of the van, type of security doors and a brief description of the two black guys. He then read through the file and smiled. He considered that he had enough on Leroy to sink him, but thought, "The little prick will keep until the timing's spot on." The phone rang and Jack was pleasantly surprised to find Bernie on the other end. "Listen, Jack, I'm going late night shopping for the rest of my Christmas presents and wondered if you would like to join me?"

"Yes, sure, that would be great, Bernie. I'd really like that."

"Right then, give me your address and I'll pick you up"

On entering his apartment, Bernie was surprised at how clean everything looked. "Well, Jack Williams, I take back what I said previously about men not having a clue when it comes to cleaning. You're obviously in touch with your feminine side. It doesn't go as far as you having a closet full of women's clothing I hope!"

Jack replied in as gruff a voice as possible, "Now see here, Missy, you sure are looking for a good smacked butt."

"What yer gonna' use, Jackie? One of your high heel shoes?" They left, chuckling together, down to her car.

Having hit the first store, Jack began looking at baby clothes and toys. "Are you buying a present for a baby?" Bernie asked looking puzzled.

"Oh no, Bern', it's a present for Cindy. Tony advised me as she never stops talking about baby gear."

Bernie burst out into an infectious chuckle, and Jack, not knowing why, chuckled along with her. "You, men, you really do not have a clue, do you? Yes, Cindy may be talking babies all the time, but she still needs to feel special in her own right for goodness sake." With that, she grabbed his arm and pulled him along. "Come with me."

Having approached the jewelry counter, she stopped. "Now, Jack, I'm guessing you haven't a clue what her favorite perfumes are, so a good quality necklace or bracelet would mean a lot to her. Now, does she wear gold or silver or both?"

"Well, I do know that she wears a silver ring."

"There you are then, Tiger. I'll leave the rest to you. I'll be at the perfumery."

Fifteen minutes later, Bernie took a diamond shaped sampler bottle of perfume from the counter and sprayed a little onto her wrist. Having sniffed at it, she smiled and said to the attendant, "My God, that smells like a wet cat." She then offered her wrist to the attendant.

Having sniffed it herself, the attendant agreed. "Yes, you're right; I wouldn't use that as an aerosol in the John." Out of earshot, Jack, who had been watching with great interest from behind some shelving, misunderstood the situation. They enjoyed shopping together in the huge store amid the Christmas spirit, which was in abundance. Bernie ended up with a Santa hat on her head and gold sparkle sprayed across her face. Jack managed to return to the perfumery, as Bernie was trying on a dress. As the attendant was taking the money from Jack she commented, "You have actually chosen one of our most popular lines, sir."

"Really? Thank you very much, miss."

He left the perfumery as pleased as punch, leaving the attendant giggling to herself thinking, "Moments like these make it almost worthwhile working in this dump."

Eventually satisfied with their shopping, with Jack having purchased his most important item, a camcorder, they reached Jack's apartment at 10.30 p.m.

"Would you like a beer, Bern?"

"No thanks. I'd like a coffee and a sandwich though, I'm starving.

"Say no more, Madam, what would you like on your sandwich?"

"Well, I must tell you, one peanut butter sandwich and I'm anybody's."

"That's typical of my luck. All I have is cheese."

"Cheese sandwich it is then. Unfortunately, cheese does nothing for me."

Jack mockingly pursed his lips, drooped his shoulders and moaned as he moved into the kitchen area.

After supper they chattered on about various things before Bernie said, as she grabbed her bag, "I'd better be going. I'm a working girl you know."

Jack held her coat for her. "Thank you, Bern'. I really enjoyed tonight." He was only half listening as she reciprocated, as he was looking at her thinking how beautiful she looked with her silly Santa hat still on her head and the gold sparkle shimmering on her face. He could not have had a more opportune time to kiss her, but instead chickened out and felt an idiot asking, "What do you think of Benjie and Duane?"

She was puzzled by the question "Unfortunately, Benjie makes my skin crawl but Duane is really nice." She was disappointed as she left shrugging her shoulders.

Chapter 9

Jack walked to work on Christmas Eve with a spring in his step. "Not even Leroy Dalton could dampen my spirits today," he thought.

At coffee break, Benjie took every opportunity to hug and maul the cringing Bernie. Jack was again seething inside, but felt he had to keep a lid on it else all his plans for the factory could be hampered. The sound of the hooter signifying break over was music to his ears. He was really looking forward to the afternoon in the Yankee Bar. He felt as though he gelled well with most of his colleagues and in fact knew the majority of them by first name. 'Also,' Jack thought, 'Lord Spencer will be there with his prat of a son Nigel, so the afternoon promises to be interesting.'

The hooter eventually sounded and they were all off to the Yankee Bar. Benjie was practically glued to Bernie, as was Lila to Jack. Because of the regular hints from Lila, most of the women thought she and Jack were an item. Arriving at the bar, they found Lord Spencer and his son Nigel waiting. Jack thought that Nigel was already looking rough, his eyes looked blurry. Lord Spencer took out his wallet in front of everyone and passed over $500 to the manager of the bar, then turning to his workforce, said, "When that runs out, you chaps, I'm afraid you are on your own." Although most of Lord Spencer's employees couldn't stand the sight of him, they all clapped and cheered.

As they were waiting for their first drink to be served, Jack looked across at Bernie, who had her hand on Duane's shoulder. As she stretched up, she whispered in Duane's ear, "Please don't leave me alone with Benjie today." Jack of course read the situation totally wrong.

Just at that moment, the beautiful Della walked in with Drew Rickets and made a beeline straight for Jack. Flashing her eyes at him, she stretched up onto her toes in her tiny mini skirt and kissed his cheek. "Hi," she said as practically every man in the bar looked on with envy.

"Hi, yourself, would you like a drink?"

"No thanks, Jack, Lord Spencer is waiting for his annual grope and, if I keep him waiting much longer, I think he'll wet himself."

As Della walked away, still with the hungry male eyes following her every movement, Drew pulled up his sleeve. "Do you like my new watch, Jack?"

Jack looked at the watch, which had a picture of a scantily clad female in a tight fitting black, dress. "Yeah, Drew, it's cool."

Drew gently tapped his watch. "Ah, but look now."

Jack smiled as the tight, black dress slowly peeled off, leaving the girl naked.

"That's the best $50 I've spent in a long time," Drew said, pulling down his sleeve. "By the way, how many of these black beauties have you shagged?"

"Well, none actually, Drew."

"None? Have you seen yourself, Jack? I mean, don't you realize what you look like?"

"Well, there is one that I like, but she doesn't seem interested. I think she's about to get it together with another guy."

Just then, the bar door opened and in walked a tall, stunning looking brunette in a tight little Santa dress. She walked straight over and kissed Drew on the cheek before flashing her big brown eyes at Jack. In her high heels, she was actually taller than both of them. With her eyes not moving from Jack, she then asked, "Are you going to introduce me to your friend, Drew?"

As Drew introduced them, she took hold of Jack's hand and held it with a teasing look in her eye. She then turned sharply away and walked off to join Lord Spencer at the bar.

"Wow, she's quite a looker that Grace, isn't she Drew?"

"Yes, my friend, she's also the infamous daughter of Lord Spencer.

"Lord Spencer's daughter?"

"Yep, and if I were you, I would give her a wide berth."

"Oh, come on, Drew, you have to tell me more. Why infamous?"

"One thing I did learn from my predecessor was not to talk to anyone about Grace or Nigel Spencer and I do mean anyone."

As the afternoon wore on, the drinks really flowed and the happy workforce were feeling the effects, apart from Jack, that is. He was keeping himself sharp. As he looked closely at Nigel, he became convinced, "Lord Spencer's little boy," he thought, "has a monkey on his back, and doesn't look capable of managing a shoe shine boy, never mind a large factory."

Jack had not been able to approach Bernie, as she constantly had Benjie on one side of her and the doting Duane on the other. He did, however, enjoy the banter with Drew. Looking across at Lord Spencer, whom he very much wanted to speak to, he decided the time was right. He had waited patiently in order for the Lord to be pleasantly tipsy, but not plastered, as he wanted him to remember Jack Williams. As he approached the bar, his own mind was razor sharp. He had decided to use Grace in order to make contact with her father. She was leaning against the bar looking totally bored. Walking over to her, he whispered in her ear, "I was just wondering, Santa, do you have a present in the 'sack' for me?"

She smiled. "Well, Jack the lad; you are a dirty little bastard, are you not?"

Jack laughed himself. "I don't know about the 'little' part,"

"Where has my father been hiding you, Jack?"

"As a matter of fact, Grace, I've not actually met your father yet."

"Well then, in that case we must put that right. Quinton, darling," she said pulling on her father's arm. "I want you to meet Jack, a friend of mine and one of your employees."

As the two men shook hands, Lord Spencer looked at Jack, peering over his bifocals. "Ah, you're the new lad. How do you do, old boy. Have you settled down with us so far?"

"Yes, sir, really well."

"And how is old Tony doing? I like him; he's a good sort."

"He's very well, sir. Actually, he's going to be a daddy soon. He and Cindy are delighted."

"Wonderful, wonderful, my boy. Please pass on my congratulations."

"I will, sir, and by the way, I would like you to know how much all of these people here today appreciate your generosity."

"Well, it is the least I could do," Quinton said, pushing out his chest.

Grace then pulled Jack away from her father. "Well, that was a surprise. By the way, I noticed you didn't miss the opportunity of a little brown nosing with the old fart."

Jack smiled as he put his arm around her waist. "I really don't know what you mean, Grace,"

She responded by cuddling in to him. "Unfortunately, Jack, I have to go now, but I will be back in about two hours. Will you still be here?"

"I sure will, Santa, I've not forgotten the present you have for me in the sack."

"What kind of a girl do you think I am?" She replied, as she then walked over to her father and kissed him on the cheek before leaving.

Jack looked across at Bernie, who was fending off the persistent Benjie. He walked over, feeling like he wanted to smack Benjie and take her in his arms but on approaching simply said, "Bernie, come to the bar with me. I owe you a cocktail."

She broke free from the clutches of Benjie, with obvious relief, and accompanied Jack to the bar. He ordered a Manhattan Scraper cocktail, which he paid for himself as the $500 had long since gone.

Bernie sipped at her cocktail. "I noticed you talking to Grace Spencer,"

"I had to talk to somebody, Bern', I couldn't get near you with all your admirers.

"Oh please, don't Jack, that Benjie is getting to be a bloody pain."

"Not to mention Duane," he replied, digging for a response.

"Oh no, Duane is really lovely."

"I wanted to speak to you anyway, Bernie. I have your Christmas present. He handed her the present with a huge smile on his face.

Oh, Jack, you shouldn't have.

"Open it, Bernie. I won't see you on Christmas day will I?"

She took the Christmas wrapping off with great care and stared dumfounded at the perfume.

"Last night, when we went Christmas shopping together, I hid behind some shelving when you were sampling this perfume. I could tell that you liked it so after you went off I moved in and bought it."

"Jack, that was so thoughtful of you. I don't know what to say?"

"You don't have to say anything. I'm just delighted that you like it."

It wasn't part of Bernie's character to lie but Jack's thoughtful offering left her with no choice. "Yes, I love it. Thank you so much." She reached up onto her toes and kissed him on the cheek.

"She then changed the subject. "When are you going over to Tony and Cindy's?"

"Cindy is picking me up tonight at eight o'clock."

"It's five thirty now. How are you getting home?"

"Lila's dad is picking her up soon. She said that they would drop me off on their way home."

"I don't know, Jack, men are such dopes. Lila's dad doesn't have to go anywhere near the Bronx, either to drive to his house or Lila's."

"Oh, I see," he replied looking across at Lila, who at that moment was flirting outrageously with Drew, who seemed to be lapping it up. Jack was well aware of Lila's intentions, as he knew New York like the back of his hand. It was convenient and he liked the game.

At that moment, Benjie approached and put his arms around Bernie, who became distressed as she tried to fend him off. Jack felt sick inside, as he wanted to help her desperately, but Lord Spencer was no more than ten feet away. The cavalry arrived in the form of Duane, who had been watching. He took hold of Benjie's shoulder. "Take your hands off her, you big sap. Can't you see, she doesn't want you messin' with her?"

Benjie spun round and landed a punch on Duane's left eye, which spurted blood before Duane had hit the floor. Pandemonium broke out. Benjie made for the exit with everyone screaming abuse at him. Bernie was on her knees cradling Duane's head in her arms, with tears running down her cheeks, oblivious of the blood on her new dress, which she had purchased with Jack just the previous night. Jack, for his part, felt foolish. He knew for sure that he could have handled the lumbering Benjie, but instead he had just stood there, allowing a close friend to take an unnecessary beating and almost certainly delivering Bernie into Duane's welcoming arms.

"What is that chap's name?" Lord Spencer called out to nobody in particular.

The heat was taken out of the situation by Duane who, with the help of Bernie, stood up. "Don't worry none, folks, it was all a to-do about nothin'. We always like to have our Christmas dog fight and of course, I always end up with a black eye, if you'll excuse the pun." He had almost certainly saved Benjie's job.

Lila approached Jack and informed him that her father was waiting outside. He was going to wish Bernie a merry Christmas, but she was so engrossed in fussing over Duane, he simply left.

Jack spent an enjoyable Christmas with Tony and Cindy, apart from one moment of panic during Christmas lunch. Tony picked up his glass of white wine. "Here's to our new baby. If it's a boy, I would like to call him Jack."

Cindy, in a nervous state anyway, knocked over her glass of water. She recovered her poise quickly, however.

"Dear me, since becoming pregnant, I seem to have become as clumsy as a man."

"Don't worry, darling," the attentive Tony said as he mopped up the water, before then refilling her glass.

Jack sat silent. The last person he would like the baby to be named after would be himself. 'That,' he thought, 'is far too dangerous.'

Cindy was thinking along the same lines. "Please don't take this the wrong way, Jack. If we have a boy, the only name I would consider would be Tony."

She had hit the right note, as Tony was beaming like a proud father.

Jack had recovered and found that he could move his jaw again. He lifted up his glass "You're right, of course, Cindy. I'll drink to that."

After the meal they decided to exchange presents. Tony went first, excitedly wheeling into the lounge a huge pram which was covered in Christmas wrapping, only to be confronted by a totally unexcited Cindy. "Don't you like it, Darling? We can change it for a different one if you want."

"No, no, Tony, its lovely and it's exactly what we needed."

Jack witnessed this scene, with a mental picture of Bernie, her Santa hat on her head and gold sparkle lighting up her face. 'She had been spot on,' he thought, looking down at the present lying on the coffee table that he was about to give Cindy

He was shaken from his thoughts by Cindy. "Here you are, Jack, this is from Tony and I." He ripped off the wrapping revealing an oblong box. Taking off the lid, his eyes nearly popped out of his head as he looked inside the box which was full of money.

"You'll find there's $2,000 there," Tony pointed out. "$1,000 from each of us. We figured this was what you most needed in order to continue on your chosen path."

As he looked at them both through grateful eyes, Cindy broke the moment. "Come on, Jack, let's have our present's now." Tony unwrapped his and was delighted with his Cuban cigars and Cindy, for her part, was almost hysterical when she tried on her silver necklace.

As the afternoon wore on, Tony and Cindy began nodding off, so Jack rang for a cab and, after leaving a note, went off to see old Tom. His old friend was delighted when he opened his door to find Jack standing there. After greeting him with a hug, he ushered him through the hall and into his sitting room. Toby, old Tom's shop assistant, was snoring away in an armchair by the fire. Tom explained that he and Toby had shared Christmas lunch "Come through and I'll pour you a drink, Jack," old Tom said as he walked to the kitchen.

"Just a coffee please, Tom. It's a bit early for me."

They spent an hour chatting away as Toby snored, oblivious of Jack's presence. Eventually, Jack spoke of his plans for the factory, the problems regarding the prototype, and his near capitulation to the dark side.

Old Tom put down his drink. "Now listen here, Jack, I have approximately $6,000 put away that I don't know what to do with. Why don't you allow me to loan you the money for the prototype?"

"No, Tom. I didn't tell you about this so that I could borrow money off you."

Tom became insistent. "I'm not offering you this loan for your sake. Having listened to your plans, I'm confident that you can pull this off. Now, here's the deal; if you borrow say, $4,000, from me and it goes belly up, you can pay me back in monthly installments over a three year period, $7,000. On the other hand, if it does work out and, consequently, your company pays for the prototype, you can pay me $5,000. Either way, I come out sitting pretty. Furthermore, we both know you have no chance of a loan from a bank, so you don't really have much choice." Old

Tom really had no intention of fleecing Jack, but he also knew that this was the only chance of him accepting the loan.

Jack was astonished "You old shark, Tom, I've been thinking all this time that butter wouldn't melt in your mouth."

"Never mind all that crap, Jack. Do we have a deal?"

"Yes we do and I won't let you down, you old con man."

As the two men shook hands on the deal, Jack's mind was racing, as he knew that the next phase of his plan could now take shape. The rest of the Christmas and New Year break dragged for Jack Williams, as he was keen to return to work, move into his new apartment and see Bernie again.

The first day back, he had a spring in his step. During the first coffee break, he was looking for signs between Bernie and Duane but, thankfully, could see none.

Benjie approached their table with two presents, one each for Bernie and Duane.

He looked genuinely sorry for his behavior and promised it wouldn't happen again.

Duane, being the kind of guy that he was, simply asked, "What won't happen again, Benjie?"

At lunchtime, Jack phoned Ted Windlass and arranged a meeting for the following evening. Having sorted that, he then went into lunch and told Bernie of his plans to begin cleaning his apartment that night. He was delighted when she insisted on helping him. However, he was then brought down to earth, as Duane offered as well, therefore raising his worst fears. After work, with all three of them walking together, the atmosphere seemed relaxed. Bernie was between the two of them happily chatting all the way to Jack's apartment.

Using the cleaning utensils purchased by Jack, they began their laborious task. After working for two hours,

Duane said, "I don't know about you guys, but I'm starvin'."

All three of them agreed, so off they went for a Pizza nearby. Eventually, having bid goodnight to Bernie, Jack and Duane shared a cab. Jack was still none the wiser as to the possibility of a relationship between his friends.

The following evening, Jack excitedly went to see Ted Windlass, carrying with him all that he thought would be necessary. Having looked at the drawings and Jack's notes, Ted took off his spectacles and was examining the slither of metal, along with the old worn punches. "Well, Ted?" Jack asked impatiently. "How long will the job take?"

"Hold your horses, Jack, these things take time. The first priority will be a report from a metallurgist. I will then be able to discuss how long the job may take. As you know, you will have to give me a deposit of $2,000. I will contact you when I have had the chance to see the report and discussed the whole project with one of my engineers. Please be patient." Jack paid the deposit and left with his receipt, feeling as though things were really moving.

The following morning, Jack's hopes regarding Bernie were raised when she asked him, "Are we cleaning tonight?"

"Yes, Bernie, if you're sure it's not too much trouble."

"Sorry, guys," Duane said, raising Jack's hopes. I can't make it tonight. I'm going bowling with a couple of friends."

Bernie smiled, as she looked at Jack. "Oh dear, Jack, how in the world are we going to manage without Duane making coffee every five minutes?" As Duane then protested his innocence, Jack's hopes took another leap. He decided right there and then that he would take the plunge and attempt to kiss Bernie that night, as soon as he felt the time appropriate.

Jack and Bernie worked tirelessly for two and a half hours, cleaning, scraping and sanding down wood in preparation for painting, during which time the two of them laughed and joked together. Eventually, he called a halt. "Come on, lazy bones, I've a bottle of wine in the refrigerator." Having settled down to have a glass of wine, Bernie dropped a bombshell on Jack with the disclosure that she had been out on a couple of dates with Duane. He could hear himself muttering the words, "Duane is a really nice guy," as his heart sank.

He could then vaguely hear Bernie adding, "It hasn't been anything serious, just a pizza and a movie," as he berated himself for being so stupid. That night in bed, he went over and over in his mind, the missed opportunities, before falling into a fitful sleep.

In the days that followed, Bernie carried on helping Jack make his apartment habitable and, as always, they laughed together. Finally, he left the Bronx behind him and moved in.

A few days later, Ted Windlass contacted Jack on his cell phone. "I've been through your project with Chris Peacock, one of my engineers. We have studied the report from the metallurgist, so all that we need to do now is arrange a time for Chris to be able to inspect the machine when it's actually working."

Jack was taken aback. "Ted," he said in desperation. "That's not possible. Can you not carry on using my drawings?"

Ted answered slowly and deliberately. "No, we cannot. We're a professional company and we don't do any job using guesswork. You're not building with Meccano sets now. If we are not able to inspect the machine, then I'm afraid the deal's off." Jack promised to contact Ted soon and turned off his cell phone feeling sick inside. He had not bargained for this and, thinking about it now, he felt as though he had been naive in thinking that the prototype could be built from his drawings. He thought about his problem all night, but was unable to come up with a simple solution. He decided to sleep on it, and so went to bed.

The following morning, feeling invigorated and, having had a shower, Jack felt much better, as he sat drinking his beloved morning coffee. "There has to be an answer," he thought. "It's just a case of thinking it through methodically." By the end of the morning, he had decided on his course of action and so, at lunchtime, went to see Leroy Dalton carrying his camcorder. Leroy was sitting eating his lunch at his desk, as Jack approached. "Mr. Dalton, can I have a word please?" Jack asked as respectfully as he possibly could, looking down at this ignorant pig of a man, who was now looking at him through blurry, drunken eyes.

"What the fuck do you want, Nancy boy?"

Jack kept himself together. "Well, it's about the ongoing problem with the hole-punching machine, Mr. Dalton. I have a good friend who is an engineer and he has offered to come in and inspect it in order to hopefully solve the problem."

Leroy looked at him with an amazed look on his face. "What the fuck's it to do with you, Nancy boy? As far as I'm concerned, you're a dog's body in this dump and a fucking pathetic one at that."

Jack felt amused by the remark but went on, "It's only that with all the breakdowns, Mr. Dalton, my colleagues are afraid of possible redundancies."

"Fuck off, Williams, go and eat your pig swill."

Jack placed the camcorder on the desk in full view and looked closely at Leroy's eyes as he then went on slowly and deliberately, "I came to see you last week, Mr. Dalton, but you were busy loading security doors into an unmarked van. You had two big black guys helping. The van took my eye, as I noticed it had a strange registration. Vehicle registrations are a hobby of mine you see. Having seen one, it sticks in my mind."

Leroy stood up and glared at him, then at the camcorder with his jaw unable to move. Jack allowed what he thought was enough time, for this hateful little man to digest his veiled threat, before then going on to remove it. "As I said, Mr. Dalton, I'm only worried about my fellow workers. If you allow my friend to inspect the machine and it goes well, you will come out of it looking real good. I wouldn't have to disturb you in your lunch break anymore. You could carry on with whatever you wanted."

Leroy's eyes told Jack all that he needed to know. It was obvious that his veiled threat had hit home. The fire had been knocked out of Leroy as he sat down saying, "Well, I don't suppose it would do any harm. When would he want to come?"

"Thursday morning, Mr. Dalton."

"Okay, Williams, but make sure he doesn't get under my fucking feet."

Jack walked back to the canteen smiling; he was enjoying the challenge more and more as time went on. He then contacted Ted Windlass and made arrangements to meet Chris Peacock by reception at 10.15 Thursday morning. He then joined his friends in the canteen.

"You're a dark horse, Jack Williams," Bernie said smiling. "You seem to have something to attend to every lunch break these days."

"Well, you know how it is when you have lots of friends," Jack replied. "People to contact, arrangements to be made, not to mention the advertising companies trying to sign me up as a male model." Jack's two friends laughed, as he walked into the locker room with his head held high and his chest pushed out. In actual fact, he had not missed one lunch break without a look around the loading bays since he had witnessed Leroy up to no good. He put the small camcorder into his locker and quickly rejoined his friends for what remained of the lunch break.

"I was going to bring your new curtains up tonight and hang them, Jack, but Duane has asked me to go to the movies with him. You're welcome to come with us if you want to."

"Yes, sure, man," Duane joined in, "of course you are." His pleading eyes praying that Jack would decline, which of course, he did.

Thursday morning at 10.15, Jack met Chris Peacock, as arranged, by reception and was surprised by the amount of equipment the engineer had with him. Arriving at the hole-punching machine, with all the puzzled eyes glued to the scene, Jack introduced Chris to Glen saying, "Glen knows everything there is to know about this machine, Chris." Then, turning to Glen, he went on, "Mr. Peacock has apparently come to sort out the problems. Will you give him any assistance that he needs?"

Glen naturally thought that Chris had been sent by the company "Yes, yes of course, if I can help, sure."

Jack helped Chris set up the expensive looking camera equipment and then watched, as he patiently took close up shots with the machine working, then even closer shots with it shut down. They eventually packed away the cameras, along with the lights that they had set up. Chris then opened a square box containing calipers, spirit levels, measuring tapes, sketching pads and a variety of other equipment. Jack watched as Chris, in regular consultation with Glen, completed his task.

It was just before lunch by the time Jack and Chris loaded the equipment back into the car. Leroy Dalton had kept out of the machine shop the whole time that Chris had been there. As the car left through the main gate, the hooter sounded. Jack was relieved that this tricky part of his plan had been completed successfully. He then went for a burger at a nearby diner, as he thought there would be too many questions in the canteen and he wasn't in the mood.

That night, Bernie called and fitted Jack's new curtains. Having done so, they sat down and had a cup of coffee. "What are you up to, Jack?"

"I don't know what you mean, Bern'."

"Oh, come on, Duane and I have been trying to guess. We feel sure there is something going on with you at work."

He sat looking at Bernie thoughtfully. He had decided days ago, that she would be the first person that he would confide in, as the time was fast approaching when the balloon would go up. He figured having her on his side would be extremely beneficial as she was so respected by the whole labor force. "Okay, Bernie, what I am about to tell you will be in strict confidence," he went on to explain his plans for the factory, which would include increased productivity, culminating in more money for the whole workforce and greater job security. His future plans in regard to skin, colour or creed, playing no part in the furthering of a person's career and finally, his determination to remove Leroy Dalton. She sat looking at him with an amazed look on her face. "When I said you were a dark horse, it was the understatement of the year. By the way, who was that guy photographing Glen's machine today?"

"I wondered how long it would be before you asked me that. In a way, he was in my employ. Glen's machine is an integral part in my first breakthrough. But forgetting that for a moment, Bernie, I need to know if you trust me completely?"

"Yes, of course I do, and what do you mean, he was in your employ?"

"It's a long story, Bern', but if my plans are to be successful, I will need the whole workforce on side and that is where Duane and your good self can be so important. You are both well respected and trusted and they will need to be convinced about the necessity for a change in working practices. No demarcation, the possibility of flexible coffee breaks, shift work, and so on. If you can convince them that I have their best interests at heart, then we can go a long way together."

Jack waited as Bernie sat open mouthed, trying to come to terms with all that he had just said, until finally she uttered, "How will you get rid of Leroy?"

"He won't be a problem. Trust me."

"Yes, Jack, I do trust you, and I will do all I can to convince any doubters."

He kissed her on the cheek as he stood up. "Thanks, Bernie. You're not bad for a half Russian, half Iraqi nut case."

"Careful, Honkey," she replied, as she kissed him on the cheek very close to his lips "Any more sass, and I'll take my curtains back."

The following few days dragged for Jack, as he waited for Ted Windlass to contact him. His continued surveillance of the loading bay each lunch period bore fruit as he captured Leroy on the camcorder, loading more security doors into the same unmarked van. 'That,' he thought, as he put his camcorder into his locker, 'completes Leroy's dossier.' It had been three weeks since Chris Peacock had visited the factory, when finally Ted Windlass sent a text to Jack asking him to make contact, which he did immediately. "Hi Ted, Jack Williams, you asked me to contact you."

"Yes, you'll be happy to know that your project is complete. We now need to fix up a time for Chris to try it out on the machine."

This time he was not in the least surprised. "I'll ring you this afternoon, Ted." He switched off his cell phone and, as it was lunch time, went to see Leroy, who as usual was sitting at his desk. "Excuse me, Mr. Dalton, can I have another word?" Leroy didn't bother to answer as he glared at him. Jack looked into his eyes and for the first time since he had met him, they were clear. 'Good,' Jack thought. 'If his mind is clear, it will make it easier to put the frighteners on him.' Taking his camcorder out of his pocket and holding it in full view of Leroy, Jack went on. "I came to see you Monday lunchtime, but you were busy in the loading bay again."

Leroy's eyes narrowed and the veins stood out in his neck as he looked firstly at the camcorder, then hatefully into Jack's eyes. Jack broke the silence. "Good news, Mr. Dalton. My friend, the engineer who inspected the hole-punching machine, has come up with a remedy and he would like to come in and try it out on Friday morning. I told him I would check with you first. So will that be okay? I promise to keep him from under your feet, as I know you're a very busy man."

After a long delay, Leroy said, "Yeah, now fuck off."

Having fixed the appointment with Ted Windlass, Jack went back to have lunch with Bernie and Duane. Bernie whispered in his ear. "I've told Duane and he's promised his full support." Jack looked at them both wide eyed. "Don't worry, Duane and I won't say a word to anyone else until you have given us the go ahead. You have our word on it." At 10.15 a.m., on Friday the eighth of February, Jack stood shivering by reception waiting for Chris, who eventually turned up a little late at 10.25. "Sorry I'm late, Jack, I couldn't get my car started."

"Some engineer you are," Jack said, laughing as they carried the equipment from the car into the machine shop. All eyes were on them as Glen and Chris shook hands. It had taken Foggo, the maintenance man, the best part of the morning to remove the old punch from the machine, which seemed even more stubborn than usual, in readiness for the arrival of Chris. This of course had brought everything to a standstill. It took Chris less than five minutes to fit the new prototype and, with Jack looking on with his fingers crossed, Glen turned on the machine. The new prototype punched through the metal door like it was going through paper. There was much less noise than before and almost no vibration. Glen turned off the machine with a huge grin on his face. Jack shook Chris warmly by the hand and thanked him.

Chris explained to Jack that he needed to examine the prototype after it had punched through quite a few doors, so he was going to leave it on for the rest of the day. He removed the prototype in about ten seconds and immediately replaced it back again so that Foggo would know how to remove it later that day. Foggo looked on in amazement. Jack promised Chris just before he left, that he would call in to see Ted Windlass on his way home from work with the used prototype.

Glen restarted the machine and began working through the backlog with relish.

Jack, of course, felt ten feet tall as he examined the spare prototype that Chris had left with him. He held it lovingly in his hands as though it were his baby, which in a way, it was. He ran his finger along what he thought was an inbuilt shock absorber, before then putting it back into its case. Placing it safely in his locker, he then went back to work.

Leroy Dalton had not been seen all morning and usually that meant he would be drunk in the afternoon, but not this time. He was quiet but, to Jack, looked sober.

Late in the afternoon, Foggo removed the spring loaded prototype in seconds and gave it to Jack before then replacing it with the old punch. Jack, having put the prototype in his locker, was on his way back to work when Leroy called him over. "What are you up to, Williams?"

"Nothing, Mr. Dalton."

"You can drop the Mr. Dalton crap and come outside. I want a private word." Jack followed him outside ready and willing to give Leroy the hiding of his life. They stood face to face in the cold drizzle. "Right Williams," Leroy said with a snarl on his face. "Give it to me straight or I'll put you through the fucking wall."

Jack looked at his mad eyes and coolly and slowly replied. "Nobody puts Jack Williams through any wall, certainly not you. The fact is, my friend Chris has developed a new punch that won't break down every day and is easily replaceable in seconds. I'll bring it to you along with the drawings, technical data, and the name of the company that you will need to deal with. You can take all the credit for it if you want; I'm only interested in job security for my friends and myself." With that, he left Leroy standing there wondering what to say and went back to work.

When he had finished work and was on his way home, Jack called in to see Ted and Chris. He had with him the two Prototypes. Having examined the used one, they both agreed on its 100% success. Jack paid them the balance in full and they, in turn, provided the whole file, which included all the technical data, an official document from the Patent office in the name of Jack Williams, details of ongoing replacement punches, and of course, the two prototypes. The whole weekend, he could think of nothing else but his plans for the following Monday morning, plus back up plans, should anything not go as expected. At last the weekend was over, and Jack was in work at 9.15 a.m. He was on the phone to Drew Rickets, who answered as usual with a simple, "Yeah?"

"Hi, Drew. It's Jack Williams. Is there any chance of my coming to see you at lunch time?"

"Sure, Jack, what's goin' down?"

"I'll tell you when I see you, Drew. It's very important though."

"I await with anticipation, Jack."

At lunchtime, he tapped on Drew's door and almost immediately heard Drew call out. "Come in, Jack, come in."

Sitting down in front of an astonished Drew Rickets, he went through the whole story of the hole-punching machine, its continuing problems, how he had come to the point of contacting Windlass engineering, the cost, the ensuing trial of the prototypes on the machine and so on. He then showed Drew the two prototypes, the drawings, and the document from the Patent office and finished off by asking, "What do you think?"

Drew took a deep breath and exhaled exaggeratedly through pursed lips, "What do I think? Well I'm staggered! First of all, how did you manage to get this engineer past Leroy Dalton?"

"That part was easy, Drew, Leroy has been a naughty boy and I have proof."

"I see. At least I think I do. This is all amazing. I knew as soon as I met you that you were nobody's fool, but this has me gob smacked. What do you want me to do?"

Jack leaned back and relaxed in his seat. "Well, Drew, first off, I'd like your advice. What's the normal procedure for a case like this?"

Drew began to laugh. "The normal procedure for a case like this? There is no normal procedure for a case like this. I suppose you could let me pass this on to dick head Nigel. Alternatively, you could go through Leroy."

"Now here's the thing, Drew, if I went through Leroy, would Nigel bring you on board to discuss it?"

"Yes, he would, definitely. No doubt whatsoever."

"In that case, Drew, that's what I'll do. It might just kill two birds with one stone."

Jack left Drew in shock and went straight to Leroy who, having finished his lunch, was sitting by his desk dozing. Jack banged the Prototype on his desk which woke him with a start. He looked at the prototype and then at Jack quizzically.

"I think you should see what I have here," Jack said deliberately not calling him Mr. Dalton anymore as that charade was now over. He then showed Leroy everything but the document from the Patent office. Leroy took in as much as he was capable of and then looking at Jack asked. "What exactly do you want me to do with this crap?"

"This crap, as you have just called it, could really turn this company around and, as you told me yourself, I'm just a dog's body around here, so nobody would ever take it seriously if it were to come from me. On the other hand, if you put your name to it, its chances of success would be much greater."

Leroy sat back in his seat thinking before saying. "What if I just tell you to take all your crap and fuck off, wanker?"

"Don't even go there, Mr. fucking Dalton, I have enough evidence to put you down for a long stretch. However, having said all that, you're probably wondering why I'm allowing you to become flavor of the century. It's simple really. I want in on your little racket with the doors, and don't forget I have the evidence."

Leroy sat there not knowing what to do next. He knew that Jack had him stitched up. He also knew that Jack wasn't afraid of him, so threats were useless. In any case, if he gave him a good beating, as he dearly would love to, he was in no doubt he would shop him to the cops. The only answer was to kill him, so that, he decided, was what he would do.

A smiling Jack, who was way ahead of him, broke Leroy's thoughts. "By the way, dick head. I have copies of everything that is on, or indeed in, your desk. I'm going to lodge them in a safety deposit box in the bank with full instructions as to what to do with them in the event of my death or disappearance." Jack then looked into Leroy's eyes for a few seconds, before ending the conversation in a cool clear voice leaving Leroy in no doubt. "My terms are not negotiable. You will bring all this to the attention of the company this very afternoon. As regards my partnership in your racket, we will discuss that further in a couple of days. If my instructions are not carried out, then I will shop you at the end of this working day."

As Leroy looked at him through hate-filled eyes, Jack turned on his heel and walked away. By the time he reached his locker, the hooter sounded and he went back to work. The whole afternoon, Jack's insides were jumping as the adrenalin pumped through his body as he thought of the events unfolding.

Meanwhile, at 2.30 p.m., Leroy, on one of his many visits to the locker room, flushing out unauthorized fag breaks, searched Jacks locker using his master key. A huge grin spread across his face as his hunch was proved correct. He left Jack's locker as he had found it containing all the evidence against him, before going outside and making a couple of phone calls.

The longest afternoon of Jack's life came to an end when Leroy called him over to his desk at 4.30. "Right, Williams," he whispered. "I've been through all your stuff with Nigel Spencer. I've told him it's all your work and he wants to meet you and me in the Hyde Park bar in thirty minutes. To find the bar, you go out of the main gate, turn right and the…"

Jack interrupted him at that point. "I know where the bar is. What I want to know is firstly, what was Nigel's reaction and why you have disobeyed my instructions and what exactly is goin' on?"

Leroy leant a little closer to his ear and whispered. "Because Nigel is the main man in our little scam, so don't wait for the hooter, get yourself off and we'll meet as I said in about thirty minutes." Jack hadn't bargained for this, but he thought, "Of course, Nigel has to make a lot of dough to feed his habit, so what better way than to knock off his old man, as it would be risk free?" Taking his coat out of his locker, he slipped out. As he was walking briskly along to the bar, his mind was racing. This was turning out better than he could have dreamed, he thought. The more he could get on Nigel the better as, at a later date, the ability to discredit him in his father's eyes, obviously meant there was more chance of he himself ending up at the helm of the Spencer empire.

The minute that Jack had left the factory, Leroy had slipped into the locker room and filled his leather bag with all the incriminating evidence that Jack had on him out of the locker. Happy that he had everything, he went out and stuffed the leather bag into the bottom drawer of his desk along with all the stuff that Jack had given him at lunchtime, which of course, had never been anywhere near Nigel Spencer.

Jack sat on the bar stool with a glass of beer, getting more and more irritated as the minutes went by. At 6 p.m. he gave up the wait and, putting his empty glass onto the bar, went out into the miserable night. The cold wind cut right through him so he zipped up his jacket and walked briskly through the dark street with his head bowed against the driving rain. His body then froze as he passed an entrance to an alley. There were two pairs of boots standing directly in his path. As he raised his head, peering through the driving rain, two big, black guys advanced toward him. Instinctively, he ducked as a fist fitted with a metal knuckleduster narrowly missed his head. At the same time, he sank his own fist into the solar plexus of his would be assailant, who went down into a heap. The dropping body gave Jack the split second that he needed as the other black guy, along with Leroy Dalton, had to avoid it as they attacked with metal bars in their hands. Jack dodged Leroy and at the same time, pushed him into the other thug before running away as fast as his legs would take him. The whole incident had taken no more than a couple of seconds. Jack, running at full pelt with only survival on his mind, was gradually leaving the black guy a few yards behind and as he turned a corner, he could see that Leroy was a further twenty to twenty five yards further back. With his lungs at bursting point, Jack spun round and as the big black guy came panting round the corner, he burst his nose with his right fist, badly hurting two fingers in the act. The job not done, Jack picked up the metal bar that the thug had dropped and, as he lay squealing holding his nose, knocked him out cold with it. Leroy appeared panting only to suffer the same fate, as Jack expertly dispensed with him with one blow then stood crouched waiting for the third one to arrive. After a couple of seconds he peeked round the corner but there was no sign of the other one.

Jack cursed himself as he searched Leroy's pockets for the keys to his car and the factory. He had underestimated this little bully of a man but hopefully, he thought, it wasn't too late to put things right. Finding the keys, he quickly retraced his steps. Leroy's car was parked where they had attacked him. There was no sign of the other brute, so he drove Leroy's car back to the factory. Jack's sharp mind had worked out that the only way they would have risked attacking him, would have been because they had the evidence from his locker and he hoped, as he drove the car, that Leroy had left the evidence either in the boot or in his desk at work.

Having parked in a side street, he searched the car but found nothing. He now had no option but to try Leroy's desk. Having worked overtime a couple of times, he knew that there was no alarm, but there was always some contracted security guard. Quickly checking the keys, as he walked briskly toward the main gate, the first hurdle was easy, as there was only one key that could possibly fit the lock on the inset door. The rain was falling heavily and he thought, as he locked the gate behind him, that the guard would probably remain indoors in this foul weather. Crossing the yard, he decided to try the door to the main garage and breathed a sigh of relief as he hit the jackpot. Closing the door quietly behind him he panicked as he couldn't see anything in the pitch darkness. Even though he knew every second counted with the possibility of Leroy being on his way, he remained calm as he waited for his eyes to adjust. Gradually he began to make out the shapes of the vehicles. It helped that he knew the geography of the garage. He made his way across to the door on the other side as he knew it was only yards from Leroy's desk.

Trying the keys in the dark was difficult while wearing gloves. He had to go through them methodically but quickly. Eventually, he went sick inside as he realized he didn't possess a key to the door. He didn't feel that he had enough time to go trying other entrances, so he decided it was time for positive action. His eyes now fully adjusted to the darkness, he made his way over to the workbench in the opposite corner, where he knew there was usually a tyre lever. With great relief he found it was there. Returning to the door, he pushed the sharp end of the tyre lever into the door jam and, with his heart thumping, forced open the door making very little noise. He waited for a few moments in case he had alerted the guard, before slipping into the machine shop.

He now felt remarkably calm, as he went through the keys. Opening the right hand drawer, he was disappointed, but pressed on, hoping against hope. He then felt a surge of relief, as he grabbed a leather bag in the left hand one. Opening it up, he found that it contained what he had hoped for. Holding the leather bag, he heard a locker door being closed followed by footsteps. He didn't have time to make it to the garage door so he hid behind press number one. He had only just made it to the press before suddenly, the machine shop flooded with light. Peering through gaps in the press, he could see the female guard getting closer and

242

closer, trying doors and checking windows. Jack knew that it was only a matter of time before the guard discovered the forced door, and sure enough, with Jack looking on, she suddenly took her gun from its holster. With her left hand against the door, she began to push it slowly open. Beads of perspiration were forming on Jack's forehead, as the guard suddenly stopped pushing and looked around as though she had heard something. Fear ripped through his body as he peered through the gap in the press. He was under no illusions as to his fate, if his presence became known. The guard, he felt sure, would gun him down.

Having looked all around, the guard then walked up the machine shop and having returned with a torch, turned off all the lights. Putting the torch against the door, she turned it off, and Jack could only hear the creaking of the door, as it was being pushed open. Jack figured the guard had been concerned about being a sitting duck, if she opened the door with the machine shop lights behind her. After a couple of seconds, the garage lights flickered on, and Jack could hear the probable sound of the guard's footsteps crossing the garage. This was his chance. With cold sweat on his brow, he quickly and quietly as possible made his way up to the locker room, which he knew like the palm of his hand. The darkness was no barrier to him now, as he made his way to the fire door. Pushing the bar, he was mightily relieved when it opened.

After peeking out into the rain-lashed night to make sure the coast was clear, Jack gingerly made his way across the yard, having closed the fire door behind him. Stepping into a shadow, he sorted out the key to the inset door of the main gate. He then looked carefully around for any sign of the guard and made his move. Within seconds he had opened the door and breathing a sigh of relief, slipped through and made his getaway into the night. Underestimating Leroy was a mistake, he thought, and one that he wouldn't make again, as he realized that a sober Leroy was no fool. With that in mind he decided going to his apartment was too dangerous, as Leroy would probably know his address, so he rang for a cab on his cell phone and went to old Tom's.

Tom opened the door to find Jack standing there, saturated to the skin. "Don't ask, Tom, please," Jack said, as Tom stood aside allowing him entry.

Old Tom ran a hot bath for him and put all his clothes into the dryer, before making him a hot toddy and providing him with a dressing gown. Tom simply said, "If you want to tell me what's going on, that's fine. On the other hand, if you don't want to, then that's okay as well."

As Jack soaked in the tub gratefully drinking his hot toddy, he ran through everything that had happened that day, and how the events had changed his plans for the following morning. Eventually happy with his new plans, he dried himself before joining Tom in the sitting room. An hour later he had told Tom everything except his near miss with the guard. Tom just shook his head in amazement. "Jack Williams, How do you get yourself into so many scrapes?"

"Well, Tom, It takes a hell of a lot of practice," he replied trying to bring a bit of humour to the situation. "But seriously, old friend, if all goes well tomorrow, by next week you will have made yourself a tidy profit."

Old Tom, with a furrowed brow, replied quietly and slowly, "Jack Williams, if you try to pay me one cent more than I loaned you, I will take it as a personal insult."

"But, Tom," Jack protested.

Tom put his hand up to stop him. "Never mind, but Tom. The only reason that I said I would take profit from you was because I knew full well it was the only way past your stupid pride. But enough of all this, it's getting late and you have a big day in front of you tomorrow, so come on, off to bed."

The next morning, Jack arrived bang on time by cab. He didn't want to take a chance of an altercation with Leroy, so he asked the cab driver to drive through the main gate. He had left instructions with old Tom to bring all the evidence and meet him in reception at 9.30, just in case the now desperate Leroy and his two cronies decided on a last throw of the dice. However, there was no sign of them and Jack met old Tom in reception as planned. Having done his task, Tom left. Jack asked the beautiful Della to contact Drew. Putting down the phone, she smiled. "He said you're to go through Jack."

The door to Drew's office was already open so he went straight in and, plonking the leather bag onto Drew's desk, Jack said, "This will blow your mind."

An hour later, Drew looked at Jack with a stunned look on his face as he picked up the phone and dialled a number. Eventually, he said. "Nigel, Drew here. I need to see you urgently; can I come through? Good, I'll be there pronto." Putting the phone down, Drew then said, "Right, Jack, I want you to come with me, but let me do all the talking. I know how to handle Nigel."

Sometime later, a startled Nigel looked at Drew. "What shall we do?" he asked.

Drew shrugged his shoulders. "Well I think we need to firstly contact your father, don't, you?"

Nigel picked up the phone. "Good morning, father," he said, after a couple of minutes. Something very important has come up and I need to see you urgently. Would it be convenient if we popped over forthwith? Yes, yes. Oh, Drew Rickets and Jack Williams, one of the employees. Thank you, Father." He then put the phone down and they left.

At 12 noon, Drew Rickets drove his blue Buick through Lord Spencer's tree lined drive and parked in front of the magnificent manor house. As Jack stepped out of the car, he looked all around him, his eyes taking everything in.

'Tony Martin's house and grounds are impressive,' he thought, 'but this? This is in an entirely different league.' He clutched the leather bag close into his side. He had decided that no matter what, he was going to deliver the whole story to Lord Spencer himself. 'After all,' he thought. 'It was my brainchild from the beginning, and I am fully intent on Lord Spencer being aware of it.'

The huge, oak front door opened and the butler, who was wearing a tuxedo and white gloves, invited them in. Addressing Nigel, he said, "Lord Spencer awaits you in the drawing room, sir." They walked through a huge hallway with oak panelling and a thick woollen carpet, before then entering a corridor, with beautiful paintings adorning the walls on both sides. Finally, they stopped at a door on which the butler lightly tapped before pushing it open. Lord Spencer was sitting behind a huge, leather-covered desk. "That will be all, Jenkins," he said. "Please sit down, gentlemen." Looking around at the three nervous faces, Lord Spencer smiled. "Good day, gentlemen, I'm sure this must be extremely important, otherwise you would not be here." Drew began to introduce Jack, only to be stopped by a seemingly irritated Quinton Spencer. "Mr. Williams and I have met. Now can we proceed? I am a very busy man."

Drew asked Jack for the leather bag, but he clutched it to him and said, "With the greatest respect, Mr. Rickets, I believe that I am the person who should present all of this to Lord Spencer." Drew smiled and made a gesture with his hands for Jack to carry on, as he himself sat down. Standing up and placing the bag on the desk in front of him, Jack, while looking Lord Spencer square in the eye, said. "I have irrefutable evidence in this bag, sir, which proves Leroy Dalton's guilt in ripping off your company." Leaving a moment of silence deliberately in order that Quinton would be gagging for more (something that he had learned from Winston Smyth) he then went on. "However, if you don't mind, sir, I would like to fill in the whole picture from the beginning."

Quinton was indeed hooked. Getting out a box of Cuban cigars, he offered them to each guest. Of them, only Jack declined. Quinton relaxed back into his seat. "Carry on, old chap," he said to Jack. "And please take as long as you wish."

Jack went through the whole story from the very first day that he began working for Spencer Security Doors and, on completion, opened the leather bag. He first showed Quinton the evidence that he had on Leroy. Quinton, red in the face said. "Why, this dammed rotter will go to prison for this. I don't know how to thank you, Jack."

Opening the bag, Jack took out one of the prototypes and placed it carefully on the desk in front of Quinton, before going on. "Well sir, I mentioned earlier about the problems associated with the hole-punching machine that continuously brings the factory to a standstill, and my endeavours to find a cure. The prototype in front of you has completed the punching of countless doors on trial, with fantastic results. It only takes seconds to remove instead of hours, and lasts much longer than the old punches. I believe, sir, that this could be the making of your company, as research has shown me that your main competitors in this field suffer the same massive delays."

Lord Spencer looked at Nigel, who was shifting about in his seat uncomfortably. "Is this correct, my boy?" he asked disbelievingly.

Struggling with the words, Nigel replied. "To tell you the truth, father, I don't really know." Quinton then looked at Drew who simply shrugged his shoulders.

Lord Spencer then turned back to Jack, who was really enjoying this. "Well, young man, I would like to see this in action for myself first thing tomorrow morning. If it is as you say, I would then obviously have to speak to Windlass Engineering regarding costing."

Jack felt the time was right for him to go for the break through. "Well, sir, you asked me earlier how you could thank me. I hope you don't think me out of order, but I would very much like to have Leroy Dalton's position. During the period that I have worked for you, I have studied his job and I can promise you, there are many areas where improvements on productivity would be really easy."

Lord Spencer smiled at Jack and rubbed his chin as he stood up. "Well," he offered. "We will see what happens tomorrow morning. How is that?"

"That's fine, sir," Jack replied as he got to his feet with everyone else.

Lord Spencer shook Jack by the hand. "You do realize, my boy," he said to him. "You will probably be required as a witness for the prosecution of Leroy Dalton?"

"Yes, sir, I look forward to it."

"Oh jolly good. Right, I will see you in the morning." As they were leaving, Lord Spencer was dealing the police. As Jack walked along the corridor with the strong smell of beeswax in his nostrils, he felt that at last, he had his foot firmly on the bottom rung of the ladder.

Drew dropped Jack off at his apartment. Before getting out of the car, Jack asked Drew if he would look after the leather bag for him, which now only contained the two prototypes, plus technical data, as all the evidence against Leroy had been left with Lord Spencer. This will be safer with you, Drew," he explained.

"Sure, Jack, I understand." Drew replied. "I'll see you in the morning and, by the way, congratulations!" As Drew drove off, Jack looked around carefully for the slightest possibility of trouble. Satisfied, he made his way up to the apartment. As he unlocked his door and entered, he thought to himself that the cops should have Leroy locked up within twenty-four hours and then it should be plain sailing.

At 6 p.m., having showered and changed, Jack knocked on Bernie's door and was gutted when Duane answered with a quizzical look on his face. "Hi, man, what the hell's goin' down?"

Jack told Bernie and Duane over a cup of coffee what he thought they needed to know. "All being well," he finished, "You'll have a new foreman tomorrow."

Bernie, with a flashing smile, ordered Duane to go to the drugstore and bring back a couple of packs of beer, plus some wine. "We're going to celebrate," she said. "I'm going to make us all a lovely meal."

Duane left, and Bernie, taking various ingredients out of the cupboards, began preparing the meal. Jack looked at her admiringly as she went about the preparations. She was only wearing a pair of jeans with a sloppy Tee shirt, but still she took his breath away. He thought that she looked stunningly beautiful and, all of a sudden, he felt a desperate need to tell her of his true feelings. She broke his thoughts, saying in a mocking tone, "What shall I call you from tomorrow? Boss man? Sir? Mr. Williams? Your lordship?"

"All of the above, wench," he replied smiling.

As she left the kitchen, she had flour on one of her cheeks. She walked over to him saying. "Seriously though, Jack, I'm delighted for you." She then reached up onto her tiptoes and putting her arms around his neck, kissed him on the cheek.

Warm feelings of love and desire engulfed him. She released her hands from behind his neck and stood back smiling. "Bernie," he said. "There's something I simply must tell you even though it's maybe too late."

"What's that, boss man?" she chided.

He had just managed to get out "Well, Bernie, it's simply that..."

When the door banging, and Duane's booming voice shouting from the hall interrupted him. "Let's get this party goin'."

Jack watched as Duane put the box of booze down onto the table and the keys from Bernie's front door into his pocket. The realization that Duane had not needed to knock on the door, or ring the bell, made him feel sick inside.

Duane took the booze and began loading it into the refrigerator. Bernie whispered to Jack. "Well? What is it?"

With the realization that Bernie and Duane were obviously now an item, Jack chickened out. "Bernie, I was thinking of making you a leading hand if and when I get Leroy's job."

"I see," she replied, looking both puzzled and disappointed.

The following morning, Jack informed Glen about the trial run that was planned at 9.30 for the benefit of Lord Spencer.

Glen looked at him puzzled. "That means Foggo will only have an hour and a half to remove the old punch. It could take him longer than that."

"Listen, Glen," Jack replied. "I don't want Foggo to be able to manage it. In fact, I don't want him to know anything about it until 9.15."

Glen looked at him as though he were barking mad. "You don't want him to know until 9.15?"

"Just trust me, Glen, please, I know what I'm doing."

Glen shrugged his shoulders. "Okay, Jack, I'll have him over here at 9.15."

At 9.30, Lord Spencer, Nigel, Drew, and Jack stood watching Foggo struggling with the old punch, which as usual seemed like it was practically welded on. Jack decided it was time to say something. Addressing Lord Spencer he said. "The old punch usually takes about two hours to remove, sir. If you like, I'll come and fetch you when we are in a position to fit the new prototype."

Lord Spencer's eyebrows lifted as he asked Jack. "Two hours? And how often is this necessary?"

"Most days," Jack replied feeling smug inside.

Lord Spencer looked around him at all the workers standing idle because of this hold up and shook his head. "Right, we will be in Nigel's office," he said, as he walked off with Drew and Nigel scurrying behind him.

Jack knocked on Nigel's door at 11.30. Foggo had actually removed the punch at eleven, but he wanted the maximum delay. With the group gathered again, they watched as Jack expertly fitted the new prototype in seconds, before then standing up and giving Glen the thumbs up. Glen turned on the machine, and proceeded to work his way through the security doors. Jack, having quickly removed the prototype, then proudly showed it to Lord Spencer. He then replaced it back onto the machine, again in seconds.

Lord Spencer indicated to Glen with his hand that he wanted to see him. Glen approached looking terrified. "Now listen here, my man," Lord Spencer said to him. "I would like your honest opinion of what we have just witnessed here this morning."

Jack smiled to himself as he heard Glen reply. "Yes, sir, my opinion is simple; I think this new punch is fantastic. It has less vibration so it is better for the machine. It punches much neater holes, so there will be less to do on the filing and trim bay. It only takes seconds to replace, which means no more hold ups, and it punches through the metal like it was going through tissue paper, so will obviously last much longer than the old model that we have struggled with for years."

"Righto, righto, old chap," Lord Spencer said, laughing. "I think you have made your point admirably." Jack was delighted. On any other subject, Glen lived up to his name as the quiet man, but now talking about his machine, he could not have been more convincing.

As the group started off back to Nigel's office, Lord Spencer made a point of inviting Jack to join them. Having settled down in the office, Jack had to stop himself laughing as Lord Spencer instructed Nigel to organize coffee for them. This done, Lord Spencer was then eager to get down to business. "Right, Jack," he began. "You will of course from this moment be foreman of the machine shop." Then turning to Drew, he went on, "I would like you to sort out a salary package for Jack today." Drew simply nodded his head. His Lordship then carried on. "Jack, you will no doubt be relieved to know that the police took Leroy Dalton into custody this morning, along with another chap. Alas, they're still looking for the other man. Enough of that; however, I was most impressed this morning so I need to speak to the engineering company as soon as possible, in order to purchase the equipment that you so admirably displayed. You are probably not aware of it, but this place is only one of eight outlets that I have across the U.S.A. "Therefore, if all goes well here, I will need the new prototype for all of them."

Jack's astute mind was quickly calculating a new direction for his ambitions. "Well, sir," he said, "would it be possible to speak to you in private?"

"Yes of course, my boy," said the smiling lord, who was now really impressed with him. "You can come back to the house with me. Nigel, tell Perkins to bring the car round."

This left Jack with another opportunity to impress. "Unfortunately, sir," he said. "I need to pick something up from my apartment, and I'm also concerned about problems that need my immediate attention here. Would it be okay if I leave your invitation until I finish work tonight?"

"Yes, my boy, whatever you say. Perkins will pick you up."

Jack left the office and went straight to the canteen where the lunch period had just begun. He quickly had a chat with Bernie and Duane over a cup of coffee, bringing them up to date. He then stood up in order to give his first ever presentation to a group of people feeling strangely calm. He stood up on his seat and gradually, as the murmurings ceased, had their full attention. "I won't keep you long folks," he began. "Firstly, I can tell you that Leroy Dalton won't be here anymore. As from now, I'm afraid you're stuck with me as your new foreman." A look of relief spread across the faces looking up at him, as they whistled and clapped. He put the palms of his hands up in order to reclaim their attention, before carrying on. "I plan to make this company successful. In order to do so, I'll need you all with me. It will inevitably mean changes, some you won't like, but I need you all to believe that I have your best interests at heart. My aim for all of you, and myself of course, is job security, increased pay, and a much better working environment. No longer will the colour of a person's skin be a factor in whether he or she achieves promotion." After another bout of clapping and cheering, he went on. "With that in mind and, as soon as I get clearance from above, I'm going to make Bernie team leader, with an improved salary to go with her greater responsibility."

He stopped for a few seconds in order to settle himself, as he knew his next disclosure would not be as welcome and, in fact, would be the first acid test. "In time, I want every person here to be more flexible, in that every job in this factory, can be done by each and every one of you. This can easily be achieved with good training." The clapping stopped and the atmosphere changed, with murmurings of discontent. Jack went on, "Look, guys, I know each and every one of you personally. None of what I have said is set in stone and I would be grateful for any productive suggestions. What I have just mapped out is a flexible blueprint, no more. Having said that, I believe the option to stay as we are would mean certain unemployment for each and every one of us." He stopped for a moment in order for reality to sink in, before going on. "What do you say? Can we move on as a team? Are you all with me?"

At first there was a silence as they all tried to come to terms with what they had just heard. Bernie stood up and pleaded. "What are you all waiting for? This is a fantastic opportunity for all of us that Jack has made possible."

Gradually, murmurings of agreement turned into unanimous support, with clapping and cheering. Jack felt good. His first public speech had gone really well, and he had actually enjoyed it. "By the way," he finished. "If any of you ever want to talk to me, just come to my desk. As you know, I don't have an office." Having finished on a comical note, they all resumed their lunch break.

Jack spent his first afternoon as foreman letting Bernie know what was to be expected of her in her new position, checking stock, ordering from suppliers and sorting out everyday problems. He was that busy, that he had to tell Drew another day would have to be found for contractual talks. He went home feeling shattered both mentally and physically. Having had a shower, he sat down with a cup of coffee, his mind buzzing with excitement, at the thought of the next phase in his plans.

Chapter 10

Before being picked up at his apartment by Perkins in a Rolls Royce, Jack assured Bernie that he would call in on his return in order to let her know how he had fared with Lord Spencer.

With his form from the Patent Office in his possession, he stepped out of the car feeling like a million dollars. The butler opened the huge front door and bowed slightly, before inviting Jack to follow him. They went through the large hall and down a corridor. On entering the drawing room, the Butler bowed his head in the direction of Lord Spencer and announced, "Mr. Jack Williams, milord." He then left closing the door behind him.

Lord Spencer took the phone from his ear and cupped one hand over the mouthpiece. "I'm so sorry, old boy, I have some business to attend to which will take about a half hour. Why don't you go and make yourself a coffee in the kitchen? I will call for you as soon as I have finished. If you turn right as you go out, the kitchen is three doors down on your left."

"Certainly, sir," Jack said, as he turned and went out gently closing the door behind him.

When he opened the door to the kitchen, he was surprised to see Grace Spencer sitting on the worktop wearing a loose mini skirt. She had a glass of wine in one hand and a cigarette in the other. "Well, well, Jack Williams, this is a surprise." She deliberately opened her legs a little in order to titillate Jack and then chuckled to herself as she looked at him with his mouth open. She loved the power that she felt she had over men. "I suppose you are here sucking up to the old fart again, Jack?"

Reluctantly dragging his eyes from her crotch and with his face now flushed, he replied, "I'm here for a business meeting with your father as he has recently promoted me and we have some very important points to discuss with him."

"Oh, Jack, please stop being so boring and come and help me down from here." He walked over and putting his hands around her waist, lifted her off the worktop effortlessly like a little doll. She put her hands around his neck and slowly allowed her body to slide down against him. Having stopped when she could feel his manhood, she whispered in his ear. "Is that a gun you are carrying, Jack the lad? Or are you pleased to feel me?" Before he could answer, she bit him on the neck and proceeded to unbutton his fly.

"No, no," he protested, "Don't. Your father could walk in at any moment."

Undeterred, she carried on. He grabbed her wrists. "No, Grace, what about your father?"

She ignored him and pushed her swollen breasts into him. "That just makes it all the more exciting, Mr. Williams."

Jack, although feeling aroused, was terrified of Lord Spencer catching him in a compromising position with his daughter so he said laughing. "This is neither the time nor the place."

"Okay, you win. Come back here when you have finished sucking up to him and I will drive you home. Now, can I get you a drink?"

"Yes please, just a cup of coffee. I want to keep my wits about me."

A few minutes later, Lord Spencer entered. "I really am sorry, old chap, what must you think of me?"

Don't worry, Daddy, I have been seeing to his needs for you. Isn't that right, Jack?"

Looking a bit flushed, Jack simply nodded his head.

"Thank you, darling, that was very good of you. Jack, please bring your coffee with you, I am eager to hear what you have to say."

Having settled himself into his seat facing Lord Spencer across the desk, Jack took out his business plan for the factory which he immediately passed over. "If you would read through this plan, sir, and give me your views on it, I would be grateful."

Lord Spencer's face took on an astonished look as he read through the plans that Jack had painstakingly put together. The document outlined a complete overhaul of the working practices, transportation and sales. It also went on to point out the need for a future bonus scheme. He finally put down the document and looked up. "Well, my boy, I really don't know where to begin."

Jack picked up the plan and held it up in front of him. "This, of course, is a long term business plan. I do realize that we'll have to take things one step at a time, but I do believe that what I have outlined is achievable."

Quinton rubbed his chin as he thought about Jack's ideas. "Well, young man, how would you propose to get the workforce to agree to such radical changes?"

"Actually, sir, I've already had an impromptu meeting with them outlining the necessity for change in order to protect our employment prospects for both now and in the future. I'm pleased to be able to say, the response was quite positive."

Lord Spencer now had a smile on his face. "Tell me, you have highlighted a need to change the whole transport system. Could you enlarge on that?"

"Yes, sir, as we streamline, we will of course increase output, probably by as much as 60%, so there will be a need, I believe, to expand the machine shop. With that in mind, I think we should consider using contract labour to deliver our security doors. That would free up the garage for the said expansion, plus, it would remove the necessity of renewing the aging vehicles. The money saved on the vehicles, I have calculated, would be enough to pay for the deliveries and the fitting out of the garage into another machine shop, therefore enabling us to achieve the extra output."

Lord Spencer looked stunned. "Incredible! You have obviously put a great deal of thought into all of this. Tell me, my boy, you have suggested that we restructure the sales department. Could you enlarge on that?"

"Ah, yes, I don't know whether or not you will agree with me on this, but I think that Drew Rickets is wasted in personnel. He looks bored and in need of a new challenge. I think with his personality, he would be fantastic heading a sales team."

"Have you spoken to Mr. Rickets about this?"

"No, sir, not a word. I thought it would be best coming from you."

Lord Spencer sank back into his seat laughing heartily. "My dear boy, this has been the most enlightening and enjoyable business meeting I have ever had."

"For me as well, sir, in fact, it's the only business meeting that I've had." Both men had a laugh at this before Jack went on. "Can we now discuss the new prototype that you witnessed today in action?"

"Yes, of course, I will need to talk to the engineering company. What did you say their name was?"

"Well, sir, actually, things are not quite as you think." Jack then went on to explain how he had gambled with his own money, employing Windlass Engineering. He then took out the form issued by the Patent office naming him as the owner. He passed it over to Quinton, who, having examined it looked up quizzically. "The figures that you have seen, sir, regarding purchase of the Prototype and ongoing renewal of punches, are correct. However, you wouldn't be buying them off Windlass Engineering, you would in fact, be buying them from me. I am the sole owner, as the form from the patent office that you are holding proves. Now, as I see it, there are two ways that this could be achieved. One, I could set up a small company to supply you and working on the fact that you have eight outlets, which you undoubtedly will wish to service, it would eventually end up costing you $56,000 plus ongoing replacement costs. Or two, I could sell you the patent for $30,000, leaving you to deal with Windlass Engineering yourself. Their fees will eventually work out at approximately $26,000. Therefore, either method would cost you $56,000, but the second method gives you ownership of the prototype."

Lord Spencer took a deep breath and exhaled slowly. "Goodness me, I will have to think this over and put it to one of my legal eagles."

"Yes, sir, with that in mind, I've had two contracts legally compiled."

With that he handed the contracts over to Quinton, who looked at them shaking his head. "Thank you, my boy; you seem to have thought of everything. I will of course be in touch with you soon." Then, as Jack was leaving, Lord Spencer passed the comment laughing. "I do hope you are not planning to reorganize my house and my life."

"Well, funny you should say that, sir," Jack replied smiling. Lord Spencer picked up a brass paperweight and mockingly threatened to throw it at him. He quickly left, closing the door behind him.

Walking along the corridor, Jack felt that the meeting couldn't have gone better. He opened the kitchen door to find Grace in a totally different outfit. She was wearing a tight, black dress, with a gap in the front that plunged all the way down to her trim waist. It would have been easy to see anyway that she was not wearing a bra, as the material was so thin. She then passed him her jacket and turned her back to him. As he put the jacket around her shoulders, he briefly thought of Bernie, but only briefly, as he immediately then thought of Duane with her front door key. He ran his hand down her back saying. "C'mon, wench, take me home. I'm hungry."

Having left the kitchen, they were walking down the corridor when two huge, German shepherd dogs appeared and growled at Jack. Grace scolded them, telling them to be quiet. She then began to stroke them as she beckoned the nervous looking Jack closer. He approached very slowly as she carried on stroking them and talking to them in a soothing voice, as you would a child. "It's all right, my darlings, Jack is a friend of mine." He edged closer and gently stroked the nearest one to him. "Good boy, Bruno," Grace said to the dog patting him. "Now come on, Jack, don't be afraid, come and say hello to Toby." He gingerly stroked Toby as Grace made a fuss of the growling dog. Gradually, the two dogs began to warm to him as they realized he wasn't a threat. Grace then stood up. "C'mon, Jack, let's go."

When they arrived at his apartment block, she protested at having to climb the stairs instead of using a perfectly good elevator. Jack was not in the least bothered, as he walked up the stairs behind her watching her beautiful body sway to and fro under her thin dress. As soon as they entered the apartment, he put his hands around her waist and kissed her hungrily, pushing his hot tongue into her mouth. Then, as he was kissing her, he slowly lowered his hands down and on to her buttocks, pulling her into him. He was breathing heavily but all of a sudden she pulled away.

"Hold on, Jack, its bloody freezing in here. Why don't you put the heating on and pour us a drink?"

"Sure, Grace, but I only have beer. It's very rare that I drink anything else."

"Beer? I can't drink beer! I'm sorry but you will just have to go down to the liquor store and bring me back some decent dry white wine."

Jack turned on the central heating, "Okay, you make yourself comfortable. I'll be back in about fifteen minutes."

After he had gone, Grace wandered around the apartment admiring the tasteful décor. She thought it interesting that there was not one photograph to be seen. The doorbell rang and Grace thought Jack had forgotten his key. She opened the door only to find Bernie standing there with a shocked look on her face. Grace, not knowing who she was, enquired, "Can I help you?"

Bernie stood there, unable to speak at first. She knew who Grace was and felt silly as she eventually mumbled. "I'm sorry to disturb you. I just wanted a word with Jack."

Grace looked at her with narrowed eyes. "He will be back soon, would you like to come in and wait?"

Bernie, feeling extremely uncomfortable and of course gutted, replied, "No thank you. Will you just tell him Bernie called please?"

Entering her apartment, Bernie was now fuming. For weeks she had been putting off the persistent Duane, hoping against hope that Jack would at last show some romantic interest in her. Cursing herself for stupidly resisting even a kiss from Duane, she picked up the phone and rang him only to hear the engaged tone. She waited ten minutes and then rang him again, this time with success as Duane's gruff voice boomed through. "Yeah?"

"Hi, Duane, it's Bernie. Are you doing anything at the moment?"

261

"No, Bernie, nothin'. Why?"

"I wondered," she asked with her body shaking slightly, "If you would like to come over for a glass of wine?"

"Sure I would, Bern, but if you don't mind, I'll pick some tinnies up on my way over. Wine ain't my poison. I'll be as quick as I can." As he hung up, he felt a surge of excitement coursing through his body.

Bernie nervously walked to her bedroom and changed into a seductive dress, which was a red skimpy little number. Kicking off her slippers, she finished off her outfit with matching shoes and looked in the mirror. "Duane's gain is your loss, Jack Williams," she thought; as she first looked at herself front on, before then turning round to examine her rear.

As Bernie opened the door to Duane, his eyes nearly popped out of his head as he looked at her in her figure hugging dress. He then flushed a little as he stammered. "I'm sorry, Bernie, but you look so finger lickin' good."

"Don't be, Duane, I'm glad that you find me attractive." She then stood on her tiptoes and grabbing hold of his lapels, kissed him full on the lips. Duane's hands were still hanging by his sides holding his cans of beer. He had thought of little else for months now and felt almost terrified to respond. Letting go of his lapels, Bernie ordered Duane to pour himself a beer. She then put on some music. He couldn't believe his luck as he gulped down his beer straight from the can, while watching Bernie dance slowly to the music with her eyes closed. Little did he know, but Bernie had already decided that she would bed him that very night.

Meanwhile, Jack, having returned with a couple of bottles of wine, was getting a bit of a run around by the unpredictable Grace, who had not mentioned a word about Bernie's visit. One moment she would come on strong, then do a complete somersault and back off, leaving him totally confused and frustrated. Eventually fed up with her little games, Jack suggested it was getting late and perhaps they should call it a night. Having received no response from her, he fetched her jacket from the hall and held it for her to put her arms through. She gave him a puzzled look. "Don't you want me to stay the night?" Before he could answer, she began unbuttoning his shirt and kissing his bare chest. She then pulled his shirt from out of his pants and slipped it from his shoulders. He tried to put his arms around her, but true to form she stopped him.

"Not yet," she said as she led him to the bedroom, picking up her bag on the way. Having pulled Jack into the bedroom she ordered. "I want you to lie on the bed with your eyes closed. I'm going to give you the time of your life."

He did as she requested and lay down waiting with anticipation. She took out of her bag a pair of handcuffs and proceeded to cuff Jack's right wrist to the metal bed head. She then did the same with his left wrist to the other side before then ordering him to open his eyes. She stripped slowly to the music coming through from the sitting room. Then, kneeling either side of him, she began to unbuckle his belt before pulling it free from the loops and folding it over like a whip. "You had better behave yourself," she warned as she gently but firmly slapped him across the chest a couple of times. He tried to speak but she stopped him by putting her hand across his mouth. "You are not allowed to speak until I give you permission. Otherwise, I will have to punish you for being a naughty boy. Carrying on, she then unbuttoned his jeans and proceeded to pull them down, ordering him to lift his frame off the bed to facilitate this. Removing his jeans, she left him lying there in just his boxer shorts and went off to the kitchen.

She soon returned with two glasses of wine. "As you have been a good boy, I am going to reward you." Putting one of the glasses of wine onto the bedside table, she took a drink from the other one and kissed Jack, allowing the cold wine to seep into his mouth seductively. Good, boy," she said as she then inexplicably poured the other whole glass of wine all over his boxer shorts.

"What the fuck, you bitch." Jack yelled.

"That, on the other hand is a naughty boy," she shouted angrily at the top of her voice as she then picked up the leather belt and hit him as hard as she possibly could across his chest.

He yelped as he felt the stinging leather. "You, stupid bitch. Get these fucking cuffs off me." He pulled as hard as he could, but to no avail.

Grace edged to the end of the bed and began to stroke the inside of his thighs, while gently talking to him as though he were a little boy. "There, there, my darling, I'm sorry, I didn't mean to hit you so hard." She then pushed her hands up the inside of each leg of Jack's boxer shorts and began to stroke his stomach. He moaned with his eyes closed as she pleasured him but was brought sharply back to reality as she took hold of his boxer shorts and ripped them from him, leaving them in tatters. He felt both anger and excitement at the same time as she declared "I've decided you deserve a reward." With that, she drank the rest of the wine from the glass and kissed him as she had earlier. Jack was riding on the crest of pure lust, until she brought him down to earth with a jolt, biting him hard on his stomach and drawing blood. He screeched out loud so she hit him again with his belt. She then said coldly and without anger," If you screech again, you naughty boy, I will have to light my cigarette and really teach you a lesson." This brought Jack sharply to his senses; he now felt that she was capable of almost anything.

"That's better. Now you deserve a reward." She straddled across him stroking him until he became erect yet again. She then lowered herself on to him and began to make love. He completely forgot about the nonsense that had gone before as he looked up at her breasts, wanting to feel them on his lips and hands. She leaned close to his ear and whispered. "I am going to set you free so that you can give me a good fucking." She reached across and taking the key off the bedside table, unlocked both sets of handcuffs.

As soon as she had removed the handcuffs, she took on a completely different persona. Gone was the crazy woman who a few minutes earlier had been taking pleasure in painful eccentricities. In her place was a charming, sensuous, caring beautiful woman who simply wanted to love and be loved. Eventually, Jack rolled onto his back exhausted from the long nerve-racking day and certainly the strange night. He soon fell into a deep sleep. At 3 a.m. he woke up needing to go to the john. There was no sign of loony Grace, which he was relieved about, as he climbed back into bed and fell asleep almost immediately.

The next morning up early, showered and dressed, Jack could hardly wait to get to work so that he could begin the hard but exciting task of bringing his carefully laid plans to fruition. Skipping down the stairs two at a time and briskly walking along the landing, he knocked on Bernie's door only to be confronted by the gut wrenching sight of Duane opening it. "Mornin' Duane," he could hear his own voice say from a million miles away.

"Hi, man," Duane replied brightly before turning his head. "Bernie, it's our white, honkey boss man."

Bernie then appeared looking a bit perplexed and said good morning. As they were walking down the stairs in a strange atmosphere, Bernie stunned Jack. "I hope I didn't give Grace the wrong idea last night."

"Grace?"

"Yes, didn't she tell you? I called when you were out last night. I do hope I didn't make her feel uncomfortable."

"Oh I see, she didn't say. Grace had given me a lift from her father's house. That's all it was."

"You don't have to explain yourself to us, Jack," Bernie then said, the hurt in her voice not escaping him, or indeed Duane.

Yet another frustrating shock awaited Jack as they approached the factory. "Duane?" Bernie asked. "Have you still got my spare set of keys?"

"No, I've left them on your hall table. I've finished changing your electric sockets at last."

Jack shook his head at his own stupidity as he could hear Bernie offering to pay Duane for his time.

"No, no," Duane replied. "I was only too glad to help."

Jack's heart sank. He had obviously jumped to the wrong conclusion and the sight of Grace in his apartment had driven Bernie into Duane's arms and Duane, consequently, into her bed. "Why?" he thought "do I always get it wrong."

Pushing Bernie to the back of his mind, he spent his first full day as foreman seeing to routine matters. The day to day running of the machine shop had been badly interrupted and needed to be put back onto an even keel before he could even think of changes. One thing that he did find strange was taking his gear out of the locker room and relocating it to his new locker, which was just behind his desk. This act, he felt, set him aside from his colleagues.

In mid-afternoon, Jack was told that he had to go to Nigel's office as there was a phone call for him. Nigel's door was open, so he just gave a couple of taps on the glass out of respect before entering.

"Ah, Jack, my father would like a word with you," Nigel said pointing to the prostrate phone on the desk.

He picked it up and spoke into the mouthpiece. "Yes, sir, Jack Williams here."

"Hello, my boy, I have spoken to the people that I needed to and I have decided to accept your second option. The legal documents are at this moment with my legal eagle. You will receive $30,000 as soon as the output of our product doubles as agreed. I will of course respect your decision, if you decide not to use the new prototype until the documents are in your hands. You do, of course, have my word as a gentleman regarding our arrangement. I will be in touch soon. Cheerio, my boy."

The phone went dead and Jack smiled. He replaced it and went to see Foggo and instructed him to fit the new prototype as soon as possible. With Foggo struggling to remove the old punch for the last time, Jack decided to use the space to implement the first of his many planned changes. He asked Glen to accompany him to the stores.

Having entered the stores with Glen in tow, Duane looked puzzled. "Right," Jack began. "As you both know, demarcation in this machine shop needs to be a thing of the past if we are to succeed in turning this company around. The hole-punching machine from now on is going to be ahead of the rest of the machine shop, which leaves an opportunity for you both to learn each other's job."

The two men just stared at Jack in total disbelief. Finally, Glen broke the silence. "I've been running that machine for 15 years and I must point out, I have never been off work with sickness or anything else. Apart from that, I don't see myself as a store man."

Duane glared at Glen. Jack defused the situation by putting his arm on Glen's shoulder. "Look, running the store efficiently is an extremely difficult job, which Duane has made look easy. It takes intelligence, grit, a good sense of humor and lots and lots of patience. Now, I think you have all of those qualities in abundance and under the expert guidance of Duane, I believe you could carry it off. However, if you don't fancy it, then maybe a job swap with one of the girls in the file and trim bay should be considered for you."

Glen swallowed hard before backtracking. "Hold on, I didn't say I wasn't prepared to try. If Duane here is willing then so am I."

Jack contentedly left the two men chatting about their resp0ective jobs. It had been on his mind for a while that the sometimes difficult Glen Roach agreeing to job swap would mean a major breakthrough, as any reluctance from the rest of the workforce would disintegrate. He now felt that the first and most difficult hurdle had been overcome and the rest of his job swap plans would now fall into place.

Jack's last hour of a very busy day was spent in Drew's office discussing his new contract. He then went home feeling exhausted and looking forward to a quiet night watching television and listening to Louis Armstrong while enjoying a can of beer.

The rest of the week went well for Jack with regard to the running of the machine shop. His stomach turned over every time he looked at the beautiful Bernie of course.

Saturday morning saw him up early, waiting with a cup of coffee in his hand for Cindy to come and pick him up. He was going to spend the weekend with her and Tony. She arrived bang on time and whisked him away. Over lunch, Jack proudly brought Tony and Cindy up to date with his life. Cindy, for her part, proudly pointed out her new bump. The rest of the day went well. Jack felt part of the family with them and now, in many ways, he was. At least he would be when Cindy gave birth to the baby.

Saturday evening saw them joking and chatting over their starter in a beautiful restaurant, when, suddenly, the atmosphere changed completely. In walked Grace Spencer with her father and his latest woman friend, Danielle. They walked straight over. Lord Spencer, shaking Tony's hand vigorously, suggested that they ask the waiter to accommodate them all on one table. Tony could hardly say no, so the waiter was instructed and, with the table ready, they began organizing the seating arrangements.

Grace made sure that she sat next to Jack. He cringed as he thought of the damaging comments that Grace was capable of and then wondered what side of her split personality they were all going to be subjected to. She didn't keep him in suspense long, as she took off her coat revealing her practically topless dress and sat down. It was a little black number, showing her bare shoulders and all of her breasts apart from her nipples which seemed to be the only things holding the dress up. Jack thought she looked like a real tart, but that of course was how she wanted to be perceived. As soon as everyone was settled, she opened up with her first volley. "I really enjoyed myself at Jack's apartment on Wednesday evening." Then with an exaggerated wink to everyone, she went on. "He really was the perfect host but, thank goodness, he was no gentleman."

An embarrassing atmosphere fell on the group as Jack's face turned crimson. Her father cleared his throat and changed the subject. "I believe there is to be an addition to your family, Tony?"

Tony beamed with pride, "Yes, Quinton, we couldn't be happier."

Cindy was sporting a false smile, as she couldn't help but feel jealous of Grace. For his part, Jack could not look her in the eye.

All, except Grace, tried really hard to make it a relaxing evening. Every time Grace opened her mouth, it was to make them all cringe with embarrassment. "When are you going to pop the question to Danielle, father?"

"Really, darling, you are a little minx."

Danielle tried to hit back.

"Grace, you and Jack seem to be hitting it off, why don't you pop the question yourself?"

When it came to a war of sharp tongues, Danielle was out of Grace Spencer's league. Grace just laughed. "Oh no, that would never do. Our relationship is purely sexual."

Jack felt like digging a deep hole and throwing himself in. Grace was now warming to the catty quips and it was obvious to all present, that she didn't think much of Danielle. "But of course, Danielle, my father can't possibly propose to you, as you are already married are you not?"

Danielle couldn't speak; she looked like she was about to burst into tears. Tony came in to ease the situation. "Would anyone like a coffee to finish?"

"Yes, please," all but Grace chimed. Tony called the waiter over and ordered the coffee. Quinton then ordered the same waiter to bring the best bottle of Champagne in the house to toast the forthcoming baby. What was left of the evening went without incident, apart from Grace periodically putting her hand on Jack's thigh under the tablecloth. The trouble for him, however, was how much he was enjoying it in spite of himself.

"Are you all right, Jack?" Grace asked, mischievously. "Only, you look a bit flushed."

"Yes, I'm fine," he replied, blushing even more with the whole group then looking at him. He suggested they ask for the bill in order to divert the attention away from him.

"You must allow me to cover this," Tony said, looking directly at Quinton.

"No, old chap," Quinton protested, "I won't hear of it. You must all be my guests." Quinton then promptly called the waiter over and gave him his credit card. The bill paid, Jack excused himself and went to the men's room.

As he was washing his hands, the door opened and in walked Grace. She sauntered over to him and putting her hands around his neck, proceeded to kiss him passionately. She then pulled away and began rubbing her hand between his legs.

He couldn't bring himself to complain as she pulled him into a cubicle and locked the door. "Grace, this is ridiculous," he half protested, as she unbuckled his pants and pulled them down, along with his boxer shorts. He was now putty in her hands as she went down on her knees.

"But they are all out there waiting for us," he moaned, as she went about reducing his protests to a whimper. Jack subserviently leaned back against the wall. He closed his eyes with all semblance of protest now gone.

He gasped, as she then stood up and kissed him on the cheek. "There you are, you naughty boy." Opening the door, she left, leaving him standing against the wall with his pants and boxer shorts around his ankles.

"You stupid bastard," he mouthed to himself as he sorted his clothing out. "Why the hell have I allowed myself to get involved with that conniving, crazy bitch?"

The group were patiently waiting for him at the exit. "I'm sorry to have kept you" Jack said, as he stood there, wondering why they were all staring at him. Grace stepped forward with a wicked smile on her face as she proceeded to wipe his cheek with a tissue. She then gave it to him and he went bright red again as he looked at the lipstick stained tissue paper.

Jack was relieved when they hit the cold night air. Grace tried to link her arm in his but he shrugged her off. "Keep your hands off me you crazy bitch and stay out of my life." They all climbed into their respective cabs and sped off.

"I wouldn't have thought Grace Spencer was your type," Tony said, digging, after a couple of minutes.

With Cindy hanging on every word, he replied, "No, she's not, Tony. She's a nut case. In fact, I've just told her to keep out of my life."

Cindy sarcastically quipped, "Was that before or after she had covered your face with lipstick in the John?"

Jack tried in vain to defend himself. "Oh that. Yes, I couldn't get rid of the bitch."

Cindy was like a dog with a bone and wouldn't let go. "Oh, you poor man," she said sarcastically again. "I couldn't help but notice at the dinner table your attempts to ward off her close attentions. Then, to make matters worse, you had to put up with her attentions again in the men's room for an agonizing twenty minutes. She should be horse whipped for putting you through all that." Tony laughed out loud. He thought the whole thing was hilarious. "I don't know what you're laughing at," Cindy went on, now turning her wrath on him. "You dropped food on yourself twice at dinner because you couldn't keep your greedy little eyes off her tits. It was like being with a love struck school boy."

The rest of the ride home was very quiet as Cindy pondered her strange feelings of jealousy. First over Jack, the real father of her coming child and secondly over her husband Tony, who thought he was the natural parent. Having reached home, she apologized to both of them.

As the following weeks went by, Jack threw himself into his job. Gradually, his ideas were beginning to have the desired effect. Everything about the place was running smoother, so much so in fact, that Jack now felt he would have to bring forward his plans for revamping the whole sales structure. With that in mind, he went to see Drew Rickets and smiled as he placed the plans for revamping the sales structure down in front of him. "I'd like to give you the challenge of your life."

"Drew, with a puzzled look on his face, donned his spectacles and began to read through the document. Jack paced up and down the office until at last Drew put it down with the exclamation. "This is fantastic. I'm really impressed, but I don't understand, where do I come in?"

"That's simple, Drew, I want you to set the whole thing up. You are wasted here with your paperclips and dirty pictures." Then, lying through his teeth, he went on. "Lord

Spencer agrees with me. He thinks you have the charisma to pull it off."

Jack knew he had hit the right note, as Drew asked; "Did he really say that?"

"Yes, Drew he did. Now what do you say?"

Drew rubbed his chin before answering, "Oh I don't know. I've never even worked in a sales department."

"Listen to me, my friend, Lord Spencer, as you know, has seven other outlets for security doors across the U.S.A. If you get the blueprint right here, you could end up being the nationwide sales director. It's an incredible opportunity for you."

Drew sat back in his seat before answering, "I can't get my head round this at the moment, but there is something that you should know in confidence. Apart from the paperclips and dirty pictures that you pointed out in your own sledgehammer style, I do half of Nigel's job as well as my own, as he is fucking useless."

Jack smiled. "Yes, well, I had guessed as much and having given it some thought already, I think I have the answer."

"Now, why doesn't that surprise me, Jack Williams? What is it?"

Well, one of the salesmen, Sam Gordon – who I'm sure you know – seems a bright guy academically but, in my opinion, he couldn't sell ice cream on a boiling hot day to a ten year old fucking millionaire."

Drew laughed so much at the remark that tears filled his eyes. "You kill me, Jack, you really do."

Jack went on. "The way I see it is this; Sam takes over your job then, with a little help from both you and me, we should be able to bring him up to scratch quickly. What do you say?"

Drew shrugged his shoulders. "Well, I must admit, I am a bit fed up nursing Nigel and it does sound exciting. However, I'll need time to think it over. By the way and, just out of interest, Sam Gordon certainly doesn't come under your jurisdiction as foreman, so how would you influence that situation?"

"Lord Spencer would see to it for me; I have already been through my suggestions with him and he seemed in total agreement. Come on, Drew, come down off the fence. You know in your heart that this is a great opportunity. Say yes, and I'll set the whole thing in motion."

Drew stood up smiling. "You're right of course; I do need a change and a new challenge. Yes, let's go for it."

Jack was delighted. "Right, I'll contact Lord Spencer and put it in his hands. You won't regret this, Drew." He then took his cell phone out and rang Quinton Spencer in front of a startled Drew and asked if it were possible for them to meet. Having been told that Perkins would pick him up, Jack put his cell phone back into his pocket.

"You have Lord Spencer's personal number?" Drew asked in amazement.

"Yes I do," Jack replied, giving Drew a wink. "And with a bit of luck, I'll soon have his job to go with it." He smiled and gave a wave as he left, leaving Drew shaking his head in disbelief.

Jack sat down, facing Lord Spencer across his desk. His lordship looked over his spectacles at him. "Before we begin, Jack, I would like to talk to you about my daughter, Grace. Would that be all right with you?"

"Yes, sir, No problem."

"Jolly good show, old chap. Now, I don't like to interfere too much in Grace's life, but she seems to be quite taken with you and I wouldn't like to see her hurt."

Jack broke in. "With respect, sir, you may have this all wrong."

Quinton wouldn't be put off what he wanted to say. "Please bear with me, Jack, I'm not sure how well you know her, but usually people jump to the wrong conclusions about Grace. I know she can be a minx at times, but that is just innocent fun and I don't believe she means any harm. She is, in fact, a very soft-hearted girl with great sensitivity that she attempts to hide behind a somewhat brash exterior."

Jack could not believe what he was hearing. Her father quite obviously had no idea what a mixed up conniving, spoilt brat she really was. That, apart from her dark side, which left him confused never mind her father.

"I can assure you, sir, you have nothing to be concerned about regarding Grace and myself. We are good friends but nothing more."

"Oh good show, my boy," Quinton said with a relieved look on his face. "I would hate anything to interfere with our professional association." Jack took this last line as a direct threat delivered politely but firmly. "But enough of this, old boy," Quinton went on. "We have important business to attend to."

For the next hour and a half, Jack went through with Lord Spencer the changes made so far in the machine shop. He then asked for permission to erect a supply track from the sheet metal room to press 1, 2, and 3. With further capability to supply the new machine shop when work was completed. He then moved on to the reorganization of the sales structure of the company.

Lord Spencer was delighted with everything. After agreeing to sort out Sam Gordon and Drew Rickets, contractors for erection of the new track and other relevant points that Jack had requested his help on, he sat back in his leather seat. "I must tell you, Jack, if you carry on as you are and realize the level of success that you have outlined, I promise you, when I retire, which between you and me is not that far off, you could end up heading the whole business nationwide."

Jack felt pure adrenalin pump through his body. "Thank you, sir, as always, I will endeavour to do my best."

"Right," Quinton stood up. "If there is nothing else, I will tell Grace that you are ready to go."

Jack panicked. "No, sir, I don't want to be any trouble, I'll simply catch a cab."

Quinton would have none of it. "Nonsense, my boy, it won't be any trouble and in any case, Grace made me promise. I will tell her to meet you in the kitchen."

He watched Quinton leave, and then left himself a couple of minutes later thinking what an idiot he had been, getting involved with, of all people, Lord Spencer's daughter.

As Jack waited in the kitchen drinking a glass of water, he reflected on his inability to keep his brains out of his pants. The consequences of which knew no bounds when dealing with a person as unstable as Grace Spencer. His thoughts of how to remove her from his life without upsetting her father (who, of course, believed every word she said) were broken by the sound of footsteps, followed by the door handle turning. To his complete surprise, she entered looking demure in a pair of jeans and a scruffy T-shirt.

Smiling sweetly, she kissed him on the cheek. "Hi, Jack, I'm really sorry for the way I behaved the other night, I do hope you can forgive me. The only explanation that I can offer for such stupid behavior is the fact that you are so different from the nerds that I have grown up with. I have never met a guy quite like you before and I suppose in a way, I have been showing off like a love-struck schoolgirl. I'm so sorry."

Her eyes then filled up. Jack kissed her on the cheek and put his arms around her.

"Don't beat yourself up, Grace; I haven't exactly been Mr. Sensible myself."

Grace buried her head into his chest and smiled, as she thought how gullible men were. "Pet dogs," she thought, "are much more difficult to handle."

Jack, for his part, was mistakenly thinking that he had been wrong about her and indeed hoped that this could be the real Grace Spencer.

They left the kitchen holding hands. As they were passing her father's office, Grace banged hard on the door and laughed. She then let go of Jack's hand before running off as fast as she could. She disappeared at the end of the corridor as the door opened. Lord Spencer looked at him with a puzzled look on his face, as Jack stood there feeling like an idiot wishing that the floor would open up and swallow him. "Good evening, sir," he said, red-faced and then quickly followed Grace, whom he found grinning around the corner. "I felt like a right dope there," he scolded. "God knows what your father must think."

At that moment, Toby and Bruno came scampering up the hall excitedly. After making a fuss of them, Grace said, "Come on, Jack, I'll drive you home and please don't worry, I'll be a good girl."

Meanwhile, back in Lord Spencer's office, his son Nigel poured his father a whiskey. "Here you are, father. "

Quinton Spencer relaxed in his huge leather chair and had a drink. "Now, Nigel, what is this problem that has you in such a state?"

"Jack Williams is the problem, father, my position is being undermined constantly right across the board. I have worked my fingers to the bone for you and what do I get? This person comes in out of the gutter, with his sharp practices and in no time at all, I am made to look like a complete fool."

Lord Spencer gave his son a reassuring smile. "Nigel, my boy, there really is no reason for you to be concerned. This fellow Williams seems to have lived most of his life on the edge of the law, which is probably why he was able to see through Leroy Dalton's racket. In this case, there was no honour amongst thieves. The bottom line is, Nigel, he has something to offer that I intend to extract to the maximum. Naturally, it goes without saying, he is not to be trusted, so please don't get yourself into a state. Blood is thicker than water after all."

Nigel immediately relaxed, "Can I get you a refill, Father?"

"Yes, my boy, why not?"

Nigel replenished his father's glass and then went on. "How do we know that this William's person is not up to something himself?"

Quinton sat forward in his seat. "Well, first of all, Nigel, I have made him promises that I have no intention of keeping. I have also upped considerably, Grace's allowance in return for her time pretending to be infatuated with him. Having her on the inside, so to speak, reduces the chances of Jack Williams doing a Leroy Dalton with my money while I am using him."

Now, with a big smile on his face, Nigel poured himself another huge measure of whiskey, one of several that he had consumed that day before making another point. "Hold on, Father, what if Grace falls in love with the damned fellow?"

"No, I don't see that happening, Nigel," his father replied, with a smile on his face. "Grace could never take someone like Williams seriously, I mean, he probably doesn't know how to use a knife and fork for goodness sake." Both men broke out into pleats of laughter at this thought, before Quinton then went on. "I forgot to tell you, Nigel, I have given Williams a veiled threat that I will not tolerate Grace being hurt by him. That means that no matter how badly behaved she becomes and, as we both know, she can be extremely badly behaved, he will be terrified of upsetting her." Both men broke into laughter again.

"Please, Father, no more, my sides are aching."

"Just one more point, Nigel. This will kill you. He is at the moment waiting for $30,000 from me, which he is entitled to as soon as we double our production of security doors. With a little bit of creative accounting, we can keep him waiting for quite a while for his money, which by the way, won't be anywhere near $30,000." Nigel laughed again, thinking this was all hilarious. Lord Spencer went on. "Finally, Nigel, I must tell you this and it goes without saying that you keep it to yourself. I have told Williams that I am going to retire soon and, in a way, that is true." Nigel's eyes widened. "Let me explain, my boy, before this fellow turned up with all his plans, I was on the verge of selling the damned company. Having seen his plans however and listened to his ideas, I became totally convinced that he was indeed capable of doubling production right across the board. Consequently, that would double the asking price, if and when I sell up."

Nigel suddenly looked upset again. "But, Father, what will I do? What will become of me?"

Quinton walked over and put his hand on his son's shoulder. "Oh, Nigel, you are not cut out for this type of business. You are far too trusting and the likes of Williams would always take advantage. No, what you would be better doing is turning your attention to yachts as you love everything to do with sailing and I think you would be far happier."

Nigel brightened considerably. "Yes, I think you are right, Father. Does Grace know about this?"

"No, son, the little minx doesn't know all of what we have discussed regarding Williams and I don't want her to, not yet. Now let's have a toast to the savior of our company." Both men laughed as they drank their whiskey.

Chapter 11

Grace pulled up smoothly at Jack's apartment block and turned off the motor. "Here you are, Mr. Williams, is there anything else that I can do for you?"

He replied in his own humorous way. "Well, you can come up and make me a cup of coffee, run down to the drugstore for a bottle of wine, make me a nice meal and then later on clean my kitchen if you like."

Grace proceeded to tickle him but he simply sat there unmoved. "I'm not ticklish, wench." Now frustrated, she hit him across his chest a number of times and again he just sat there as though he didn't feel a thing. He then pinned her tiny hands down and kissed her tenderly on the lips, before whispering in her ear. "Or, I could do all of those things for you instead, followed by one of my special massages."

"Jack Williams, you obviously think you know me well and you would be right."

Later on, chatting away over a pasta meal and a bottle of wine, prepared and supplied by Jack, Grace was chatty, witty, polite and charming. He looked at her, wondering how she could have such a split personality. Having finished her meal, she sat back, put down her cutlery and let out a long "Mmmm, that was delicious, Mr. Williams, I don't know how I can thank you."

"I'll think of something, Miss Spencer, now, would you like a cup of coffee?"

"Yes, I would, thank you, Jack, but you must allow me to make it."

"Okay, you can," he said laughing, "but please wipe the pasta sauce off your chin that has been there for the duration of the meal."

"You pig" she scolded, wiping her chin with a napkin.

Later on, while washing the dishes together, Jack felt in a good mood as he teased Grace about her background. She flicked some soapy water onto his face and as they laughed together, the doorbell rang. "I wonder who that could be?" he said walking toward the door.

Grace following behind whispered, "Whoever it is, get rid of them quickly, you big lunk."

He opened the door to find Bernie clearly upset, with her eyes puffed up and red. As soon as she spotted Grace, she turned and ran away crying back down to her own apartment. Jack looked at Grace and shrugged his shoulders. "I'm really sorry, but Bernie is a good friend and it looks as though she needs me."

Although seething inside, Grace managed to control herself. "Don't worry, Jack, I understand." Then grabbing her jacket and purse, she kissed him on the cheek. "Will you give me a ring later?"

"Yes, Grace, I will, and thanks for being so understanding."

Getting into her car, Grace slammed the door shut before then throwing her purse violently against the windscreen. "Bastard, bastard, bastard, woman." She shouted out loud, before she then rammed the car into gear and roared up the road on screeching tyres.

Jack rang Bernie's doorbell without success so he rang it again and again until finally, he heard her faint voice from behind the door. "Who is it?"

"Bernie, open the door. It's Jack and I'm on my own." After a short delay, she opened the door and walked briskly back to the sitting room with Jack in pursuit. She stood there in front of him, her face as white as a sheet. "Oh, Jack, I've been a fool." She then put her head on his chest and sobbed and sobbed.

He waited until she had stopped trembling before getting her to sit down. Giving her some tissues, he waited patiently until she recovered her poise, before softly saying, "I don't know yet what is bothering you, but if it will help, we can have a long chat."

"But what about Grace?" she asked, as yet more tears flowed down her cheeks.

"Don't worry about Grace, she's gone home. He then took hold of her hands. "What's happened? What's wrong?"

"I'm in a terrible mess, I'm pregnant and I don't know what to do."

He gave her a hug. "I'm certainly not going to judge you on anything, Bernie, but I am a great listener and it goes without saying that anything you tell me will remain within these walls. I must just add though, Duane is one of the straightest guy's that I have ever met."

"Jack, you're going to think really badly of me, but the baby is not Duane's."

He was stunned as he held her tight while she sobbed and sobbed, not knowing what to say.

Her tears subsided a little and she went on. "This is tragic, Jack. I think I have been a victim of my drink having been spiked. I went to a nightclub with Lila and Tash last month. During the night, I began to feel ill and I told the girls that I was going home. I don't remember much after that until the next morning, when I woke up with a splitting headache. I found myself lying across the bed on top of my duvet. The top half of my body was still clothed. My skirt, however, was on the floor, along with my panties, which were ripped to shreds. On my bedside table was a twenty-dollar bill and a pair of men's boxer shorts. I felt sick inside as I tried to remember but only brief flashes came to me of a man's face in a taxi cab. Even that was really hazy. I also remember having a drink with a guy at the bar but probably that has nothing to do with it. I felt dirty inside. I showered and showered, but to no avail. I still felt the same." She then broke down again, choking back the tears, as her trembling body clung to Jack.

Jack waited patiently until she finally calmed down again. "Have you been to the cops, Bernie?"

"No, I felt too ashamed and, in any case, I don't remember any more now than I did on that morning, so what could they do? I threw the boxer shorts into the trashcan and tried to put the whole thing out of my mind."

He took hold of her shoulders firmly and looked into her tear filled eyes. "Listen to me, Bernie, you have done absolutely nothing wrong. You don't have anything to be ashamed of. Now, let's try and get things into perspective. Is it possible that Duane could be the father?"

"No, Jack, we have only been together the one time and he used a protective."

Jack was amazed at this revelation. "But I thought…" he started to say, until she cut him off.

"I know what you thought, you big idiot. As nice as Duane is, you should know more than anybody, he is not the man for me, nor could he ever be."

After a few moments, Jack suggested she looked tired and asked her if she would like to go to bed and get some sleep. "No," she replied. "I would like to talk this all through, but I feel as though I have ruined your evening."

"Don't worry about that, Bernie. Have you told Lila and Tash what happened?"

"No, I haven't."

"And Duane?"

"No, nobody."

Jack had a feeling of déjà vu. It hadn't been long since the scene with Cindy.

"Well, Bernie, I think we have to break it all down into clear options."

"Yes, Jack, I've already done that."

"Right, as I see it, you probably have three. I'm guessing from what you have told me, Duane doesn't fit in to your future plans. Is that correct?"

"Yes, absolutely."

"Right then, if you can forgive my sledgehammer diplomacy, I see option one, as having the baby, then putting it up for adoption from birth; option two, as having the baby, then bringing it up as best you can and option three, as having a termination." He then left a period of silence, waiting for a response.

"Sledgehammer diplomacy? That's putting it mildly, Jack Williams. Have you ever considered joining the Samaritans? You could have your very own string of suicides right across the state." A weak smile then appeared on Bernie's face. "You'll have to excuse me, Jack, I need to go and freshen up. When I get back, I will expect the bottle of white wine in the cooler to be open."

On Bernie's return, she looked much more in control. She had washed her face and changed her clothing. Having sat down and picked up the glass of wine that Jack had poured out for her, she noticed that he had not poured one out for himself. "Are you not having a drink with me, Jack?"

"No, Bernie. As you know, I usually only drink beer."

"Then go and get yourself some beer, man. I'm in the mood to get sloshed and you, I'm afraid, have been voted in as joint slosher."

He laughed as he stood up and made his way up to his apartment. Returning a little later, he had with him with a couple of six packs and a bottle of wine.

"Another bottle of wine? I do hope you don't have an ulterior motive in getting me drunk, Jack Williams. Oh dear, I'm so sorry, that was such a bad joke."

"Yes, Bernie, it was pretty lousy under the circumstances, but then, your jokes usually are."

She pulled a face at him and smiled. "You know, Jack, just telling you has been such a relief. I have considered my options of course, but none of them sound exactly wonderful do they?"

"No, they don't. By the way, I take it you have been to see a doctor?"

"No, not yet."

He put on his stern face. "But you must. Apart from the pregnancy, this monster may have been infected, if you see what I mean."

"Yes, I know exactly what you mean, but I'm so frightened."

He filled her glass with more wine and they carried on chatting until the early hours. Eventually exhausted and with the two wine bottles empty, they shared the last can of beer. Jack, will you stay the night with me? I don't want to be alone and before you answer, I know that you are with Grace Spencer. I just want you to hold me until I fall asleep."

"Yes, Bern', of course I will, as long as you promise to take tomorrow off and go to see your doctor."

"It's a deal, I promise."

As Bernie went off to bed, Jack stayed behind clearing up the bottles and cans to give her time to get into bed. By the time he entered her bedroom, she was fast asleep so he quietly left, closing the front door as gently as he could.

On arrival into his own apartment, he turned on his answering machine only to find a string of messages from Grace. He had completely forgotten that he had promised to give her a call. Shrugging his shoulders, he went into his bedroom, set his alarm clock and jumped into bed. The next thing he knew, his alarm was ringing and he could hardly lift his head off the pillow. Still with his head pounding, he showered and dressed. A couple of strong coffees helped, as did two painkillers. His phone rang but he was in no mood to answer it. The answer phone clicked in. "Jack, where are you? Why didn't you ring me last night? I'm very angry." The machine went dead as he left for work.

By lunchtime, he was feeling a little better. He rang Bernie and after four rings, she answered, "Hello?"

"Hi, Bernie, how are you."

"Well actually not too good, Jack. You were supposed to help me, not kill me."

"Bernie, I can tell your sense of humour is intact, but more importantly, are you going to see your doctor?"

"Yes, sir, I have an appointment this afternoon."

"Good, I will call and see you when I get home from work. By the way, wench, what time did you wake up?"

"About eleven. I felt dreadful, Jack. Seriously though, thank you for last night. You're a good man and a good friend."

"Oh, it was nothing, Bernie. I'll see you later." He put his cell phone away feeling sorry for her. Remembering Grace, he took his cell phone back out of his pocket and rang her.

"Hello, nice of you to remember that I am actually alive."

He began to apologize. "Grace, I'm sorry. I was going."

"She interrupted him. "Never mind about all that, my father wants you to have dinner with us tonight. I shall pick you up at seven thirty and by the way, it's black tie."

As he put his cell phone away he smiled. For some reason, he found domineering characteristics in women both funny and attractive.

At last the long day at work was over and Jack skipped up the steps two at a time, arriving at Bernie's door at 6.15. She made him a cup of coffee and sat facing him. "I've made a decision; I have decided to have a termination. In fact, I have an appointment to have it done on Saturday morning. I probably shouldn't ask, but will you go with me?"

"Bernie, this is very sudden. Wouldn't you be better off taking a bit more time before such drastic action?"

"No, I've made my mind up and there is no chance of my changing it, so the sooner the better."

He slowly nodded his head. "Of course I'll go with you. How long will you be staying in hospital for?"

"Staying in? I won't be staying in. My termination is booked for 10 a.m., so I imagine you will be able to pick me up some time in the afternoon."

"Oh I see, I didn't realize. Will you be able to walk?"

"Yes, I will Jack. I'll probably be shattered both mentally and physically for a couple of days but then I should be fine."

"Right, Madam, I don't want you to worry about anything. I will make myself available all day Saturday and Sunday to look after you."

Tears were now beginning to well up in her eyes. "Jack William's, you are a lovely man, thank you so much. By the way, I don't want anyone to know." Having promised to keep her confidence, he left after explaining that he was going to the Spencer's for dinner.

Grace arrived bang on time wearing jeans and a T-shirt, explaining that she would change when they reached her house. She looked him up and down, nodding with approval. "Very nice, Jack, you look quite the gentleman." Little did she know, but he was actually wearing the suit that he used to wear for the funeral scam.

"Now, before we go back to my house, I want you to sit at the table so that I can teach you the basics of dining etiquette."

Jack looked at her in amazement. "Are you joking?"

"No, Jack, far from it. I'm not having you waving a fork full of food around and speaking with your mouth full as you did last night here with me."

He sat down at the table chuckling. "Go on then, do your worst."

Having set the cutlery, plates and wine glasses on the table, Grace then spent a half hour patiently teaching him the rudiments. Order of the cutlery, use of a napkin and the absolute necessity of the need to use the serving spoons provided. Finally, she finished off by explaining why, when the port wine was served with the selection of cheeses, the port must be passed round the dining table clockwise; each person having poured their own port, before then passing it on to the person on their left.

He sat there and smiled, which made her angry. "This is very important to me, Jack. If at any time you are not sure of what to do, then please just watch me."

"Okay, Grace, don't get yourself worked up, I promise I will do my best."

An hour later, Grace pulled up and parked the car in the huge drive. They went straight to her room, where she changed into a beautiful evening gown. Jack whistled as he moved over to her, putting his arms around her waist before moving them slowly up to her breasts. "Keep your mind off my tits and on dining etiquette, or I won't allow you to undress me later."

"Yes, ma'am, anything you say."

By the time they joined the other guests, Nigel, who was accompanied by a beautiful brunette, already looked off his head either with alcohol or drugs or both.

"So glad you could join us." Lord Spencer said rather sarcastically.

Grace ignored the remark completely and proceeded to introduce Jack to Nigel's brunette. "Carolyn darling, I would like you to meet Jack Williams and do try to keep your hands off him."

Jack shook hands with her. "Nice to meet you, Carolyn."

"Nice to meet you," she replied looking into his dark eyes. "Yes, Grace, I will try my best, but he is rather wonderful. Where in the world did you find him?"

"Down down, now darling." Grace said to Carolyn, putting her arm through Jack's as though to warn off a predator.

Perkins approached with a tray of red and white wines. He offered them first to Grace. "Madam?" She took a glass of white wine. "Sir?" He then said offering the tray to Jack.

"Do you have any beer? Jack asked as Grace nearly choked on her wine.

"So sorry, sir, but I am afraid we don't."

"That's okay," Jack, said as he took a glass of white wine off the tray, which had probably cost Lord Spencer in the region of $150 a bottle. Carolyn, with a fit of the giggles, was obviously enjoying herself. To her, Jack was like a breath of fresh air to what was usually a stuffy, boring meal at the Spencer's.

Jack did the polite rounds, thanking Quinton for the invite, and saying hello again to Danielle, before finally and grudgingly, shaking Nigel's hand.

Perkins, having now discarded his tray, invited the whole assembly into the dining room. As they approached the huge table, Jack, not having noticed the place cards, promptly plonked himself at the head of the table next to the smiling Carolyn. Embarrassingly for Grace, he had also not noticed that there wasn't a place setting there anyway. Carolyn, thinking this was hilarious, leaned over and whispered in his ear. Jack flushed a little and Grace fumed as she indicated to him his correct place, holding the chair for him between Carolyn and Danielle.

Jack sat down in his designated place and smiled sweetly at his embarrassed girlfriend. He then mistakenly picked up the napkin on his right, which of course was intended for Carolyn. Grace, losing patience, tried hard to hold herself together. She deftly picked up Jack's napkin and placed it on Carolyn's left, before then moving round the table to her designated seat opposite Jack. She had Lord Spencer on her left and Nigel on her right. Jack realized that Grace had given him good advice. If in doubt, copy her, which he did by and large for the rest of the meal, despite the attentions of Carolyn, who flirted with him constantly.

The evening drew to a close with Lord Spencer pleasantly drunk and Nigel completely off his head.

Grace announced to all that she would drive Jack home. Having gone through the pleasantries of saying goodnight to everyone, they left the group, but of course, instead of going out, they went up to Grace's room.

"What did you think of Carolyn, Jack?" Grace asked, looking closely at him.

He chose his words carefully. "I thought she was friendly and welcoming."

"Yes, I'm sure she was," Grace said sarcastically. "In fact, it's a good job you had a napkin to wipe your chin as you constantly drooled over her."

He changed the subject quickly. "You looked really beautiful tonight, Grace."

She grunted as she sat down at her dressing table and began wiping off her makeup. He walked over to her and began massaging her shoulders. She leaned back in her seat sighing. He bent over her head, and kissed her.

"Take me to bed and undress me, Jack."

"Why? Are you sleepy?" he joked, as he lifted her up into his arms. She laughed as he carried over to the bed.

When Jack awoke the following morning, the unpredictable Grace was nowhere to be seen. Quickly dressing himself, he hurried down the stairs. Bruno greeted him enthusiastically at the bottom with a wagging tail and unfortunately, Lord Spencer.

Quinton looked puzzled. "I thought you went home last night, Jack?"

Flushing a little, he replied, "No, sir, Grace felt too tired to drive. I slept in one of your guest rooms, I hope you don't mind."

"No, no, not at all, my boy. I'm afraid you have missed Grace, though. Would you like Perkins to drive you home?"

"Thank you, that sure would be a big help."

After having been dropped off at his apartment by Perkins, Jack quickly showered and changed. He then half walked and half ran to work, where he arrived an hour late, furious with himself. Timekeeping had been one of the most important points that he had drilled in to the staff. Thus, he felt extremely embarrassed.

The following morning, he took Bernie to the clinic in a cab in order that she could have her termination. Before leaving her there, he gave her a hug and whispered in her ear, "Try not to worry, Bern', everything will be okay. Give me a ring on my cell phone when you want me to pick you up."

As the clinic was just a couple of miles away from Old Tom's house, Jack decided to go and spend a couple of hours with him. The moment old Tom saw him walking into his shop, his face lit up. He finished serving a customer before then joining Jack on the other side of the counter and giving him a big hug. "It's good to see you," Tom said, before shouting to his assistant, who was in the back room. "Martha, will you take care of things for a while? I'll be upstairs in my apartment."

The two men chatted on for a couple of hours before Jack's cell phone rang. "Hi, is that Jack Williams?" a voice asked through the phone.

"Yes, it is, I take it Bernie is ready to be picked up?"

"Yes, sir, she is."

"Tell her I'll be there in a few minutes." He grabbed his jacket off the back of his chair. "I'm sorry, Tom, but I must go."

Old Tom grabbed his own jacket "It's difficult getting a cab on a Saturday,

I'll drive you and, before you object, you would be wasting your breath."

"Okay, Tom. I'll shut up," he gratefully replied.

As they arrived at the clinic, Jack shouted. "Thanks, Tom, I'll give you a bell." He then ran up the steps and into the clinic. Bernie was sitting waiting in reception looking pale and drawn. "Are you okay?" he asked genuinely worried.

"Yes, Jack, thank you, but I will be glad to get home."

Jack asked the receptionist to call for a cab, which arrived thirty minutes later and ferried them to their apartment block. On this occasion, he had to forgo his fear of elevators for Bernie's sake. Entering her apartment, he made her lie on the settee.

"Right, my lady," he asked, in what he thought of as his soothing voice. "Is there anything I can do for you? I'm your personal slave for the whole weekend."

Bernie began to cry and he put his arms around her. She then sobbed into his chest until eventually, the tears abated. "Thanks, Jack, you have been a good friend to me."

"Nonsense, woman, I'm just being selfish, making sure that you'll be well enough to return to work on Monday and make my job easier. Now, I repeat, is there anything that I can do for you?"

"Well, as you are asking, I wouldn't mind a couple of pillows off my bed and a glass of red wine. The trouble is, I don't have any red wine at the moment."

He threw his arms up into the air with a smile on his face as though in exasperation saying. "I suppose I will have to go down to the liquor store and buy some. Having supplied the two pillows and settled her down, he went off to the liquor store, returning soon after with three bottles of red wine, a couple of packs of beer and a huge box of chocolates. "Right, madam, will this lot do?" Bernie's smile told him all that he needed to know. He gave her a glass of wine and then spent the rest of the afternoon fluffing up her pillows, fussing over her, trying to cheer her up.

By late afternoon, Bernie complained of feeling extremely tired and so went to bed. Jack checked his cell phone to find several messages from Grace. He put it back into his pocket as he didn't know what to say to her. He made himself a cup of coffee with his mind in a puzzled state. "How could he and Bernie have messed things up so badly?" His mind then turned to Phylamina and he sighed. With her, things had been different. Circumstances beyond his control had destroyed their relationship and sadly, a

293

lovely warm, charismatic lady, whom he had loved dearly had lost her life. Tears trickled down his cheeks as despair turned to annoyance at the thought of all the mistakes he had now made with Bernie. He heard his name being called from the bedroom. As he went in he could see in the half-light that she had been crying again. "Jack, will you do something for me? Will you just give me a cuddle?"

Not saying a word, he quickly stripped down to his boxer shorts and joined her.

They didn't speak for almost an hour as she wept into his chest again, until finally, she pulled away from him and looked into his eyes. "Thank you, Jack Williams." She said and then cupping her hands on his face, kissed him tenderly on the lips. "Right, Jack, I'm going to wash and dress because I'm going to cook us a wonderful meal."

"Hang on, lady, I thought that I would be doing the cooking?"

"I don't think so, Jack, you do the cooking?"

Later on, perched on a high stool, he watched as Bernie went about preparing a meal for them both. She was wearing a sloppy sweatshirt and an old pair of jeans. He thought she looked beautiful. Bernie seemed totally oblivious of him as she went about her task. He loved the fact that she never wore any makeup, not even lipstick, which most women would think to be absolutely essential.

She looked and smiled at him. "Are you going to open a bottle of wine, Jack or do you want me to do everything around here?"

During the meal, Bernie explained how she felt about the termination and various other things, including Duane, whom she said she liked very much but unfortunately, could never love. It was noticeable to Jack that she never once mentioned Grace, which pleased him. At the end of the evening, he kissed her on the cheek and went up to his own apartment. By the end of the following day, Bernie was feeling much better and told Jack that she intended to return to work the following morning.

The next few weeks went extremely well in the machine shop, which by now was running like clockwork. The new sales setup was beginning to bear fruit. Jack had managed to turn everything round and, remarkably, had managed to keep the respect of every man and woman that was working for him.

His relationship with Grace continued, but even though he quite often stayed over at her house, he never felt totally comfortable, even though he had been entrusted with the code for the burglar alarm. He couldn't figure out what he truly felt about her. He knew of course that he was not in love with her and he also knew that he couldn't afford to hurt her feelings, as that would incur the wrath of her father. He thought she was an extremely attractive woman, though a bit odd sometimes. He often thought, 'Will the real Grace Spencer please stand up?' He was also in two minds about when and how, or even if, he should mention to her father about the $30,000. Should he simply wait until Lord Spencer approached him? He had, after all, given him his word as a gentleman. Furthermore, he did have the security of the legal documents that they had both signed, of which they each had copies. In all this indecision, Jack simply carried on with his job and his life.

The delivery of the security doors by contract labour had proven to be a complete success. The huge garage was almost complete as regards fitting it out as a machine shop. Spencer Security Doors had even been mentioned in the press, such had been the rapid development of the company. Jack quite rightly felt extremely proud as he went about his task of pushing the company into more and more productivity. His insecure feelings resurfaced, however, on a bright spring morning when he called into reception to send a fax. The beautiful Della, who had always fancied him, asked if he was looking forward to the big, posh bash the following month.

"What posh bash is that, Della?"

"Why, Lord Spencer's 65th birthday bash at the Manhattan Banqueting suite of course," she said, with a shocked look on her face. "I'm going as Sam Gordon's partner. Even the mayor will be there."

"Oh, yes, Della, of course. It should be a gas," he replied, feeling a bit embarrassed. He was puzzled. "Why," he thought, "has Grace not mentioned anything about it?" After discreet enquiries, he found out that he was the only member of staff not to have received an invitation. He began to smell a rat. He had always had reservations about Grace and now that he thought about it, since they had been seeing each other, she had been to a number of jet set parties with her snobby friends and had never once invited him. His pride now hurt, he decided that it was time for him to have a word with Quinton Spencer about the $30,000. So, with that in mind, he made an appointment to see him that very evening. Lord Spencer told him that Perkins would pick him up from the factory.

Jack tapped on Lord Spencer's door at 6 p.m. "Come in, come in," he heard Quinton's voice shout from inside. He entered and sat down. Lord Spencer smiled at him from across his desk. "It's good to see you, my boy. Do we have a problem at the old factory?"

"No, sir," Jack replied, immediately seeing a chance to get his point across, "On the contrary, everything is running like clockwork. In fact our output has more than doubled."

"Excellent, excellent, well done, old boy!" Quinton exclaimed, with what Jack now saw as his usual sickly smile. "As a matter of fact I have been meaning to have a word with you about my other outlets."

Jack was not going to be put off. "Yes, sir, but before we go down that avenue, can I just mention our agreement regarding the doubling of production at this outlet?"

"But of course, Jack, I have your cheque right here all made out for you and, may I just say, you deserve every cent of it."

Quinton opened his desk drawer and handed him a sealed envelope. Jack at that moment felt ashamed of himself for doubting the integrity of Lord Spencer. After putting the envelope in his pocket, they carried on chatting about the other outlets. Later on, Perkins ran him home. He went straight into his apartment, sat down, took the envelope out of his pocket and kissed it. "Here we go," he said to himself, as he opened the sealed envelope. He looked at the cheque with a puzzled frown on his face as he read, "Pay Jack Williams, $5,000." Puzzlement then turned to anger as he rang Quinton's number only to hear the answering machine.

He rang Grace, who sounded very strange when asked about the whereabouts of her father. "I'm sorry, Jack, I don't know," she said nervously.

"When will I see you, Grace?" He then asked getting more and more suspicious by the minute.

"Oh, I'm not sure, I have a lot of engagements this week, darling, I will give you a call. In fact I am rather late for one now, so I had better be off. Byeee." As the phone went dead, Jack became convinced that, whatever was going on, she was in on it. He rang Quinton's number several times with anger rising with each call until, finally, he gave up and went to bed.

The following morning, after an uneasy night, Jack was up before the alarm went off. He rang Quinton yet again only to get the same response as before. After arriving at work, he became really busy with run of the mill problems that needed seeing to. As soon as he had a moment to spare, he went to Nigel's office only to find out that, strangely, he had not shown up for work.

Leaving Bernie to look after everything, Jack decided it was time for direct action and so took a cab to Quinton's house. He rang the doorbell and was mightily relieved when Perkins answered it. The butler, it seemed to him, had obviously been primed, as he nervously said, "I am sorry, sir, but Lord Spencer is not in residence."

"Is that right, Perkins?" Jack replied, as he pushed his way past the now irate butler. Perkins was red faced as he grabbed him and tried to get him to leave.

Jack took hold of the butler's lapels and shoved him hard, sending him sprawling across the hall.

"I will call the police if you don't leave," Perkins shouted at him. Jack was now a man on a mission and wouldn't be deterred. Striding purposefully down the corridor, he stopped outside Quinton's door. He could hear voices from inside, followed by laughter. He opened the door, and walked in.

Quinton, and his son, Nigel, were each sitting with a glass of whisky in their hand. They both froze at the sight of Jack. Perkins entered looking flushed. "I am sorry, sir, shall I call the police?"

Jack looked Quinton in the eye saying slowly, "Don't even think about it."

Quinton had recovered his poise. "My dear chap, I wouldn't dream of it. Perkins, bring some tea and biscuits."

Jack was not in the mood for any of Lord Spencer's smarmy games. "I have come here to see you about this cheque," he said, taking the envelope from his pocket. "You have only made it out for $5,000."

"That's right, my boy," Quinton replied with a smirk on his face. "$5,000, as we agreed and as I said, you deserve every last cent of it."

The gloves were off now off as far as Jack was concerned. "I'm not taking any more crap from you or your smack head son over there. You know, as well as I, that we agreed on $30,000. We each signed a legal document, of which I have a copy at home."

"I think there must be some misunderstanding, my boy," Quinton said as he opened his desk drawer and took out his copy of the agreement. "Now let me see," he went on, as he looked through the document. "Ah yes, this appears to be the page in question." He handed the document to Jack indicating the paragraph that he wished him to read. Jack read it and then glared at Quinton Spencer, before ripping the document to pieces and throwing them into the air.

Looking at the two Spencer's one at a time, he then said slowly and with deliberation, "You will find in time that nobody, and I do mean nobody, makes a Patsy out of Jack Williams."

Nigel was squirming in his seat, terrified, as Jack turned on his heel and left, slamming the door behind him. As soon as he arrived home, he took out his copy of the agreement and sure enough, there it was. He read it out, "$5,000." He cursed himself for being such a stupid idiot. He ran through in his mind the events of the morning when he and Lord Spencer had gone through the document, paragraph by paragraph. Having been satisfied that everything was in order, they had both shaken hands on the deal. Quinton had then asked him to go and fetch Sam Gordon, who was going to be a witness. Jack now realized that, while he was fetching Sam, Quinton had obviously switched documents and, on his return, like a dope, he had signed the agreement without first re-checking it through.

For the next couple of days, Jack went over in his mind what options were open to him. The first option that he ruled out was violence, as apart from giving him personal satisfaction, it offered very little else. Disrupting productivity at the factory would indeed hurt Quinton, but of course would also hurt all the employees and he himself would gain nothing, so that was ruled out. He tried to think methodically of any advantages that he had and how best to use them. Gradually, an embryo of an idea began to grow in his mind. Putting his idea on paper, he began to piece together a workable plan, trying to cover all eventualities. When, at last, he was totally happy with everything, he decided to try and obtain the first and most important ingredient that was needed in order for the plan to succeed. He rang his old friend Tiggy and asked him to come to his apartment, telling him that he had a profitable proposition to put to him.

Two nights later, Tiggy knocked on Jack's door and he greeted him with a genuine hug. "It's good to see you, Tigg'. Fancy a beer?"

"Sure," Tiggy replied, "but I'd prefer two or three."

Jack smiled as he went into the kitchen, returning soon after with a six-pack.

Settling down, they chatted for a while. "Listen, Jack, I want to get something straight about the job last year that you were blown out of."

"Don't worry, Tigg', I know exactly what happened and it had nothing to do with you. Now, have you anything going down at the moment?"

"No, as a matter of fact, I've just finished a job and I'm lying low. Which means, of course, I will probably have to turn down whatever proposition it is that you have for me.

"Tigg', please, just keep an open mind. My proposition, as far as you are concerned, is risk free. In fact, you won't even know from start to finish what the risk side of it is, which only involves me by the way."

"I'm intrigued," Tiggy said, now looking more interested. "Let's have the low down."

"Well, do you remember when you and I used to con the screws in that 'so called' young person's correction institute, as we looked so alike?"

"How could I forget? Apart from my red hair, they couldn't tell us apart."

"Right, Tigg', I need a cast iron alibi on Saturday the fifth of April, which to save you the job of counting on your fingers and toes, is in three weeks' time."

"Cheeky bastard," Tiggy broke in.

Jack ignored him and continued. "Anyway, this is how it goes down. You would have to shave off that ridiculous moustache and wear my brightly coloured bobble hat for about four hours. That will give me the alibi, while I do the job on my own. You would then walk away risk free, with between six to eight thousand bucks."

"This sounds okay," Tiggy said, opening another can of beer and taking a slug.

"Good," Jack went on. "Now, you were always talented at painting. Watercolours and oils, right?"

Tiggy looked at him as though he were nuts. "Jack, I don't understand."

"Bear with me, Tigg', it will all become clear. I have enrolled in a group that does outside watercolours every Saturday, rain or shine. Starting tonight, I want you to teach me the basics. I have already acquired the materials and brushes, as we don't have much time to spare. You are going to teach me in your particular style, so that by the fifth of April, you will be able to carry on with a painting that I have started. Are you beginning to see the light?"

Tiggy looked puzzled and just shrugged his shoulders so Jack carried on. "My first session with the group is this coming Saturday. They will find me to be a very quiet, private person. In fact, I won't speak to any of them and so it will follow, you won't have to either." Jack took a slug of beer and then carried on. "I have enquired as to what toilet facilities will be available, as and when required. The guy who runs the group, a Mr. Child, just laughed and said that usually the woods had to suffice or, if they were lucky, a small bar or diner nearby. That setup sounds perfect for our swap over. We will both have our cell phones, of course, so it should be easy. I would like you to come with me on both Saturdays that we have left before the big day. A dress rehearsal hopefully, on the middle Saturday. Any questions?"

"Yes, Jack, I have. Firstly, what the hell will you be doing while I am painting with the anorak brigade? Secondly, how and when will I get paid?"

"On your first point, I would like to keep our arrangement on a need to know basis. On your second point, after I have completed my task, I will contact you by text and we will swap back. I will then make a point of chatting to Mr. Child about something or other. Having finished the session, you can drive me home in your van which, by the way, will be loaded with jewellery and expensive paintings. Having dropped me off, you will take the booty to your 'Fence' and contact me as soon as he has done his dirty deed. I know that I am putting a lot of trust in you, Tigg', and I would like to say it's because you are such a good friend. You are a good friend, of course, but we both know that if you crossed me and I found out, I could have a word about things that you have done in the past to powerful people that would guarantee a swim in the river for you, with a pair of cement shoes on your feet."

Tiggy laughed out loud and had another slug of beer. "Yeah, you're right there, Jack," he said, putting his empty can onto the table. "One thing does puzzle me though. It's obvious from what you have told me, that when the shit hits the fan, you will be the most obvious suspect and therefore a cast iron alibi is crucial for you. That being so, why have you not asked me to do the job, while you have a jolly time with your painting playmates?"

"First of all, Tigg', I have inside knowledge of the property in question, in that I know exactly where to go for the booty. I know the burglar alarm number and finally, I know the two guard dogs very well. Secondly, I will enjoy doing this job very much on a personal level. Right, enough of all that, do we have a deal?"

Tiggy held his hand out for Jack to shake."Yeah, go on then, let's give this scam a rattle."

Having shook hands on the deal, Jack said, "Right, let's get the painting gear out. I want to be painting like Vincent Van fucking Gogh by the fifth of April," They then spent a couple of hours together on his first painting lesson and made arrangements for the following Saturday before Tiggy went home.

Jack opened another can of beer after Tiggy had gone and sat going over in his mind the whole plan in case he had left a stone unturned. Thinking about the $5,000 cheque, he decided to cash it in and go about his job as though nothing had happened. This, he thought, would give the Spencer's a false sense of security and leave them vulnerable. It would also mean he could pay old Tom what he owed him. His mind then turned to Grace Spencer. He decided, that given the chance, he would give her a good seeing to, as apart from the satisfaction of using her sexually, it would also keep him in touch with the two dogs, or 'three' he then thought, laughing to himself, if he included Grace. Going to bed, he could feel everything falling into place.

Chapter 12

On Jack's first morning at work, after having had the bust up with the Spencers, he continued on in his usual enthusiastic manner as though nothing had happened. Even to the point of looking in, saying good morning to a nervous looking Nigel. Bernie, he thought, was still not her old self. He asked her if she would like to see a movie with him and have a bite to eat. She accepted enthusiastically and that night they enjoyed a relaxing evening together. He thought she was terrific company, as usual, and he desperately wanted to share everything with her, including his plans for revenge. Having given it more thought, however, he decided that he didn't want her involved.

After kissing her, and going up to his own apartment at the end of the evening, he knew that he was totally in love with her and wanted to spend the rest of his life with her. He decided to deal with the Spencers before finally declaring his feelings to Bernie.

On Saturday morning Tiggy called at Jack's apartment bang on time at 9.15. As agreed, his hair was now cut short and his moustache was a distant memory. They both stood in front of the mirror wearing identical bobble hats, shoes, shirts and pants. Tiggy tried Jack's ring on his finger to make sure it was a good fit, which it was. "You know, Tigg', if we were to walk into my local bar like this, I don't think anyone would be able to tell which of us was Jack Williams."

They both laughed, as they went out into the cool morning air. During the drive into the countryside for Jack's first painting session, they discussed several points. He told Tiggy that he had been practicing his painting technique and, although he thought it was going well, he didn't think as yet that he was as good as Van Gogh.

"By the way, Tigg', any chance you could acquire a small motorbike or scooter?"

"Yeah, I suppose so. What will you need one of them for?"

"Well first off, I don't want to use your van in case some nosy bastard notices the registration and secondly, right by the job there is a small quiet walkway running into the countryside that would be perfect for a discreet getaway. I have seen people use it riding mountain bikes and scooters, so it shouldn't attract attention. Furthermore, it would give me the perfect excuse to wear a motorcycle helmet, as nobody would be able to give a description of me to the cops, even if they saw me."

"Brilliant," Tiggy said in admiration. "I must make a mental note of that for the future. Okay, leave it with me. I'll bring it in the van on the morning of the job."

Following the directions given to Jack by Mr. Child, they pulled up 100 yards from a small car park. Mr. Child had told him that the chosen position for the painting session that day was just a short stroll across a field from the meeting place. Tiggy jumped out and Jack carried on into the said car park where a short skinny guy with horn-rimmed glasses was waiting at the gate, ticking people off as they arrived. He walked over as Jack jumped out of the van.

"Mr. Williams?" the short skinny guy asked, offering his hand. Jack simply nodded his head and shook the old man's hand warmly. "Welcome to our little group Mr. Williams. I'm sure you will find us very easy to get on with. Now, as we discussed, the enrolment fee is $50. I do hope you don't mind me bringing it up, but the members are quite funny about these things and I feel it's much better to get sensitive issues out of the way."

Jack had actually been standing there with the $50 in his outstretched hand, offering it to Mr. Child practically the whole time he had been giving his nervous request. The embarrassed old man finally noticed and reached out for the money. "Oh good, good," he said, "Thank you very much. I will give you a receipt later, okay?

As soon as you are ready," he went on without waiting for a reply, "I will lead off."

Jack unloaded his easel, canvas chair and leather satchel out of the van. Then having donned his multi-colored bobble hat, joined the line following Mr. Child who was leading them all as they sang, "Hi ho, hi ho, it's off to paint we go."

After a short walk, they all stopped and, after deciding on what they each considered to be a good position, proceeded to set up their equipment. Jack decided on a spot on the outside of the group near to some trees and bushes. As he was setting up his gear, Mr. Child approached him saying, "If you need the toilet, that little wood is the best that we can offer Mr. Williams. Now, if you need any help, please don't hesitate to ask, okay?" Jack smiled and nodded his head.

Having set his gear up ready to begin painting, Jack looked at the scene in front of him and froze. He had a block and didn't have a clue how to start. So he poured himself a cup of coffee and sat back surveying the scene again. In the distance and to his right, was a church with a small cemetery surrounded by a stone wall. The sun was just about breaking through a thin layer of cloud. In front of him and a little nearer, were two horses grazing peacefully. He looked around him at his fellow painters, now engrossed in their own little world, then stood up and made his way through the small wood where he knew Tiggy would be observing everything as planned. Sure enough, there he was.

"Tigg', I haven't a clue how to start the damn painting. It might be a good idea if we swap over for a couple of hours."

"Okay," Tiggy said with an enthusiastic look on his face. "Is there anything that you need to tell me about Mr. Child, or any of the others?"

"No, not really, I've not spoken a word to any of them yet. Oh yes, Mr. Child will be coming to see you with a receipt for the $50 enrolment fee." Jack gave Tiggy his bobble hat, ring, watch, and spectacles which actually had plain glass lenses. Having donned them, Tiggy walked briskly out of the wood and over to the group. Sitting down on the small canvas chair, he poured himself a cup of coffee and surveyed the scene. A few minutes later he began sketching.

An hour passed by before Mr. Child, who had been around the whole group, now stood behind Tiggy admiring his handiwork. With Jack watching from the wood, with his heart in his mouth, Mr. Child commented, "Most interesting, most interesting, Mr. Williams. You are obviously a terrific acquisition to our little group."

"Thanks," Tiggy said, which apart from a couple of telephone conversations, was the first word Mr. Child had heard from his new member. Jack heaved a sigh of relief as Mr. Child moved on. The only thing he had to worry about, he thought, was Tiggy eating all the sandwiches that they had between them.

Another hour and a half went by with Jack looking at his watch every five minutes, until eventually, Tiggy stood up and stretched his arms out as he observed his handiwork from a few feet away. He then turned his attention to his fellow painters. Most of them were eating lunch and chatting about each other's paintings, so he slipped off and walked briskly to the waiting Jack.

"I really enjoyed that," he said enthusiastically as he took off his bobble hat, watch, glasses and ring, before placing them into Jack's hands.

"What did Mr. Child say to you?"

"He said that I was a 'terrific acquisition' to the group, so I thanked him. By the way, Jack, you had better be careful with my painting. Remember, you only have to look as though you are working on it. As a matter of fact, I think it would be better if I returned to the group for another couple of hours. You then, could finish off the final period, possibly with your bobble hat off so that they all get to see exactly what you look like. Do you agree?"

Jack looked at him, knowing he was right, but dreading the boredom of being on his own in the woods. "Yes, Tigg'," Jack agreed shrugging his shoulders. "The thing is, I'm bloody starving."

Tiggy looked at him in amazement. "This is no time for you to be thinking of your stomach. In any case, there's only one sandwich left."

Jack's eyes opened wide, "You, greedy redheaded pig. There was easily enough there for both of us."

Tiggy looked guilty. "I'm sorry, it's just that I get carried away when I'm painting and it makes me hungry."

Jack handed him back the hat, watch, glasses and ring. "You'd better go, but I'm warning you, if you eat that last sandwich, you might find that bobble hat stuffed down your throat."

Tiggy laughed as he walked back to the group and quickly restarted work on the painting.

They eventually swapped over late in the afternoon and Jack looked at Tiggy's creation with admiration. He took off his bobble hat and greedily ate the last sandwich and then swore to himself as he discovered Tiggy had finished off the rest of the coffee. He hardly touched the painting, as he went about the charade with a dry brush for the duration of the final session. Mr. Child eventually began packing his gear up, which was a signal for the rest of the group to follow suit. They then followed in single file behind their leader cringingly singing, "It's a long way to Tipperary." Having reached the car park, Jack quickly jumped into Tiggy's van and with a smile and a wave to the group, drove out of the car park, therefore avoiding unnecessary conversation with them.

He picked Tiggy up where he had dropped him off that morning and they drove to Jack's apartment, picking up a pizza on the way. "That went really well," Jack said enthusiastically as they eventually sat down with a can of beer. "By the way, Tigg', I was well impressed with your painting. I had forgotten how good you were."

"You can have it, if you want,"

Jack accepted the painting enthusiastically. They then discussed the day at length, before Tiggy went off.

Jack later called to Bernie's carrying a bottle of wine and a six-pack of beers, feeling pretty good about the way things were going. Her eyes lit up as she opened the door to find him standing there. "Well come on then, Bernie, are you going to invite me in or not?"

"Oh, I suppose I might as well. You're probably in need of some adult company after playing with your little painting friends all day." Then laughing, she ushered him through the hall.

"You can mock as much as you like, Bernie, but don't expect an invitation to my first exhibition."

They chatted and joked for a few hours before Jack left, kissing a thoroughly disappointed Bernie on the cheek. The following day, Sunday, they went for a stroll in Central Park chatting and cajoling each other. Jack was tempted to ask Bernie if she would marry him but again frustratingly decided to wait until after he had sorted out the Spencers.

The following week Jack carried on running the machine shop with enthusiasm, practiced his painting technique and spent quality time with Bernie. Saturday morning and Tiggy arrived spot on time at 9.15. He was already wearing identical clothing to Jack. "I've sorted your scooter out; it will have phony plates by the time I bring it."

"Great, Tigg', that's another problem out of the way." Jack then proudly held up his latest attempt at painting. "What do you think?"

Tiggy looked at the painting nodding his head. "That's not bad. You're coloring is still far too strong though. Tone it down."

"Yes, sir," Jack said picking his stuff up off the floor. "Let's be off. I don't want to be late." Having set off, he explained to Tiggy that there was a complication this time as the venue for the day was an hour and a half's drive. Consequently, they were all meeting in a public car park, where they would be sharing transport. Having followed Mr. Child's directions, they stopped short of the meeting place and Tiggy jumped into the back of the van.

Jack then carried on to the meeting place in the public car park. Mr. Child approached him as he stepped out of the van. "Good morning, Mr. Williams. You can jump into Alison's car if you want," he said pointing to a woman in her thirties, who was leaning against her car smiling. "Or, you can just follow me if you prefer."

"I'll follow you, Mr. Child," Jack replied as he smiled across at Alison, who he thought resembled a man. When the whole party had arrived and sorted out transport arrangements, they set off at a ridiculously slow pace.

Throughout the whole journey, there were beeping horns from irate drivers. They were finding it extremely difficult to get past the tortoise like convoy, which trundled along seemingly oblivious to the anger and, therefore, the danger they were creating. They eventually pulled into a clearing by a farm. Mr. Child indicated to the group pointing with his finger, the house and barn approximately 200 yards inside the gate where they would be setting up for the day. Jack turned the van around so that Tiggy would have a good view of the farm from the rear window, then quickly gathered his stuff together. With everyone ready, the group followed Mr. Child down a well-worn track. They chatted like a group of excited children as they slowly made their way up to the house and barn. Reaching the chosen spot, they began setting up their equipment as Mr. Child walked over to the house and chatted to the owner, a huge fat guy. Coming back to the group, he collected $5 off everyone, explaining that it was for the use of toilet facilities in an outbuilding nearby.

Jack had noticed on the way up the track that Alison was becoming too interested in him. She was now setting up her gear a little too close to him for comfort so he moved further away. The last thing he wanted right now was one of the ladies taking a shine to him. "Particularly Alison," he thought, as he smiled to himself.

Satisfied that everyone knew exactly what he looked like, Jack donned his multi coloured bobble hat, sat down on his little canvas chair and poured out a coffee. After a few minutes and with the group now totally absorbed in their work, he slipped quietly away and walked back to the van. Passing Tiggy his watch, bobble hat and so on, he said, "Go to it, boy. Just a word of warning. There is a woman named Alison, who is situated just to the left and in front of you, who fancies the pants off us. You'll know who I mean when you see her as she looks like she needs a shave. Give her a wide berth, as she could make things difficult for us."

Jack looked out of the dirty rear window of the van as Tiggy walked up the track and took his place. As soon as Tiggy sat down and looked at the view in front of him, he became excited and began sketching. Jack was bored sitting in the van but this time at least, he had his own sandwiches and flask. As lunch came and went, Tiggy became

311

oblivious to Jack as he sat painting the scene in front of him. He did, however, return to the van in late afternoon for the swap over. "Any problems, Tigg'?"

Tiggy passed all the accessories across to him. "No, none at all. Now don't you go and ruin my painting. I want to frame this one for myself."

When Jack reached the group, he sat down on the little canvas chair and marvelled at the painting in front of him that Tiggy had created. He took off his bobble hat as planned and pretended to be touching up the painting with dry brushes. Out of the corner of his eye he could see Alison, the male look-alike, turning round and glancing at him. He ignored her but at the same time, made a mental note to engage her in conversation the following week on his return from the job, as she would be perfect for his alibi.

At 5.30 p.m., they all packed up their equipment and Jack made sure to be the first down the track. Having put his gear on the passenger seat, he was pulling away as the first of the group were getting to their respective cars. He just gave them a friendly wave. Once out of sight, he turned down a dirt road in order that Tiggy could join him up front. They waited patiently until the convoy had gone past as they were afraid that any hold up ahead might give the group a chance of seeing them together. It meant a laborious drive home, but it was safer. Having reached Jack's apartment block, Tiggy went straight off, taking his painting with him.

Jack ran up the stairs, dumped his gear in the hall and jumped into the shower. Bernie had promised to cook him a meal and he was looking forward to it. He was pleased at the way the day had developed as, so far, everything was going to plan.

With the weekend over, Jack returned to work and carried on as though he were perfectly happy. Each afternoon he left Bernie in charge for an hour, as he himself went off to Central Park with an old baseball. He had paced out and put markers down at 20ft 25ft and 30ft from a two-foot wide tree. Each day he had practiced throwing the baseball while wearing a motorcycle helmet, until he could hit the tree dead center from each distance, ten times out of ten.

The big day arrived and Tiggy turned up at 9 a.m. as agreed. Jack had a knot in his stomach, as they stood side by side in front of the mirror, as usual checking for any irregularities. Satisfied, they picked up the gear, which now included a large square backpack to carry the paintings and a small bag that held the tools that Jack needed for the break in. Finally, Jack picked up the motorcycle helmet and the old baseball.

"What's that for, Jack?"

Putting the ball into the bag, he replied, "I'll need it to set off the burglar alarm before making my getaway."

Tiggy looked at him in amazement. "Set off the burglar alarm? Are you mad?"

"Well, Tigg', I happen to know that it is automatically wired to the cop station, so it will guarantee that the robbery will have taken place between 11 a.m. and 5 p.m. making my alibi watertight.

"Ah, I see, Jack, but how's the baseball going to do that?"

"You don't need to know, Tigg'," Jack answered impatiently.

They went down to the van, which now had a scooter in the back. Jack was not expecting any problems with the painting situation as Mr. Child had told him, when giving directions, that they would be in the countryside. Jack read out the list from his notebook and ticked everything off that they needed. Finally, putting the notebook into his pocket, he said. "Right, this is it, let's go."

With Tiggy in the back of the van, Jack drove along following Mr. Child's meticulous directions until he pulled into a clearing in the woods where, as usual, Mr. Child was waiting with just a few cars. He waved to him and proceeded to tick him off the list. The rest of the cars gradually arrived and, once packed up and ready, the group followed their leader mercifully, as far as Jack was concerned, not singing.

They trundled slowly along with Tiggy a safe distance away, until they reached a stream and began setting up for the day. Jack waited until everyone had chosen their spot, before then positioning himself at the rear of the group. It was a beautiful spring day. Having donned his bobble hat, he sat and looked at the scene in front of him. A stream wound its way snake like through the countryside. The different colored trees bathed in the sunshine, made it a tranquil setting. This, along with the blue sky broken up by fluffy white clouds here and there and the hills climbing in the distance would, he thought, bring the very best out of Tiggy. He looked at his watch and then at his fellow artists. Satisfied that they were oblivious to him, he quietly slipped down the track and met Tiggy. Swapping the ring, watches, and other accessories for the last time, they shook hands.

"I'll text you as soon as I get back,"

Tiggy looked at him concerned. "The bike is out of the van and ready for you, for pity's sake, man, don't get stopped for speeding."

Wearing his thin, black gloves, which he would wear right through the job, Jack drove the bike carefully making sure he was within the speed limit at all times. Arriving at Lord Spencer's house, he looked around to see if the coast was clear. Satisfied, he then jumped up and grabbed the top of the exterior wall. Peering over, he could see that both cars belonging to the Spencers were not there. Knowing that they never ever put the cars in the garage, he was satisfied that they had left for Quinton's 65th birthday bash. He knew the party was scheduled to begin at noon and it was now five minutes past. He was then further convinced when he saw Toby and Bruno roaming loose in the grounds, as he knew the only time they were ever left outside was for guard duty. After yet another glance round to see if anyone was looking, he hauled himself over the wall. Dropping to the ground, he was immediately greeted by the two excited dogs. He gave them some dog biscuits and then made his way to the side door.

Taking the jemmy bar out of his backpack, he forced the door open and immediately the beeps from the burglar alarm sounded. He knew he then had just fifteen seconds to cancel the alarm. Having done so, he closed the door behind him and made his way quickly to Quinton's office. Within minutes he had in his possession the original agreement between himself and Quinton Spencer. Gathering together the form from the Patent office with his name on it, the technical drawings and the spare prototype, he then made his way up to Grace's room, where he pocketed her valuable jewelry. Making his way back down stairs, he went straight to the most valuable paintings, which were quite small and easily fitted into his backpack. He was enjoying himself, as he felt nothing but revulsion for whom he now considered to be conceited morons. Satisfied, he then made his way back to the side door where he had entered. The dogs were waiting excitedly for him. He gave them some more biscuits and typed in the numbers resetting the alarm. Leaving the door wide open, he made his way over to the wall. Jumping up and grabbing the top of the wall, he peeked over to make sure the coast was clear, before then sitting on top.

Taking the baseball out of his pocket, he took aim and threw it accurately through the center of the doorway 25 yards away. With the dogs in pursuit of the ball, he jumped down and started the scooter. He laughed as right on cue; the alarm went off after fifteen seconds, set off by his innocent partners in crime, Toby and Bruno. He then drove down the narrow pathway onto the dirt track road and away. There was nobody about as he drove along, but he wouldn't have been concerned anyway as he had on his motorcycle helmet. The whole plan had gone as smooth as silk. Jack thought that, Tony Martin - his mentor, would have been proud of him.

He then began his return journey back to the painting venue, meticulously checking his speed. Arriving in plenty of time at the clearing in the woods, Jack lowered the ramp down and drove the scooter up and into the back of the van.

Tiggy, who at this time was engrossed in another masterpiece was really enjoying himself. He sat back in his seat as his cell phone gave off two beeps indicating a text message. A smile came to his face as he read, "The eagle has landed. Operation successfully completed." He looked around at the group who, as usual, were totally absorbed and, standing up, he slipped away and walked quickly down the track, where he met Jack.

Having swapped the various personal items, Jack returned to the group for the last time. He sat down in the canvas seat with a satisfied smile on his face and then removing his bobble hat, walked over to where Alison was busy painting. Looking at her work, which he thought was rubbish compared to Tiggy's, he remarked, "I really like that, Alison."

She flushed noticeably. "That's very nice of you to say so, but I'm sure it's not as good as yours."

Jack pressed on, as he wanted her to remember this moment. "Well, I think you have a very individual approach, Alison. By the way, we haven't really been introduced properly, my name is Jack Williams." She flushed again as she stood up and put her tiny hand inside Jack's and shook it enthusiastically. He flirted with her by keeping hold of her hand as he asked. "Any idea where the venue is next week, Alison?"

"Oh dear, let me see," she was really nervous, as she rummaged through her bag for her copy of the club booklet. "Let's see, today is the fifth of April, so Saturday the

316

twelfth is unfortunately a blank week. If you like, I could show you a wonderful landscape that we could paint together."

"That sounds interesting, Alison, why don't you give me your telephone number and I'll give you a call?"

Her hands were shaking as she wrote out her number and gave it to him. "I'm just going to have a word with our beloved leader," he said as he walked away with the tool that he could use on the cops, her telephone number. He then walked through the group saying 'hi' here and there, making his presence felt. After a brief conversation with Mr. Child, he returned to his canvas chair.

Alison was over in a second. "Jack, that is a wonderful piece of work, I look forward to seeing it finished."

"Well, I seem to have a block at the moment, Alison, which as you know is an artist's nightmare. Do you ever get them?"

"Yes," she laughed "but unfortunately mine seem to last all day." She went back to her seat, giggling like a schoolgirl with her first crush.

Jack was delighted that phase one was complete and now he was anxious to complete phase two. Just after five o'clock, Mr. Child stood up and stretched, which was a clear sign that he had had enough. Packing his gear up quickly, Jack was off down the track as most of the group were only just getting their gear together. He and Tiggy were into the van and away in a flash. Sitting outside the apartment block, they went through the day's events.

"Now look," Jack said. "One of the paintings is valued at $40,000 and the other at $30,000. The jewelry is all top notch stuff, so don't let the Fence con you."

"Don't worry, I've been dealing with the same guy for four years now. He's the straightest bent bastard that I have ever met."

They both laughed before Tiggy went on, "He naturally doesn't like hot stuff on his hands and so doesn't usually take long to shift it."

Tiggy went off and the first thing Jack did, as he entered his apartment, was strip off and jump under the hot shower. Having changed his clothes, he relaxed with a cup of coffee in order to settle himself down and clear his mind. A few hours later, looking out of the window into the dark, he took a deep breath and wearily stood up. There was one more piece of the jigsaw that needed removing from the Spencer's, the second prototype that was mounted on Glen's machine. Then, he thought, he would have them by the balls. Revenge, he felt, would be sweet, when he approached Spencer Security Doors main competitors.

Grabbing his bunch of keys to the factory, Jack went out into the cool, cloudless night. On reaching the main gate, he took out the keys and opened the inner door. Obviously not wanting to be seen, he went through the pitch black, converted garage, that was now a machine shop, using his pen torch. Reaching Glen's machine and, firstly making sure that it was disconnected electrically, he jumped down into the belly of it in order to remove the prototype.

A short distance away, however, the agency security guard, having been alerted by a noise, was stealthily inching his way through the dark towards the flickering light of Jack's pen torch, drawn like a moth to a flame.

Jack, having removed the prototype, had stuffed it into his backpack and was ready to make his getaway, when suddenly, he was gripped by fear as a torch was shone into his eyes. He raised his hands in the form of surrender, but then tried to dive out of the way as he heard a gun being cocked. A bullet smashed through his shoulder, knocking him back, with his head colliding violently against the metal frame of the machine.

The cold hateful eyes of Antonio Berezi looked down at Jack's prostrate, bleeding body without pity. Putting his gun back into its holster, Antonio smiled sardonically. Then, panicking at the realization of what he had done, rang the police, who, on arriving, found that Jack still had a pulse. They held a pressure pad on each side of his wound trying to stem the blood loss as they waited for the paramedics.

Jack was taken to hospital and underwent surgery within two hours of being shot. The police, having searched his clothing, found a small address book and consequently contacted old Tom, Tony Martin, Bernie and Lord Spencer.

Quinton Spencer accused Jack of burglary so the police, armed with a warrant, searched his apartment. They found nothing of course, as Tiggy had taken everything away.

As Jack lay in a coma, hovering between life and death, his friends sat in the hospital white faced and shaken. The consultant, speaking to all of them suggested they pray and stay positive as Jack, in his opinion, had a 60-40 chance of recovery.

As hours became days, Jack's body gradually grew stronger and he was taken out of intensive care, although still in a deep coma. As he lay there on the bed, his friends took it in turn talking to him and trying to bring him around. After six days their prayers were answered as his eyes flickered open for a few seconds. Bernie, old Tom, Tony and Cindy waited anxiously in anticipation.

The next morning, looking pale and exhausted, they were allowed in to see Jack, who was slowly responding to treatment. He didn't seem to know them, as he drifted in and out of consciousness, until after twenty-four hours of his eyes first opening, he smiled weakly at Bernie, who consequently broke down in tears. Old Tom thanked God under his breath while comforting Bernie with his arms around her shoulders.

Gradually, over the following days, Jack, although extremely weak, slowly became more like his old self as he began to swap banter with his friends. The police were allowed in to ask him about his whereabouts on the day that he had been shot. He told them about the painting group and furnished them with the telephone numbers of Mr. Child and Alison. They then went off to check his story. Jack knew by now, of course, what had happened to him and consequently what he had been through.

When old Tom had Jack on his own, he explained to him that Bernie had never left his side through all those days and nights.

The following day, the police returned with Mr. Child and Alison in tow. They both backed up Jack's story without hesitation and confirmed that, if called upon, they would be willing to testify in court. This left him with his phony, but watertight alibi.

As soon as they had left, old Tom, suddenly looking serious, sat down on a small stool by Jack's bedside. "There's something I have been meaning to tell you, I have decided to retire and I know this is going to be a big shock, but I would like to give my store to you, lock, stock and barrel."

"Tom, I can't accept that from you."

Tom wouldn't be deterred. "Yes, you can. Knowing you, of course, you will probably turn it into a chain of stores right across the state. I hope you do."

Jack began to protest but Tom would have none of it. "Please don't stop me now. I should have told you this years ago." Beads of sweat were now appearing on Tom's baldpate as he went on. "The fact is, Jack, I'm actually your father."

The silence was almost deafening, as Jack struggled to take this in. "But my mother told me that my father was a student who had done a runner, in any case, why have you left it this long, Tom? And, if what you say is true, how could you have left her struggling on her own?"

At this point Bernie became extremely uncomfortable and stood up. "I think it would be best if I left you two in private."

Old Tom put his hands up, "No, Bernie, I would like you to stay." After a brief silence as Tom wiped more beads of sweat from his brow, he went on. "It's quite complicated, but she didn't want me. She always hoped that she would get back with her previous boyfriend, who she was infatuated with, and bring you up as his son. I swear, Jack, I begged her but she would have none of it, as she said she wasn't in love with me. The longer we kept the truth from you, the harder it became. Unfortunately, she then began to drink more and more"

There was then a silence as tears of relief flowed from the old man's eyes. Bernie gave him a tissue and he wiped his eyes before going on. "I know you must have many questions to ask me, but for now, will you consider my offer of the store? I have left it to you in my will anyway."

"The strange thing is," Jack said, looking shell-shocked, "I suppose I have always felt like a son to you in a way."

At that point Bernie stood up. "Right, as it appears to be cards on the table time, I'm going to play mine. I should really leave this to you, Jack Williams, but so far you have been less than useless. The fact is, I want to be your wife and I'm not going to take no for an answer."

Jack smiled. "Bossy little madam ain't she, Tom? The sass of it calling me less than useless. I don't know, it's been a right couple of weeks for me. I get a hole blown through me and I endure the mother of all headaches, then I'm forced into a shotgun wedding and, finally and worst of all, because of you, Tom, I find out that I'll probably be bald by the time I'm forty."

All three of them ended up laughing out loud. The duty nurse, looking through a small window in the door wondering what all the laughing was about, shook her head and smiled.

END